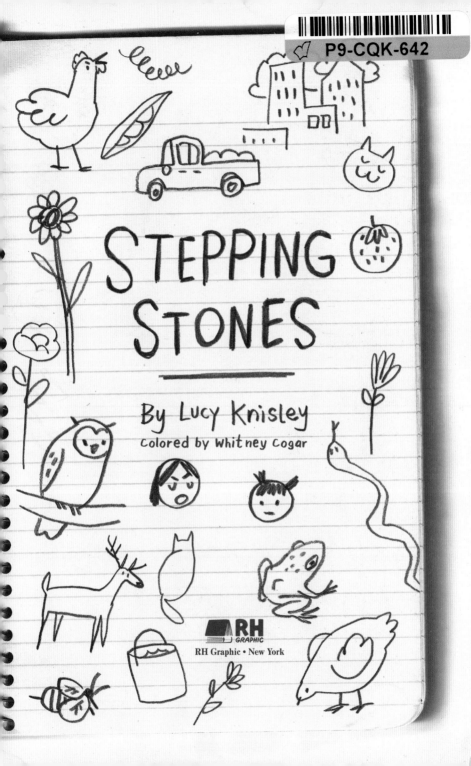

STEPPING STONES

By Lucy Knisley

Colored by Whitney Cogar

RH GRAPHIC

RH Graphic • New York

Text, cover art, and interior art copyright © 2020 by Lucy Knisley
All rights reserved. Published in the United States by RH Graphic, an imprint of Random House Children's Books, a division of Penguin Random House LLC, New York.

RH Graphic with the book design is a trademark of Penguin Random House LLC.

Visit us on the Web! RHKidsGraphic.com • @RHKidsGraphic

Educators and librarians, for a variety of teaching tools, visit us at RHTeachersLibrarians.com

Library of Congress Cataloging-in-Publication Data
Names: Knisley, Lucy, author, artist. Title: Stepping stones / Lucy Knisley.
Description: First edition. | New York : RH Graphic, [2020] | Audience: Ages 8–12 | Audience: Grades 4–6 |
Summary: "Jen moves out to the country and has to put up with her mom and her mom's new boyfriend, as well as his kids. Suddenly part of a larger family in a new place, Jen isn't sure there is a place for her in this different world"—Provided by publisher.
Identifiers: LCCN 2019026160 | ISBN 978-1-9848-9684-1 (paperback) | ISBN 978-0-593-12524-3 (hardcover) | ISBN 978-1-9848-9685-8 (library binding) | ISBN 978-1-9848-9686-5 (ebook)
Subjects: LCSH: Graphic novels. | CYAC: Graphic novels. | Families—Fiction. | Country life—Fiction.
Classification: LCC PZ7.7.K663 St 2020 | DDC 741.5/973—dc23

Designed by Patrick Crotty
Colored by Whitney Cogar

MANUFACTURED IN CHINA
10 9 8 7 6 5 4 3 2 1
First Edition

A comic on every bookshelf.

Stepping Stones was drawn with Blackwing *602* pencils on bristol and colored digitally.

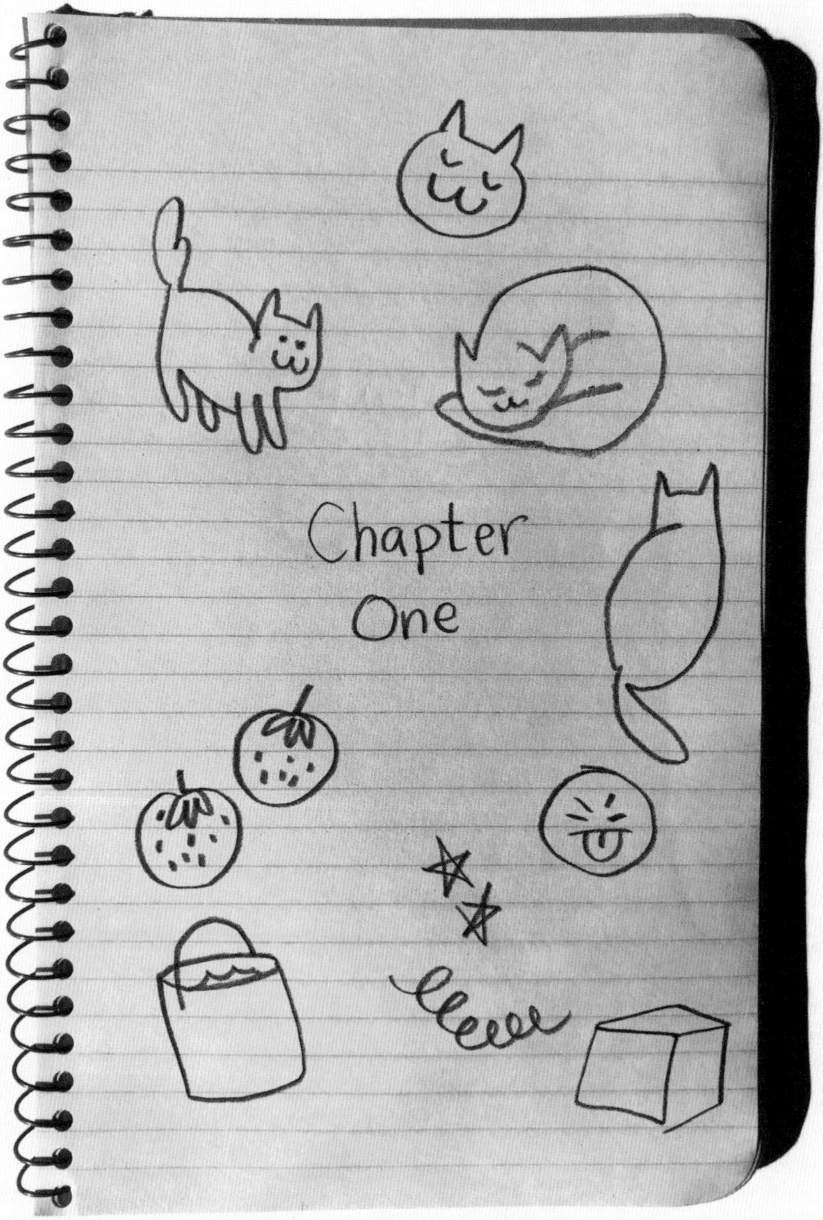
Chapter
One

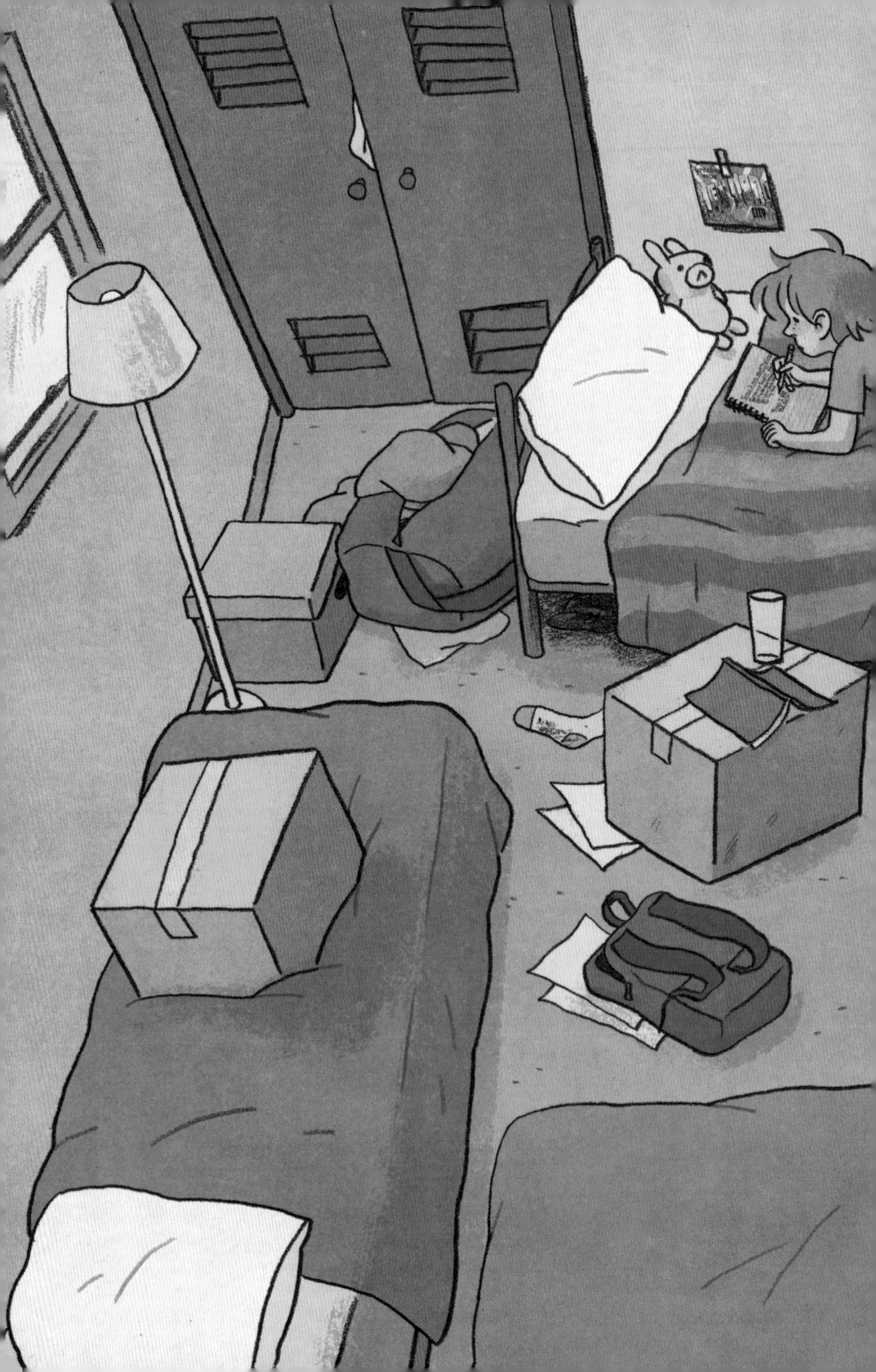

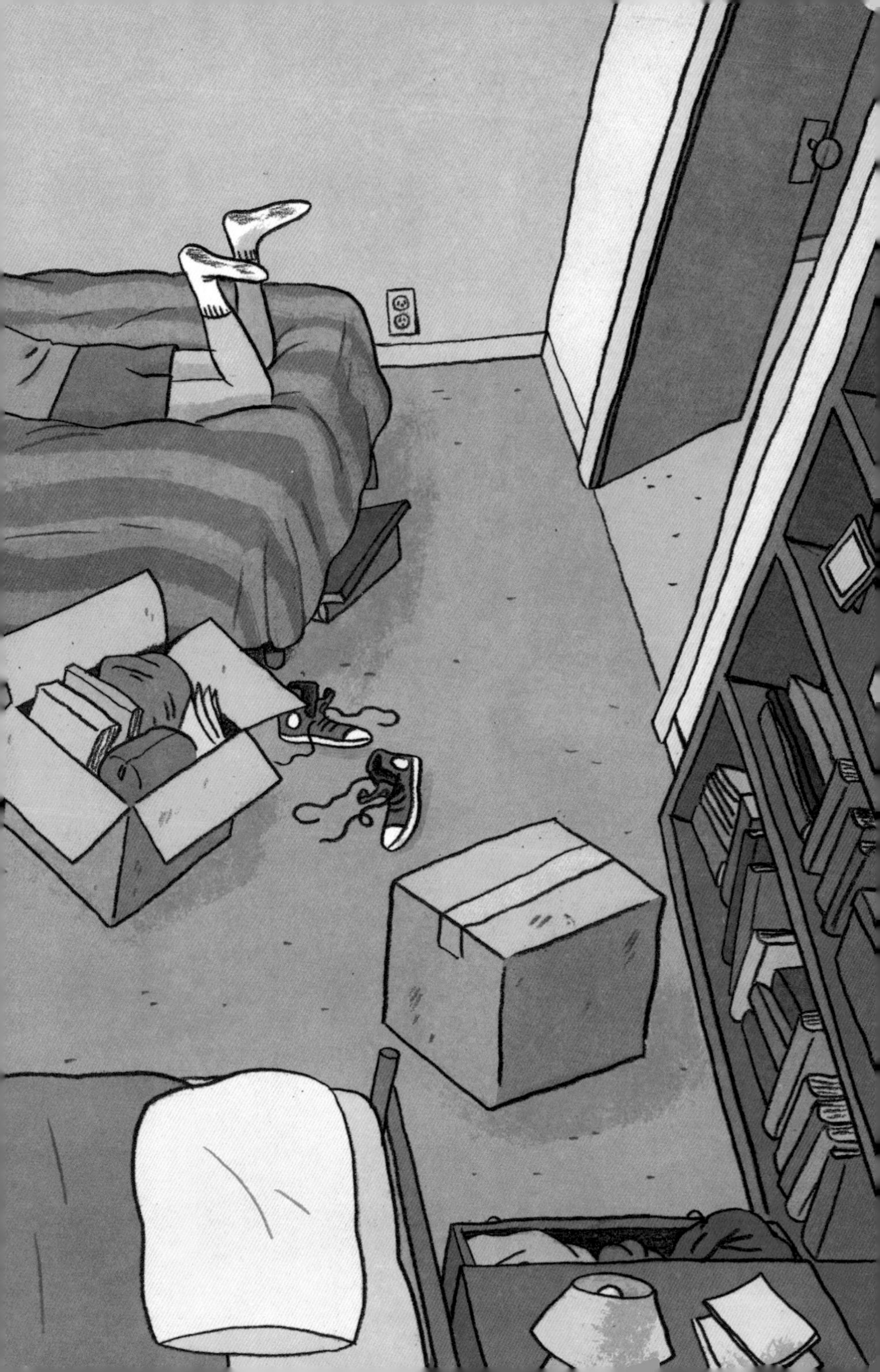

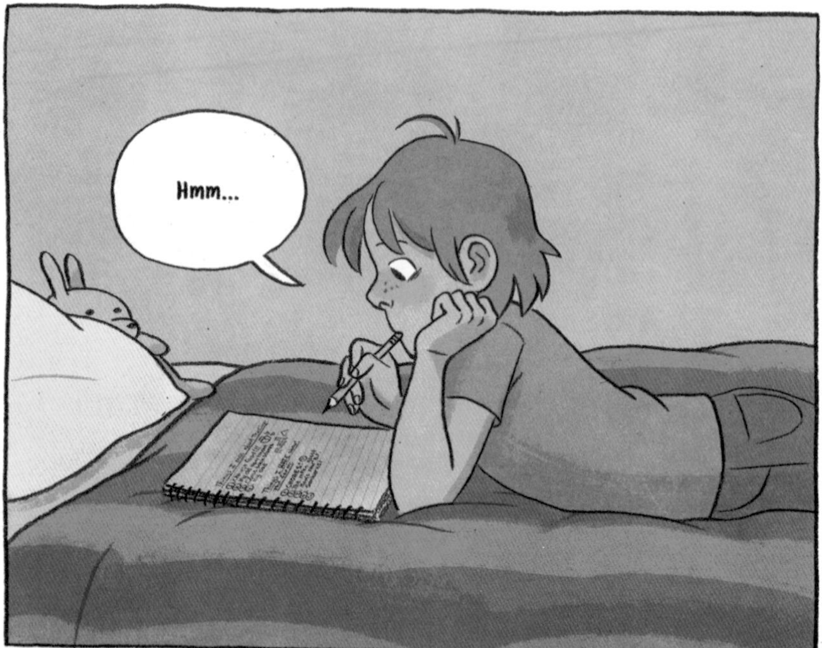
Hmm...

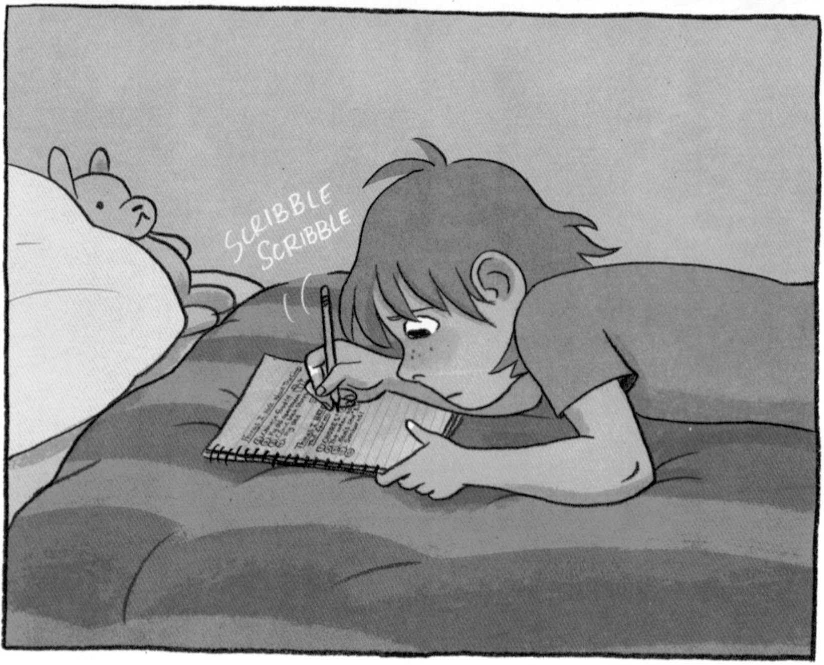
SCRIBBLE
SCRIBBLE

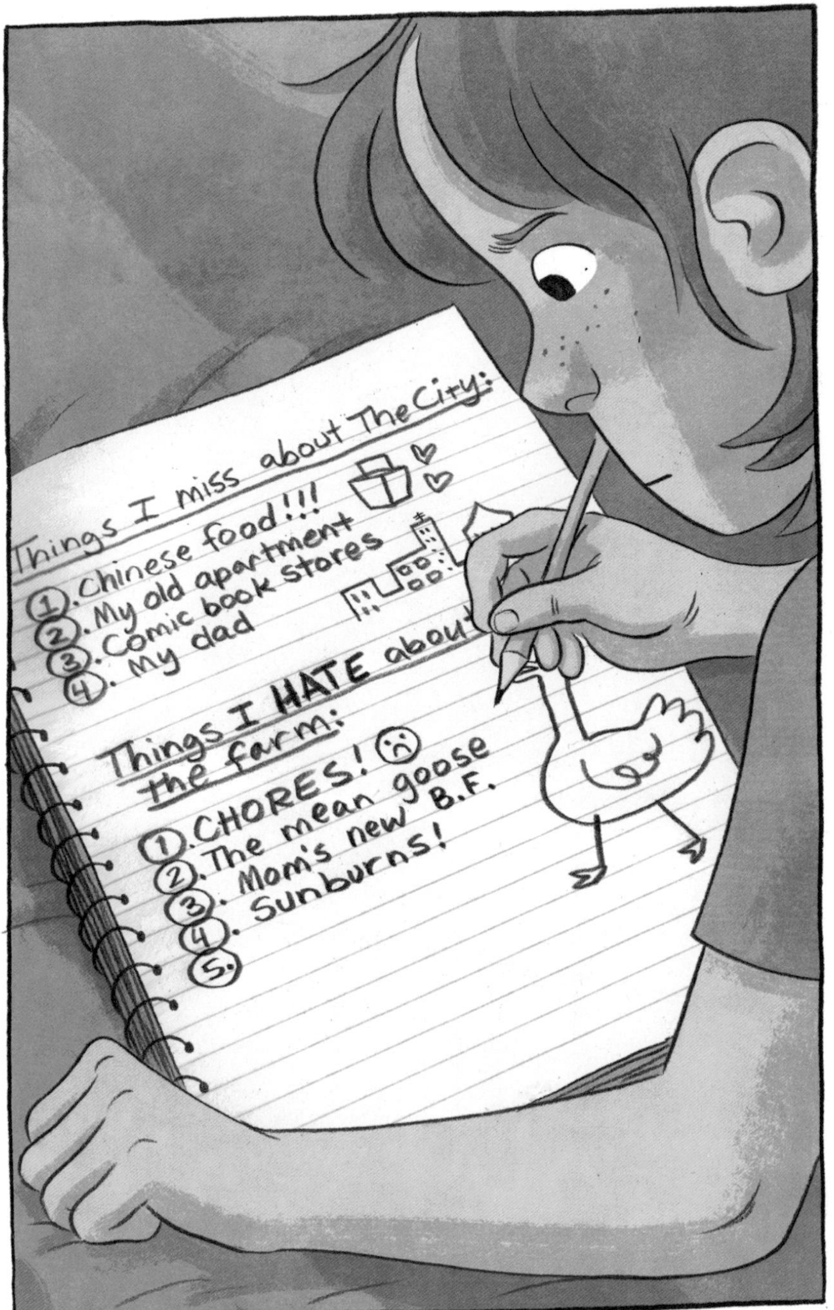
Things I miss about The City:
1. Chinese food!!!
2. My old apartment
3. Comic book stores
4. My dad
Things I HATE about the farm:
1. CHORES!
2. The mean goose
3. Mom's new B.F.
4. Sunburns!
5.

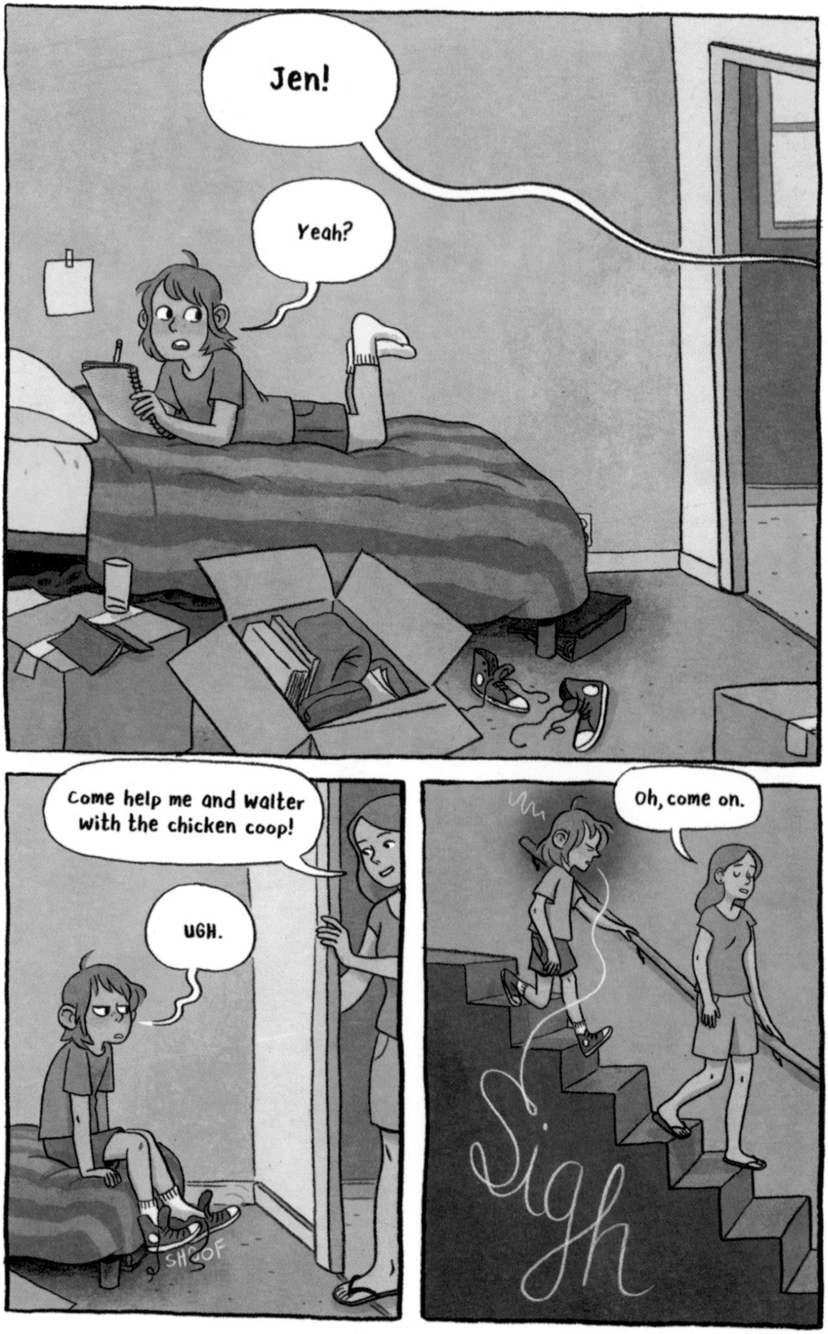

Jen!
Yeah?
Come help me and Walter with the chicken coop!
UGH.
SHOOF
Oh, come on.
Sigh

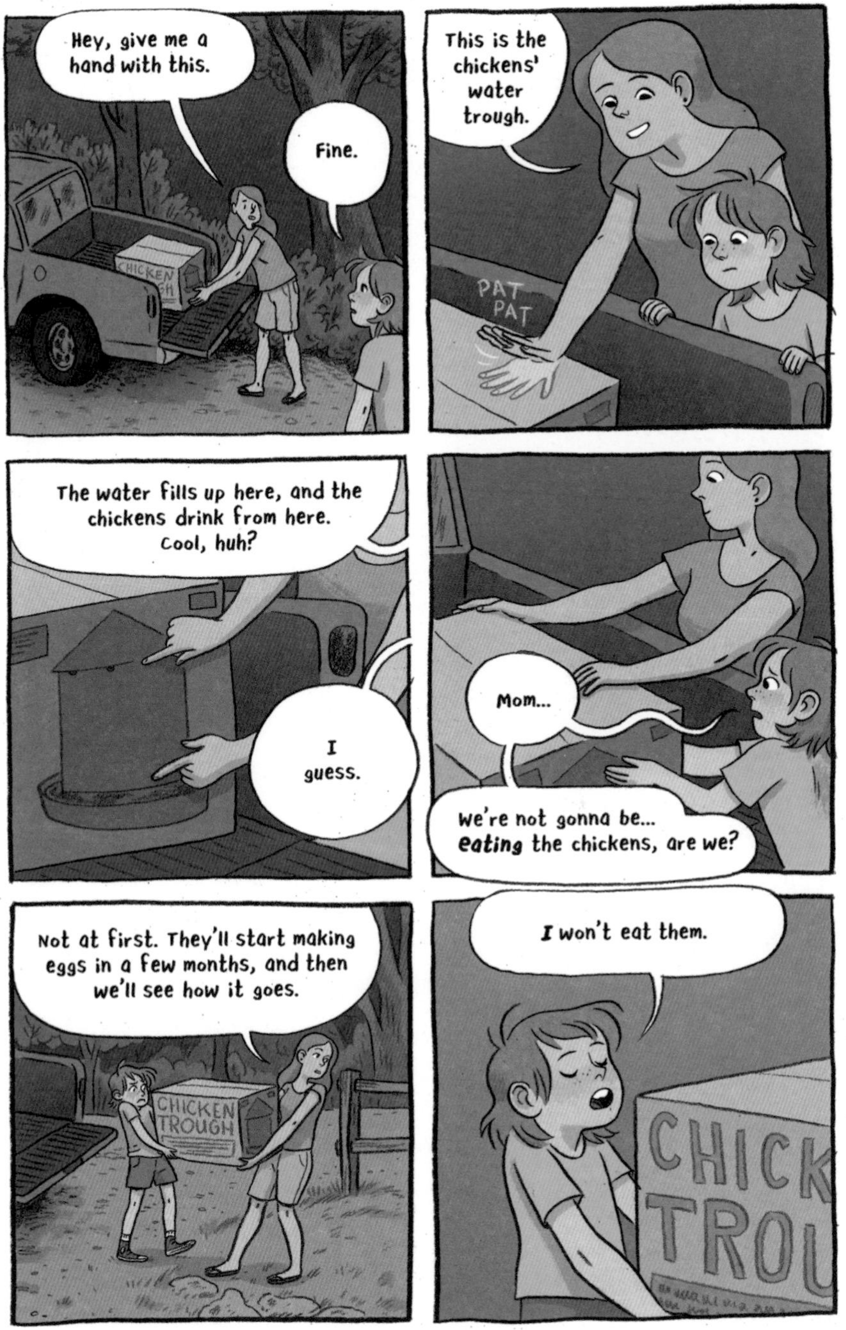
Hey, give me a hand with this.
Fine.
CHICKEN TROUGH
This is the chickens' water trough.
PAT PAT
The water fills up here, and the chickens drink from here. Cool, huh?
I guess.
Mom...
We're not gonna be... eating the chickens, are we?
Not at first. They'll start making eggs in a few months, and then we'll see how it goes.
CHICKEN TROUGH
I won't eat them.
CHICK TROU

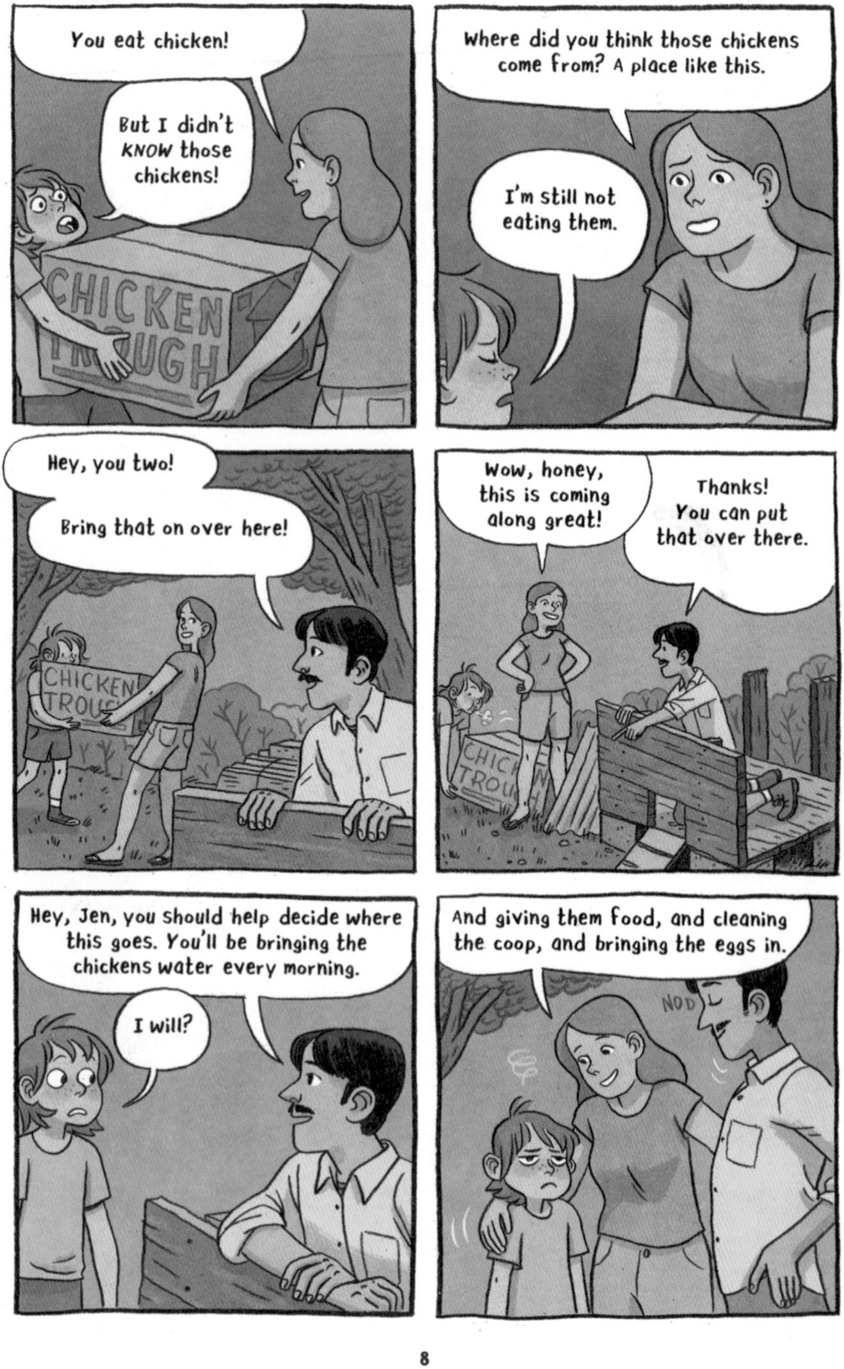
You eat chicken!
But I didn't KNOW those chickens!
CHICKEN TROUGH
Where did you think those chickens come from? A place like this.
I'm still not eating them.
Hey, you two!
Bring that on over here!
Wow, honey, this is coming along great!
Thanks! You can put that over there.
Hey, Jen, you should help decide where this goes. You'll be bringing the chickens water every morning.
I will?
And giving them food, and cleaning the coop, and bringing the eggs in.
NOD

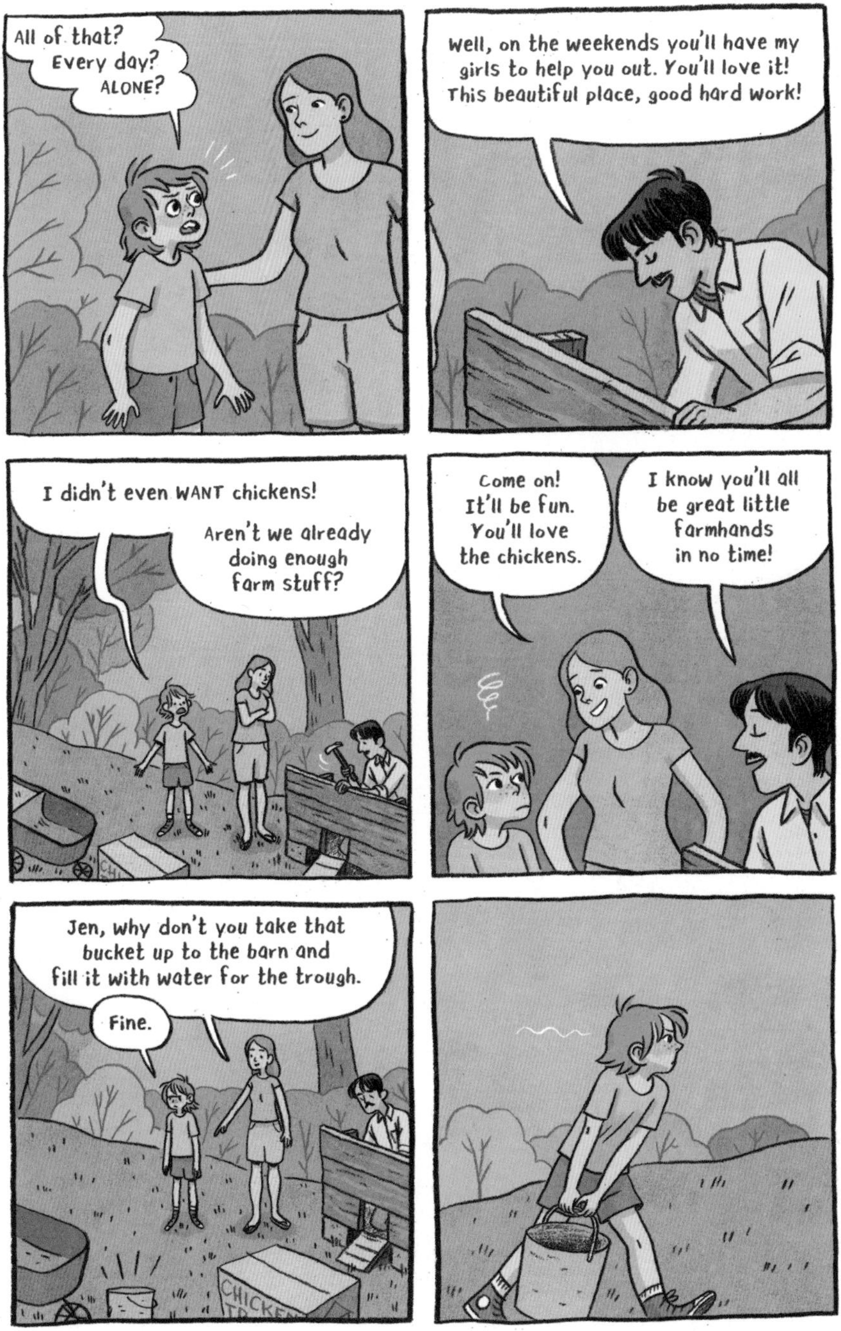
All of that? Every day? ALONE?
Well, on the weekends you'll have my girls to help you out. You'll love it! This beautiful place, good hard work!
I didn't even WANT chickens!
Aren't we already doing enough farm stuff?
Come on! It'll be fun. You'll love the chickens.
I know you'll all be great little farmhands in no time!
Jen, why don't you take that bucket up to the barn and fill it with water for the trough.
Fine.

Map of Peapod Farm
Barn
House
Water Spout
Mom's garden
me
(Future) Chicken coop
mean goose
Pond
Woods

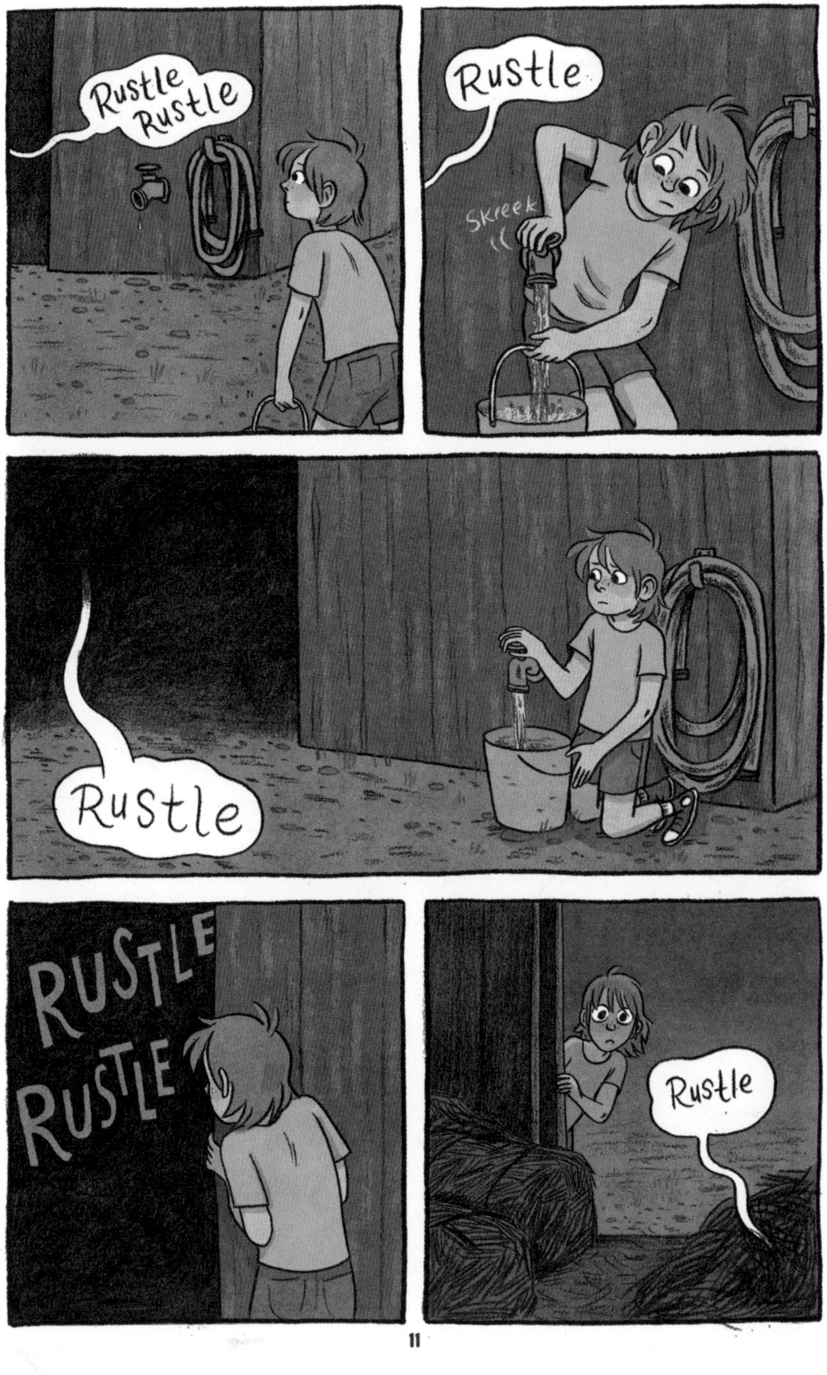
Rustle Rustle
Rustle
Skreek
Rustle
RUSTLE RUSTLE
Rustle

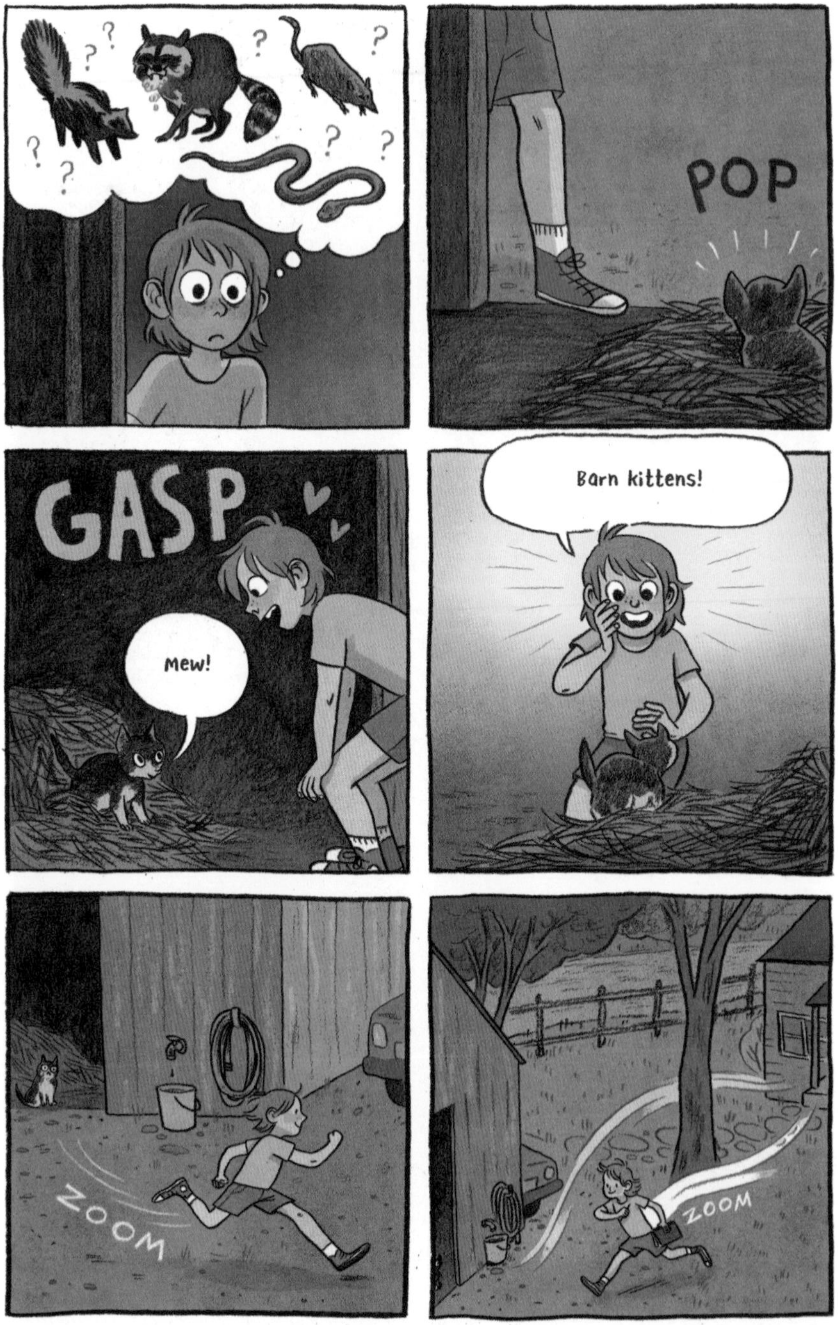
POP
GASP
Mew!
Barn kittens!
ZOOM
ZOOM

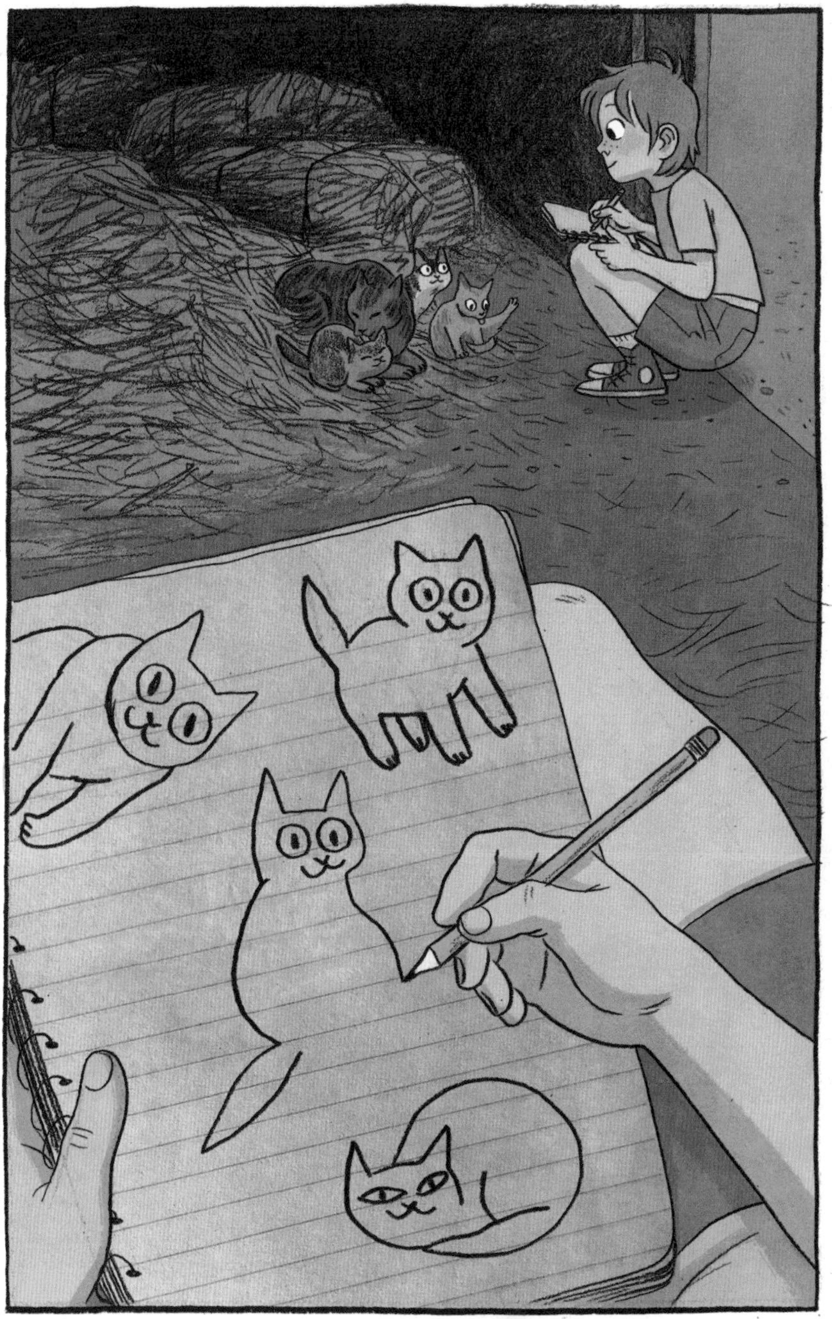

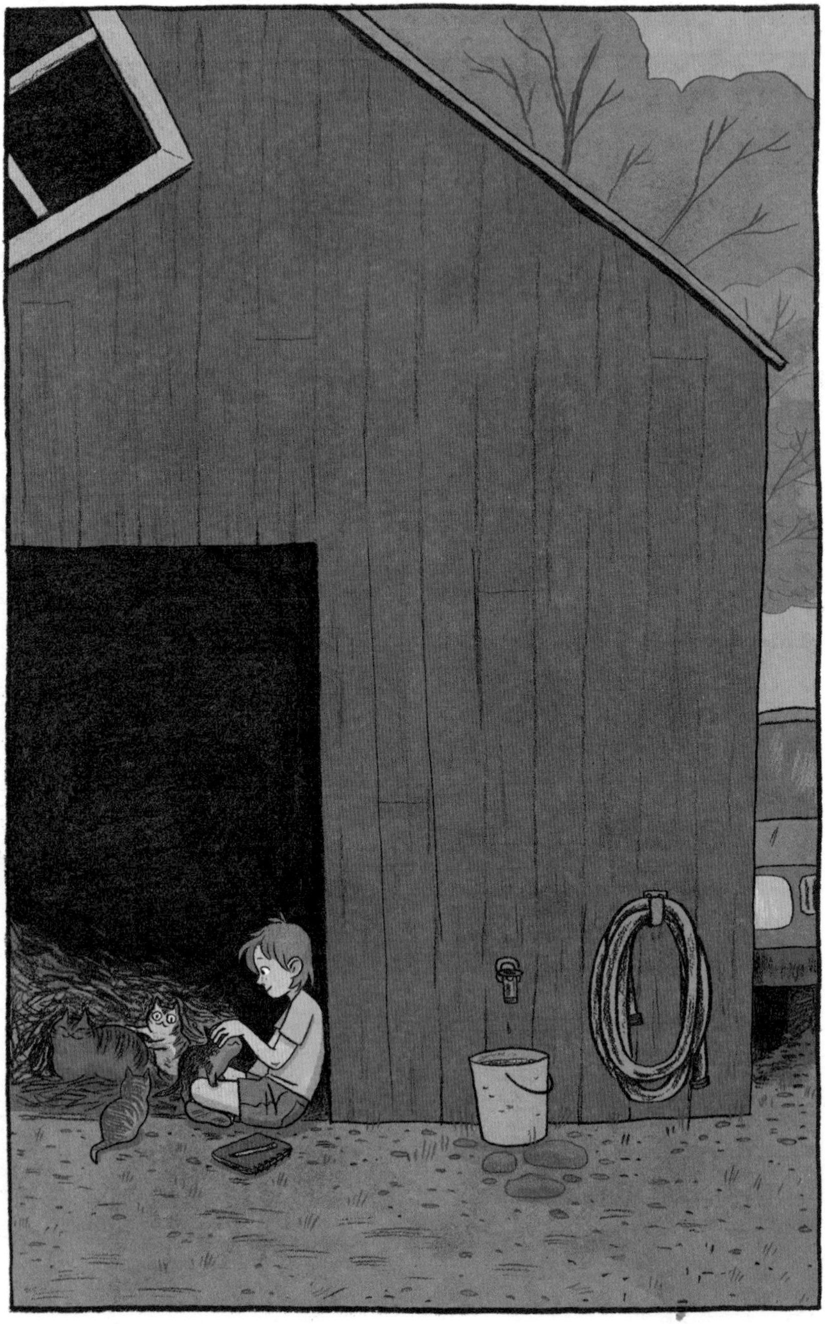

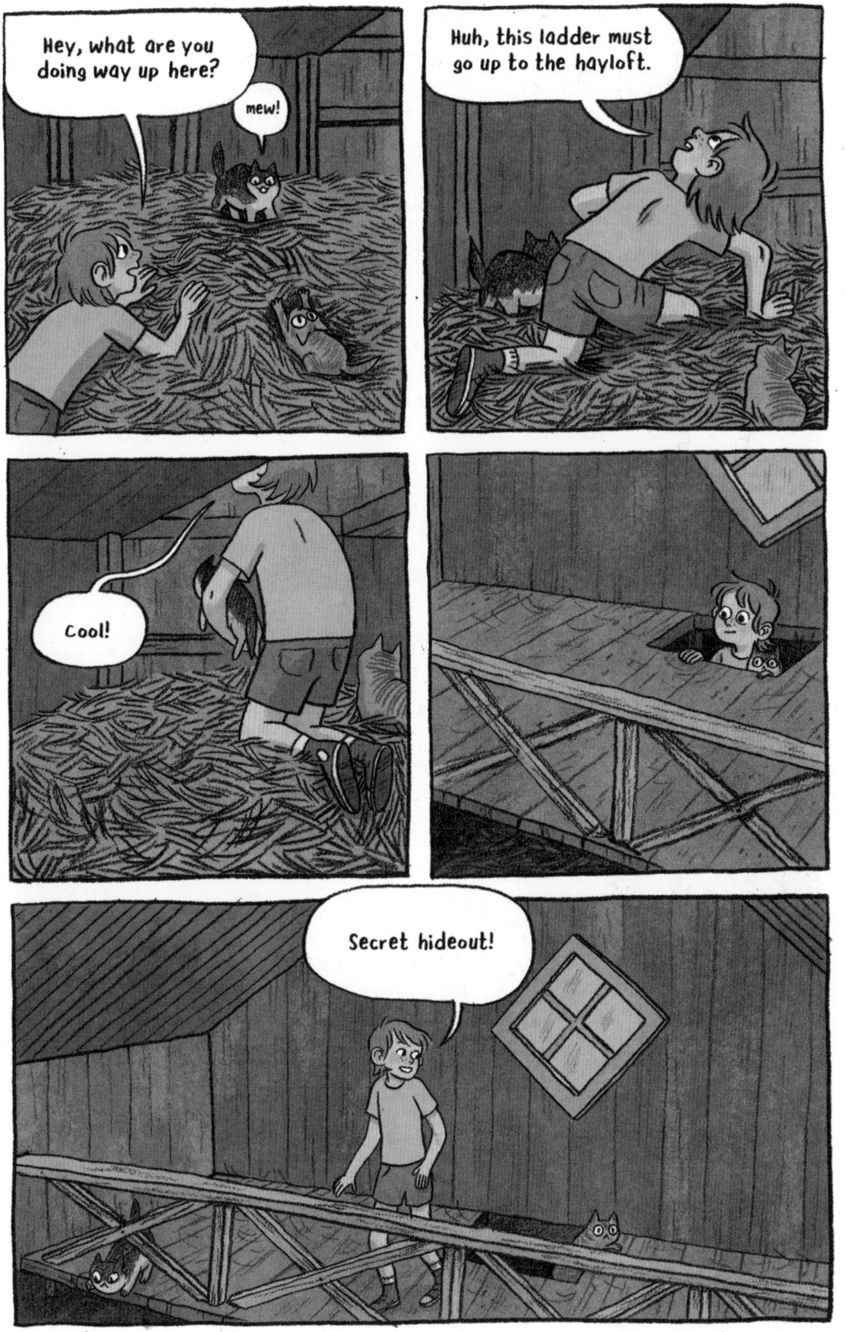
Hey, what are you doing way up here?
mew!
Huh, this ladder must go up to the hayloft.
Cool!
Secret hideout!

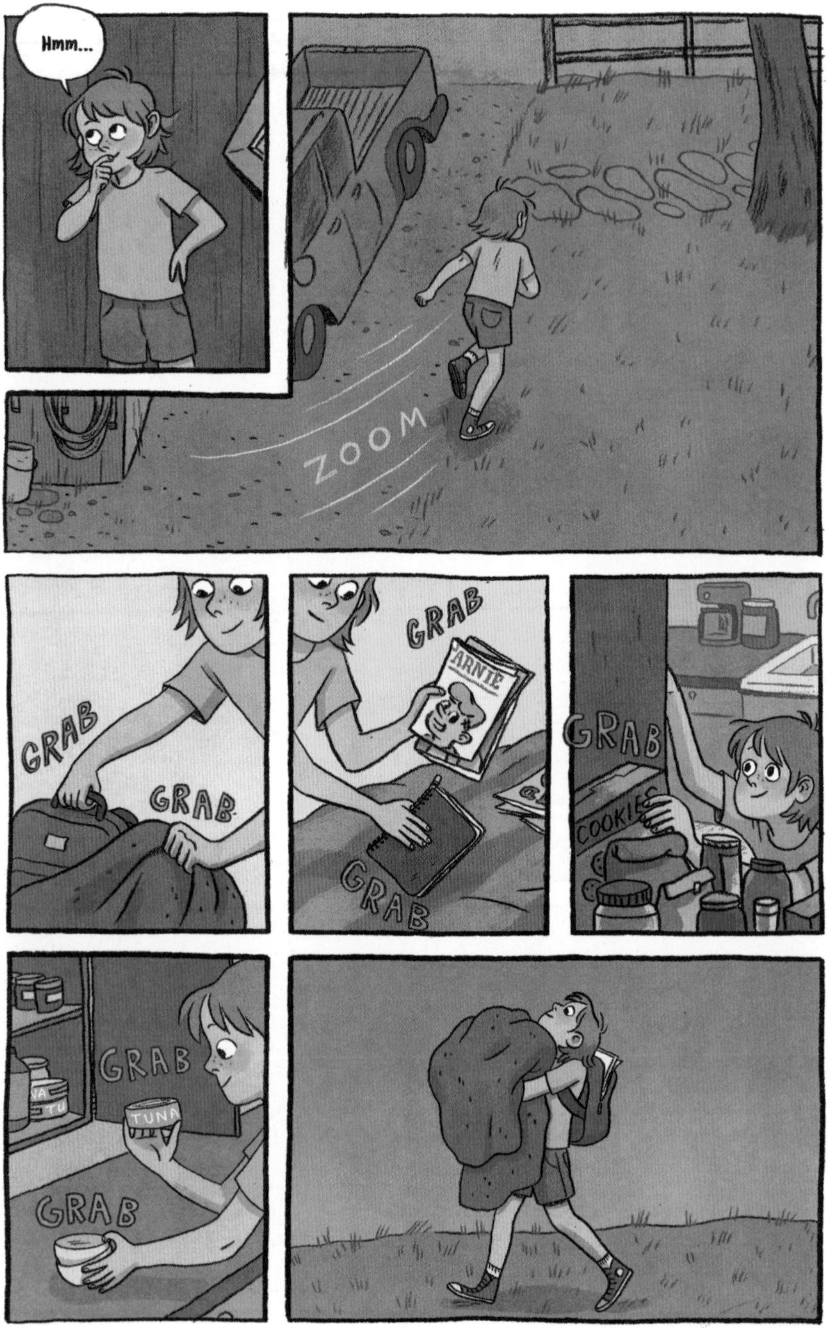
Hmm...
ZOOM
GRAB
GRAB
GRAB
ARNIE
GRAB
GRAB
COOKIES
GRAB
TUNA
GRAB

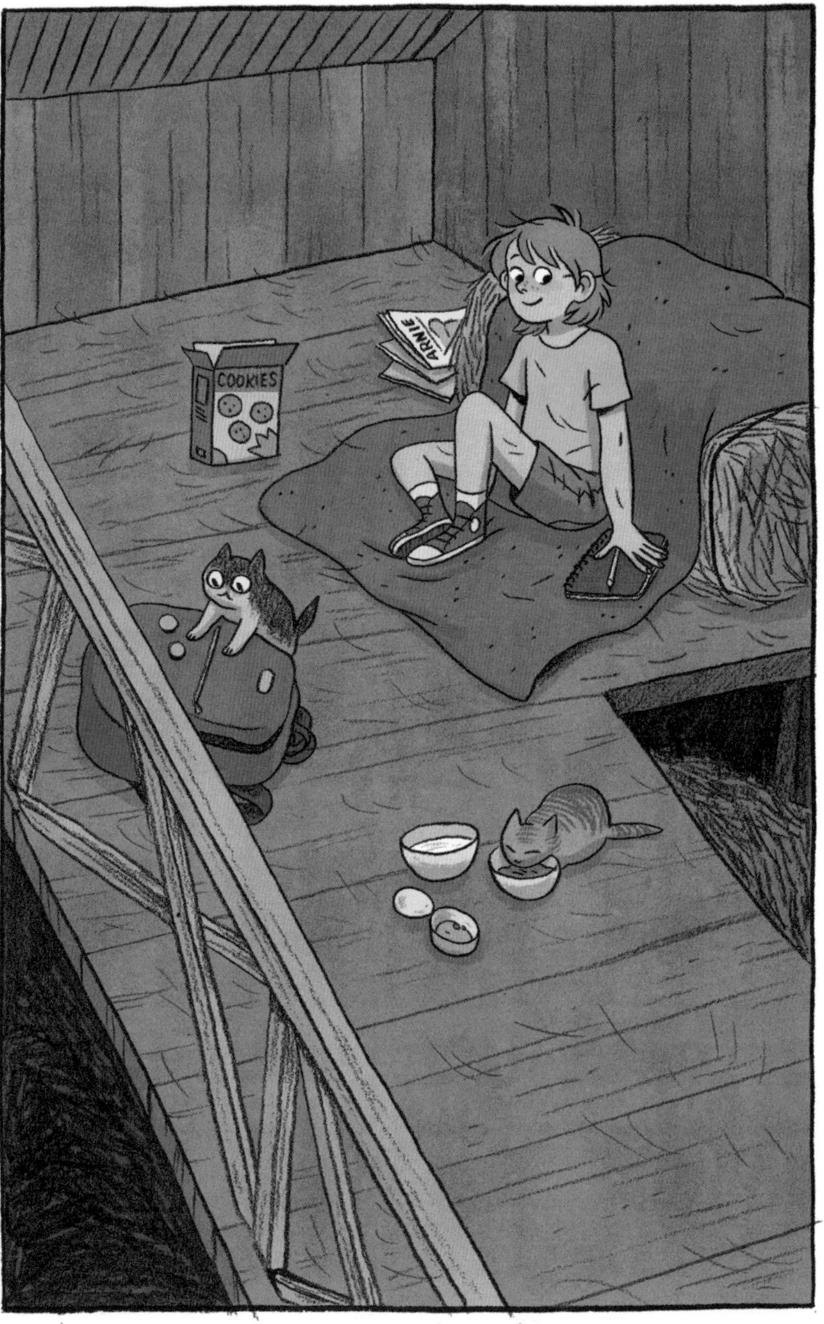

COOKIES
ARNIE

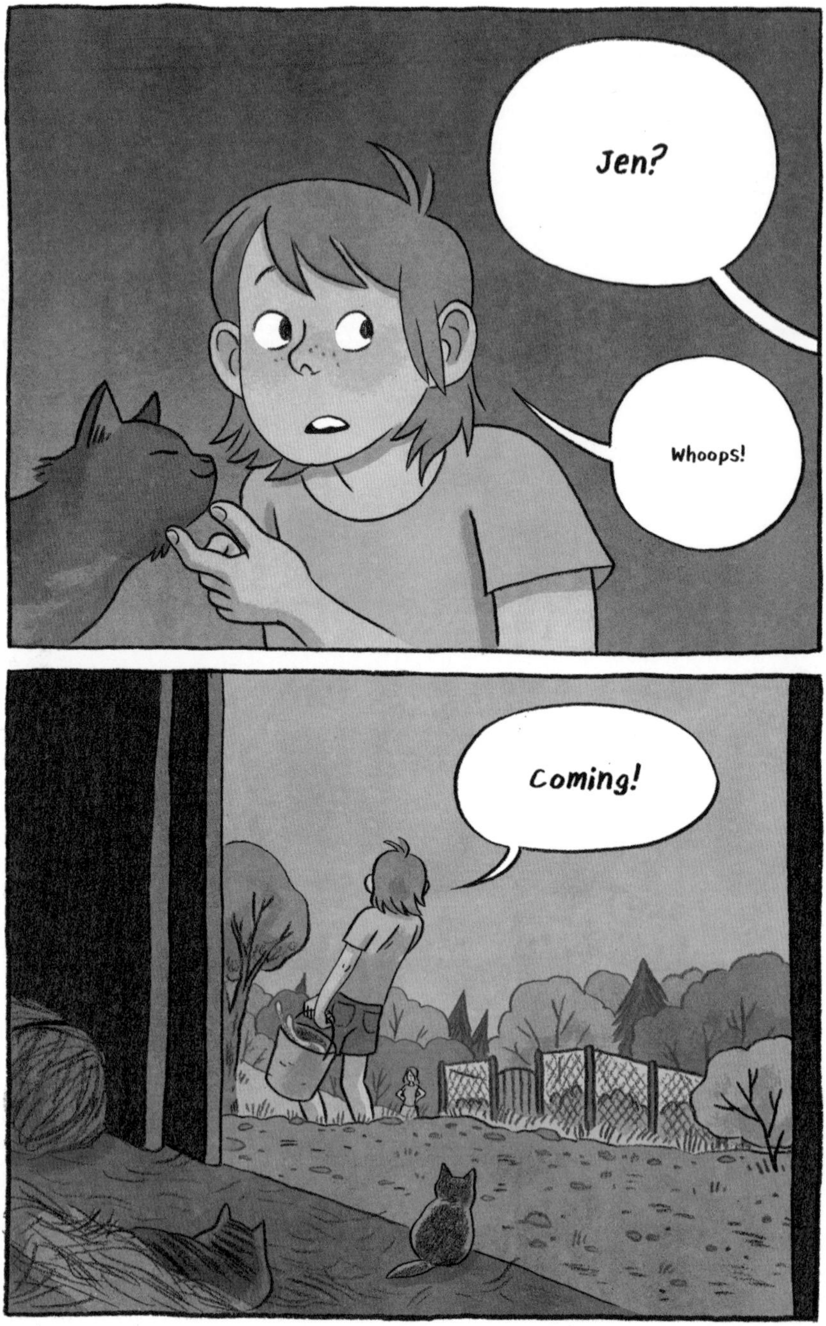
Jen?
Whoops!
Coming!

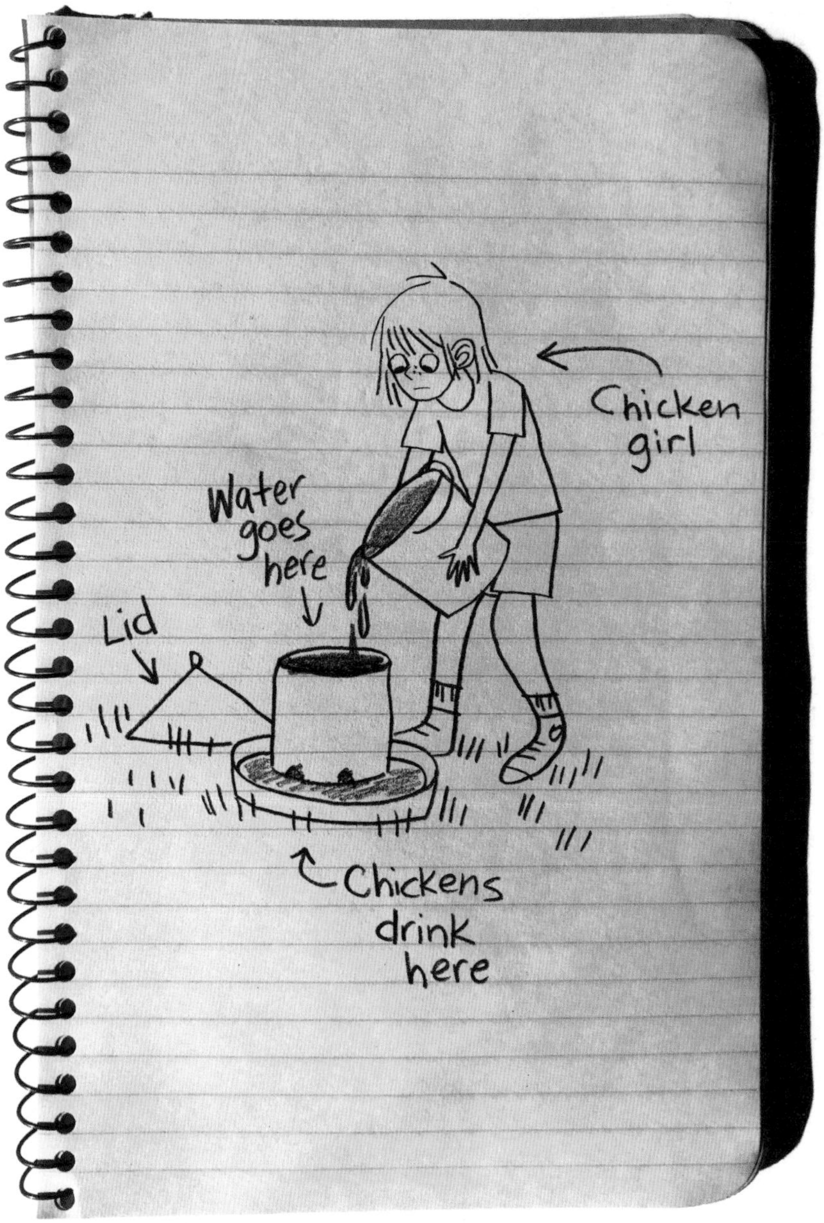
Chicken girl
Water goes here
Lid
Chickens drink here

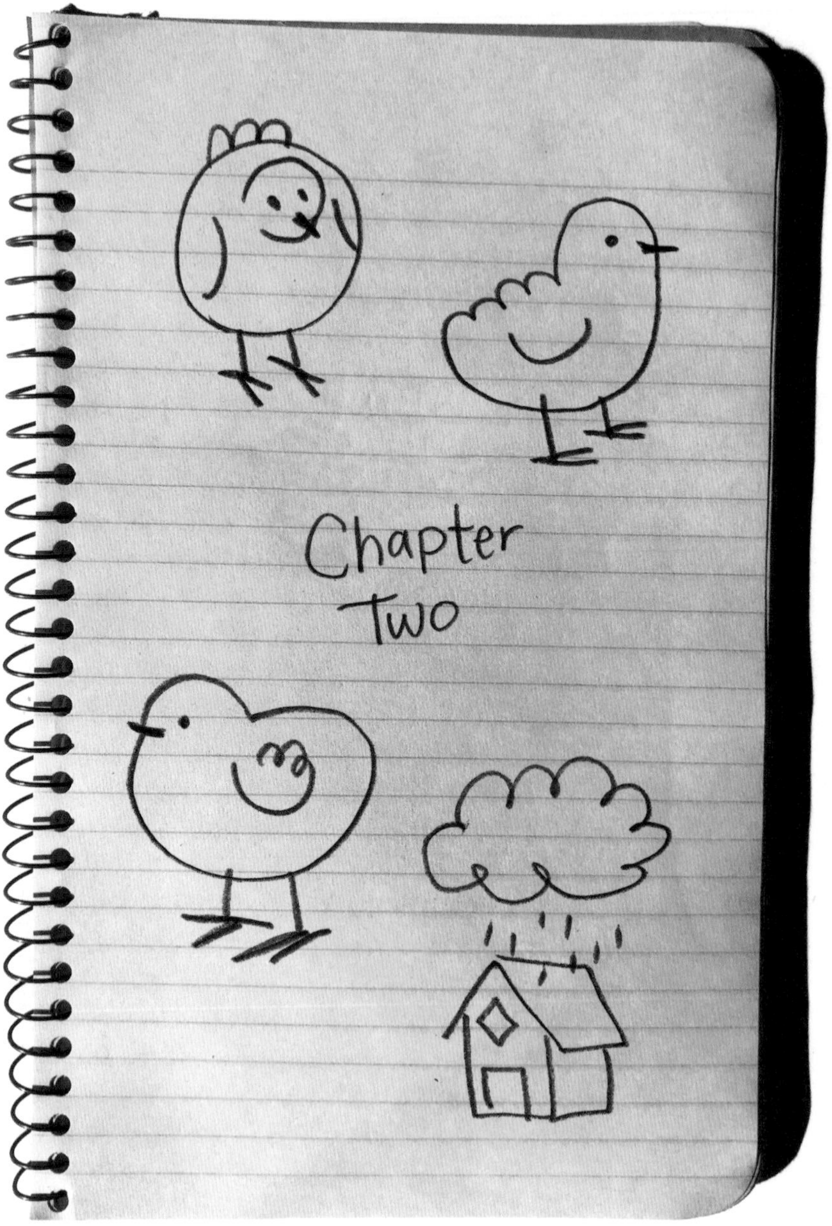
Chapter
Two

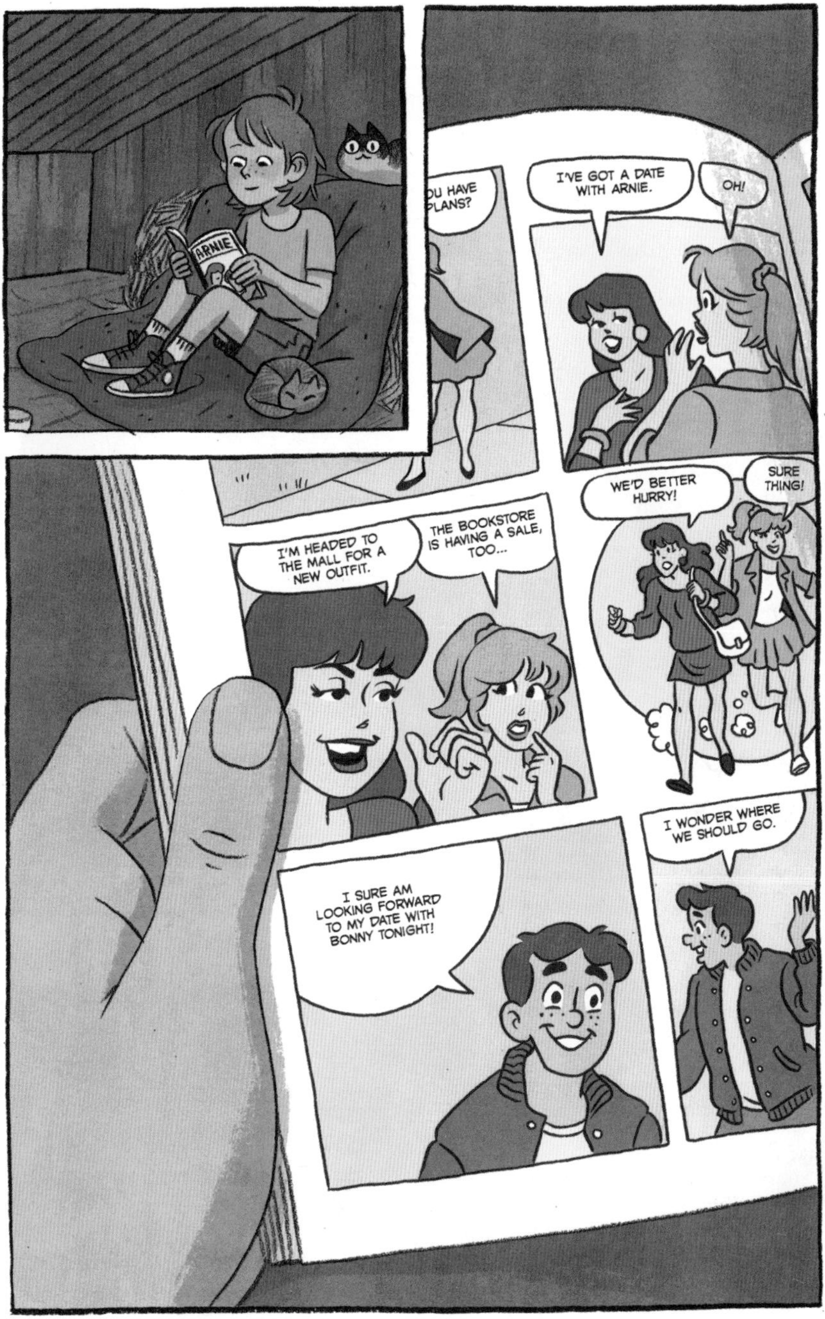
ARNIE
...U HAVE PLANS?
I'VE GOT A DATE WITH ARNIE.
OH!
I'M HEADED TO THE MALL FOR A NEW OUTFIT.
THE BOOKSTORE IS HAVING A SALE, TOO...
WE'D BETTER HURRY!
SURE THING!
I SURE AM LOOKING FORWARD TO MY DATE WITH BONNY TONIGHT!
I WONDER WHERE WE SHOULD GO.

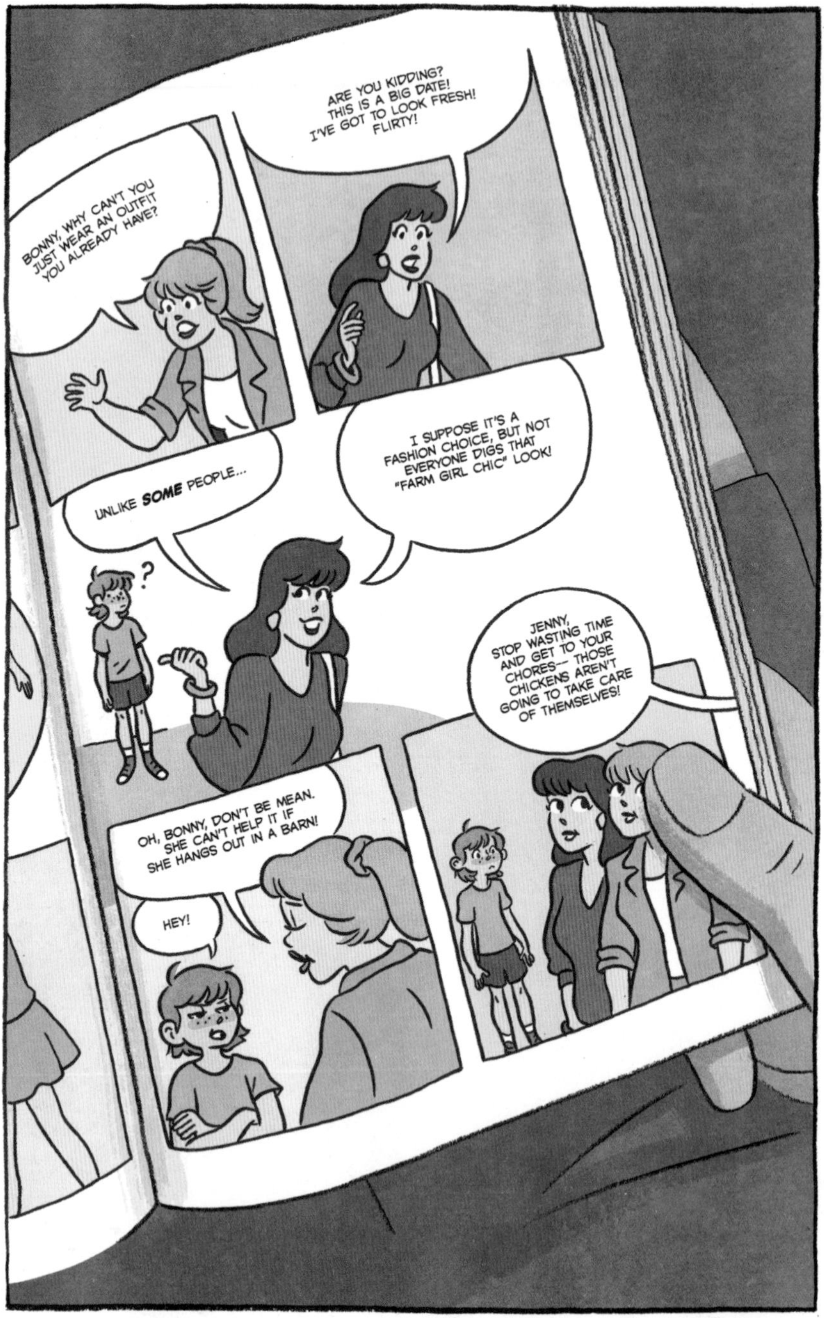
BONNY, WHY CAN'T YOU JUST WEAR AN OUTFIT YOU ALREADY HAVE?
ARE YOU KIDDING? THIS IS A BIG DATE! I'VE GOT TO LOOK FRESH! FLIRTY!
UNLIKE SOME PEOPLE...
I SUPPOSE IT'S A FASHION CHOICE, BUT NOT EVERYONE DIGS THAT "FARM GIRL CHIC" LOOK!
?
JENNY, STOP WASTING TIME AND GET TO YOUR CHORES-- THOSE CHICKENS AREN'T GOING TO TAKE CARE OF THEMSELVES!
OH, BONNY, DON'T BE MEAN. SHE CAN'T HELP IT IF SHE HANGS OUT IN A BARN!
HEY!

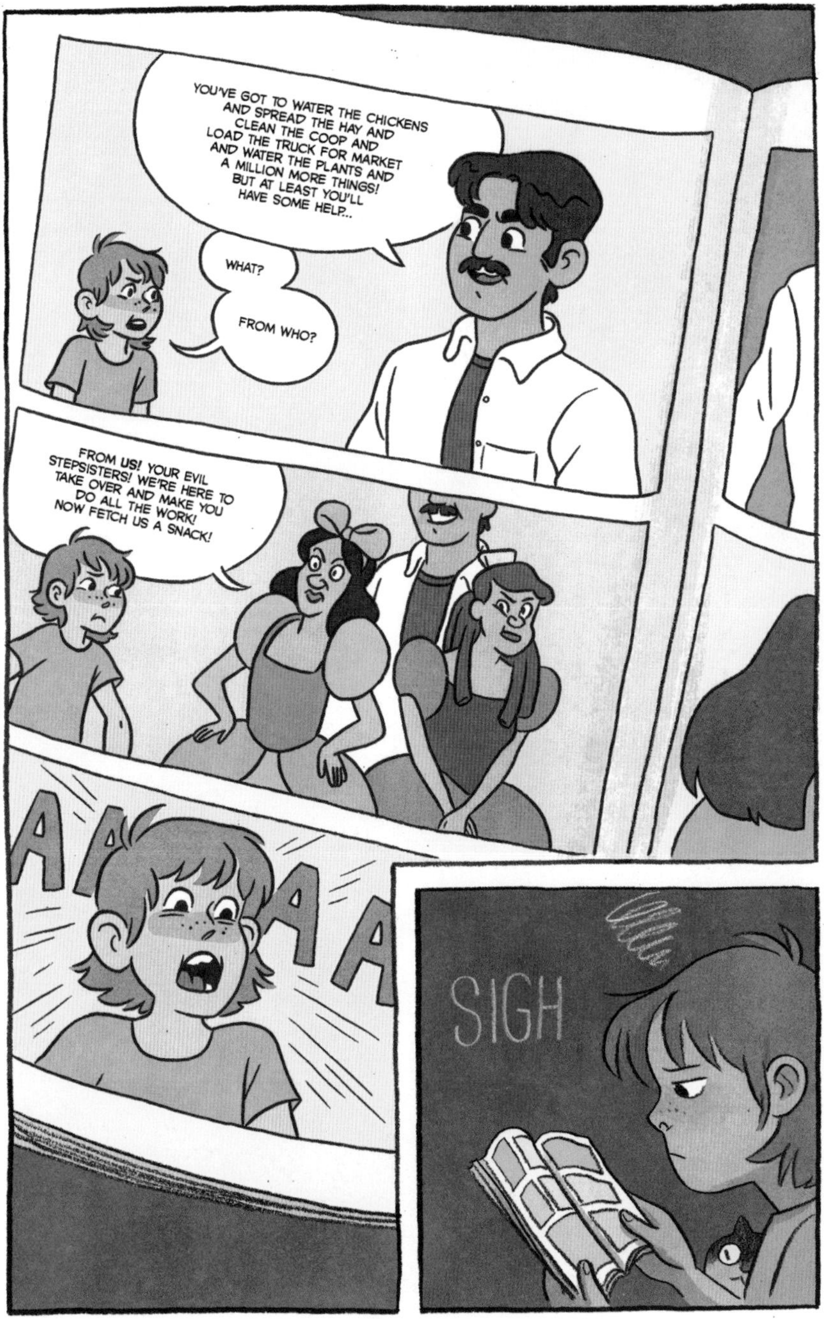
YOU'VE GOT TO WATER THE CHICKENS AND SPREAD THE HAY AND CLEAN THE COOP AND LOAD THE TRUCK FOR MARKET AND WATER THE PLANTS AND A MILLION MORE THINGS! BUT AT LEAST YOU'LL HAVE SOME HELP...
WHAT?
FROM WHO?
FROM US! YOUR EVIL STEPSISTERS! WE'RE HERE TO TAKE OVER AND MAKE YOU DO ALL THE WORK! NOW FETCH US A SNACK!
AAAA
SIGH

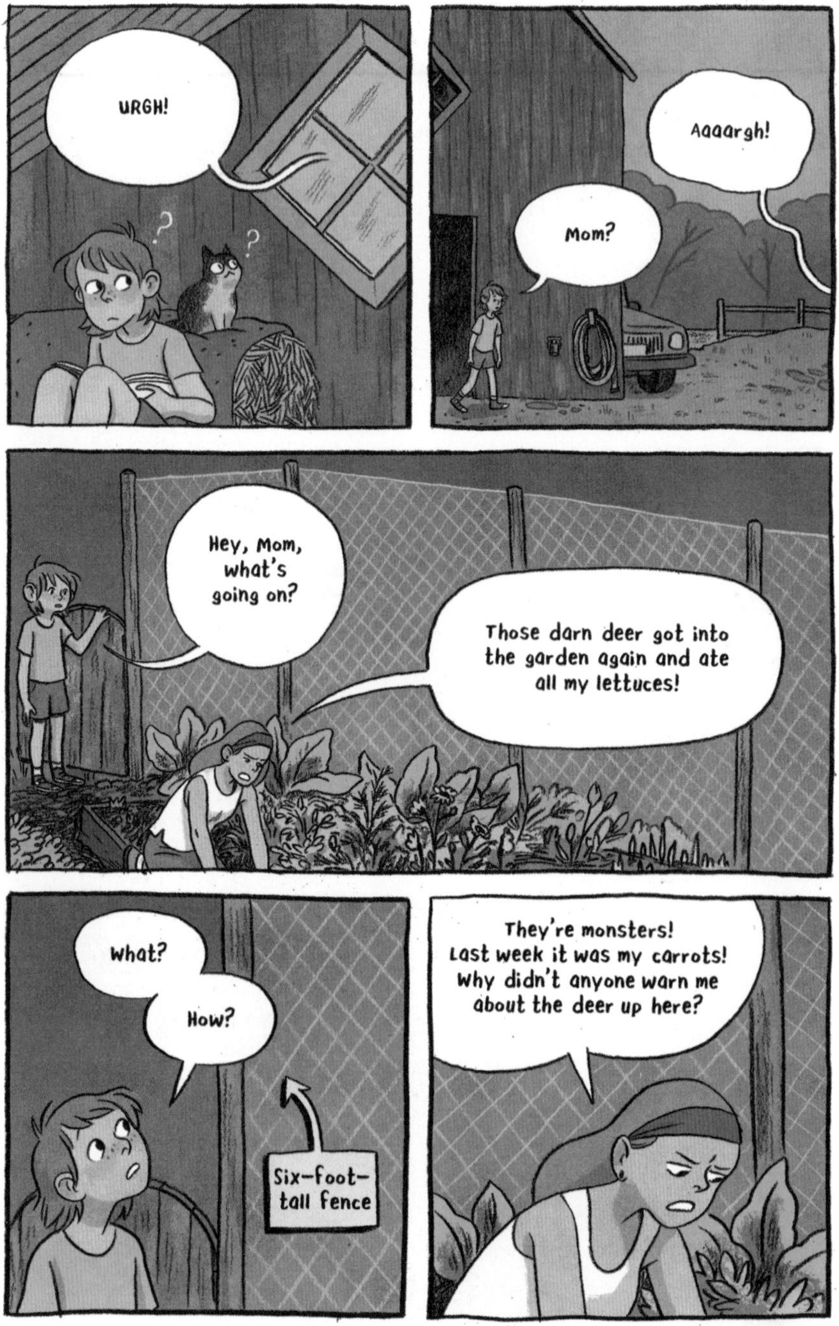
URGH!
Aaaargh!
Mom?
Hey, Mom, what's going on?
Those darn deer got into the garden again and ate all my lettuces!
What?
How?
Six-foot-tall fence
They're monsters! Last week it was my carrots! Why didn't anyone warn me about the deer up here?

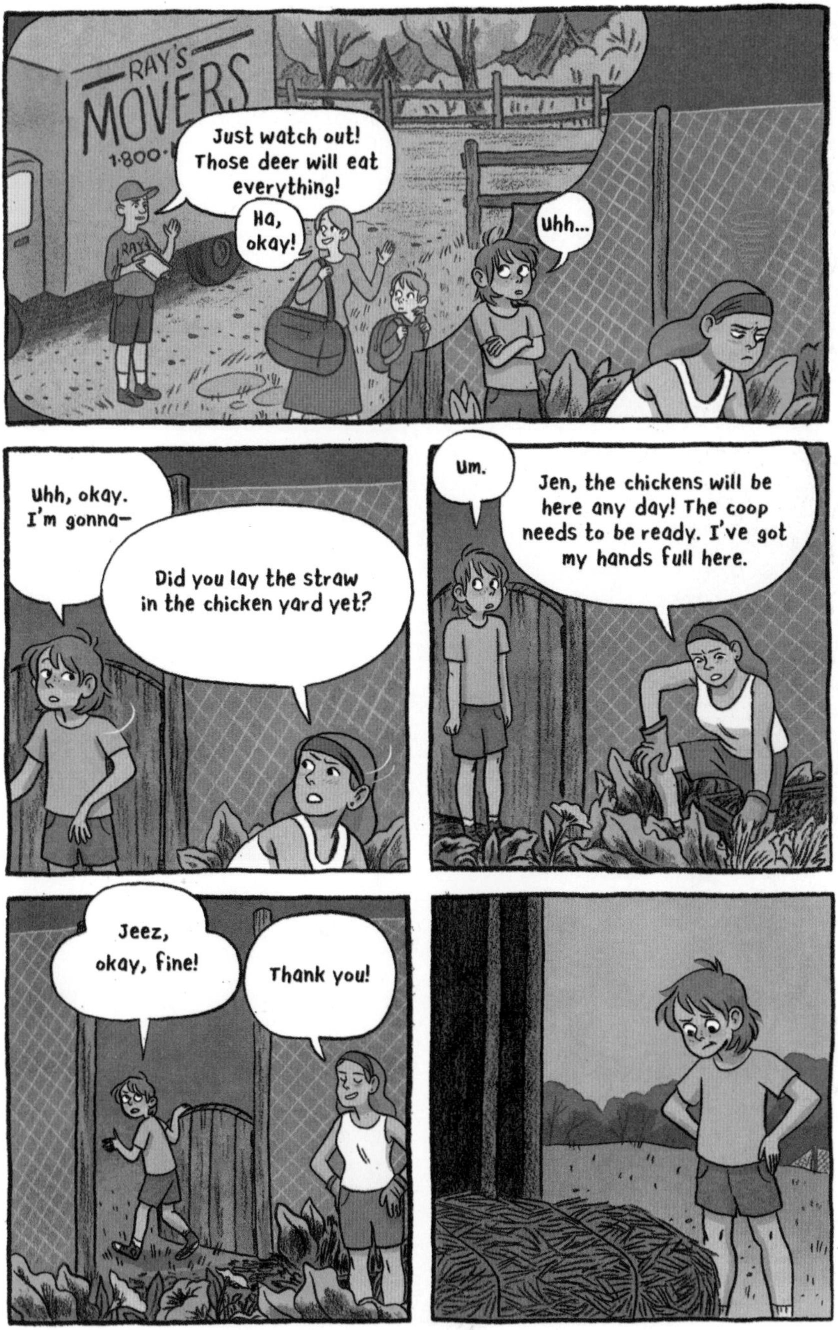
RAY'S MOVERS 1·800·
Just watch out! Those deer will eat everything!
Ha, okay!
Uhh...
Uhh, okay. I'm gonna–
Did you lay the straw in the chicken yard yet?
Um.
Jen, the chickens will be here any day! The coop needs to be ready. I've got my hands full here.
Jeez, okay, fine!
Thank you!

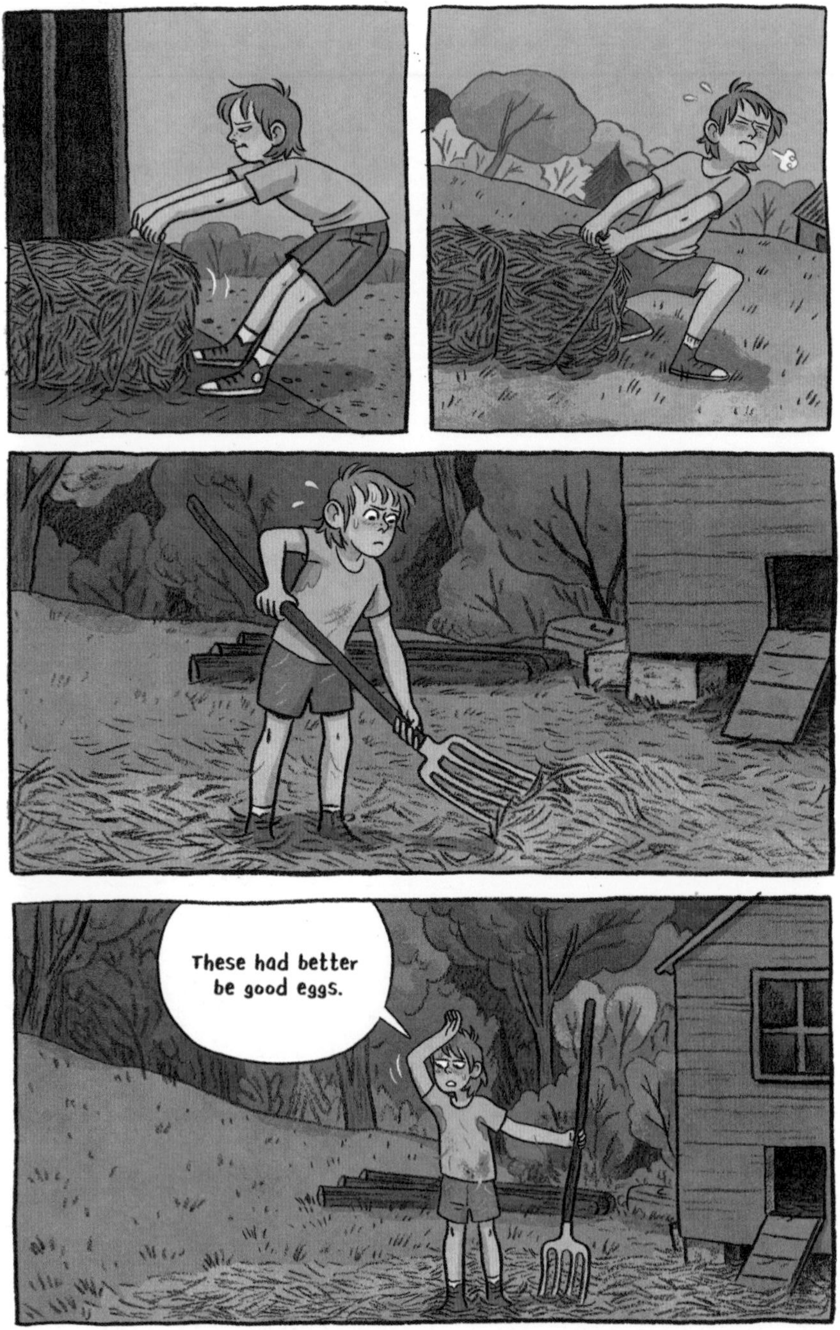
These had better be good eggs.

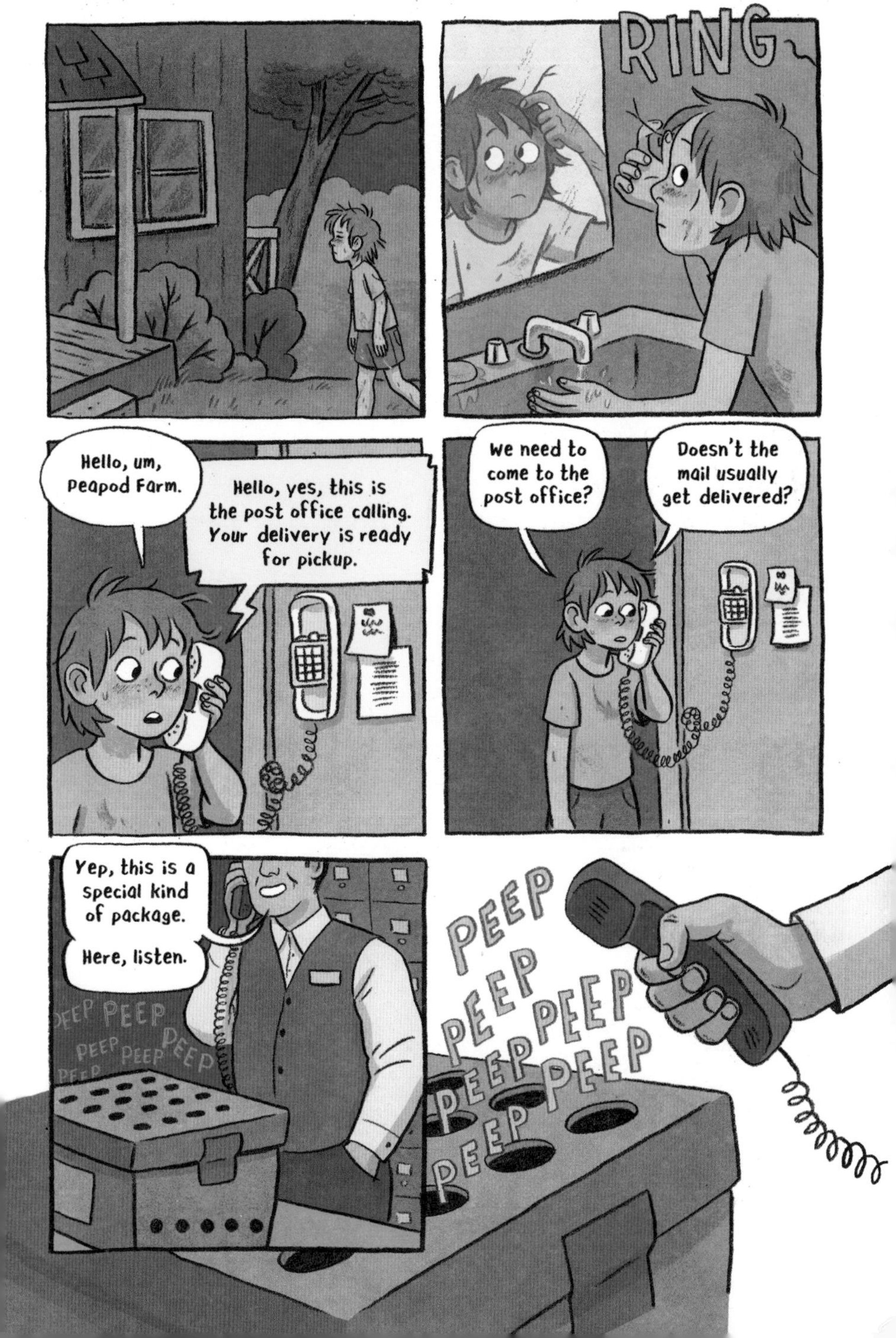
RING
Hello, um, Peapod Farm.
Hello, yes, this is the post office calling. Your delivery is ready for pickup.
We need to come to the post office?
Doesn't the mail usually get delivered?
Yep, this is a special kind of package.
Here, listen.
PEEP PEEP PEEP PEEP PEEP PEEP
PEEP PEEP PEEP PEEP PEEP PEEP PEEP

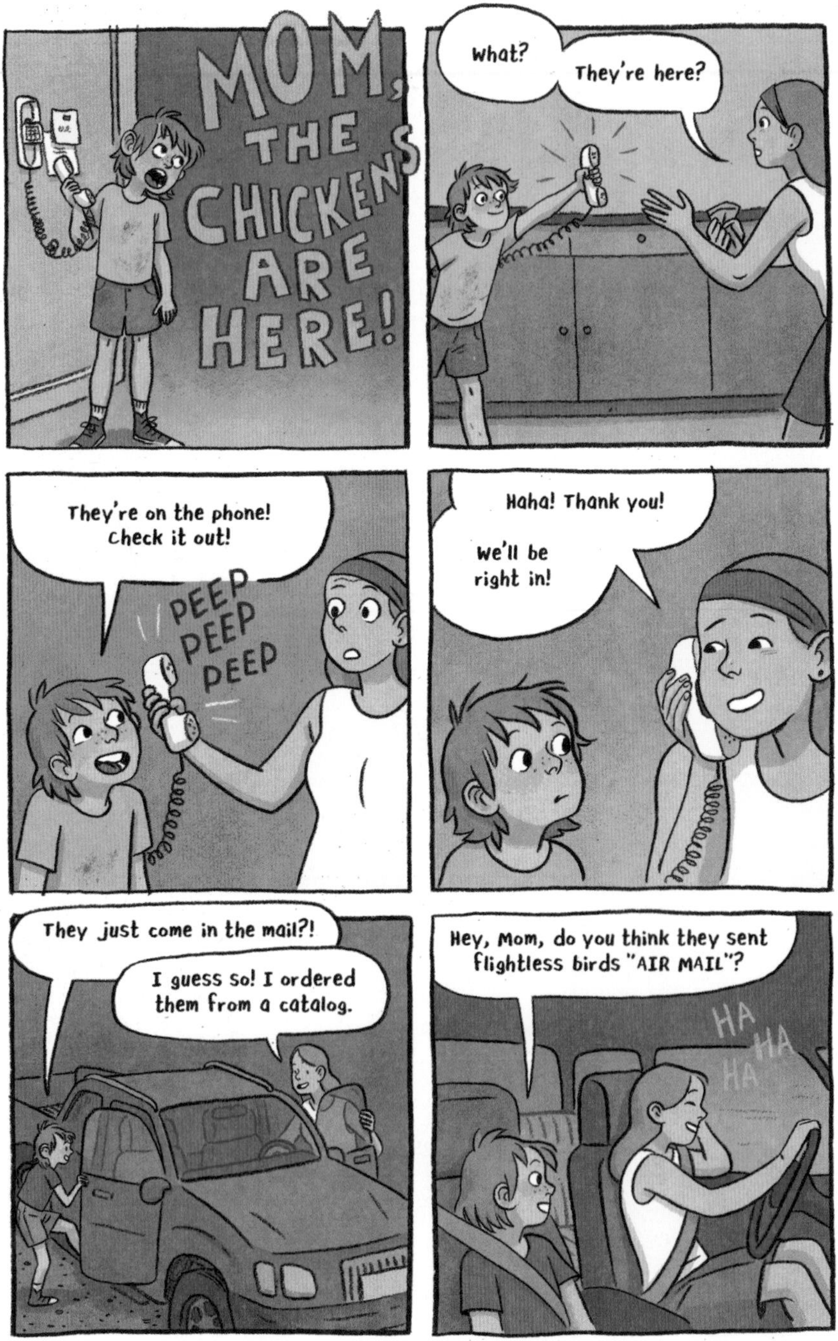
MOM, THE CHICKENS ARE HERE!
What?
They're here?
They're on the phone! Check it out!
PEEP PEEP PEEP
Haha! Thank you!
We'll be right in!
They just come in the mail?!
I guess so! I ordered them from a catalog.
Hey, Mom, do you think they sent flightless birds "AIR MAIL"?
HA HA HA

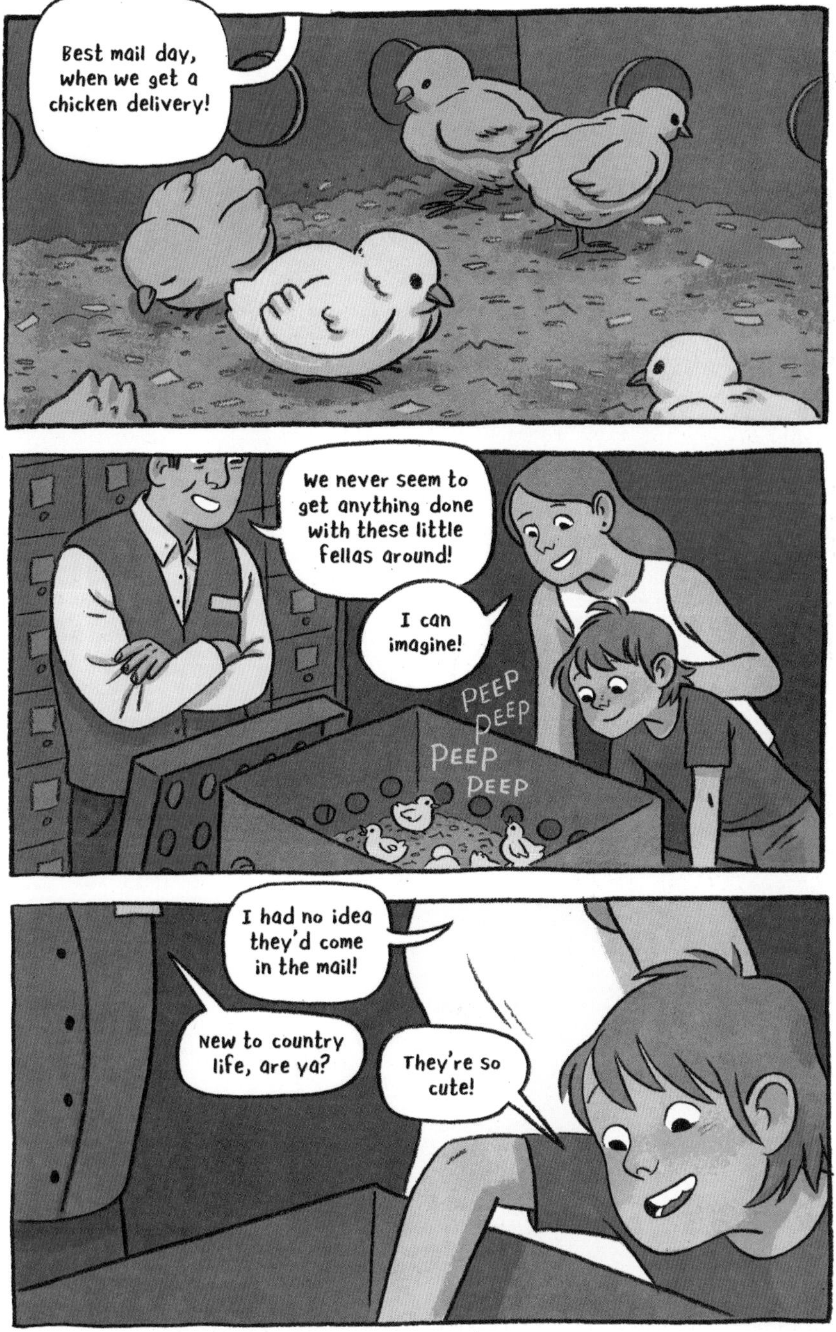
Best mail day, when we get a chicken delivery!
We never seem to get anything done with these little fellas around!
I can imagine!
PEEP PEEP PEEP PEEP
I had no idea they'd come in the mail!
New to country life, are ya?
They're so cute!

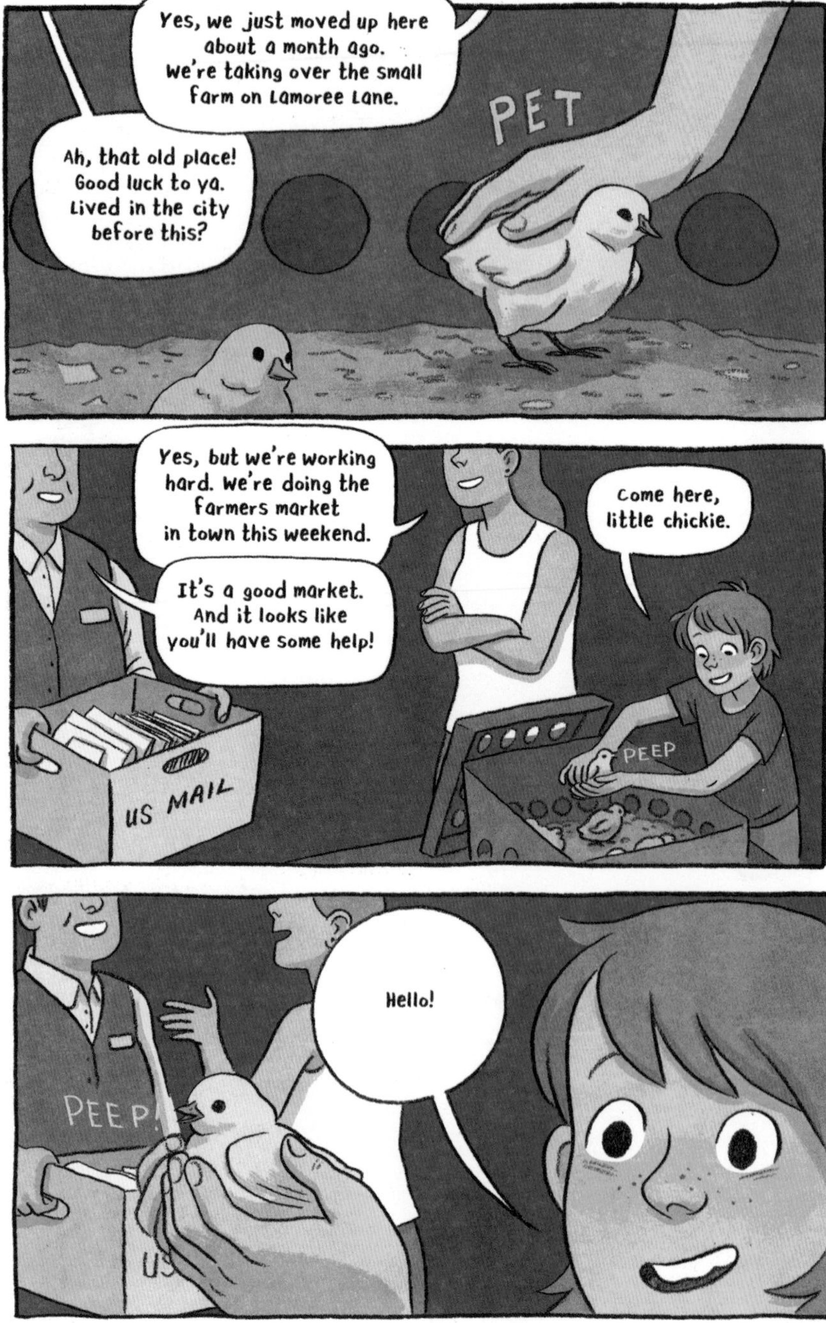
Yes, we just moved up here about a month ago. We're taking over the small farm on Lamoree Lane.
Ah, that old place! Good luck to ya. Lived in the city before this?
PET
Yes, but we're working hard. We're doing the farmers market in town this weekend.
It's a good market. And it looks like you'll have some help!
Come here, little chickie.
US MAIL
PEEP
Hello!
PEEP!

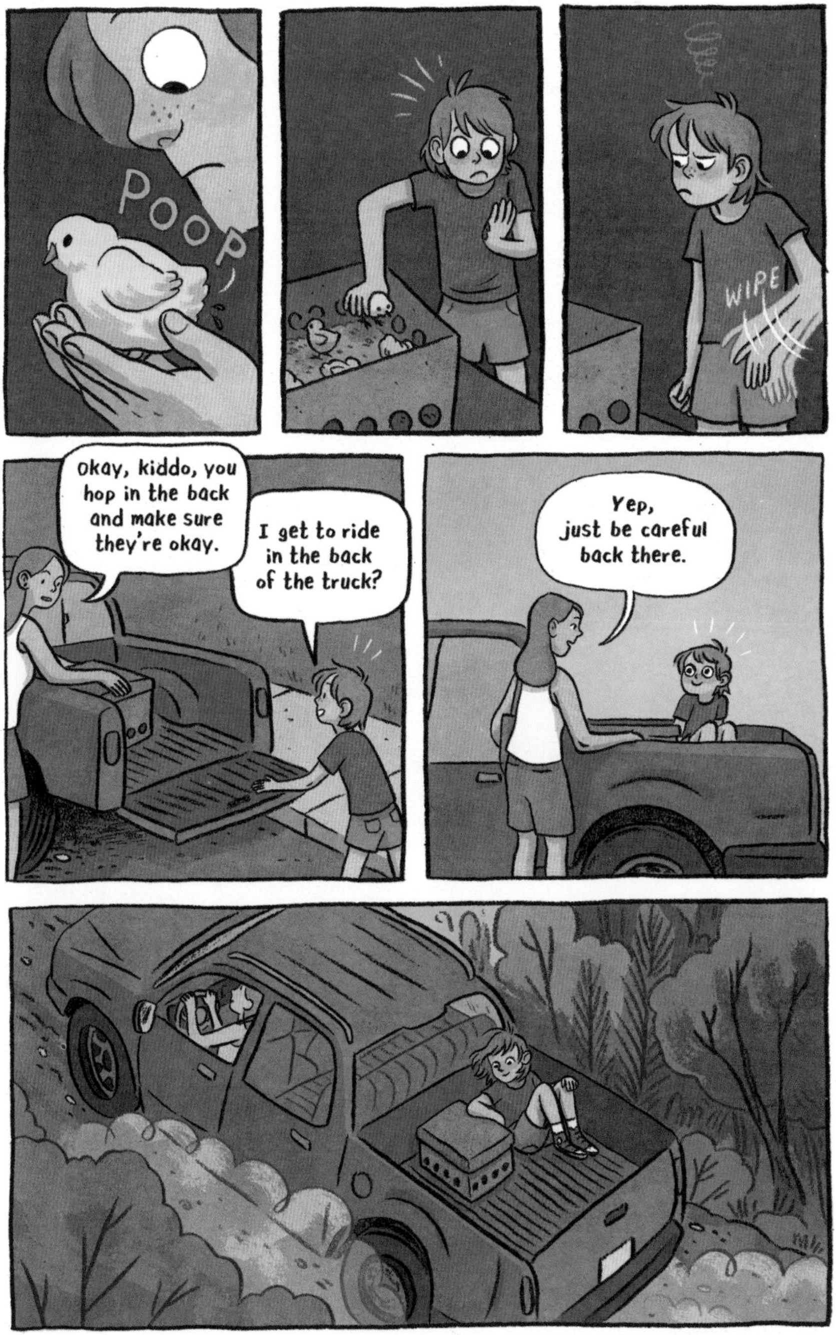
POOP
WIPE
Okay, kiddo, you hop in the back and make sure they're okay.
I get to ride in the back of the truck?
Yep, just be careful back there.

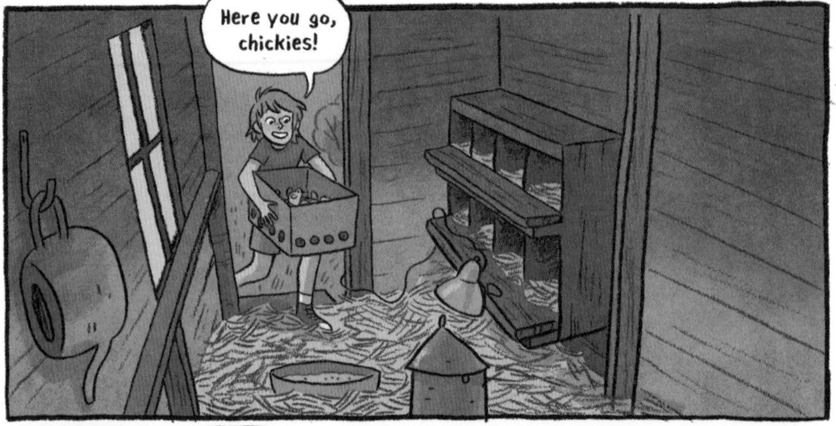
Here you go, chickies!

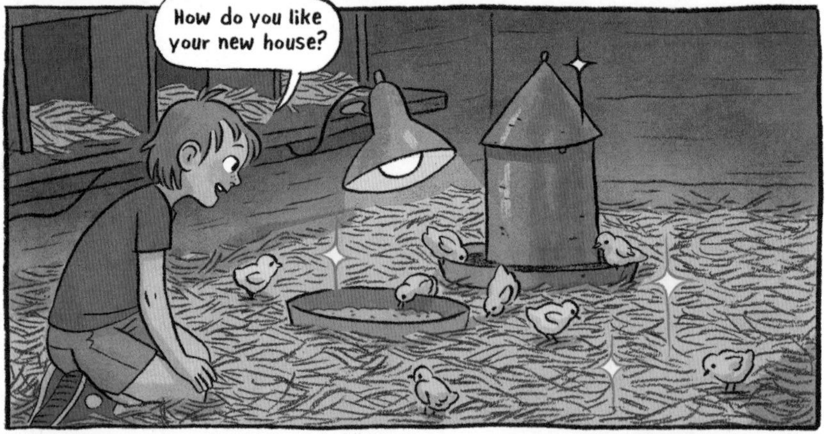
How do you like your new house?

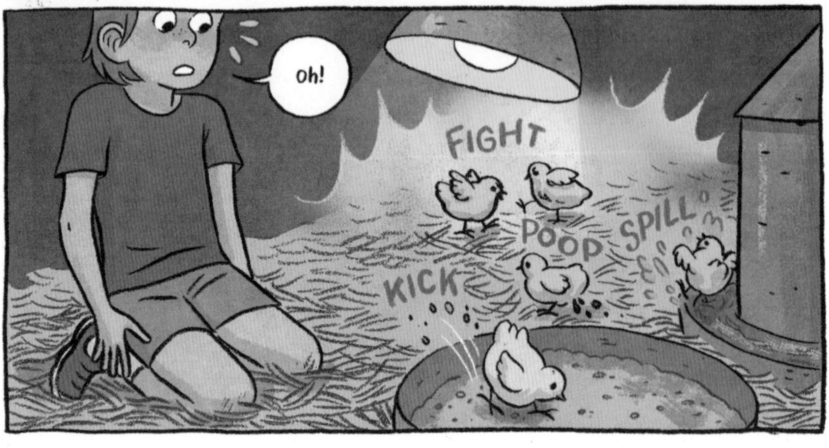
Oh!
FIGHT
POOP
SPILL
KICK

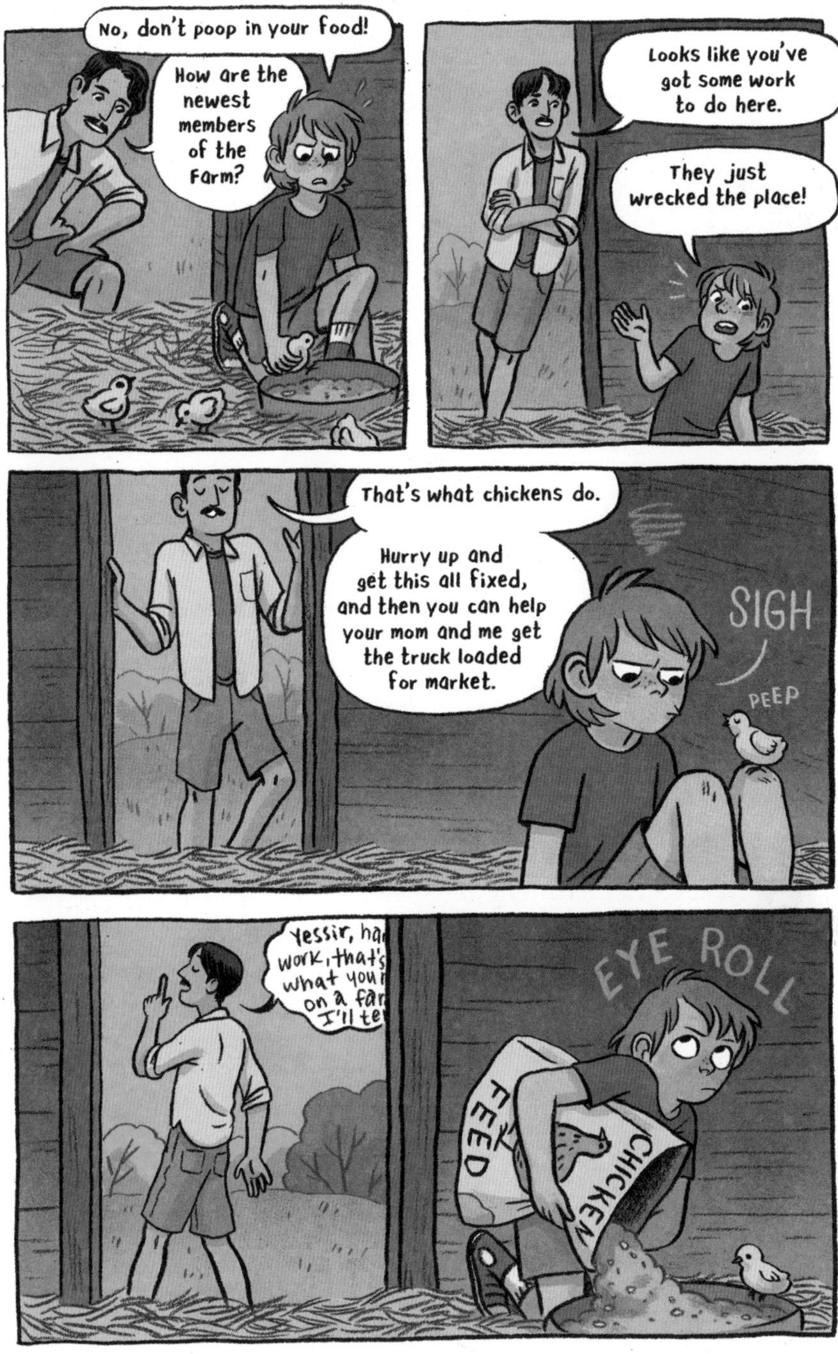
No, don't poop in your food!
How are the newest members of the Farm?
Looks like you've got some work to do here.
They just wrecked the place!
That's what chickens do.
Hurry up and get this all fixed, and then you can help your mom and me get the truck loaded for market.
SIGH
PEEP
Yessir, ha
work, that's
what you
on a far
I'll te
EYE ROLL
CHICKEN FEED

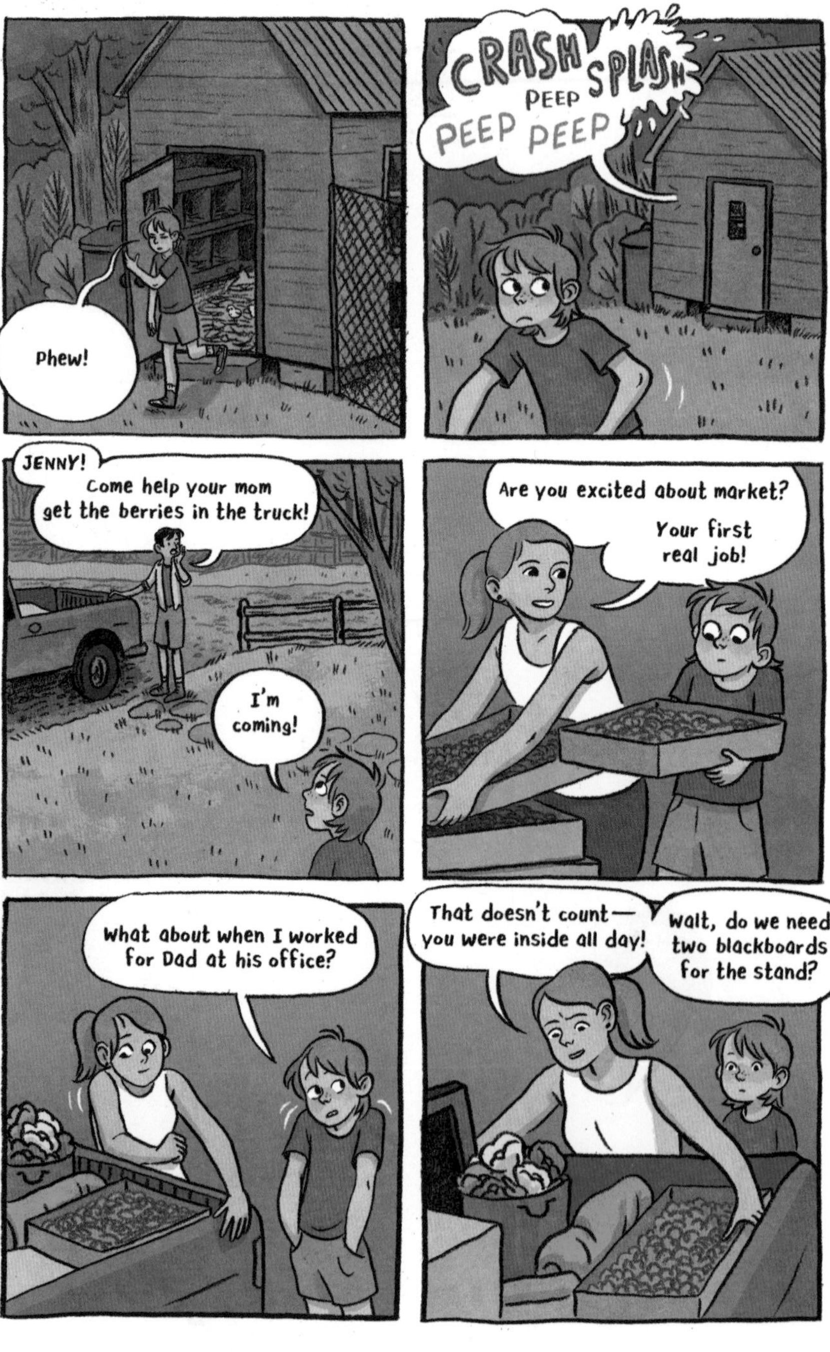
Phew!
CRASH
PEEP
PEEP PEEP
SPLASH
JENNY!
Come help your mom get the berries in the truck!
I'm coming!
Are you excited about market?
Your first real job!
What about when I worked for Dad at his office?
That doesn't count— you were inside all day!
Walt, do we need two blackboards for the stand?

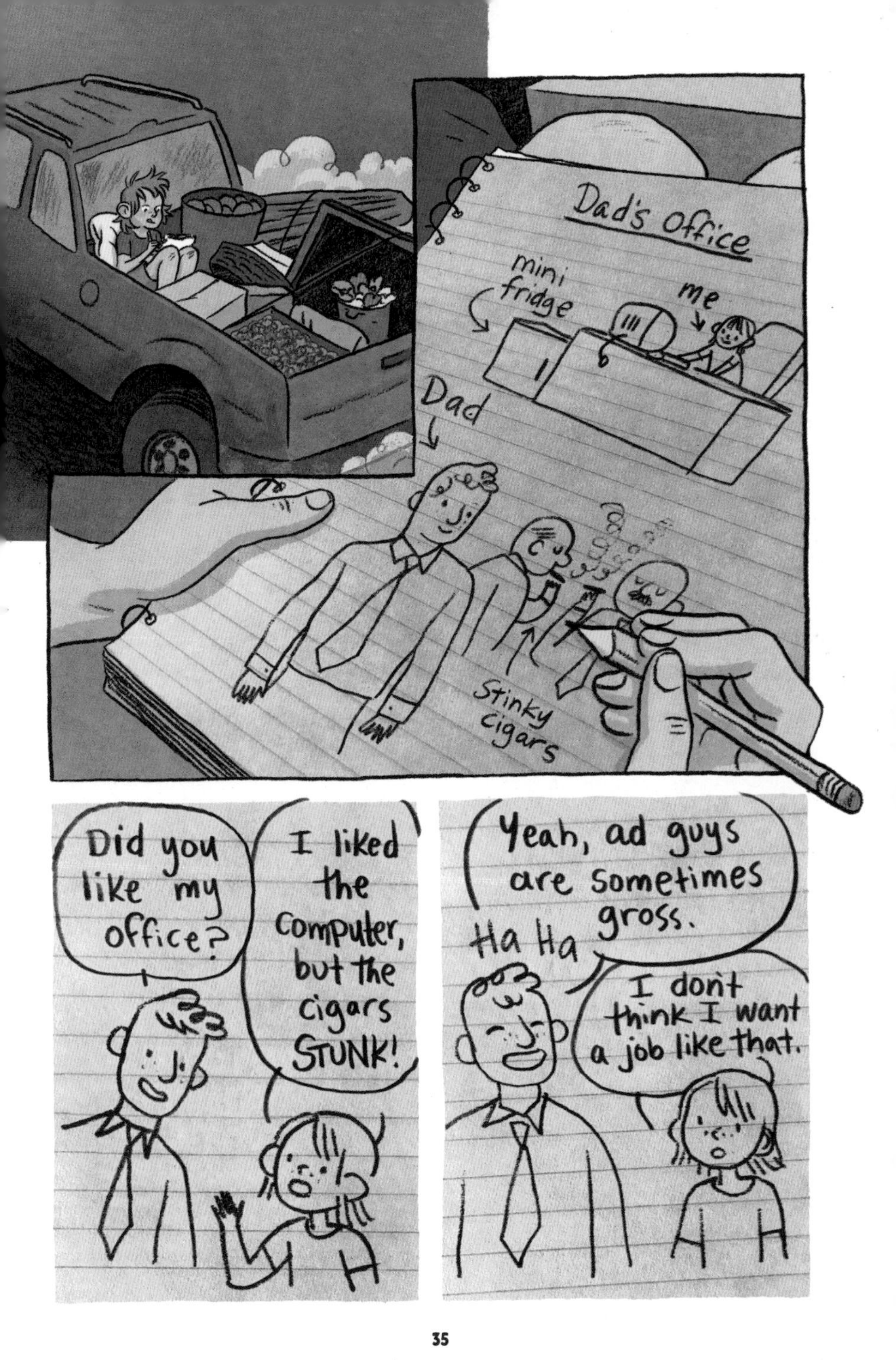
Dad's Office
mini fridge
me
Dad
Stinky cigars
Did you like my office?
I liked the computer, but the cigars STUNK!
Yeah, ad guys are sometimes gross.
Ha Ha
I don't think I want a job like that.

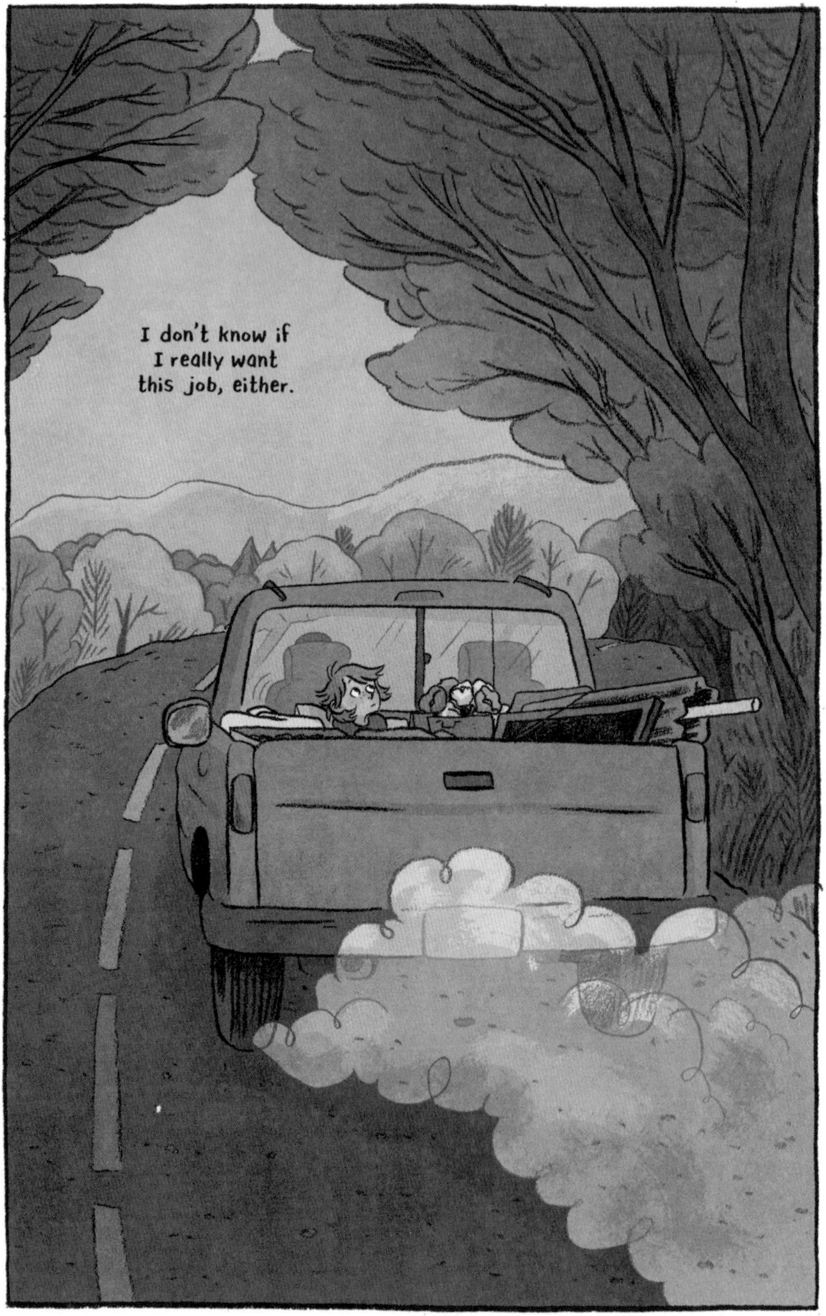
I don't know if
I really want
this job, either.

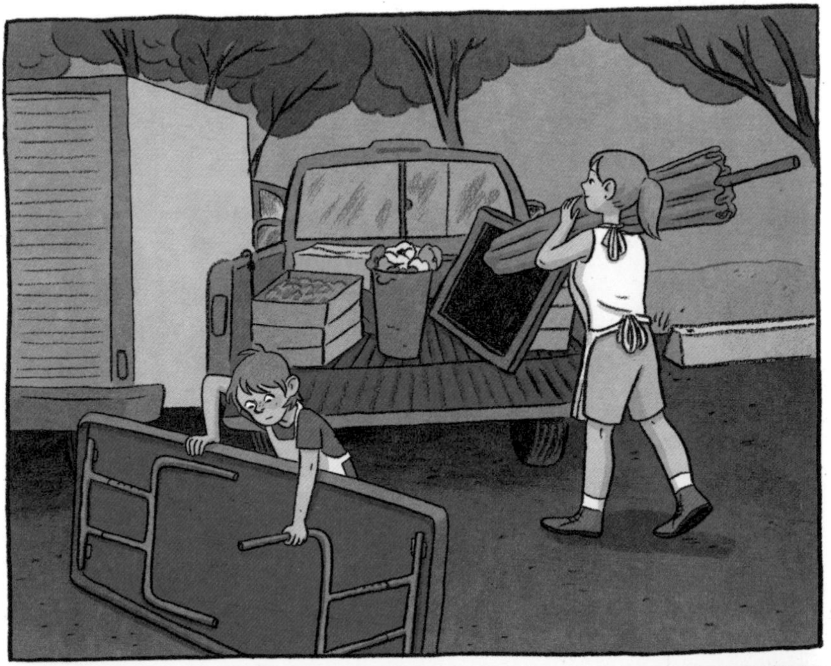

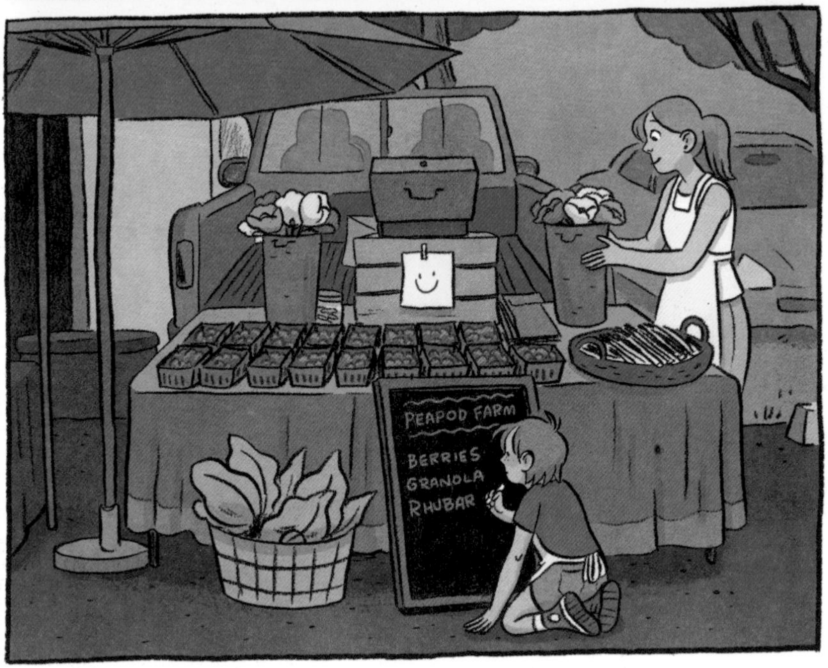
PEAPOD FARM
BERRIES
GRANOLA
RHUBAR

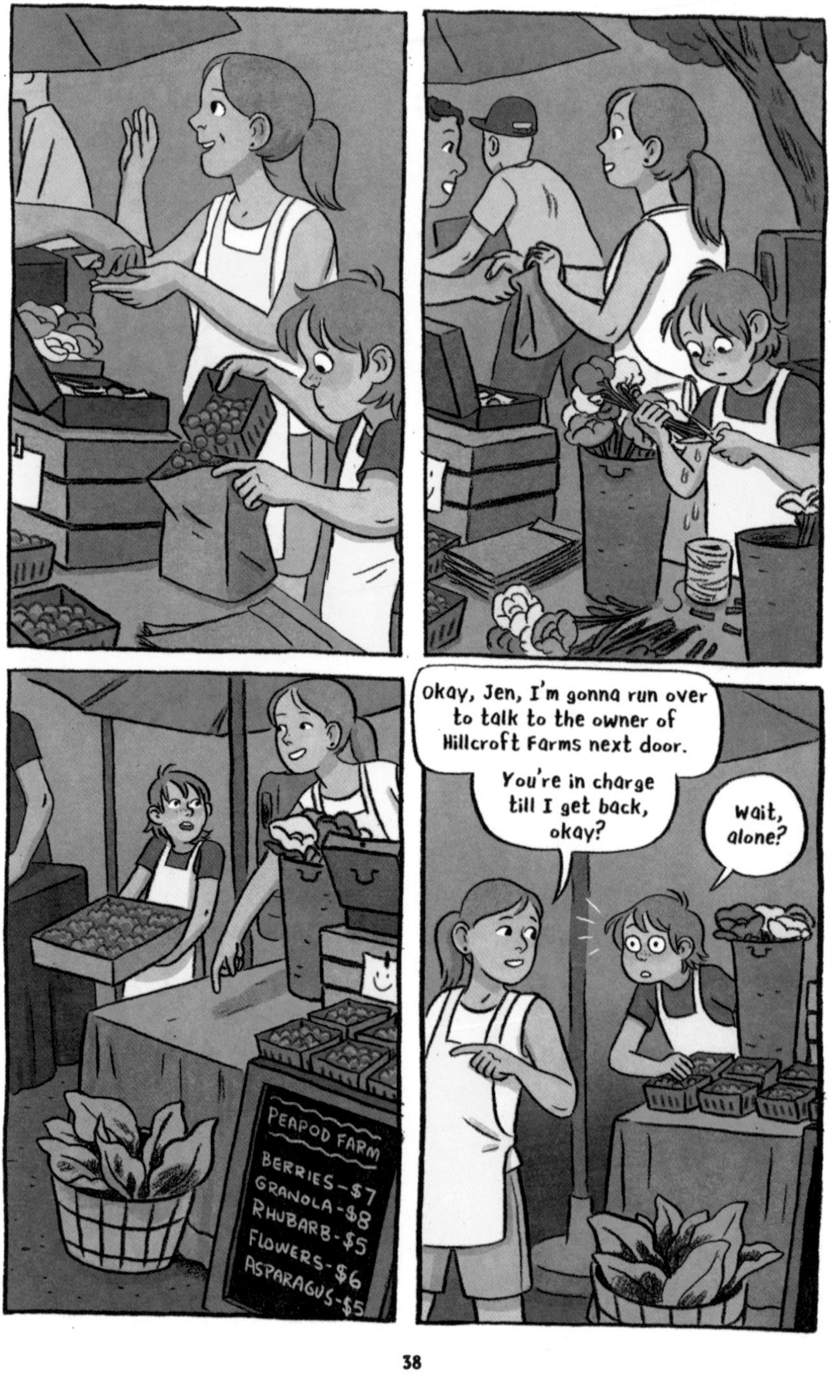
PEAPOD FARM
BERRIES - $7
GRANOLA - $8
RHUBARB - $5
FLOWERS - $6
ASPARAGUS - $5
Okay, Jen, I'm gonna run over to talk to the owner of Hillcroft Farms next door.
You're in charge till I get back, okay?
Wait, alone?

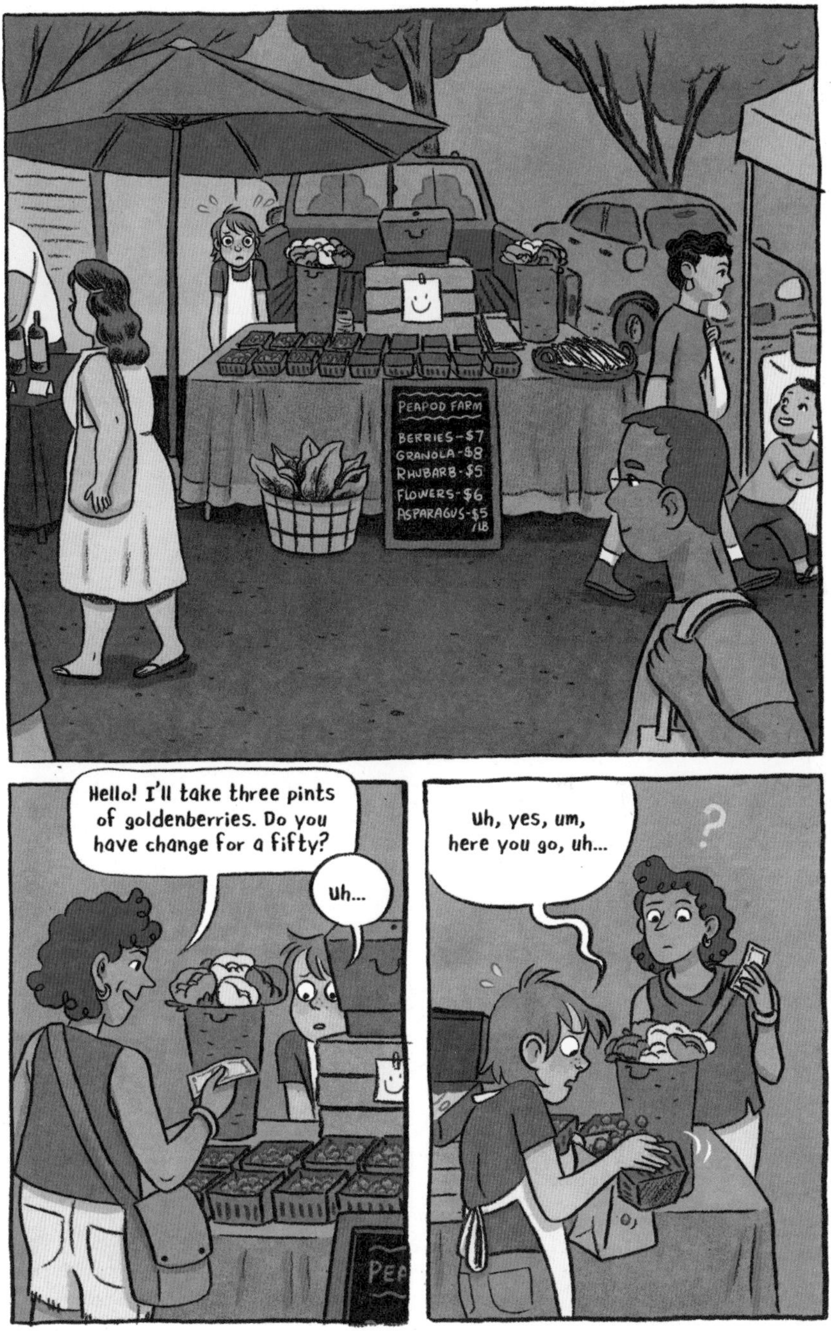
PEAPOD FARM
BERRIES - $7
GRANOLA - $8
RHUBARB - $5
FLOWERS - $6
ASPARAGUS - $5 /LB
Hello! I'll take three pints of goldenberries. Do you have change for a fifty?
uh...
uh, yes, um, here you go, uh...
?

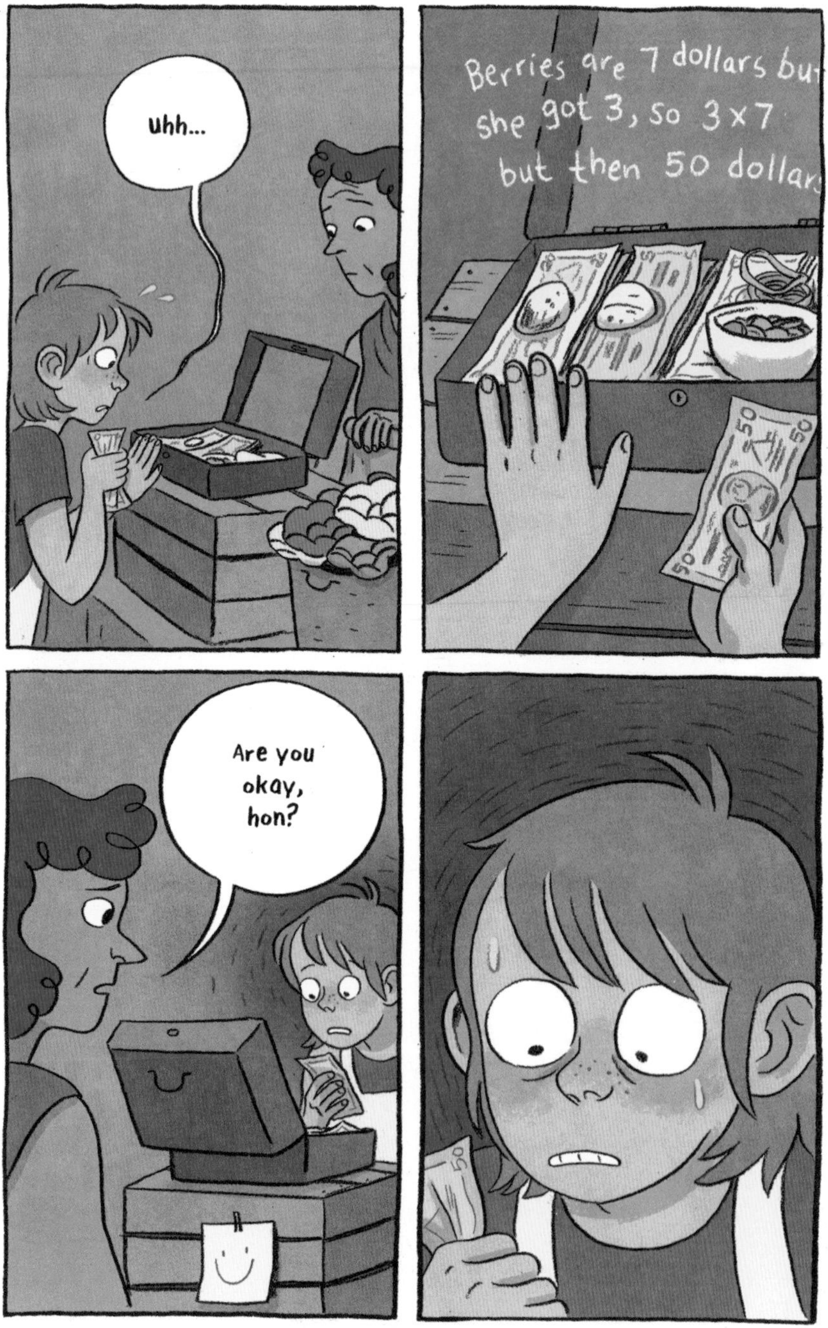
uhh...
Berries are 7 dollars but she got 3, so 3x7 but then 50 dollars
50
Are you okay, hon?
50

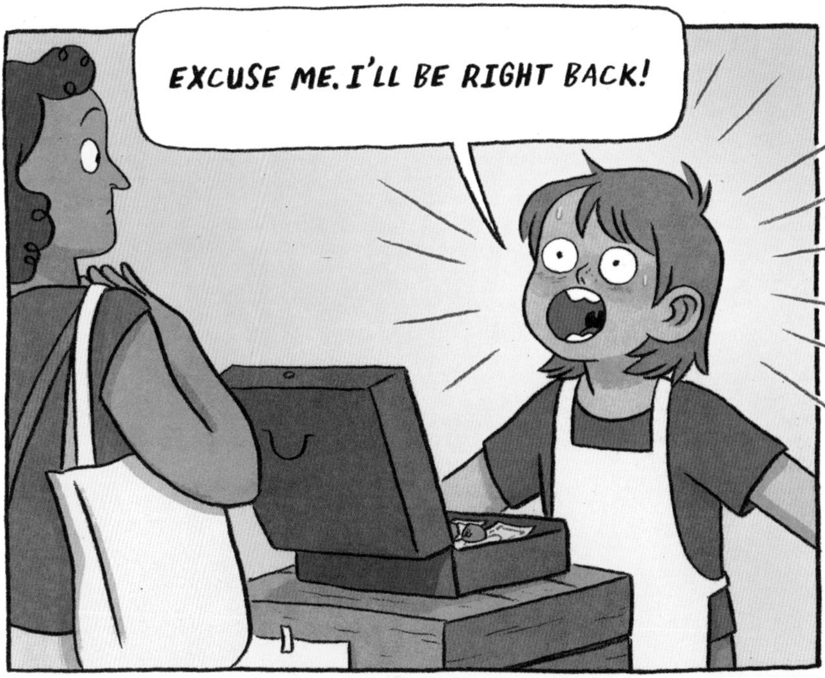
EXCUSE ME. I'LL BE RIGHT BACK!

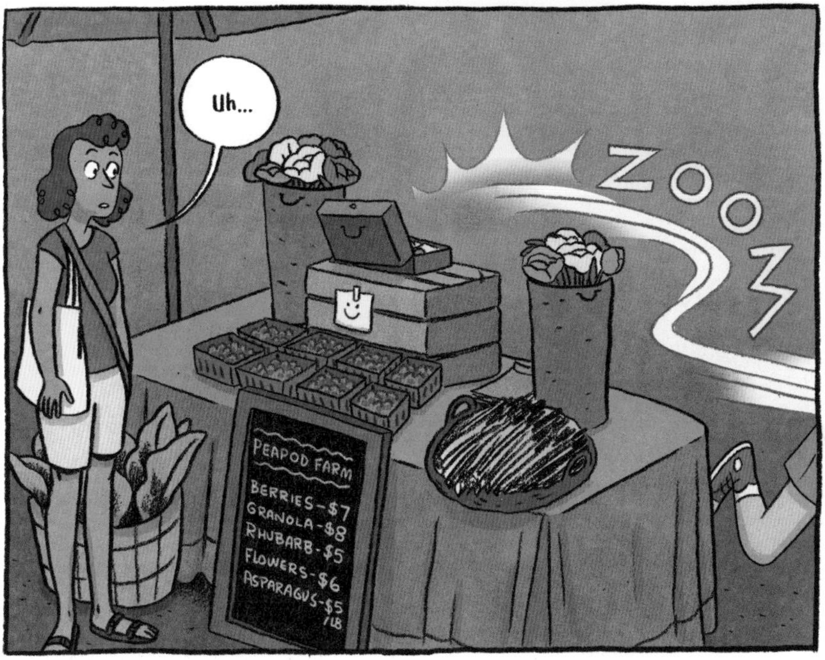
Uh...
ZOOOM
PEAPOD FARM
BERRIES-$7
GRANOLA-$8
RHUBARB-$5
FLOWERS-$6
ASPARAGUS-$5 /LB

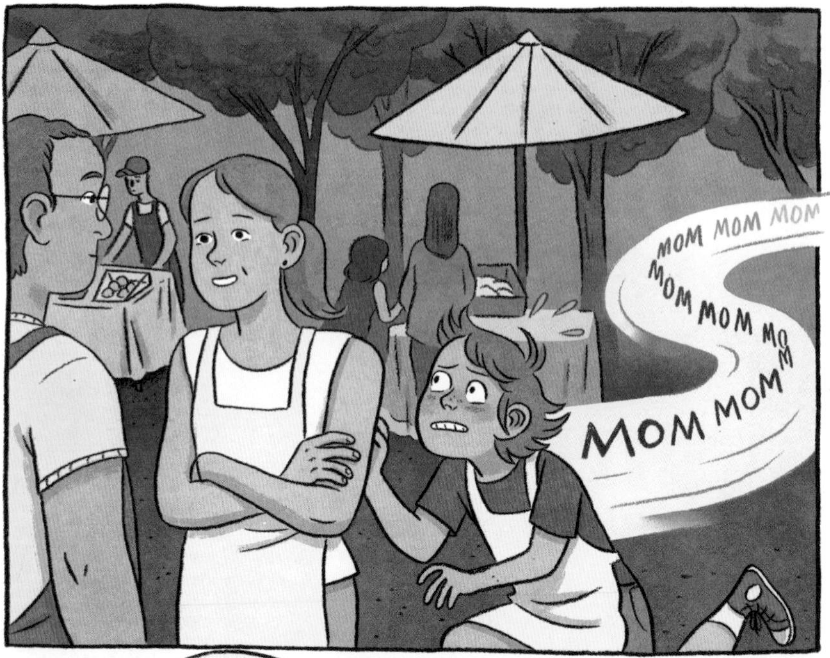
MOM MOM MOM
MOM MOM MOM MOM
MOM MOM

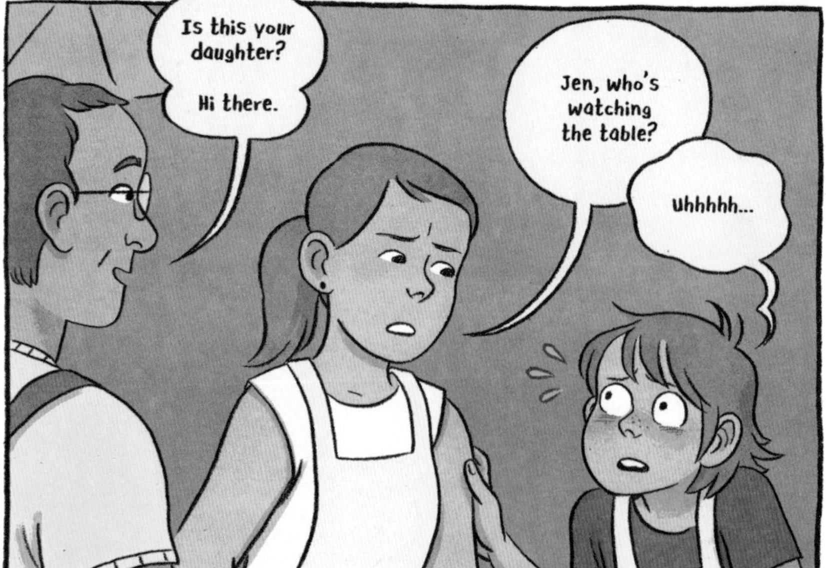
Is this your daughter?
Hi there.
Jen, who's watching the table?
Uhhhhh...

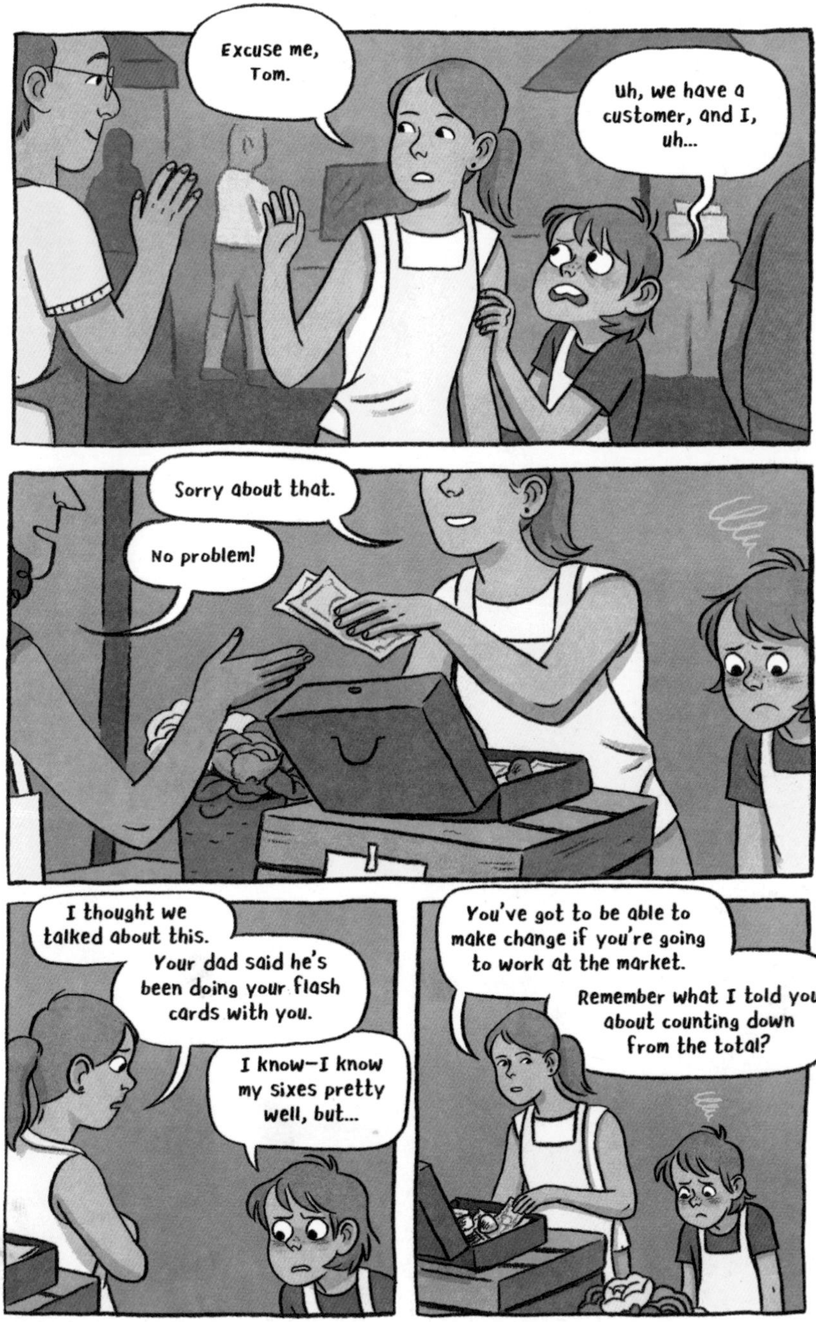

Excuse me, Tom.
Uh, we have a customer, and I, uh...
Sorry about that.
No problem!
I thought we talked about this.
Your dad said he's been doing your flash cards with you.
I know—I know my sixes pretty well, but...
You've got to be able to make change if you're going to work at the market.
Remember what I told you about counting down from the total?

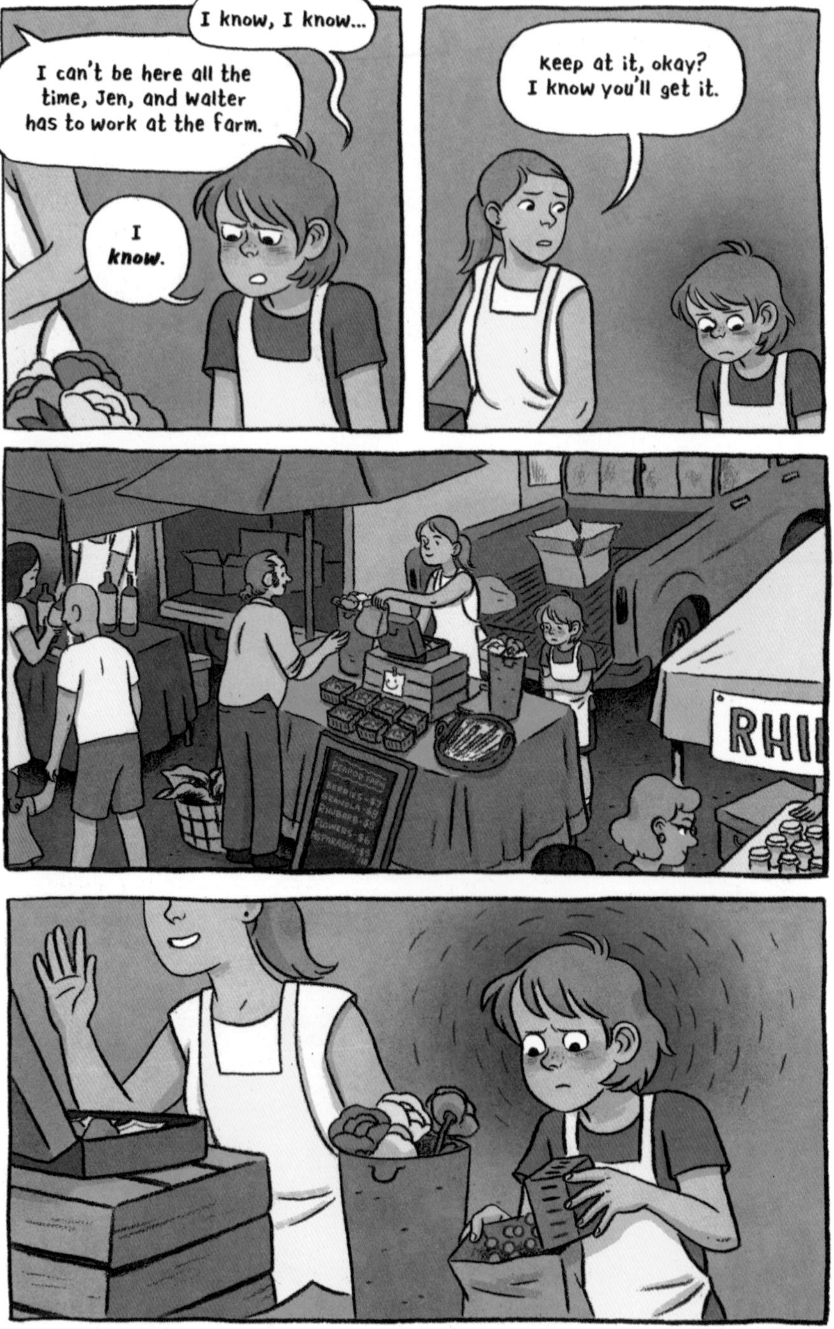
I can't be here all the time, Jen, and Walter has to work at the farm.
I know, I know...
I know.
Keep at it, okay? I know you'll get it.
RHI

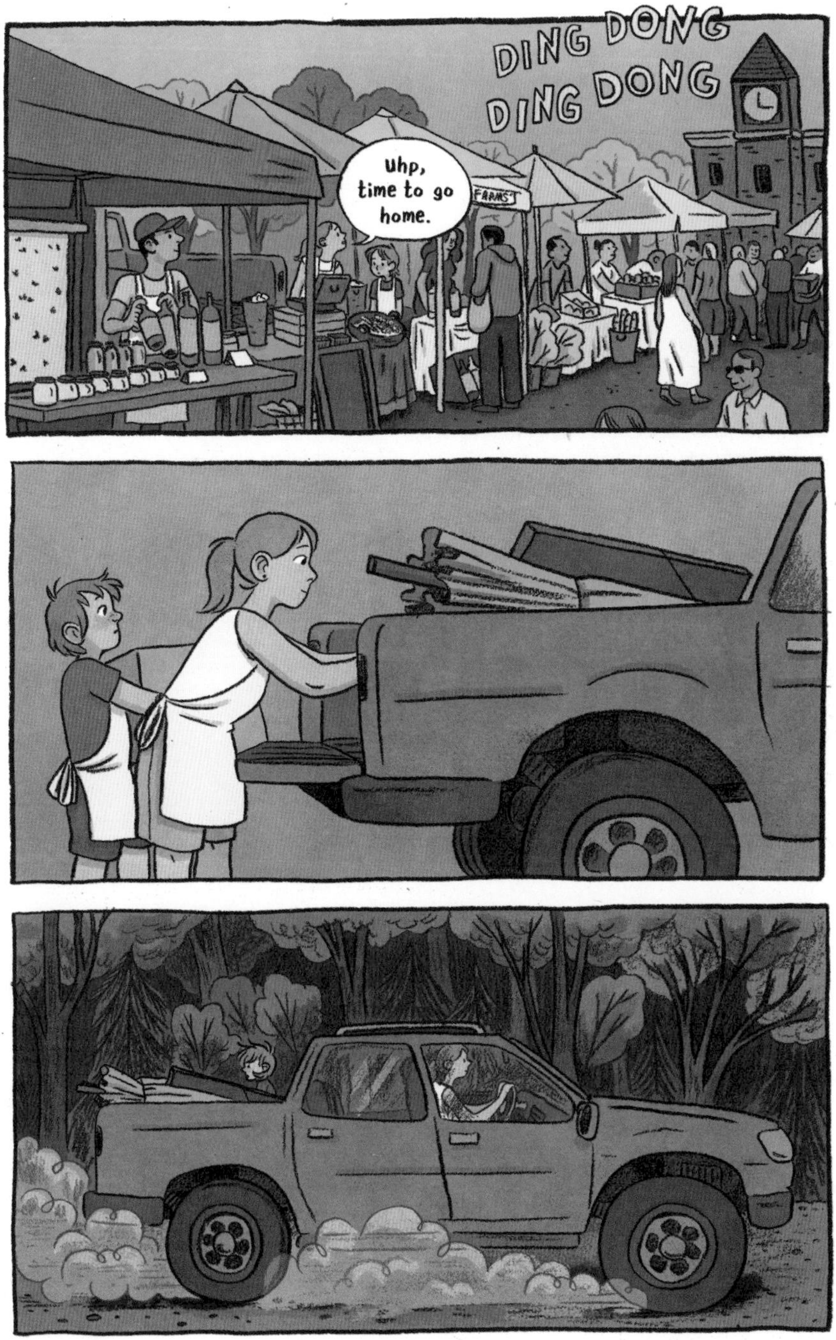
DING DONG
DING DONG
uhp, time to go home.
FARMS

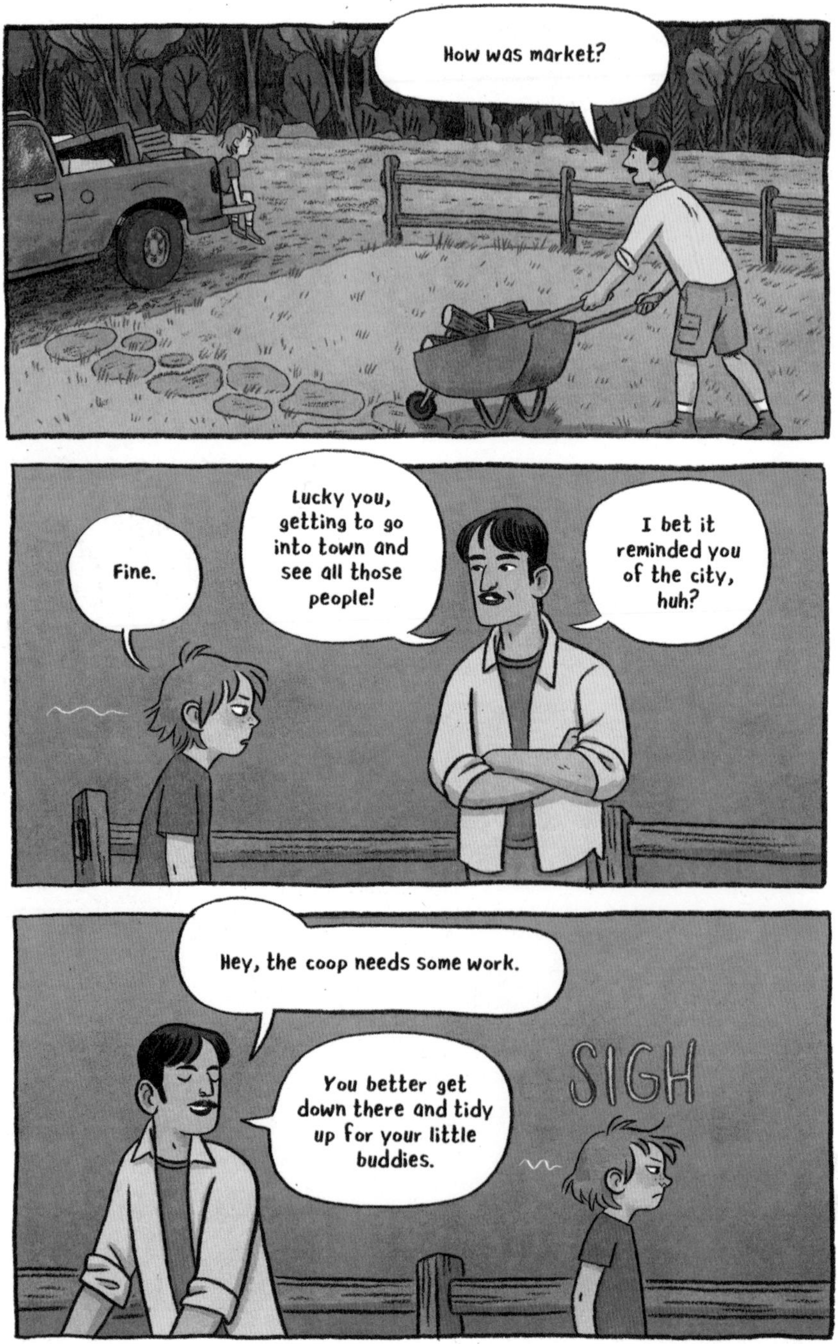
How was market?
Fine.
Lucky you, getting to go into town and see all those people!
I bet it reminded you of the city, huh?
Hey, the coop needs some work.
You better get down there and tidy up for your little buddies.
SIGH

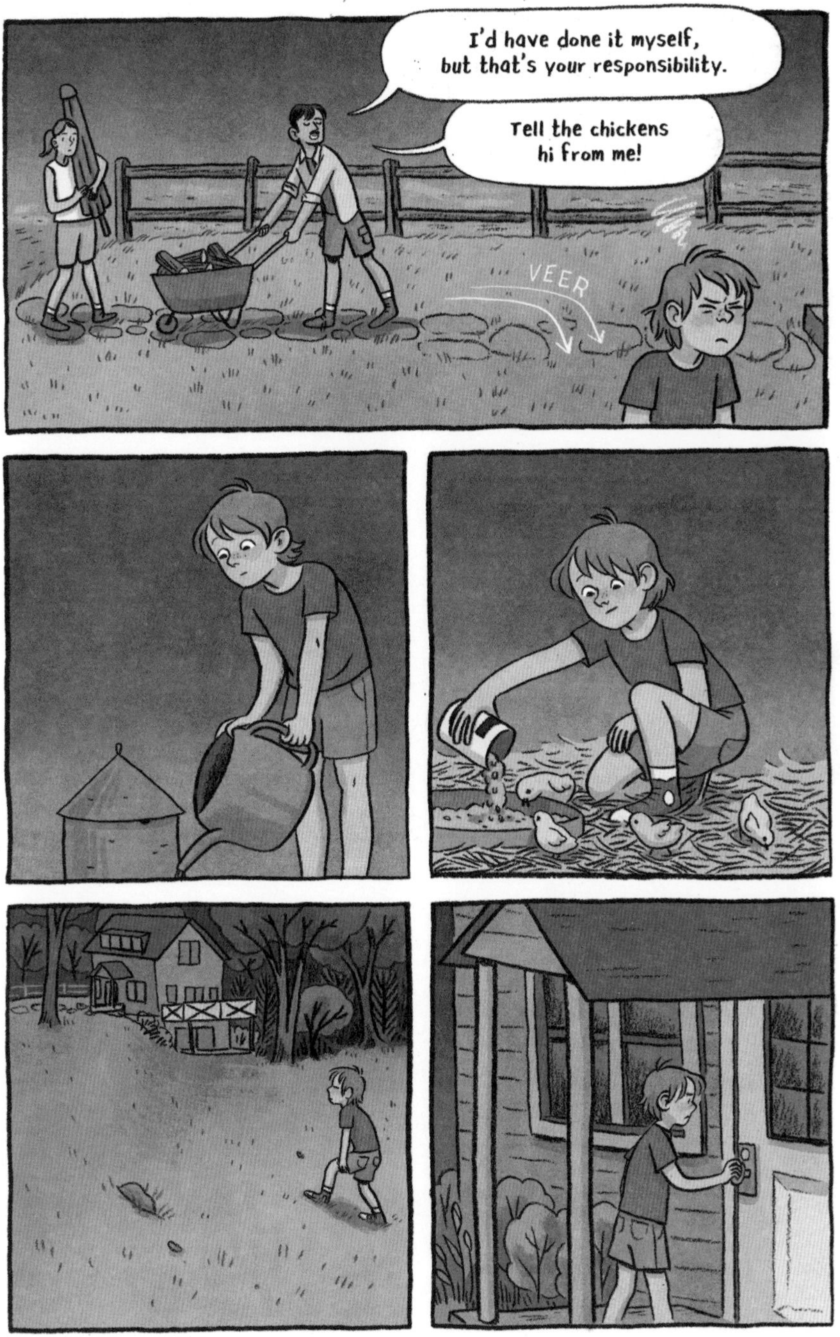
I'd have done it myself, but that's your responsibility.
Tell the chickens hi from me!
VEER

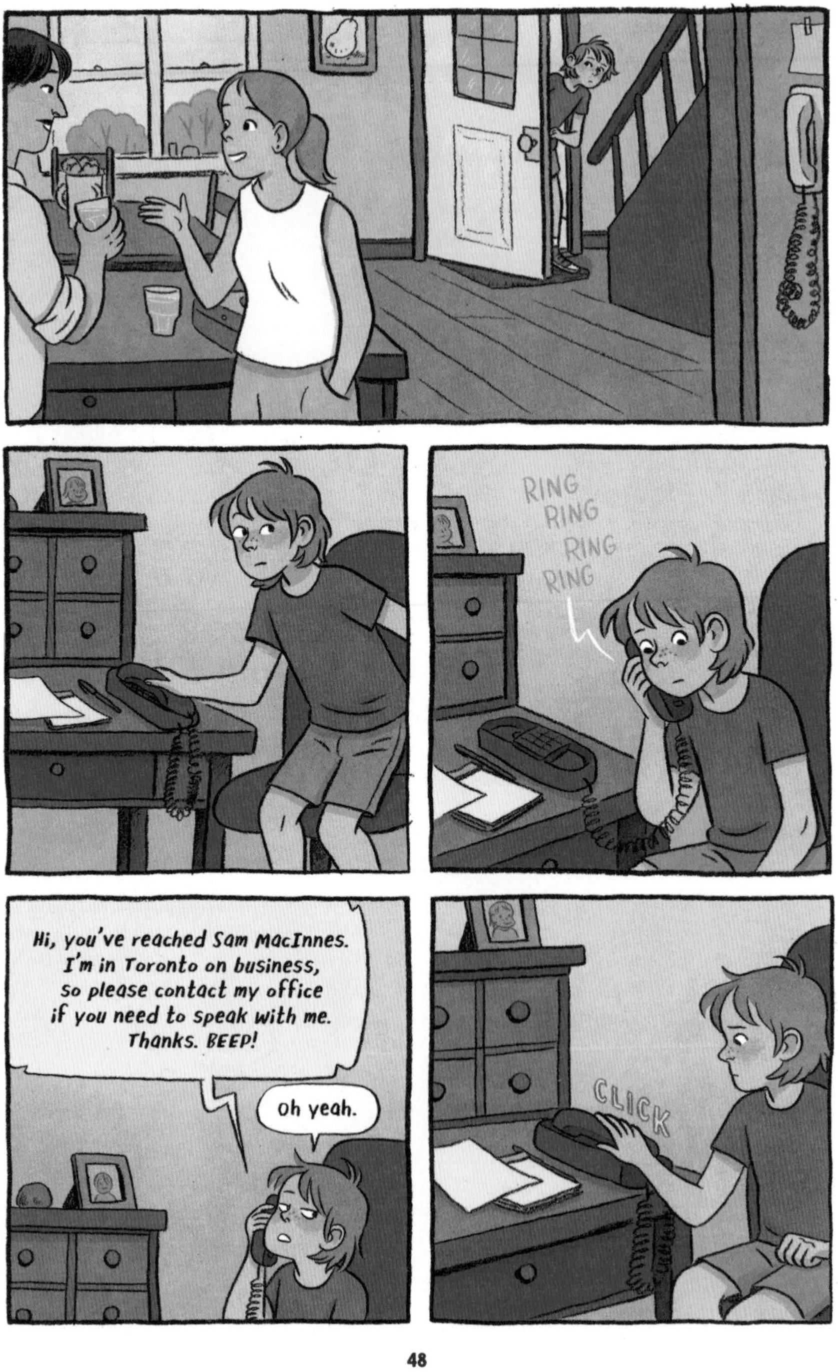
RING
RING
RING
RING
Hi, you've reached Sam MacInnes. I'm in Toronto on business, so please contact my office if you need to speak with me. Thanks. BEEP!
Oh yeah.
CLICK

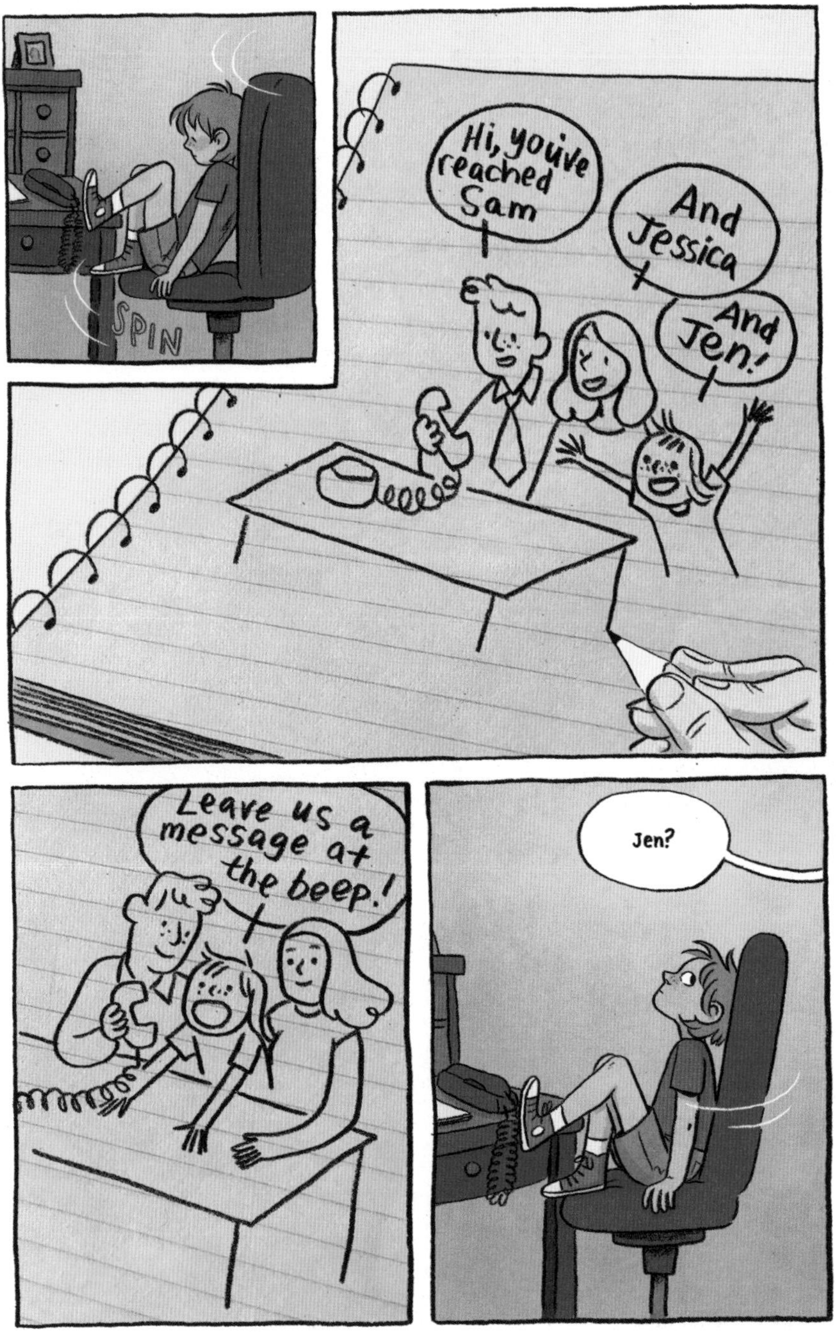
SPIN
Hi, you've reached Sam
And Jessica
And Jen!
Leave us a message at the beep!
Jen?

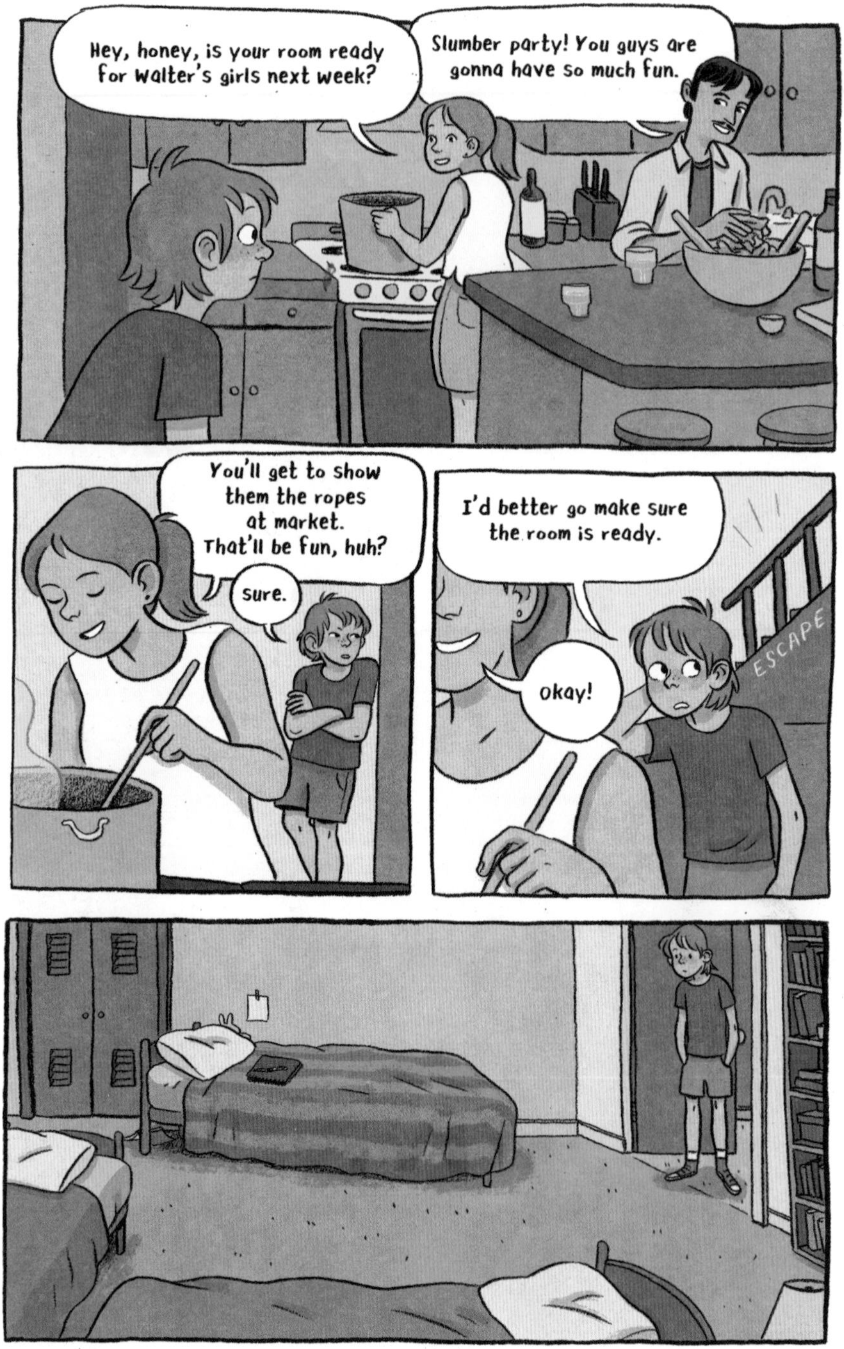
Hey, honey, is your room ready for Walter's girls next week?
Slumber party! You guys are gonna have so much fun.
You'll get to show them the ropes at market. That'll be fun, huh?
sure.
I'd better go make sure the room is ready.
Okay!
ESCAPE

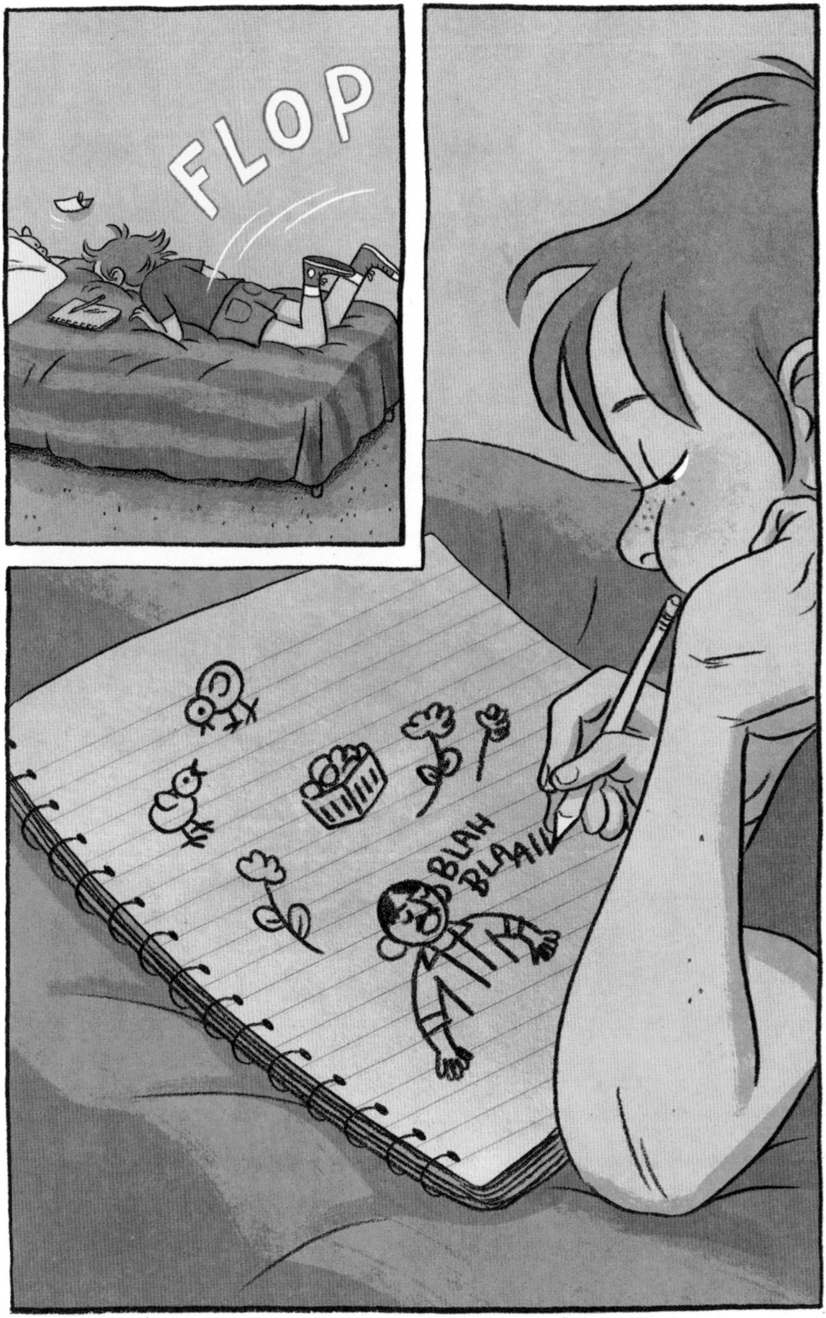
FLOP
BLAH
BLAAH

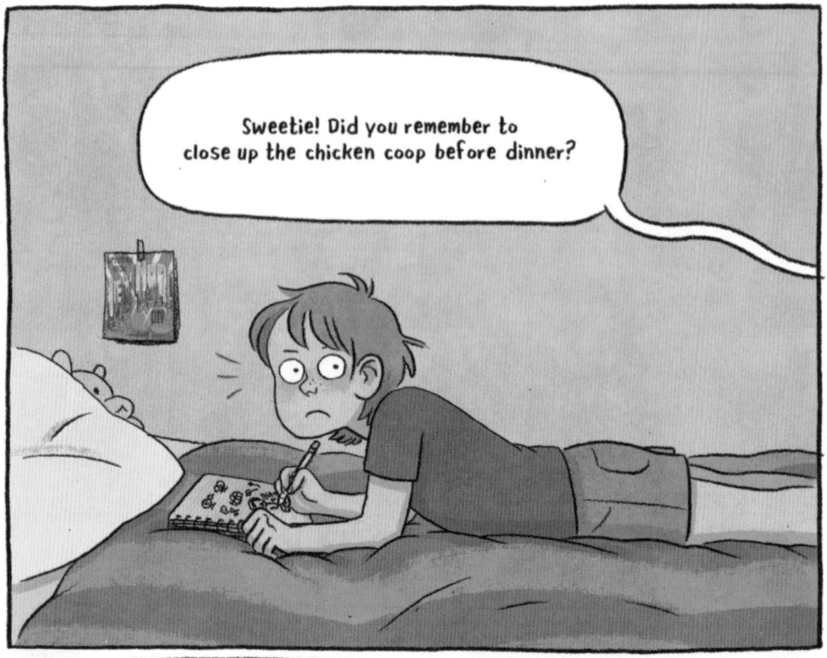
Sweetie! Did you remember to close up the chicken coop before dinner?

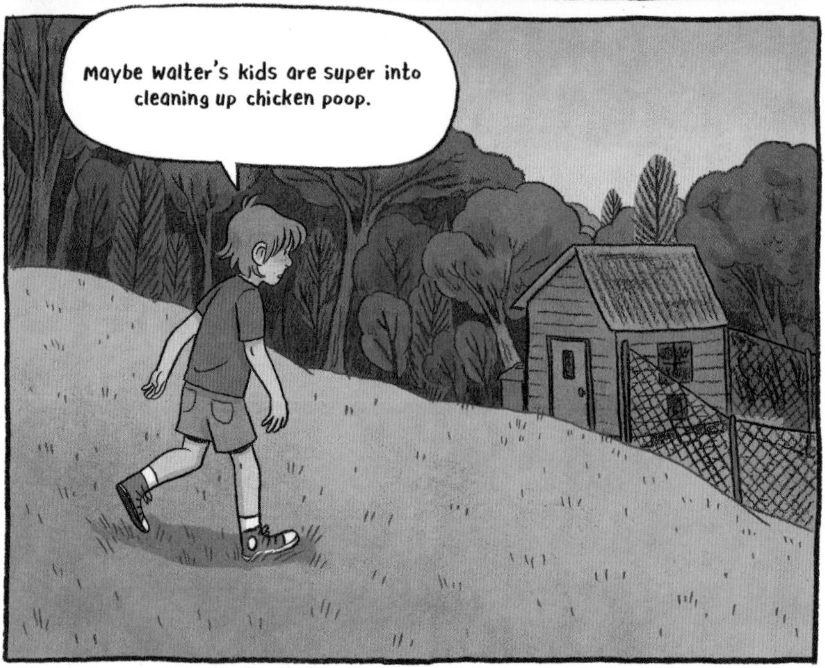
Maybe Walter's kids are super into cleaning up chicken poop.

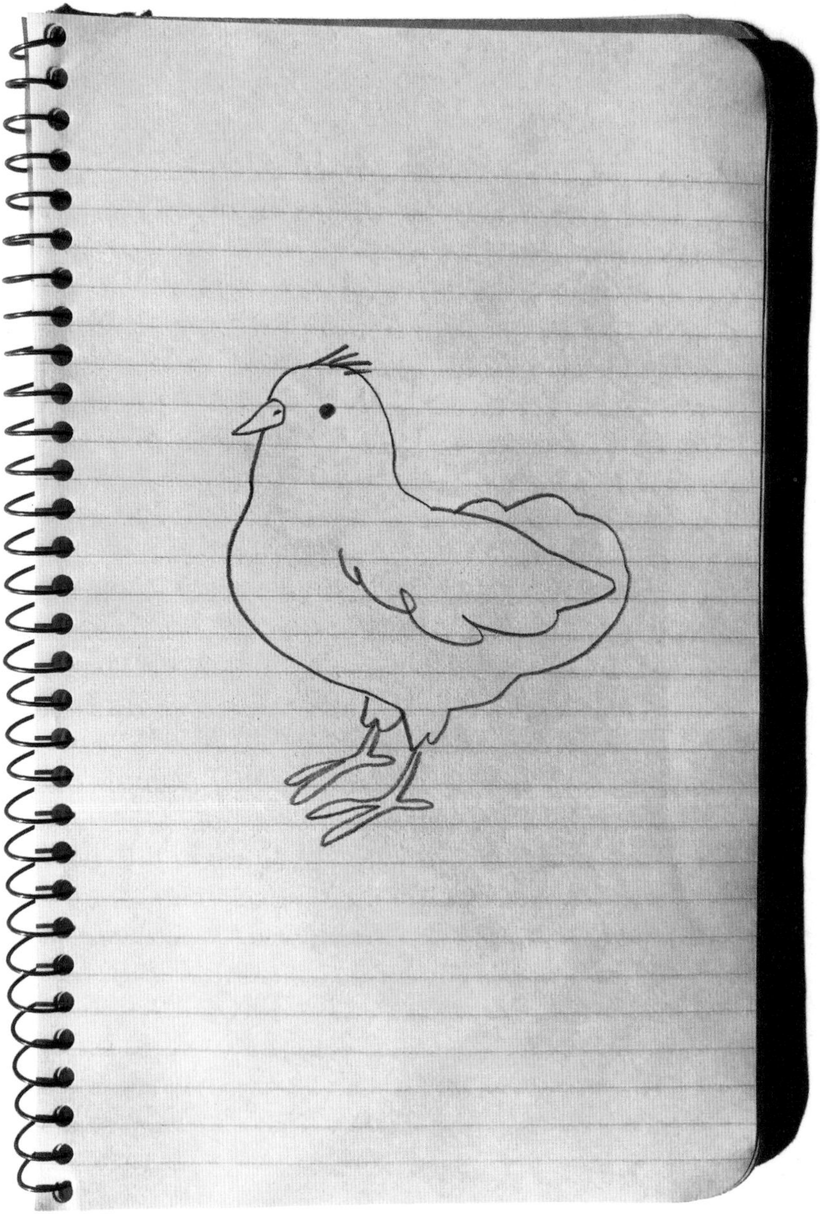

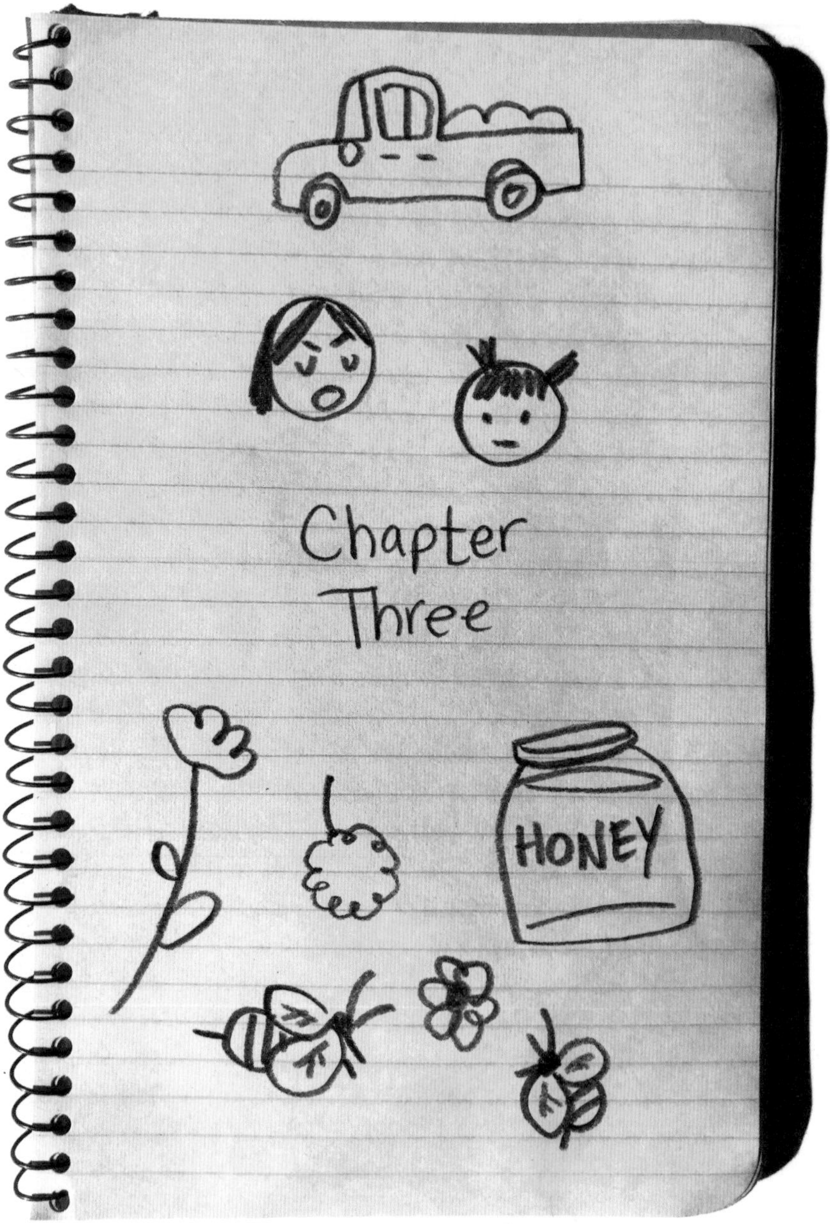
Chapter
Three
HONEY

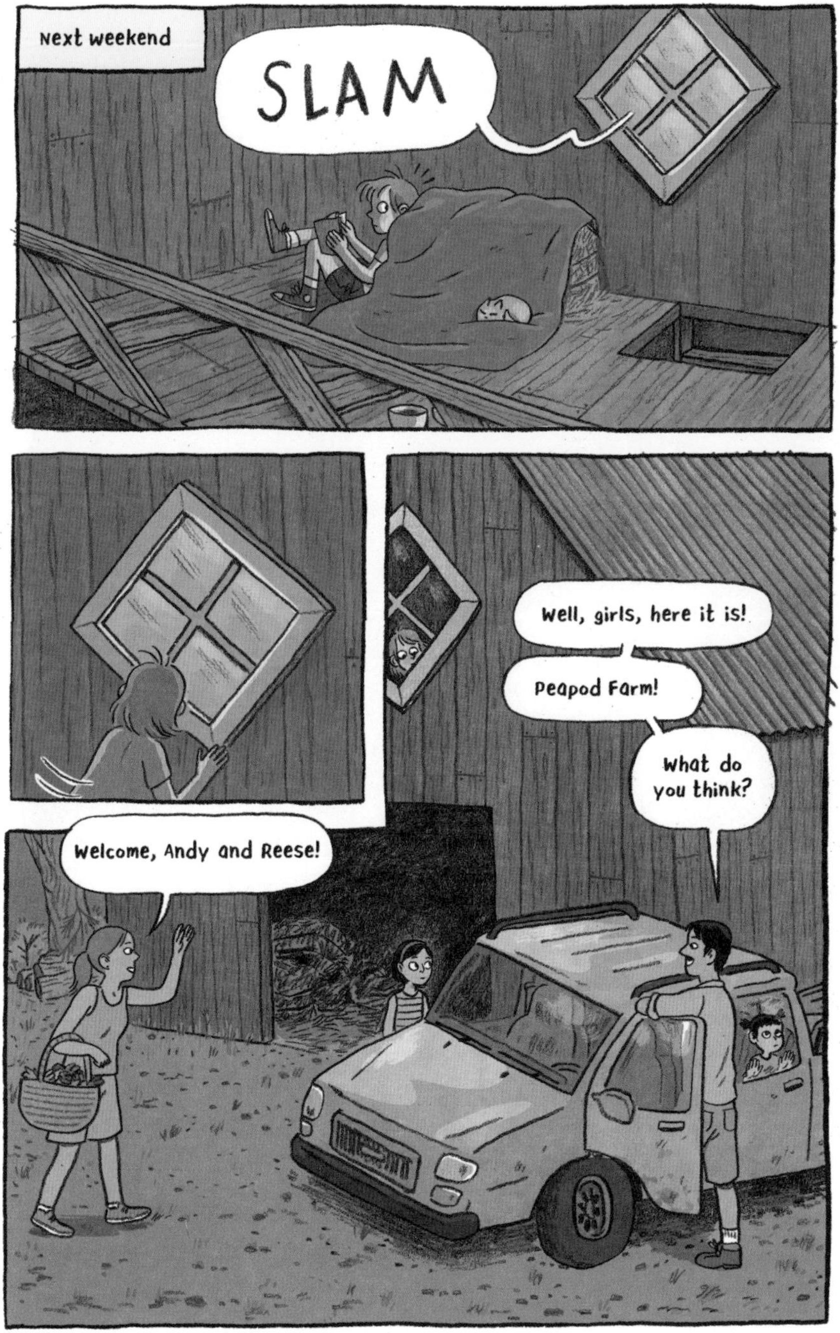
Next weekend
SLAM
Well, girls, here it is!
Peapod Farm!
What do you think?
Welcome, Andy and Reese!

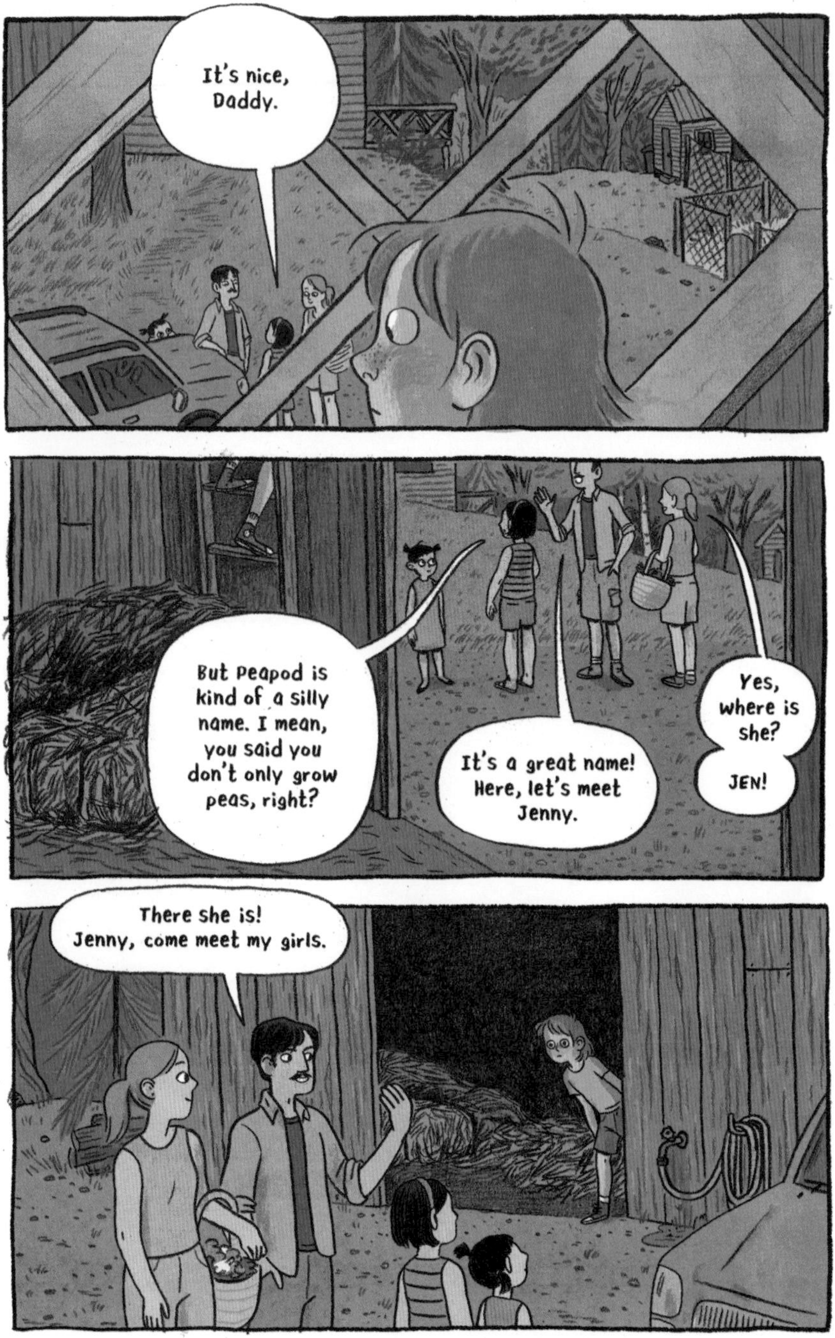

It's nice, Daddy.
But Peapod is kind of a silly name. I mean, you said you don't only grow peas, right?
It's a great name! Here, let's meet Jenny.
Yes, where is she?
JEN!
There she is! Jenny, come meet my girls.

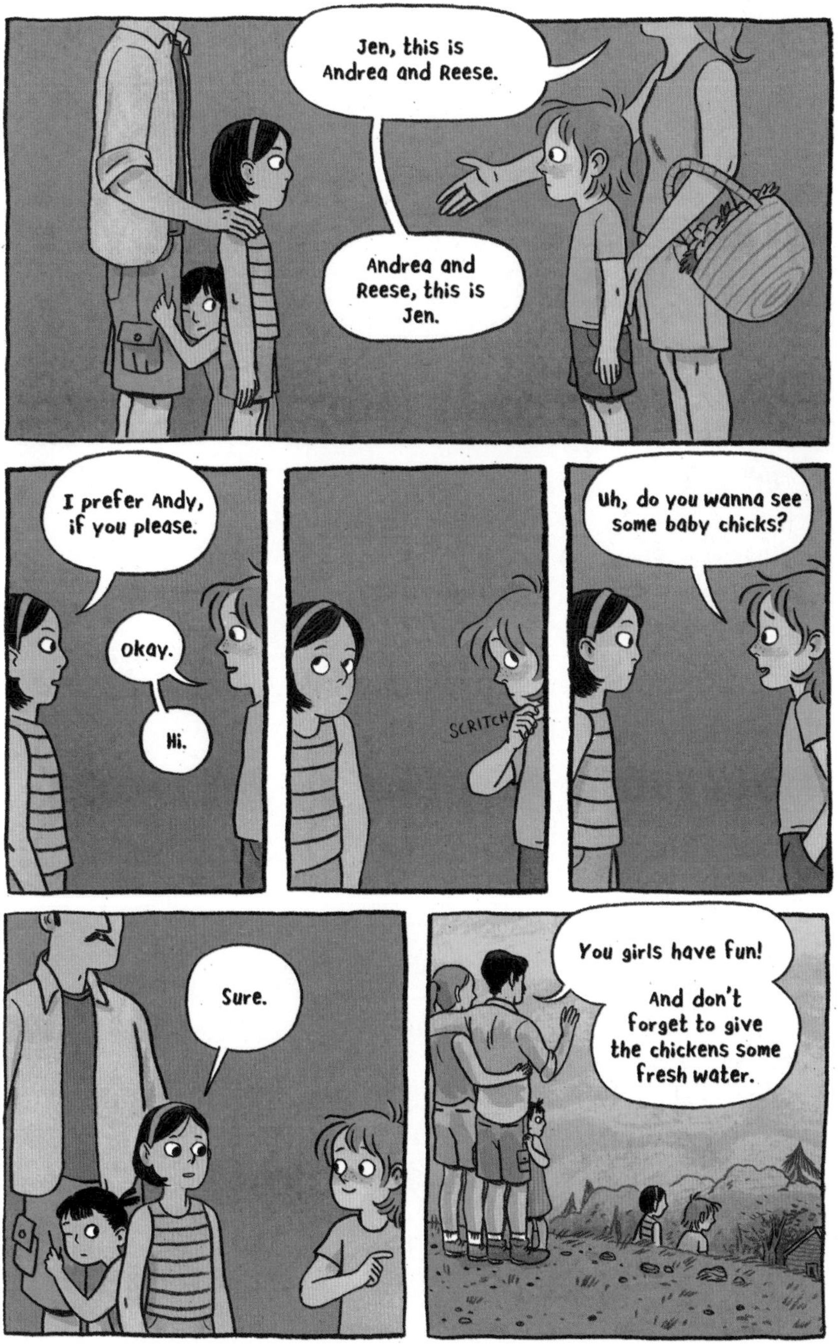
Jen, this is Andrea and Reese.
Andrea and Reese, this is Jen.
I prefer Andy, if you please.
Okay.
Hi.
SCRITCH
Uh, do you wanna see some baby chicks?
Sure.
You girls have fun!
And don't forget to give the chickens some fresh water.

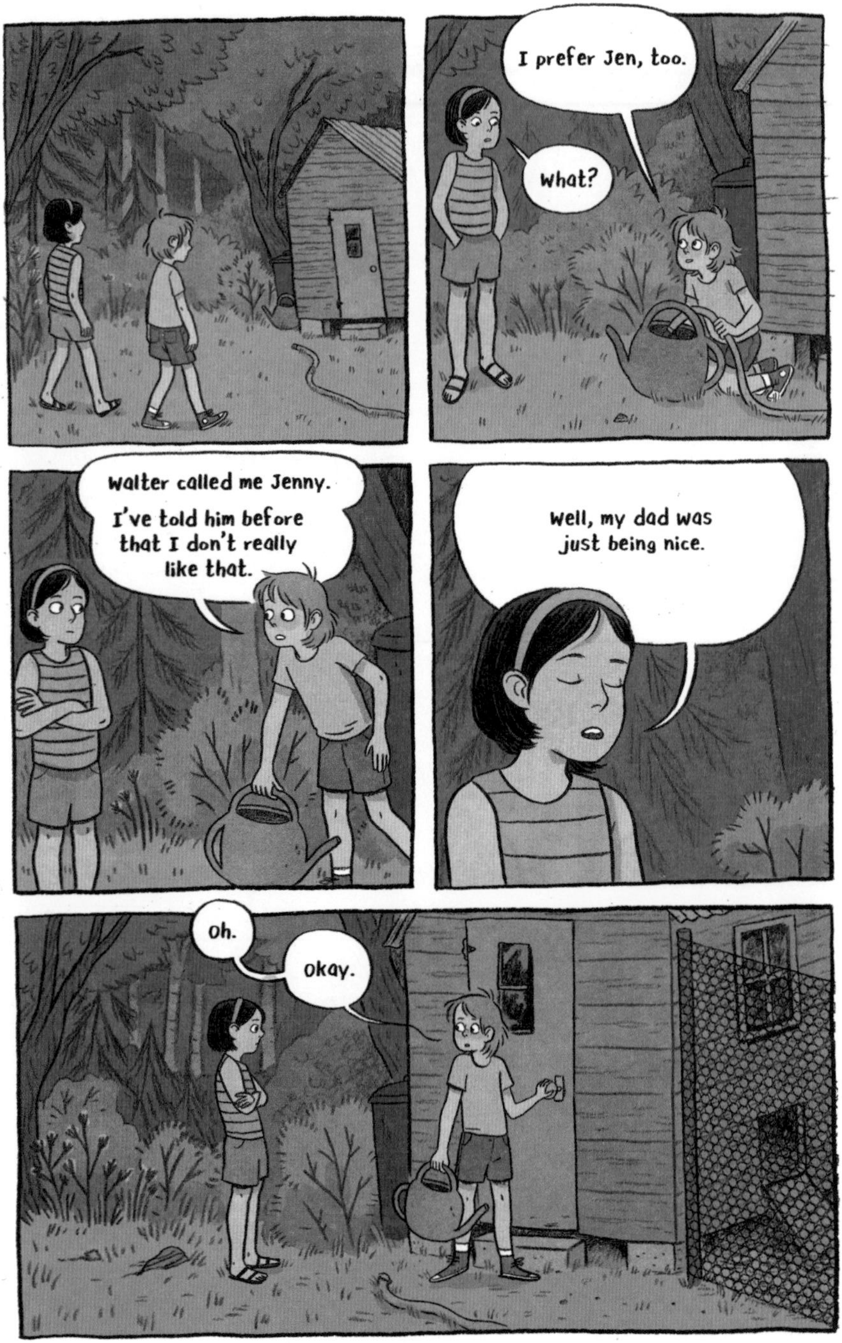
I prefer Jen, too.
What?
Walter called me Jenny.
I've told him before that I don't really like that.
Well, my dad was just being nice.
Oh.
Okay.

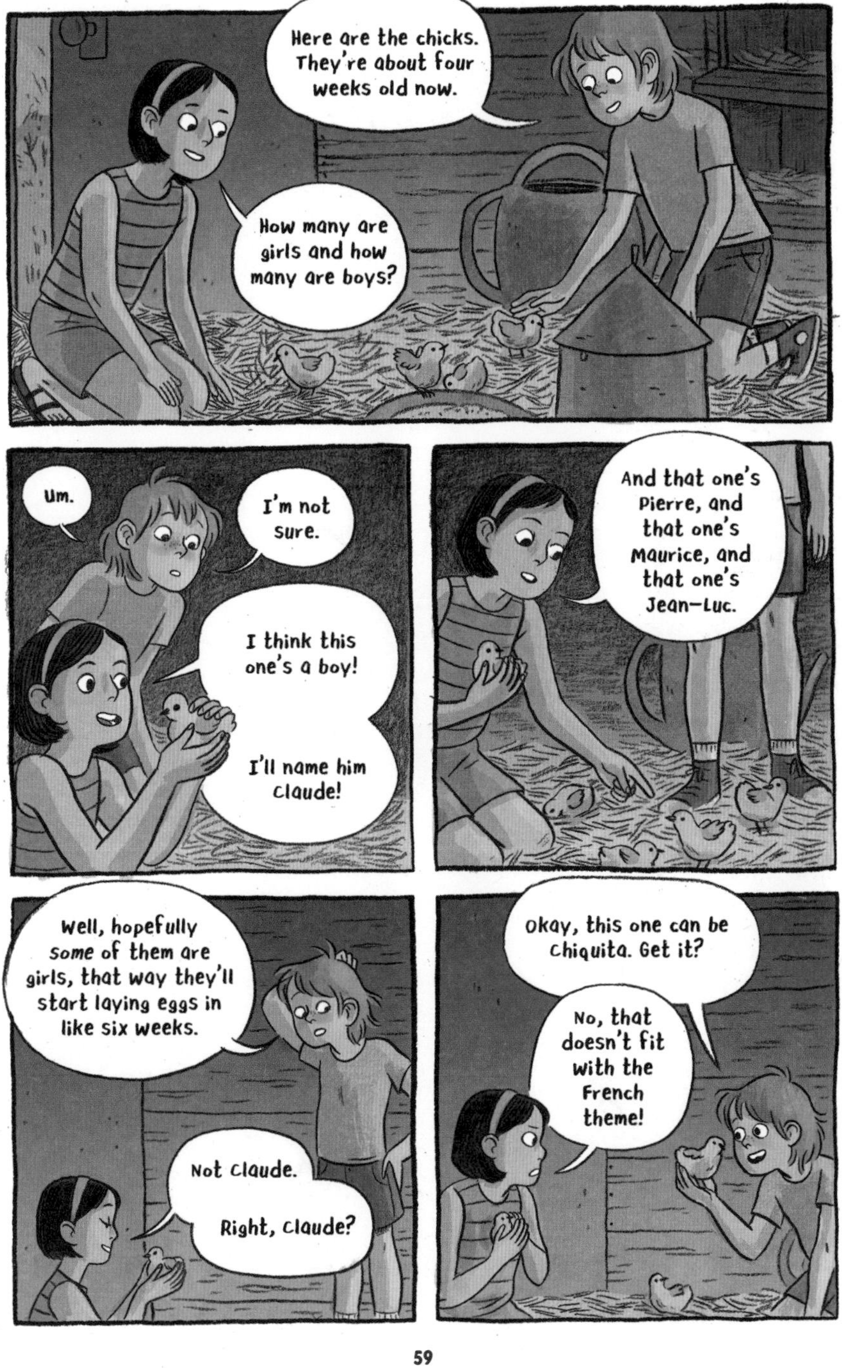
Here are the chicks. They're about four weeks old now.
How many are girls and how many are boys?
Um.
I'm not sure.
I think this one's a boy!
I'll name him Claude!
And that one's Pierre, and that one's Maurice, and that one's Jean-Luc.
Well, hopefully some of them are girls, that way they'll start laying eggs in like six weeks.
Not Claude.
Right, Claude?
Okay, this one can be Chiquita. Get it?
No, that doesn't fit with the French theme!

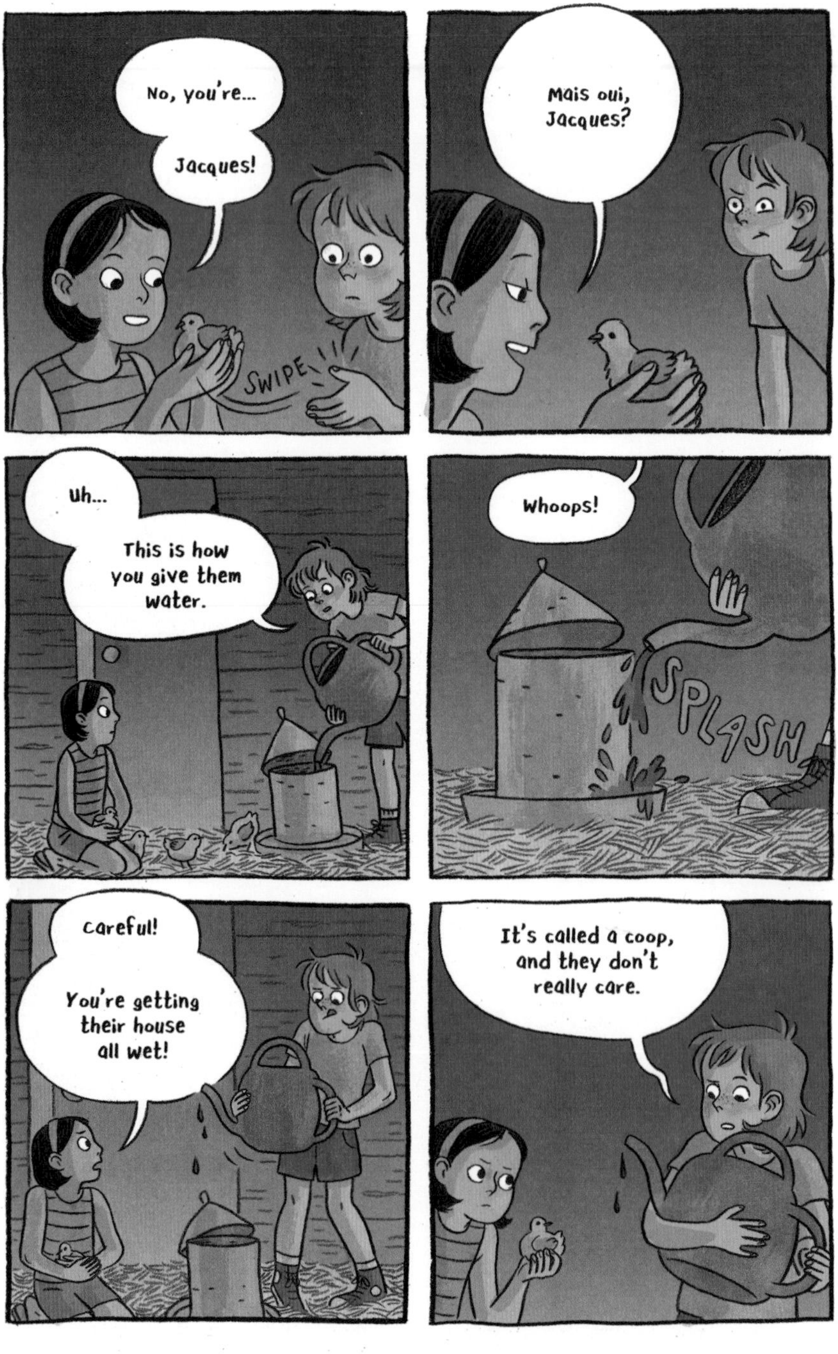
No, you're...
Jacques!
SWIPE
Mais oui, Jacques?
Uh...
This is how you give them water.
Whoops!
SPLASH
Careful!
You're getting their house all wet!
It's called a coop, and they don't really care.

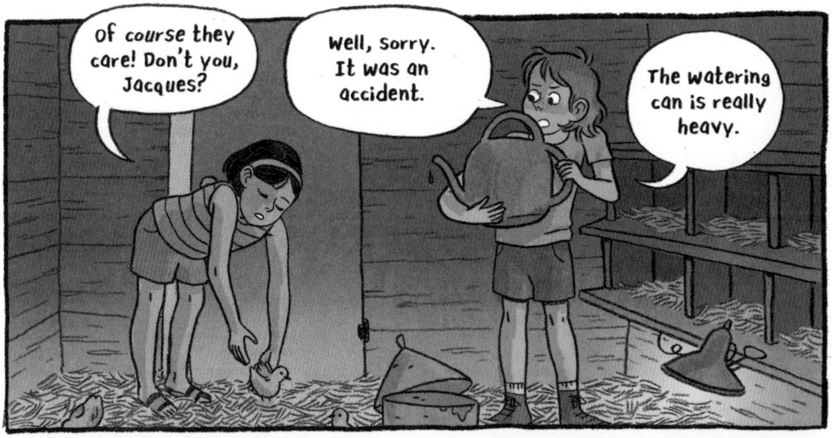
Of course they care! Don't you, Jacques?
Well, sorry. It was an accident.
The watering can is really heavy.

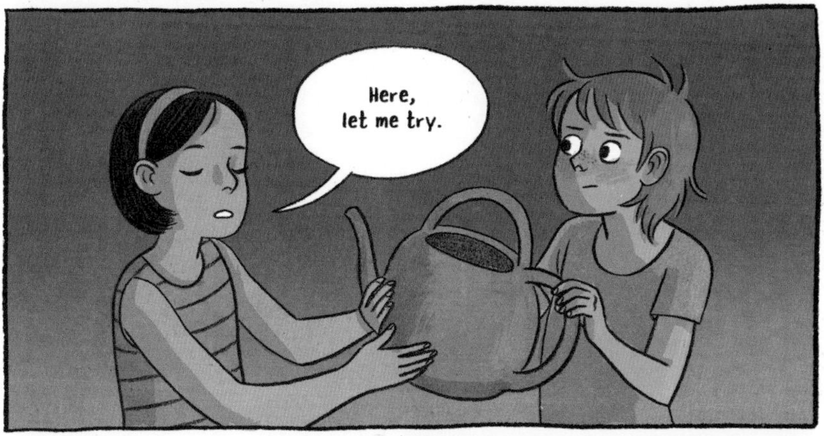
Here, let me try.

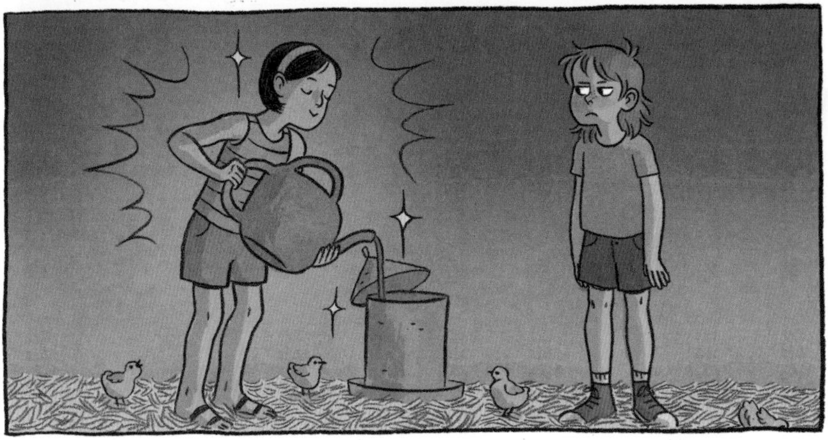

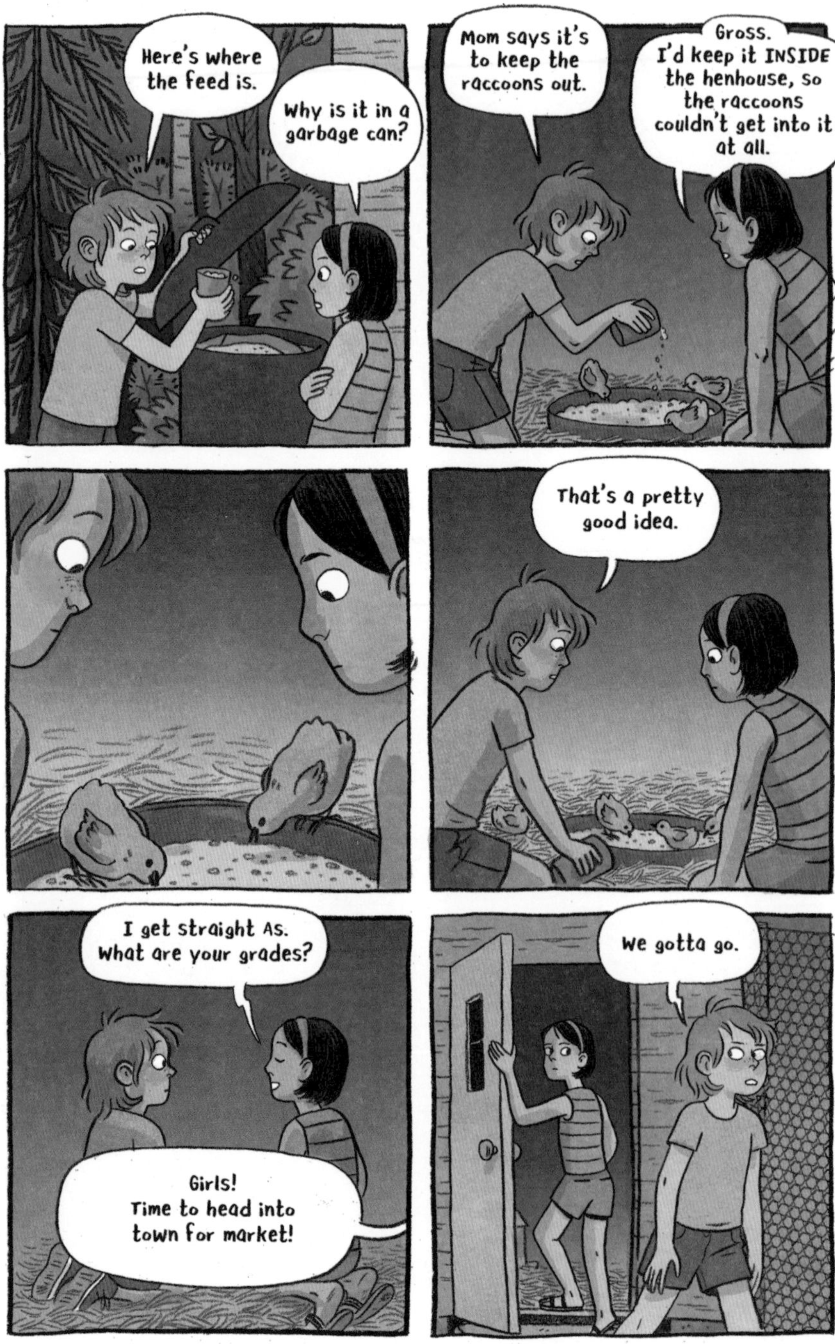
Here's where the feed is.
Why is it in a garbage can?
Mom says it's to keep the raccoons out.
Gross. I'd keep it INSIDE the henhouse, so the raccoons couldn't get into it at all.
That's a pretty good idea.
I get straight As. What are your grades?
Girls! Time to head into town for market!
We gotta go.

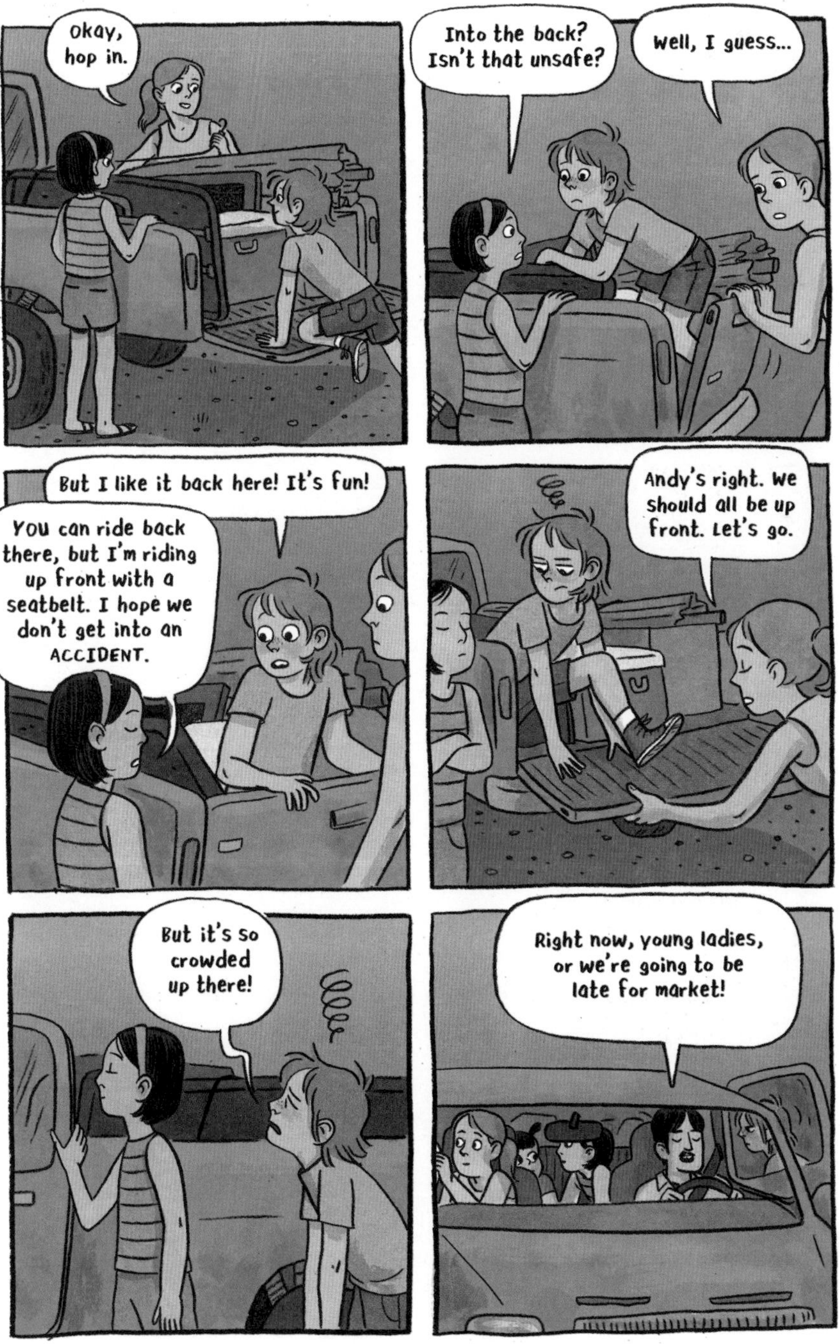
Okay, hop in.
Into the back? Isn't that unsafe?
Well, I guess...
But I like it back here! It's fun!
You can ride back there, but I'm riding up front with a seatbelt. I hope we don't get into an ACCIDENT.
Andy's right. We should all be up front. Let's go.
But it's so crowded up there!
Right now, young ladies, or we're going to be late for market!

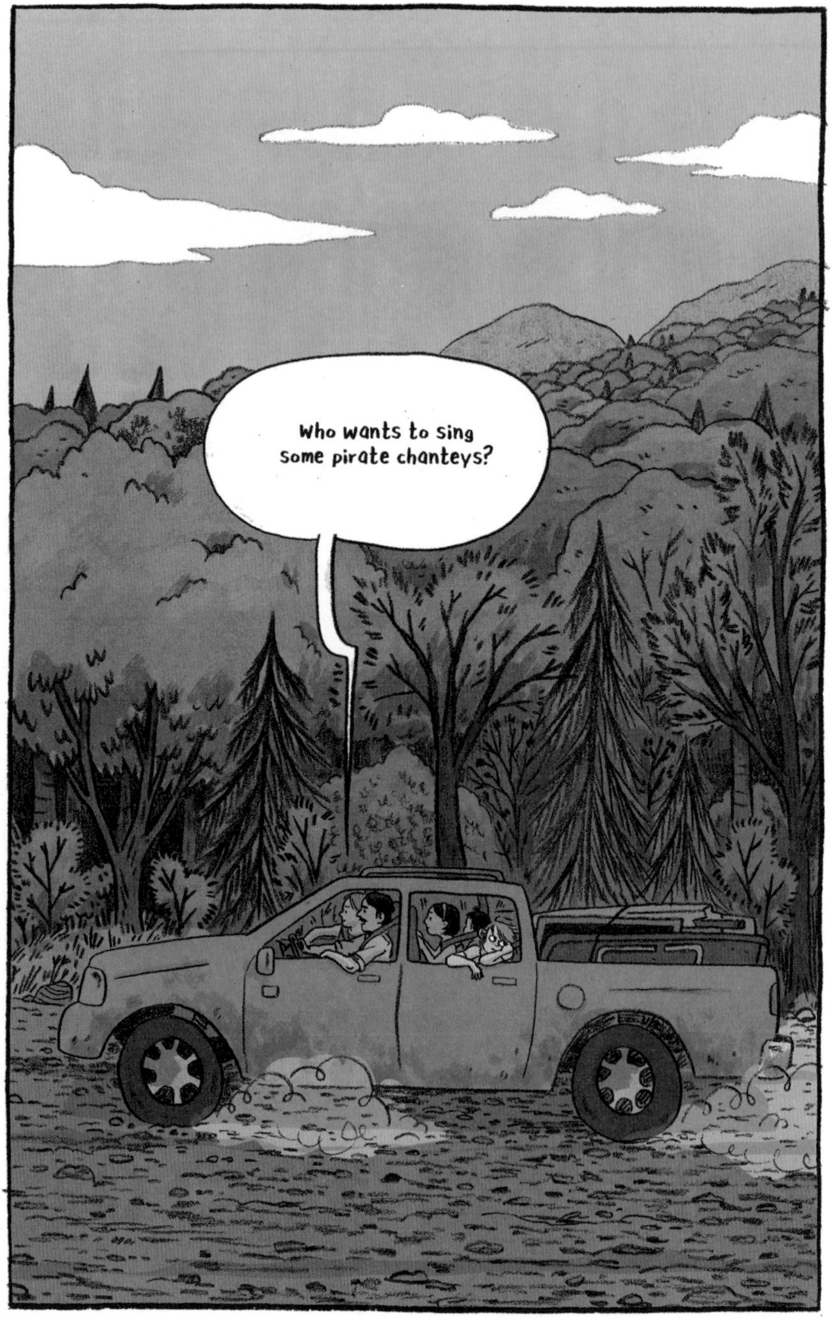
Who wants to sing some pirate chanteys?

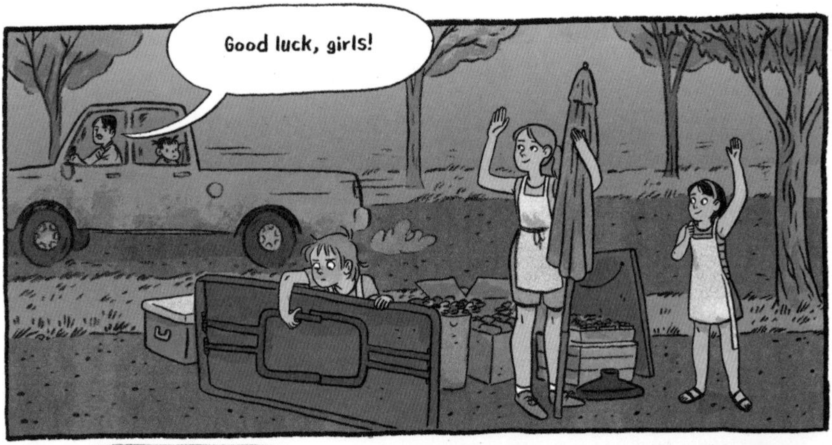
Good luck, girls!

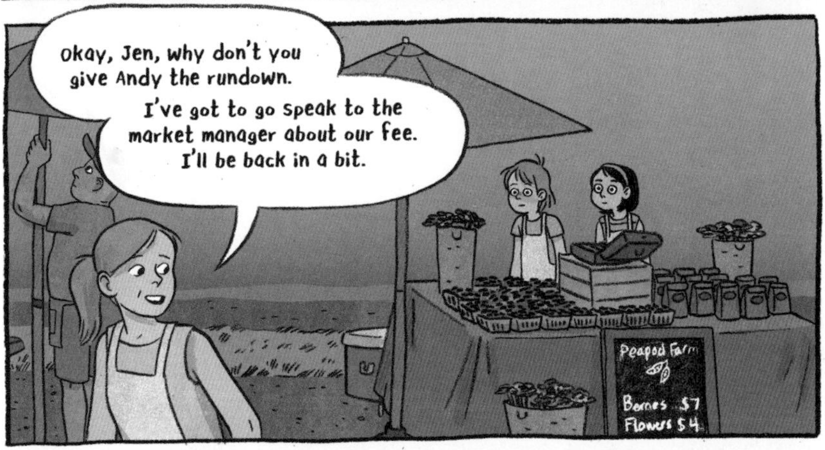
Okay, Jen, why don't you give Andy the rundown.
I've got to go speak to the market manager about our fee. I'll be back in a bit.
Peapod Farm
Berries $7
Flowers $4

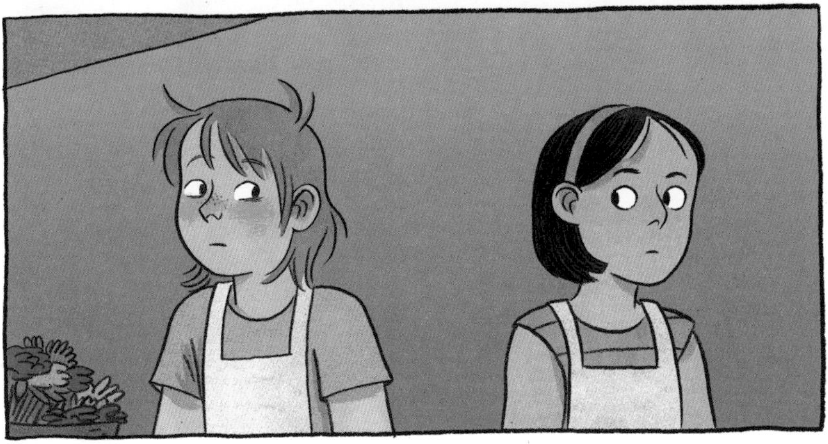

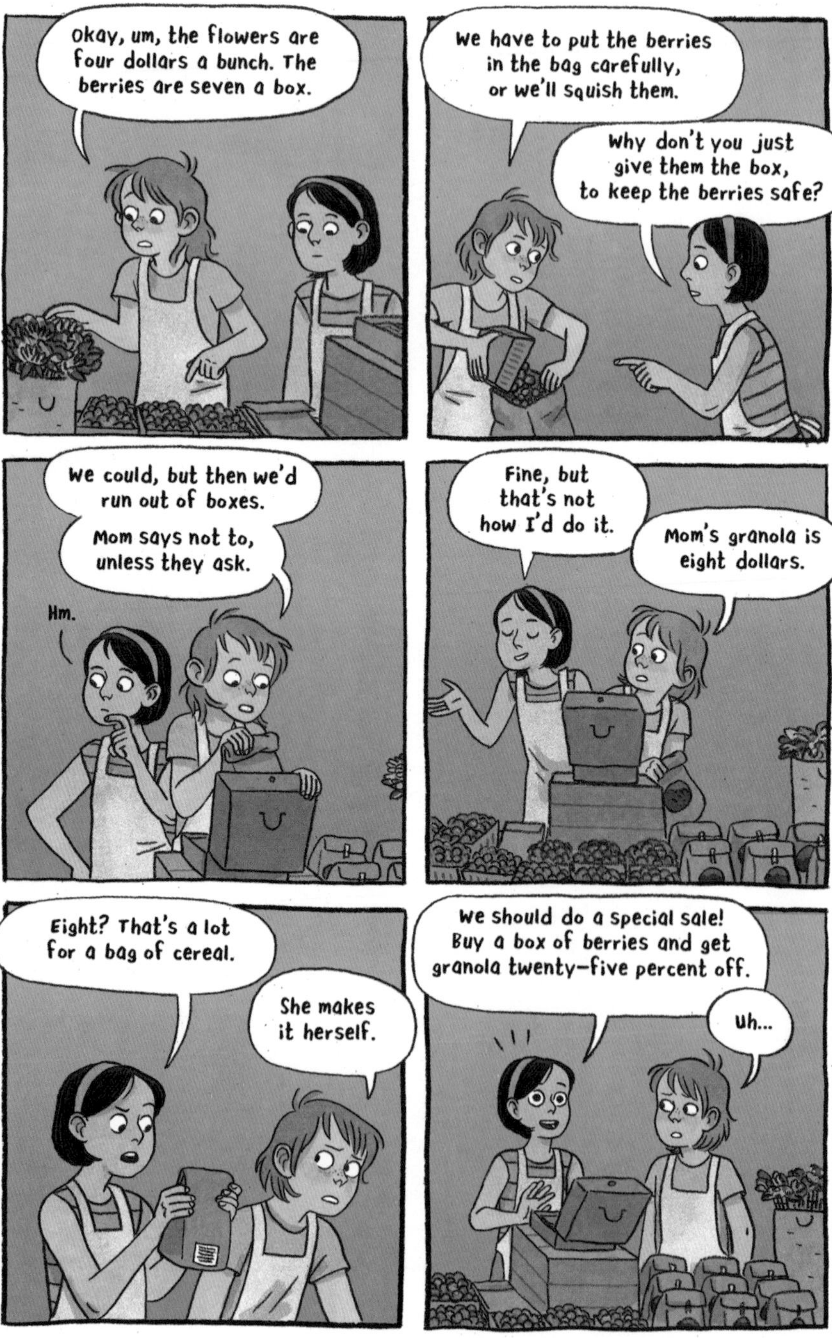
Okay, um, the flowers are four dollars a bunch. The berries are seven a box.
We have to put the berries in the bag carefully, or we'll squish them.
Why don't you just give them the box, to keep the berries safe?
We could, but then we'd run out of boxes.
Mom says not to, unless they ask.
Hm.
Fine, but that's not how I'd do it.
Mom's granola is eight dollars.
Eight? That's a lot for a bag of cereal.
She makes it herself.
We should do a special sale! Buy a box of berries and get granola twenty-five percent off.
Uh...

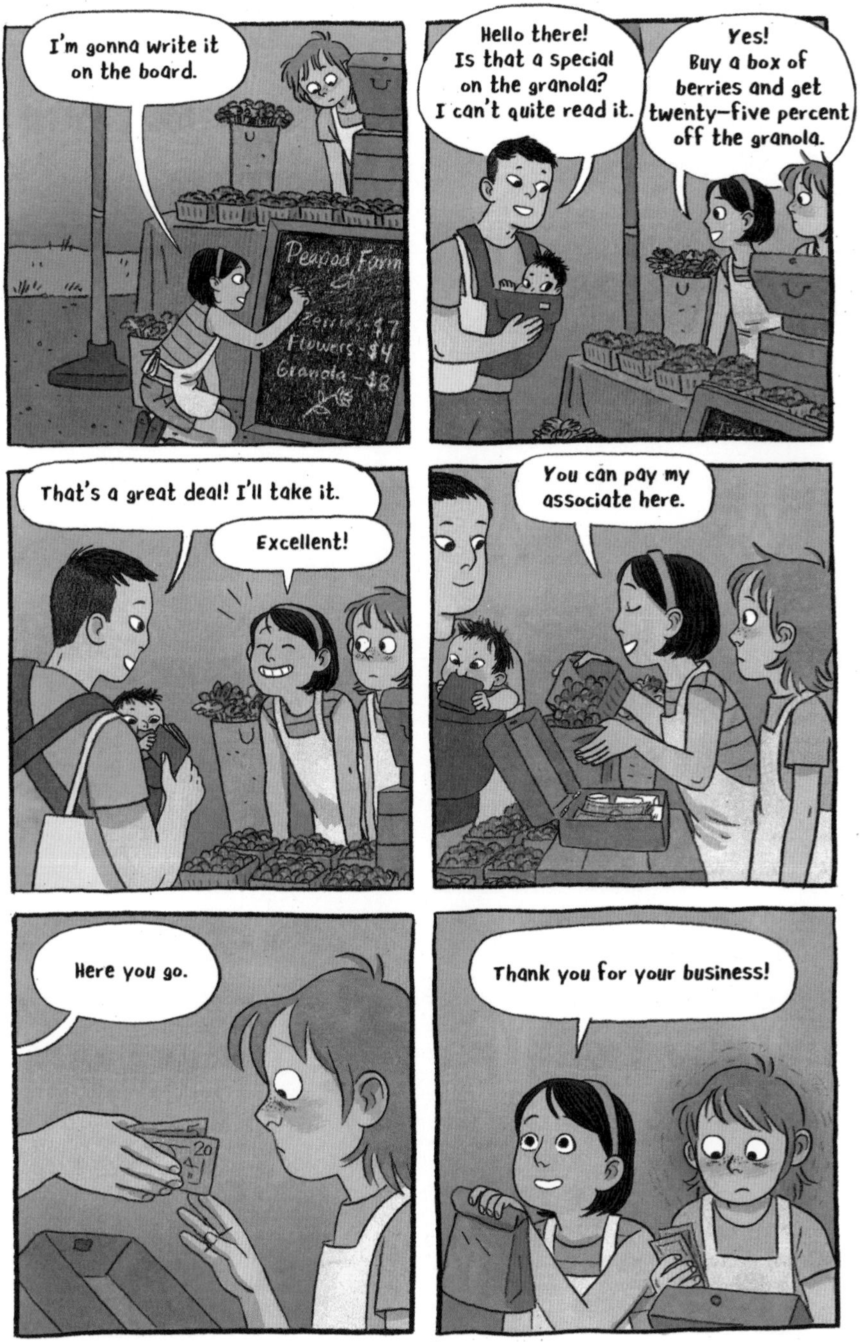
I'm gonna write it on the board.
Peapod Farm
Berries - $7
Flowers - $4
Granola - $8
Hello there! Is that a special on the granola? I can't quite read it.
Yes! Buy a box of berries and get twenty-five percent off the granola.
That's a great deal! I'll take it.
Excellent!
You can pay my associate here.
Here you go.
Thank you for your business!

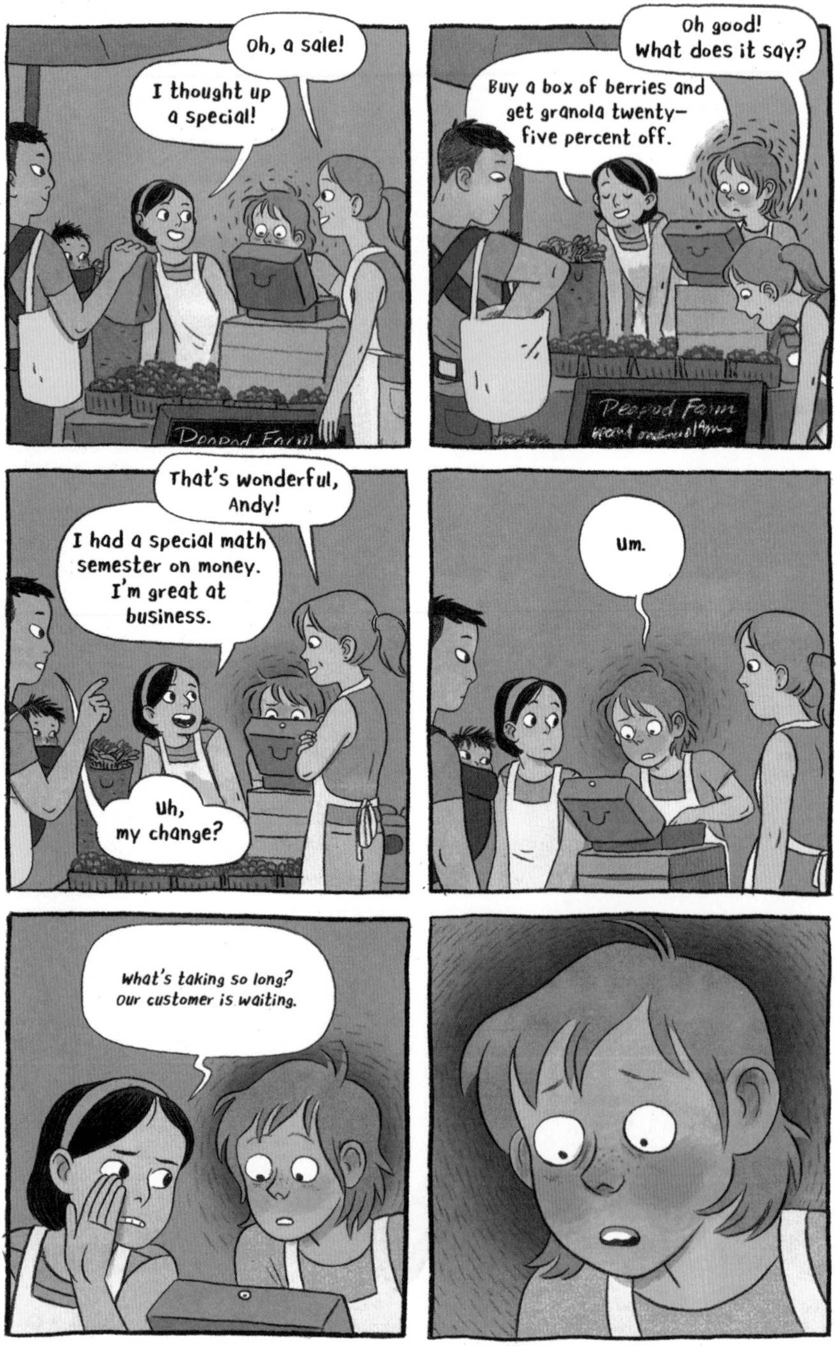
Oh, a sale!
I thought up a special!
Oh good! What does it say?
Buy a box of berries and get granola twenty-five percent off.
Peapod Farm
That's wonderful, Andy!
I had a special math semester on money. I'm great at business.
Uh, my change?
Um.
What's taking so long? Our customer is waiting.

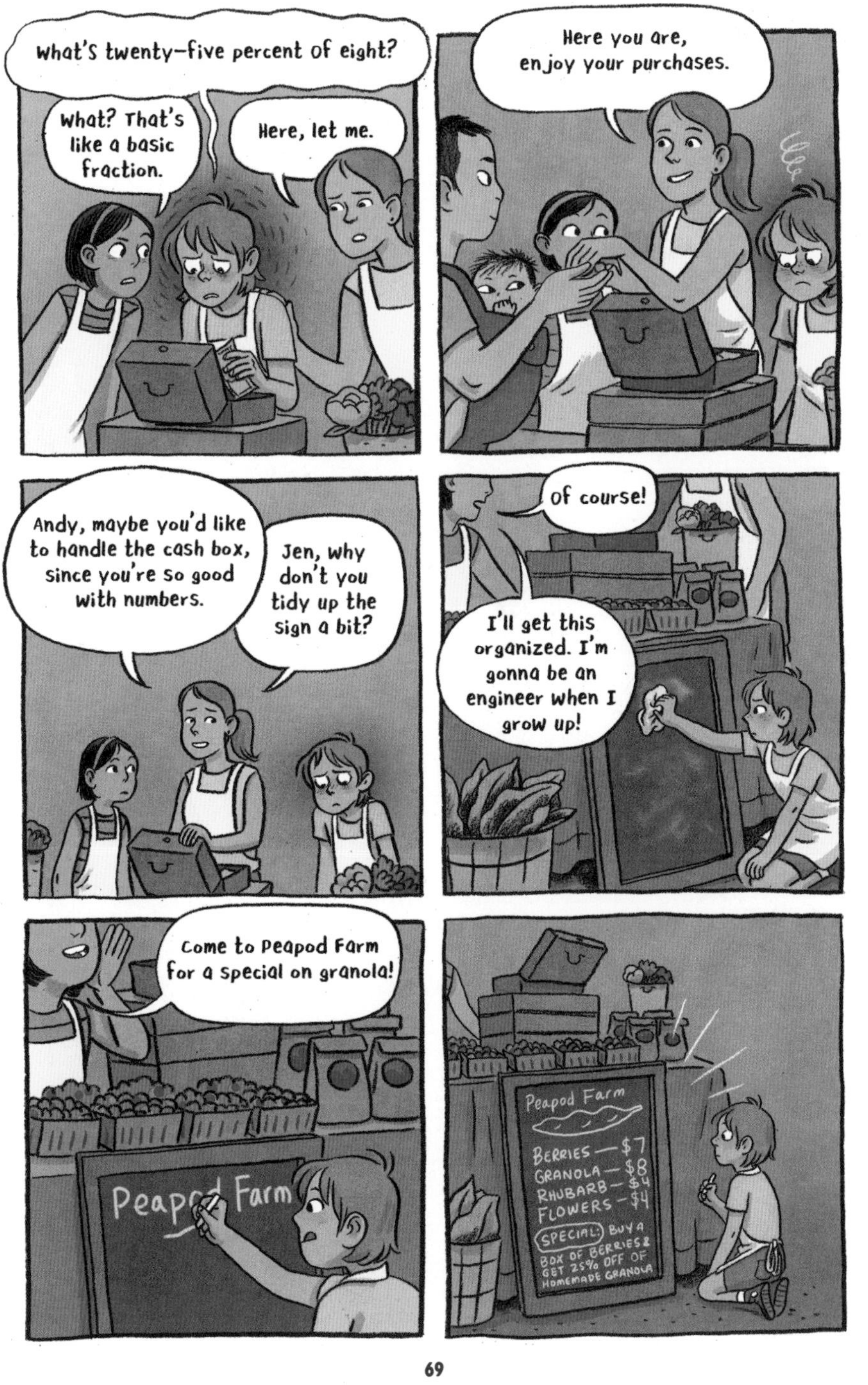

What's twenty-five percent of eight?
What? That's like a basic fraction.
Here, let me.
Here you are, enjoy your purchases.
Andy, maybe you'd like to handle the cash box, since you're so good with numbers.
Jen, why don't you tidy up the sign a bit?
Of course!
I'll get this organized. I'm gonna be an engineer when I grow up!
Come to Peapod Farm for a special on granola!
Peapod Farm
Peapod Farm
BERRIES — $7
GRANOLA — $8
RHUBARB — $4
FLOWERS — $4
SPECIAL: BUY A BOX OF BERRIES & GET 25% OFF OF HOMEMADE GRANOLA

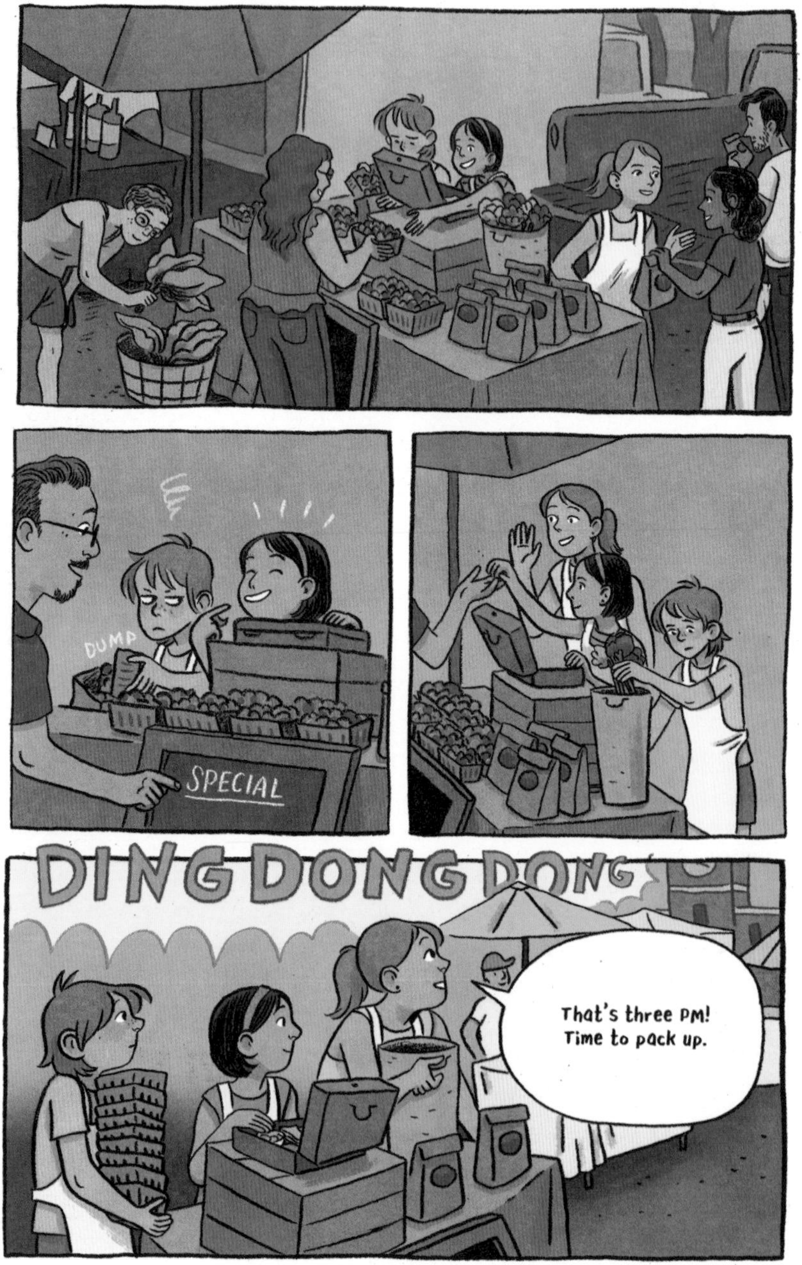
DUMP
SPECIAL
DING DONG DONG
That's three PM!
Time to pack up.

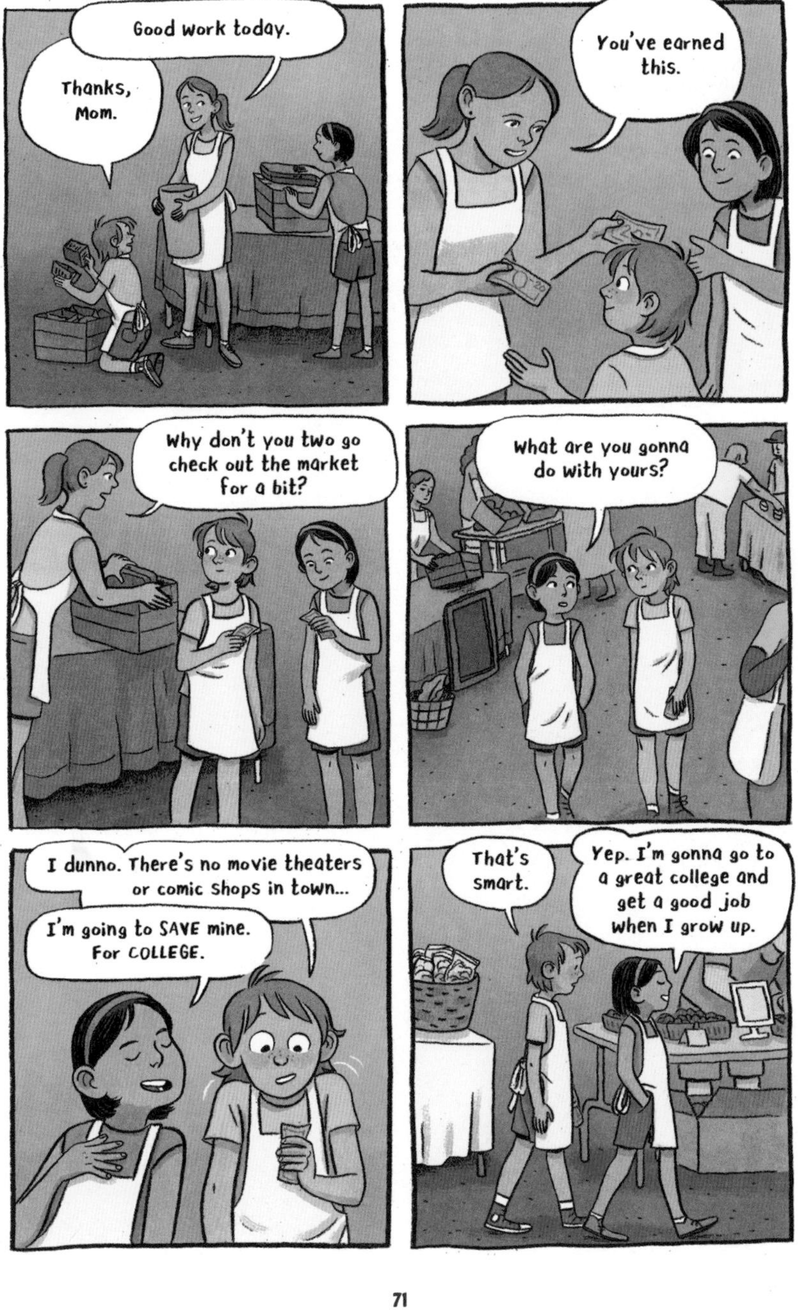

Good work today.
Thanks, Mom.
You've earned this.
Why don't you two go check out the market for a bit?
What are you gonna do with yours?
I dunno. There's no movie theaters or comic shops in town...
I'm going to SAVE mine. For COLLEGE.
That's smart.
Yep. I'm gonna go to a great college and get a good job when I grow up.

But you can go ahead and spend yours if you'd like.

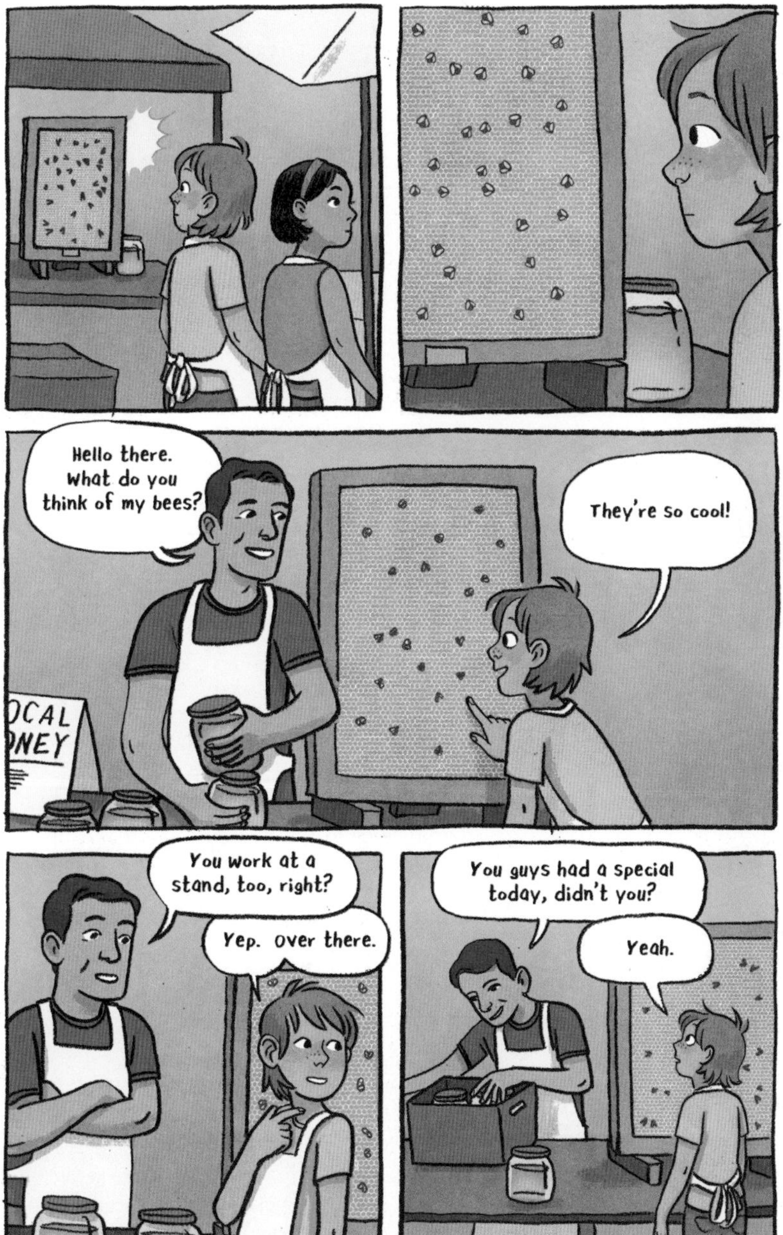
Hello there. What do you think of my bees?
They're so cool!
LOCAL HONEY
You work at a stand, too, right?
Yep. Over there.
You guys had a special today, didn't you?
Yeah.

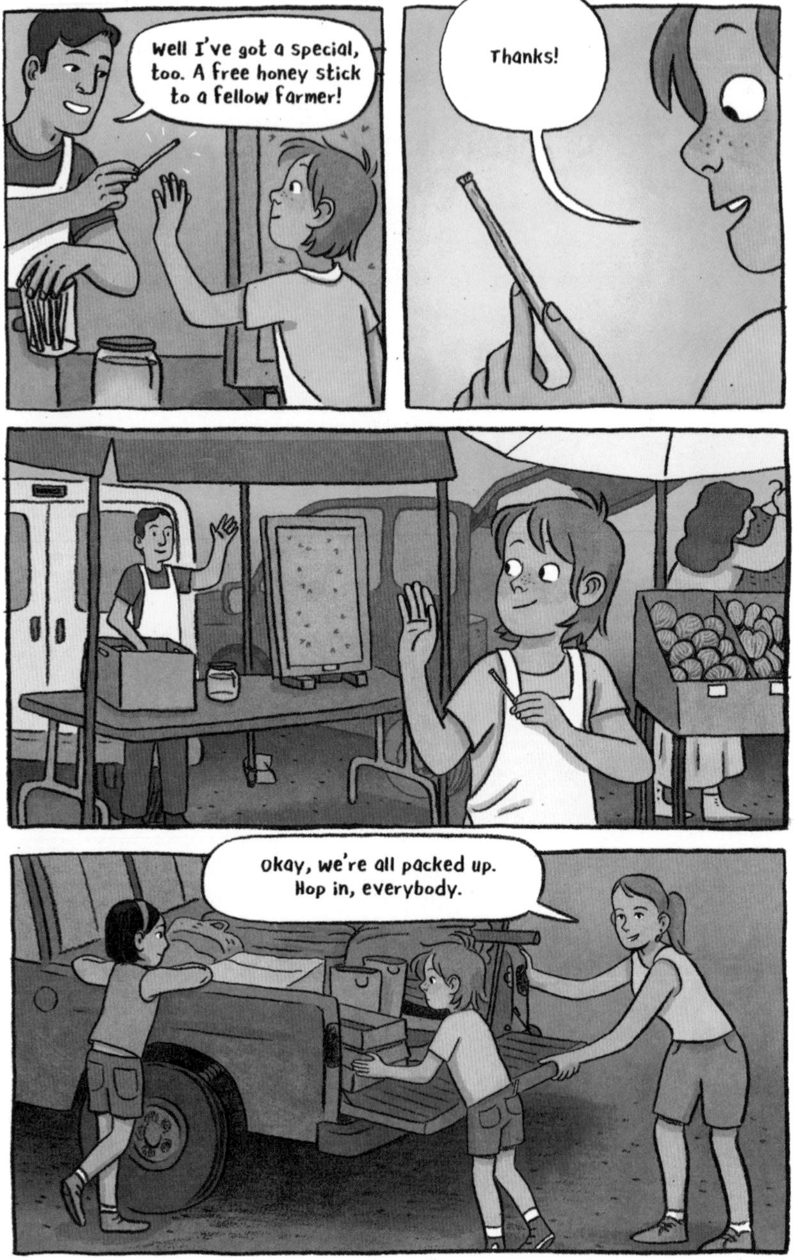
Well I've got a special, too. A free honey stick to a fellow farmer!
Thanks!
Okay, we're all packed up. Hop in, everybody.

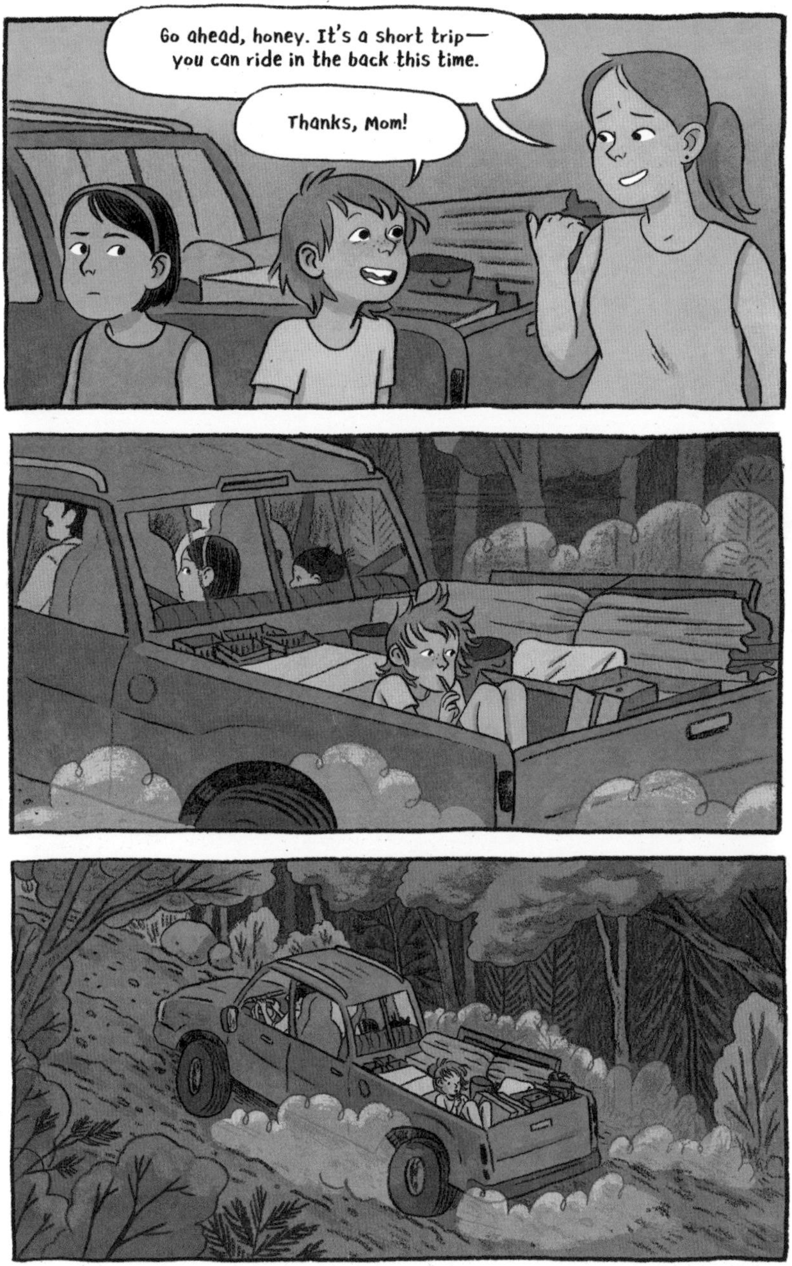
Go ahead, honey. It's a short trip—you can ride in the back this time.
Thanks, Mom!

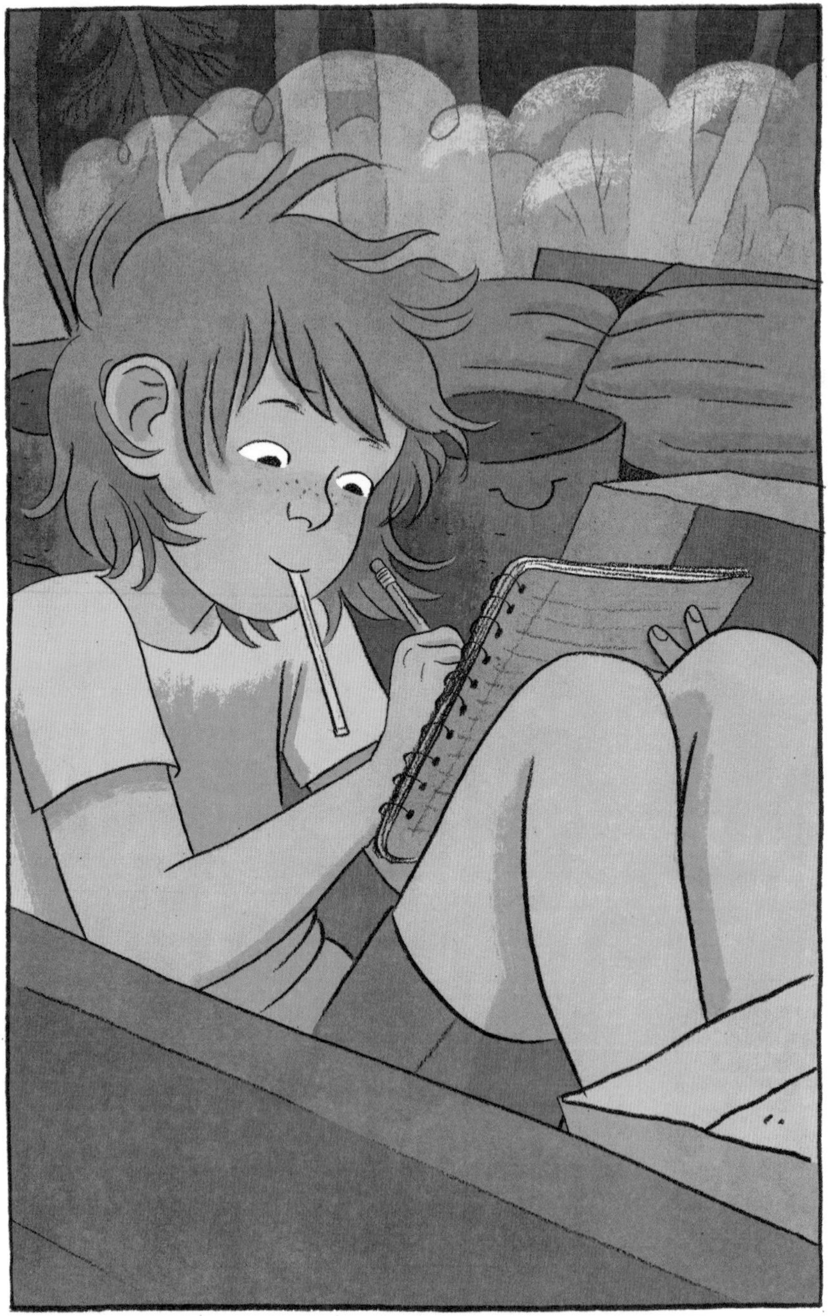

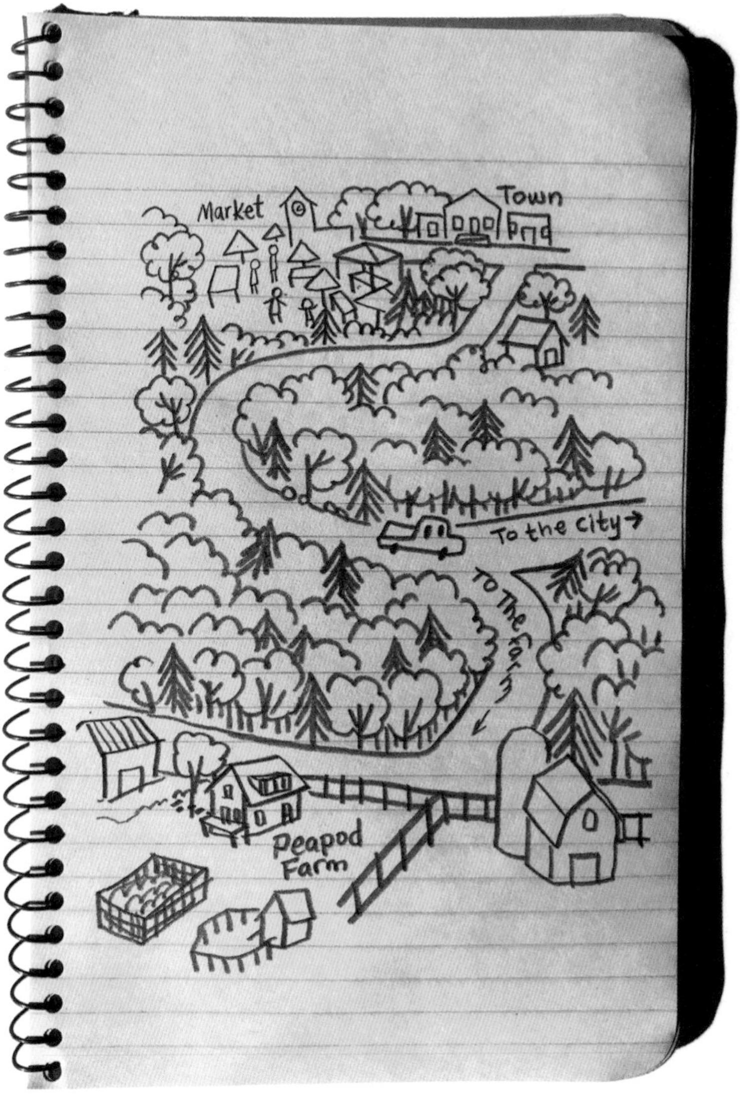
Market
Town
To the city →
To the farm
Peapod
Farm

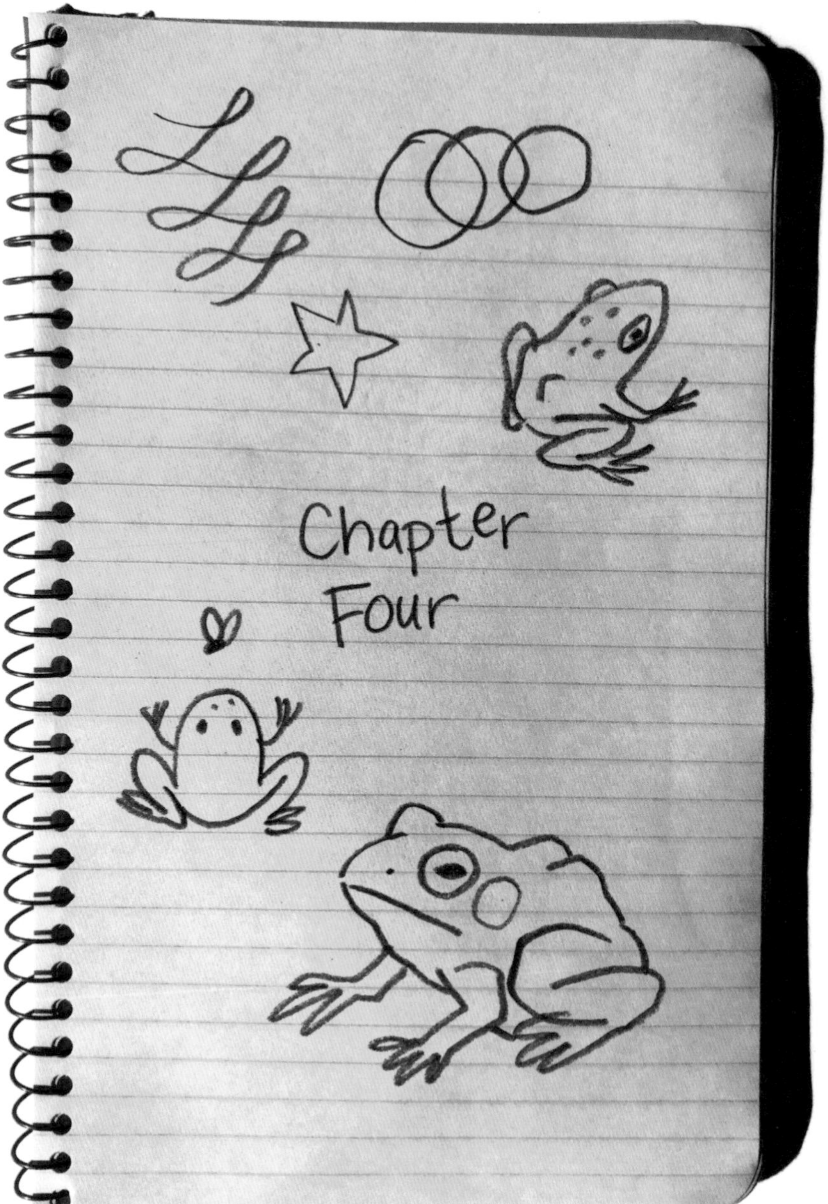
Chapter
Four

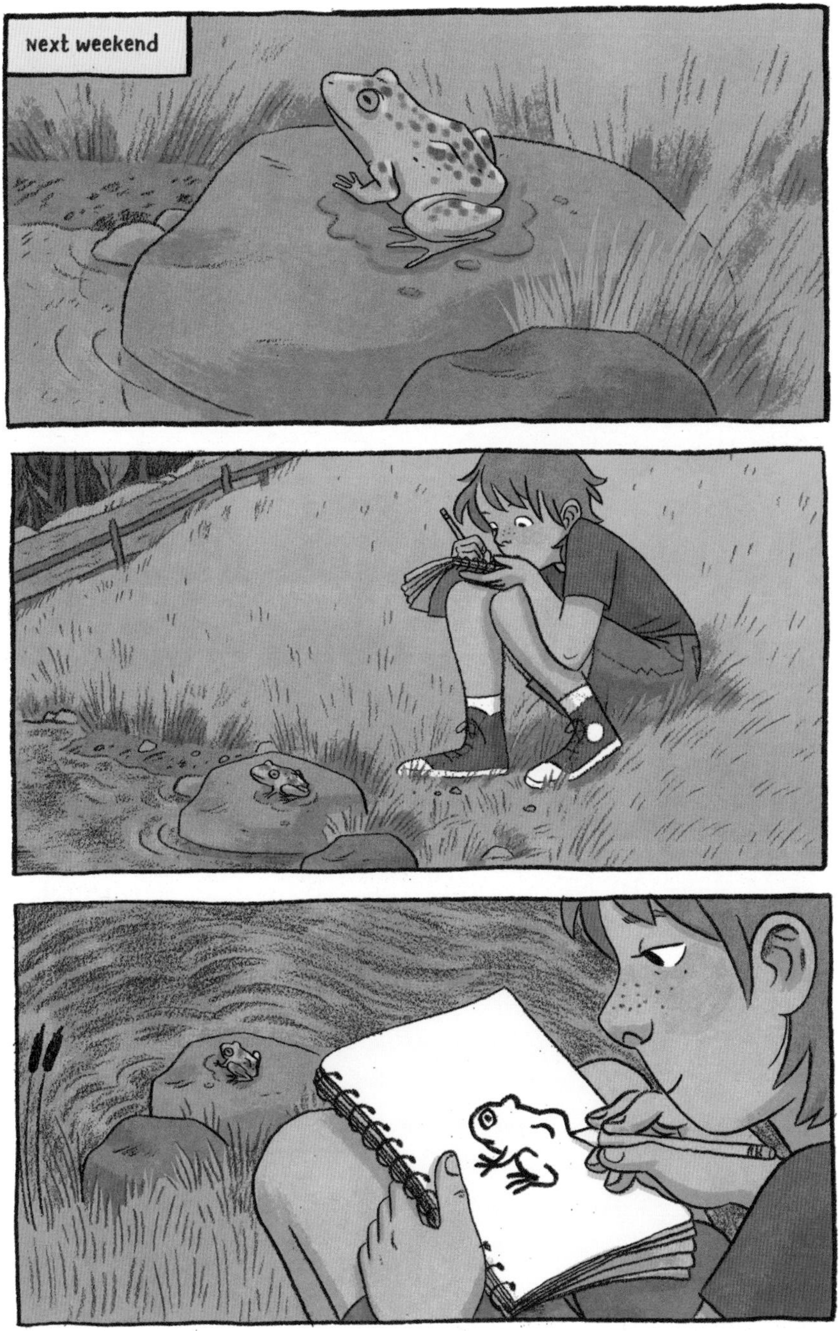
Next weekend

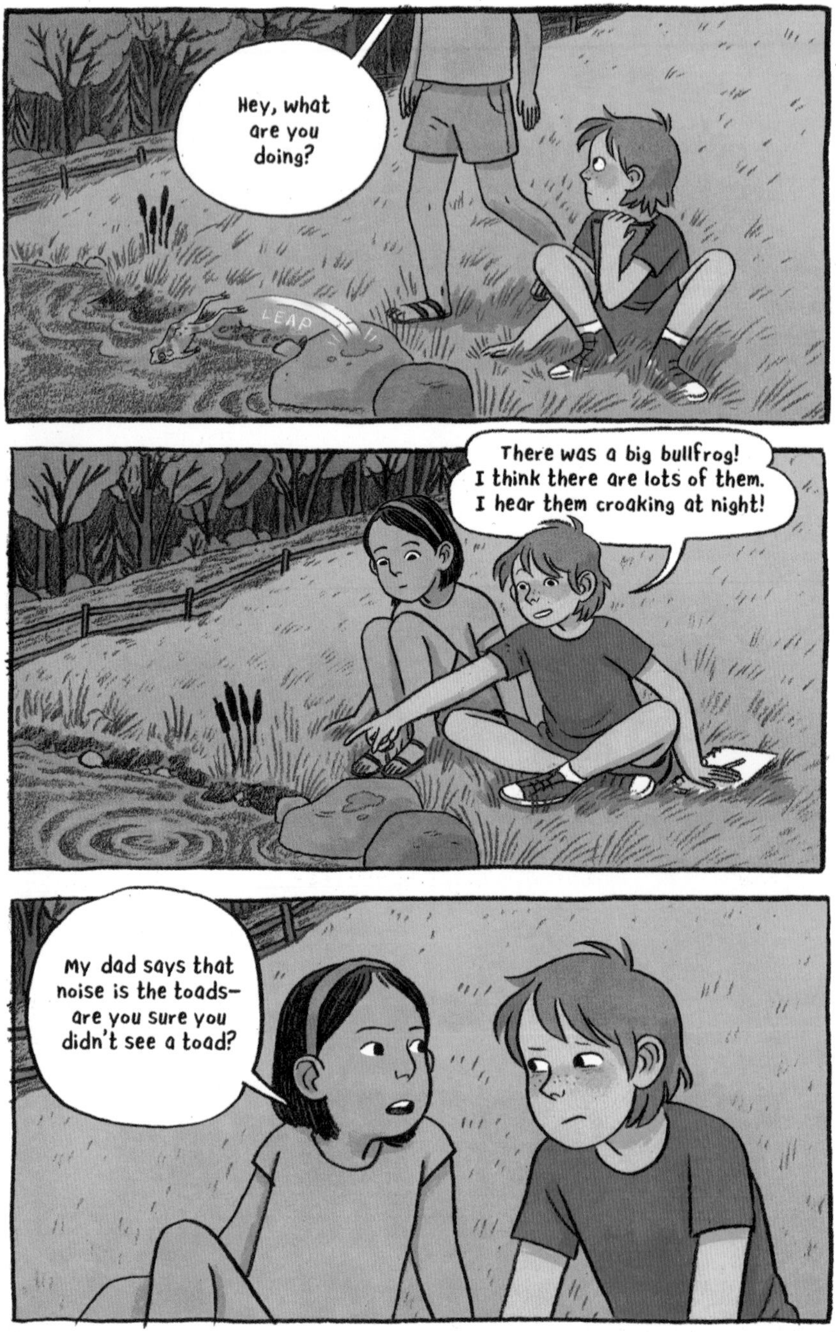
Hey, what are you doing?
LEAP
There was a big bullfrog! I think there are lots of them. I hear them croaking at night!
My dad says that noise is the toads- are you sure you didn't see a toad?

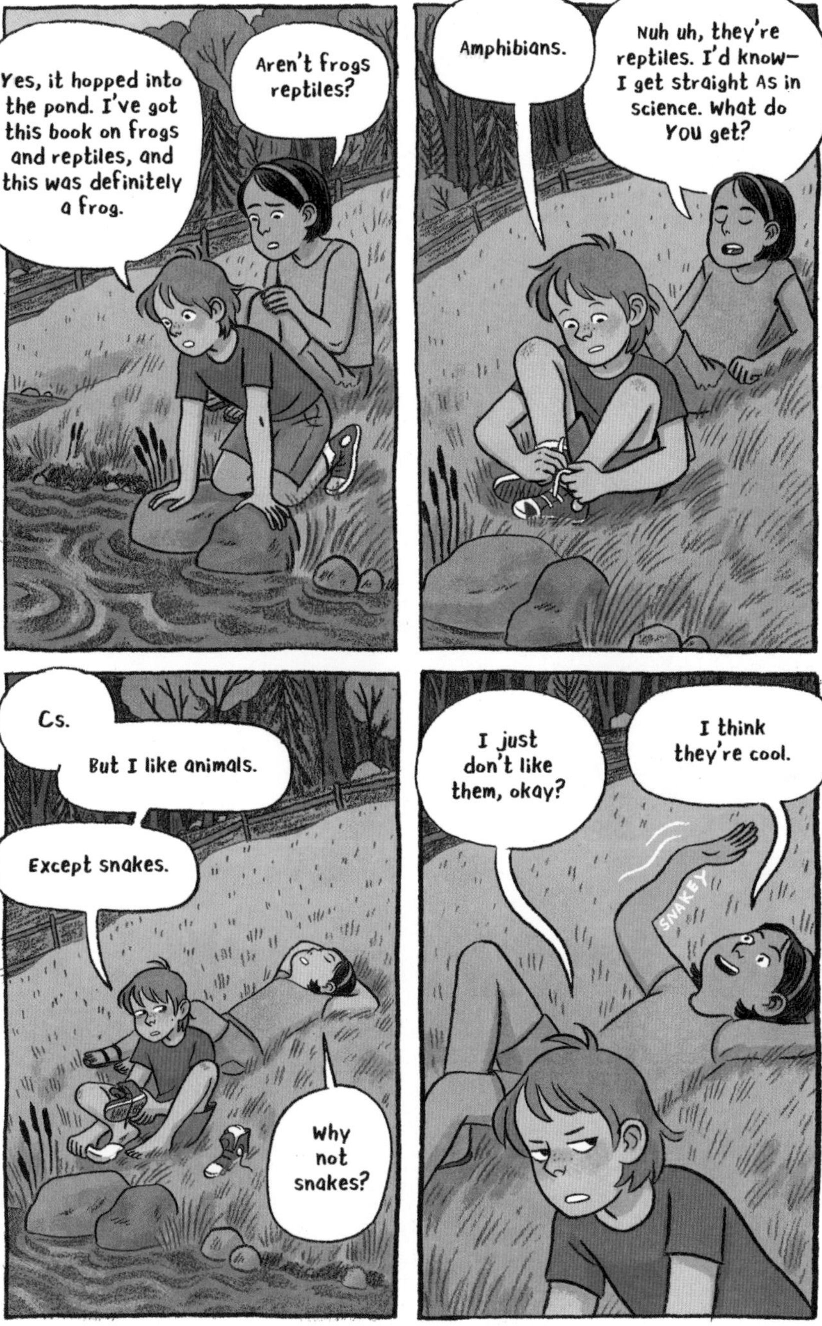
Yes, it hopped into the pond. I've got this book on frogs and reptiles, and this was definitely a frog.
Aren't frogs reptiles?
Amphibians.
Nuh uh, they're reptiles. I'd know—I get straight As in science. What do YOU get?
Cs.
But I like animals.
Except snakes.
Why not snakes?
I just don't like them, okay?
I think they're cool.
SNAKEY

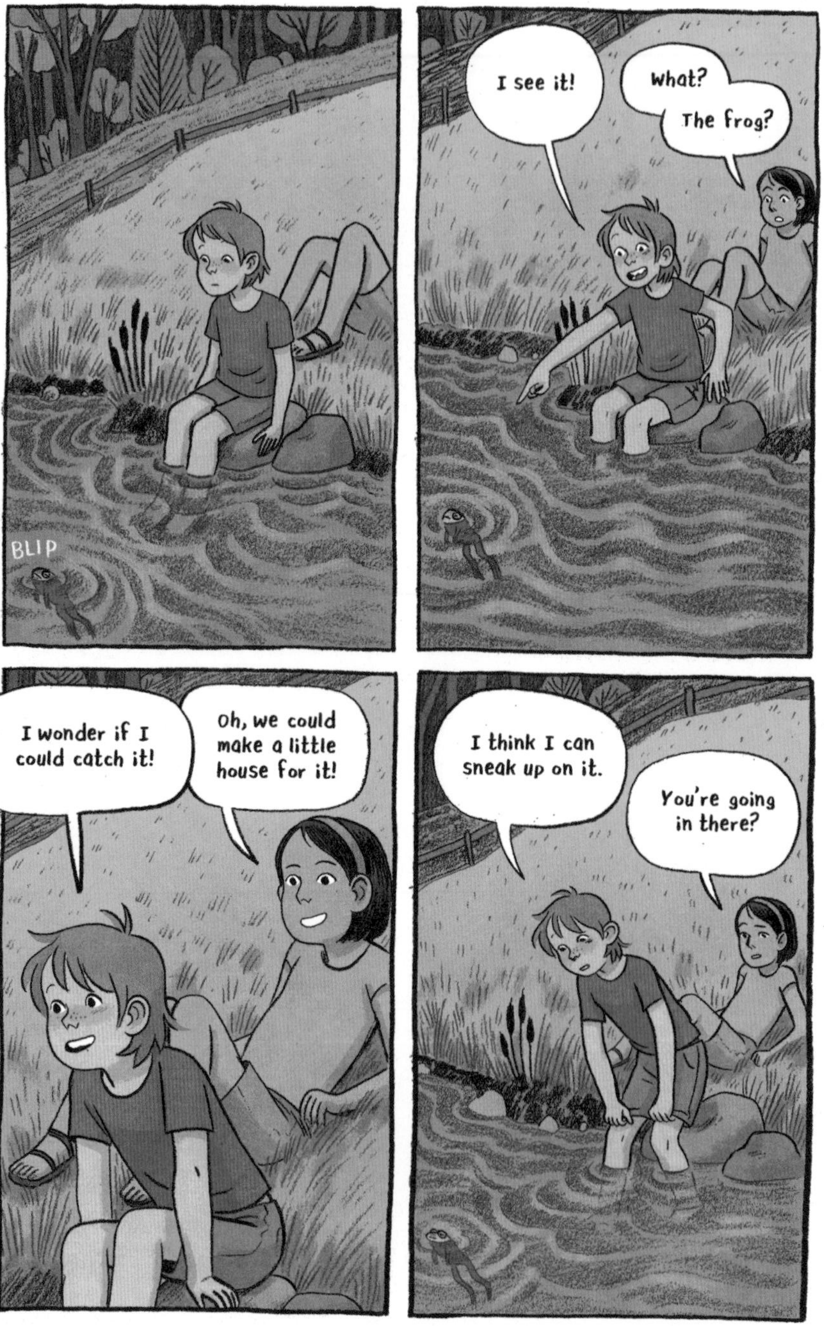
BLIP
I see it!
What?
The frog?
I wonder if I could catch it!
Oh, we could make a little house for it!
I think I can sneak up on it.
You're going in there?

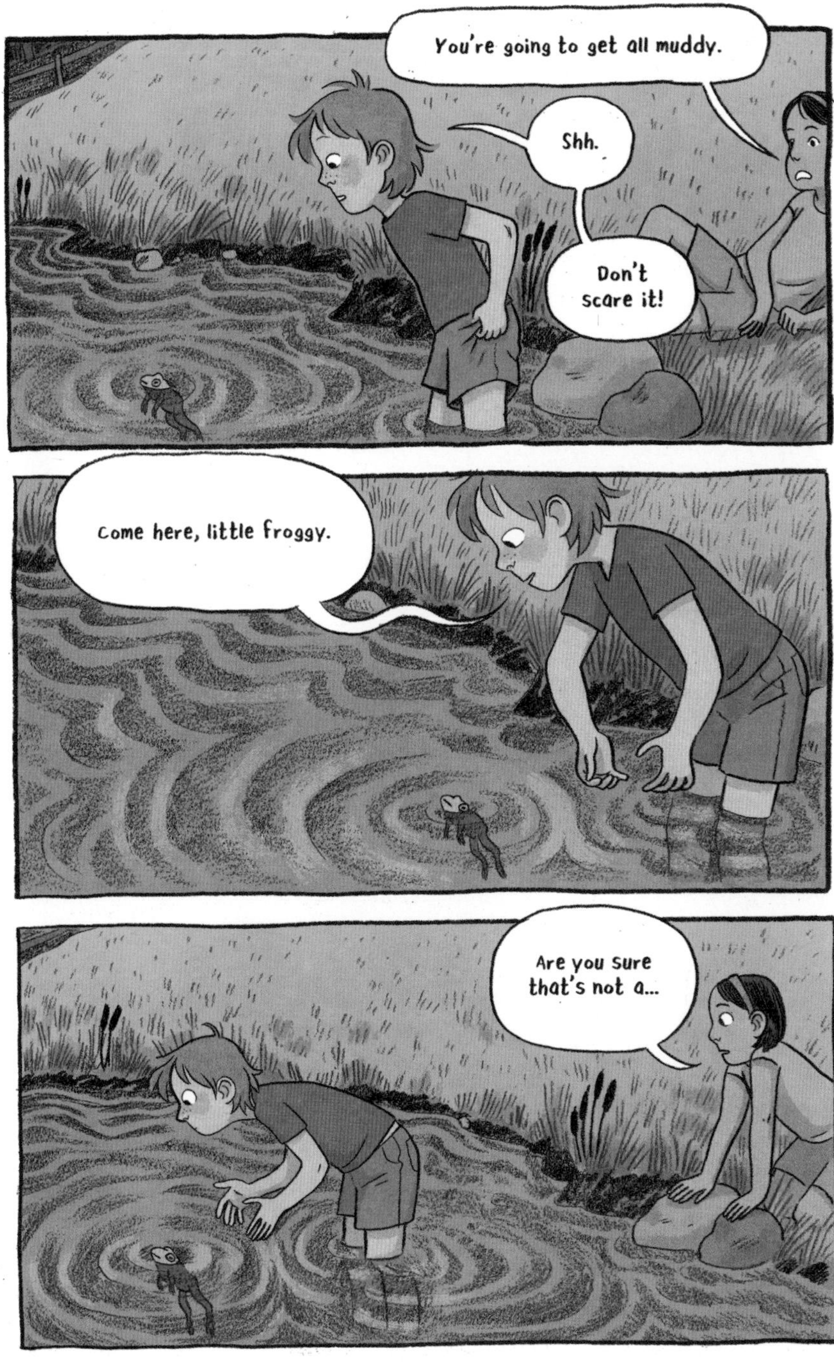
You're going to get all muddy.
Shh.
Don't scare it!
Come here, little froggy.
Are you sure that's not a...

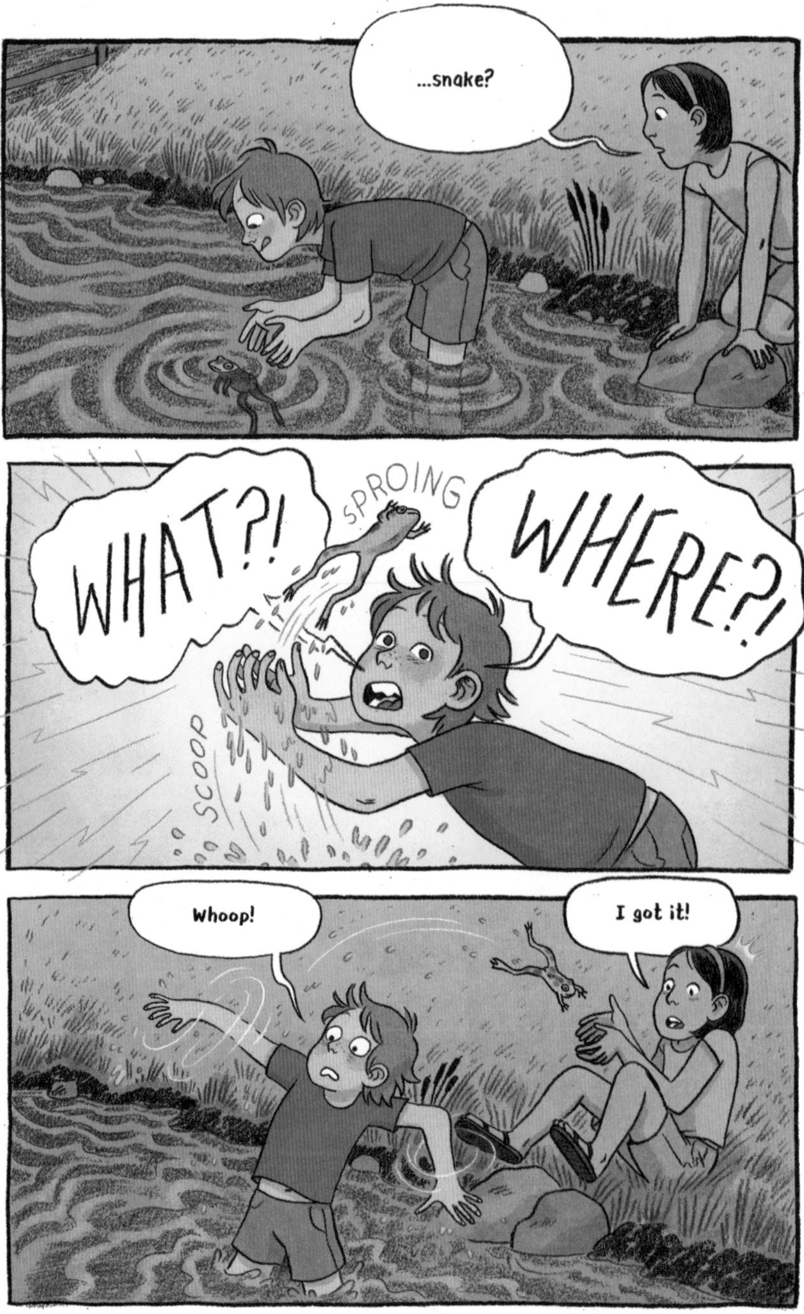
...snake?
WHAT?!
SPROING
WHERE?!
SCOOP
Whoop!
I got it!

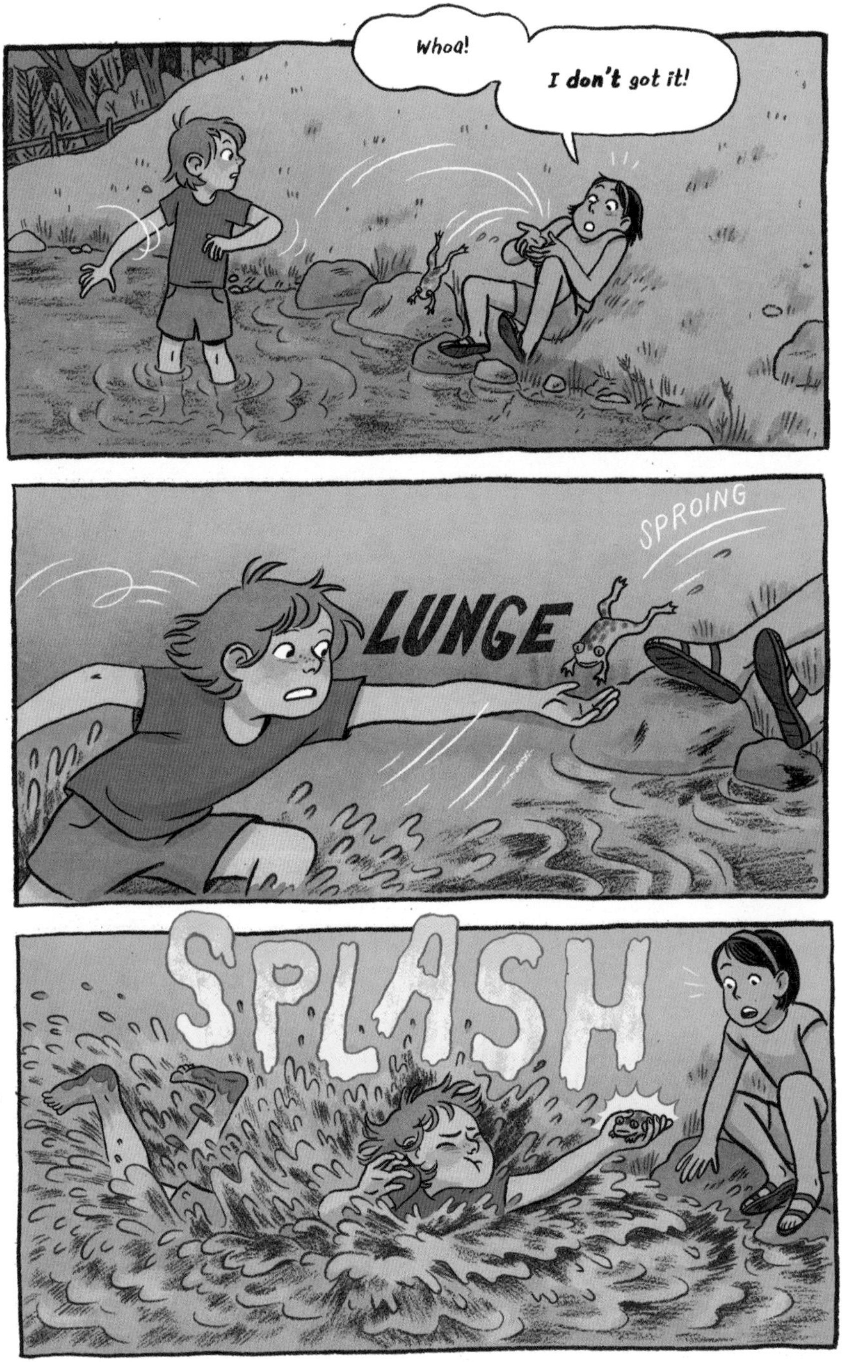
Whoa!
I don't got it!
LUNGE
SPROING
SPLASH

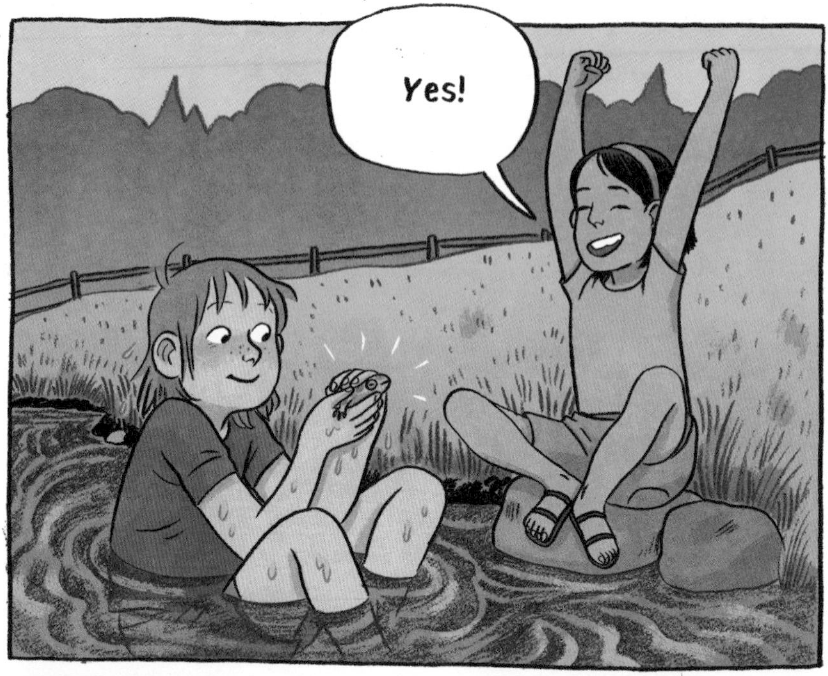
Yes!

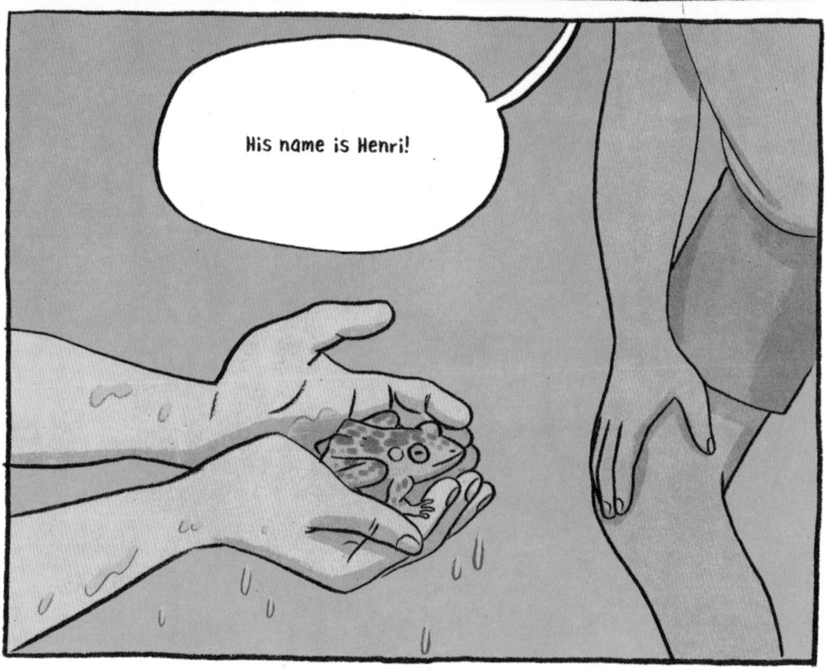
His name is Henri!

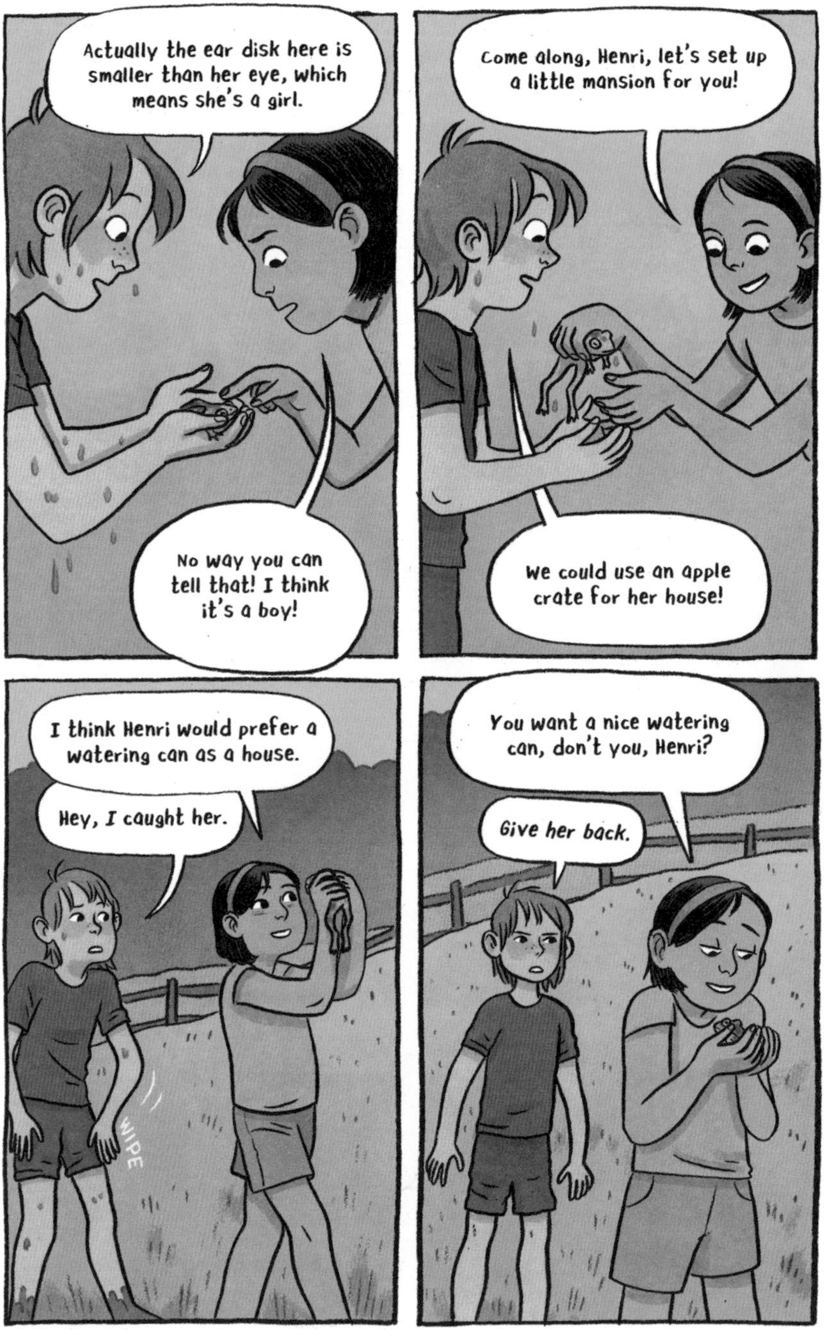

Actually the ear disk here is smaller than her eye, which means she's a girl.
No way you can tell that! I think it's a boy!
Come along, Henri, let's set up a little mansion for you!
We could use an apple crate for her house!
I think Henri would prefer a watering can as a house.
Hey, I caught her.
WIPE
You want a nice watering can, don't you, Henri?
Give her back.

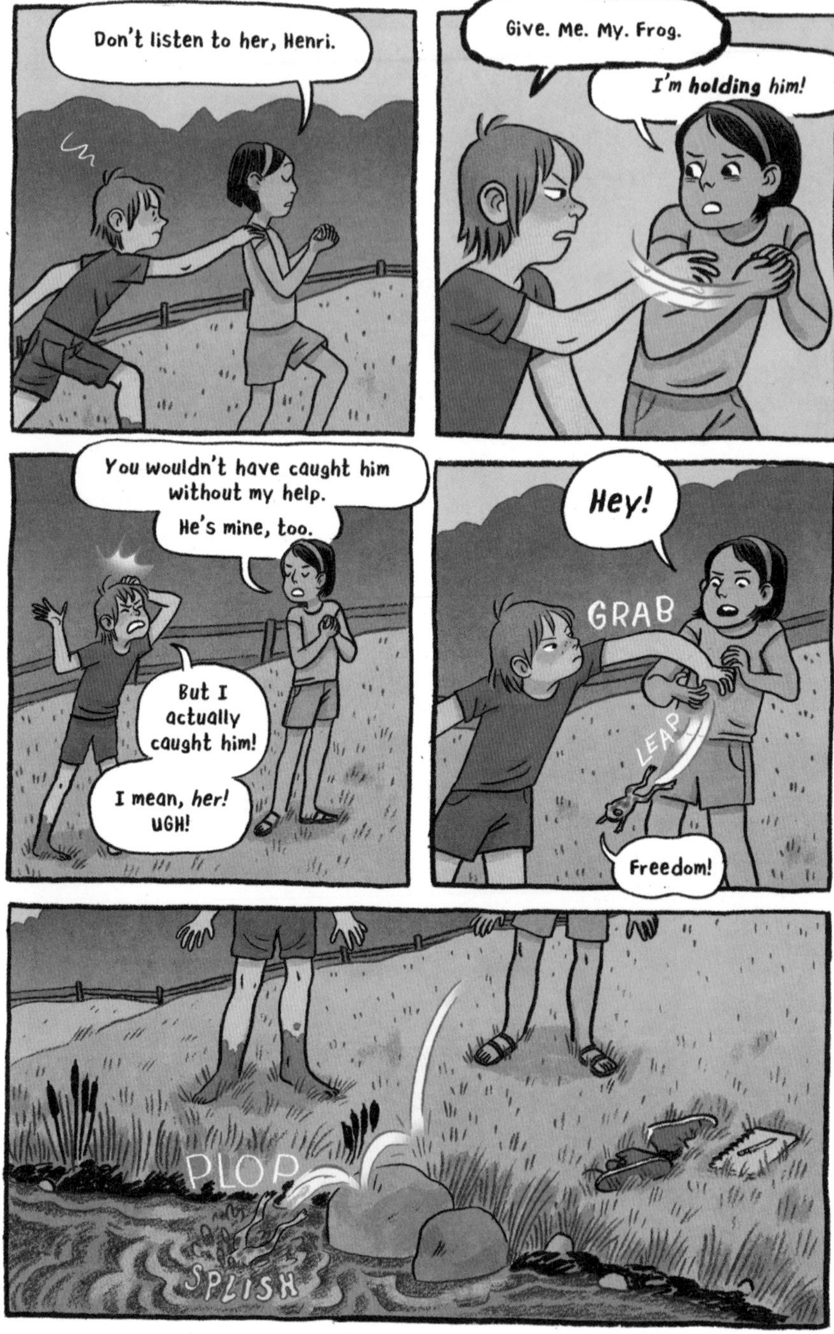
Don't listen to her, Henri.
Give. Me. My. Frog.
I'm *holding* him!
You wouldn't have caught him without my help.
He's mine, too.
But I actually caught him!
I mean, *her!* UGH!
Hey!
GRAB
LEAP
Freedom!
PLOP
SPLISH

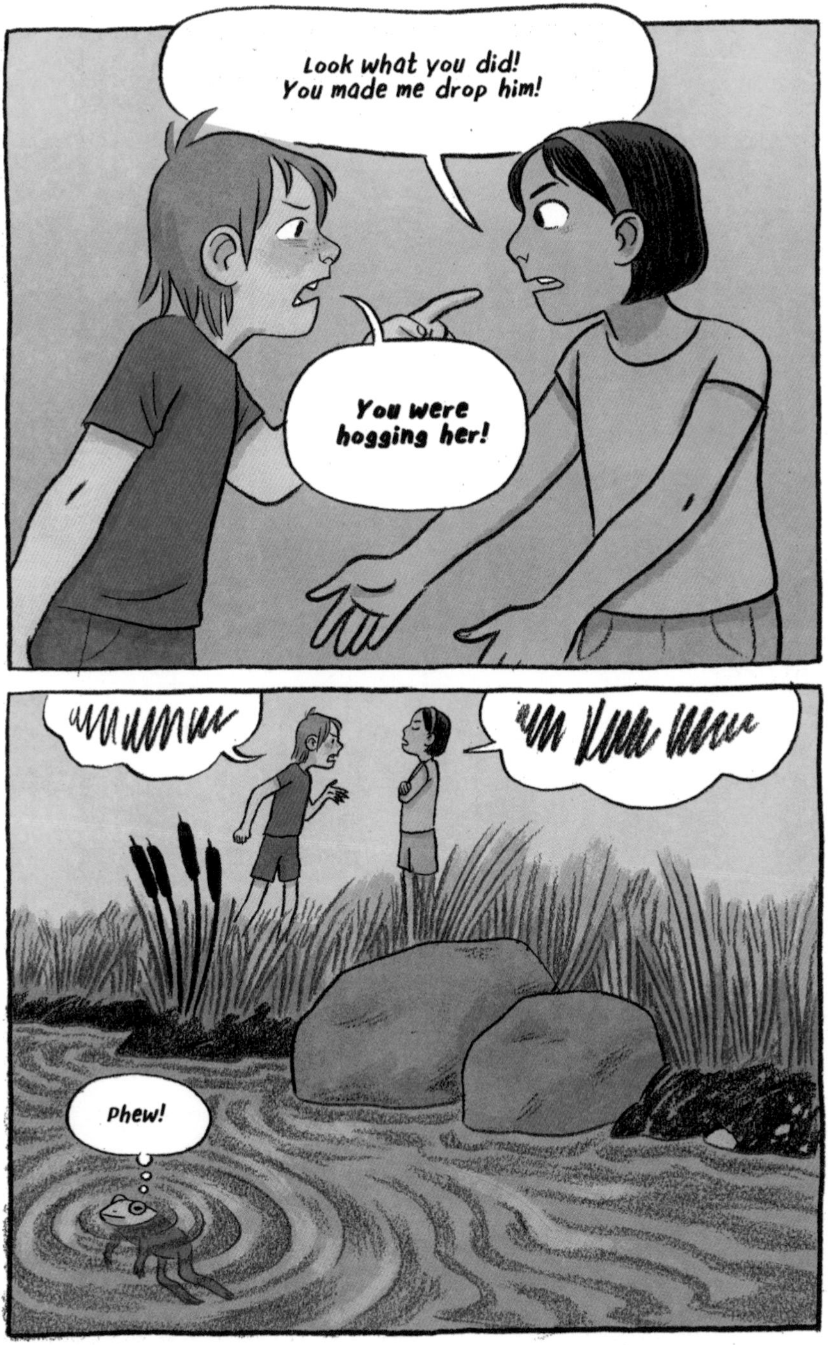
Look what you did!
You made me drop him!
You were hogging her!
Phew!

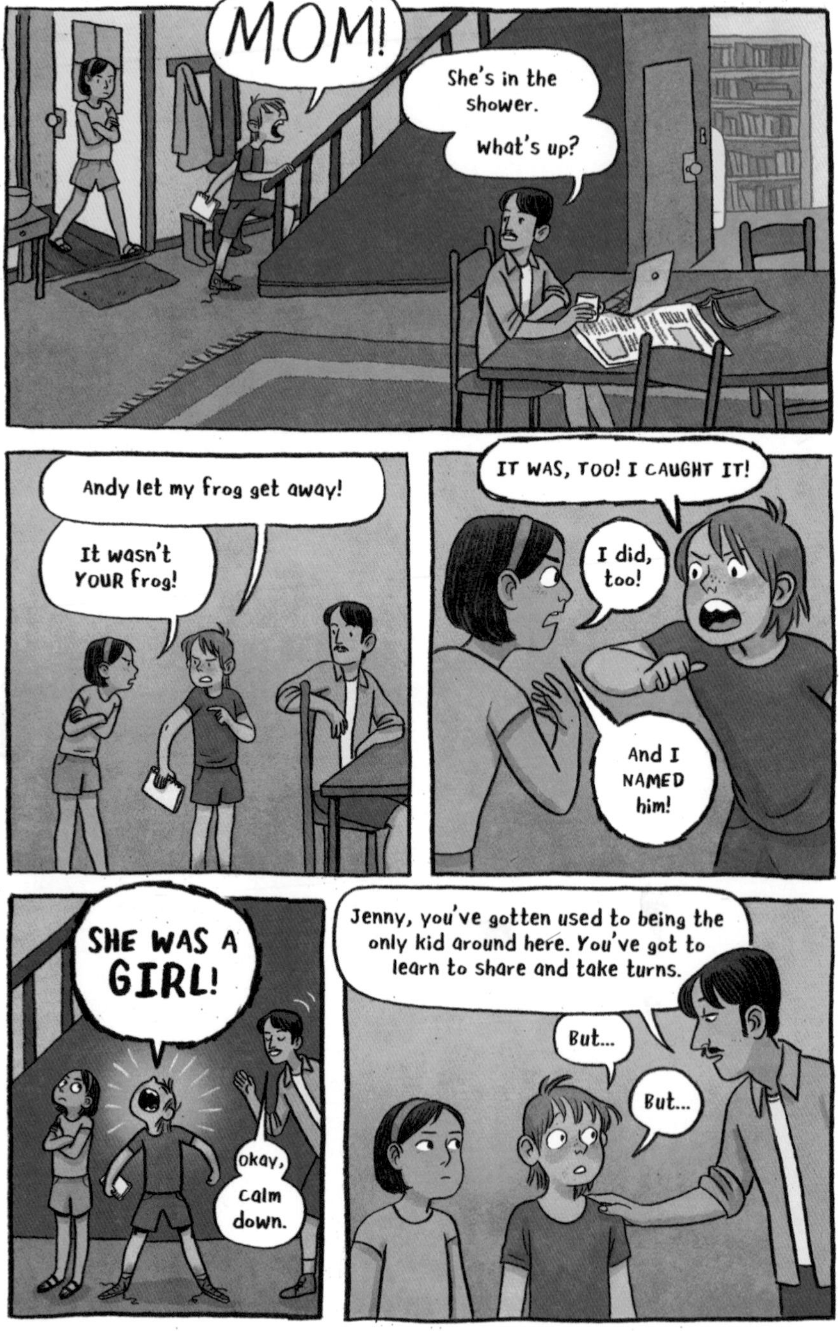
MOM!
She's in the shower.
What's up?
Andy let my frog get away!
It wasn't YOUR frog!
IT WAS, TOO! I CAUGHT IT!
I did, too!
And I NAMED him!
SHE WAS A GIRL!
Okay, calm down.
Jenny, you've gotten used to being the only kid around here. You've got to learn to share and take turns.
But...
But...

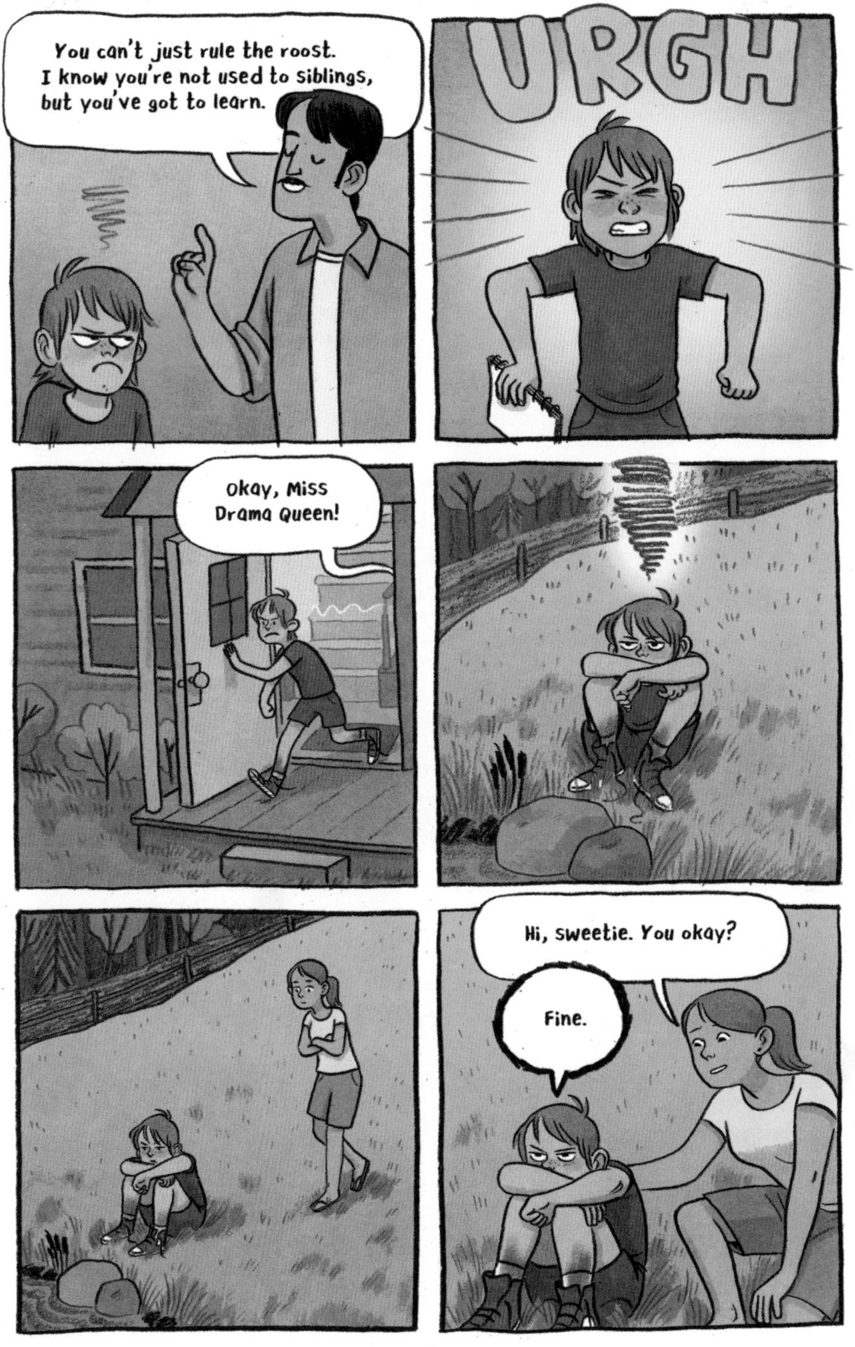
You can't just rule the roost. I know you're not used to siblings, but you've got to learn.
URGH
Okay, Miss Drama Queen!
Hi, sweetie. You okay?
Fine.

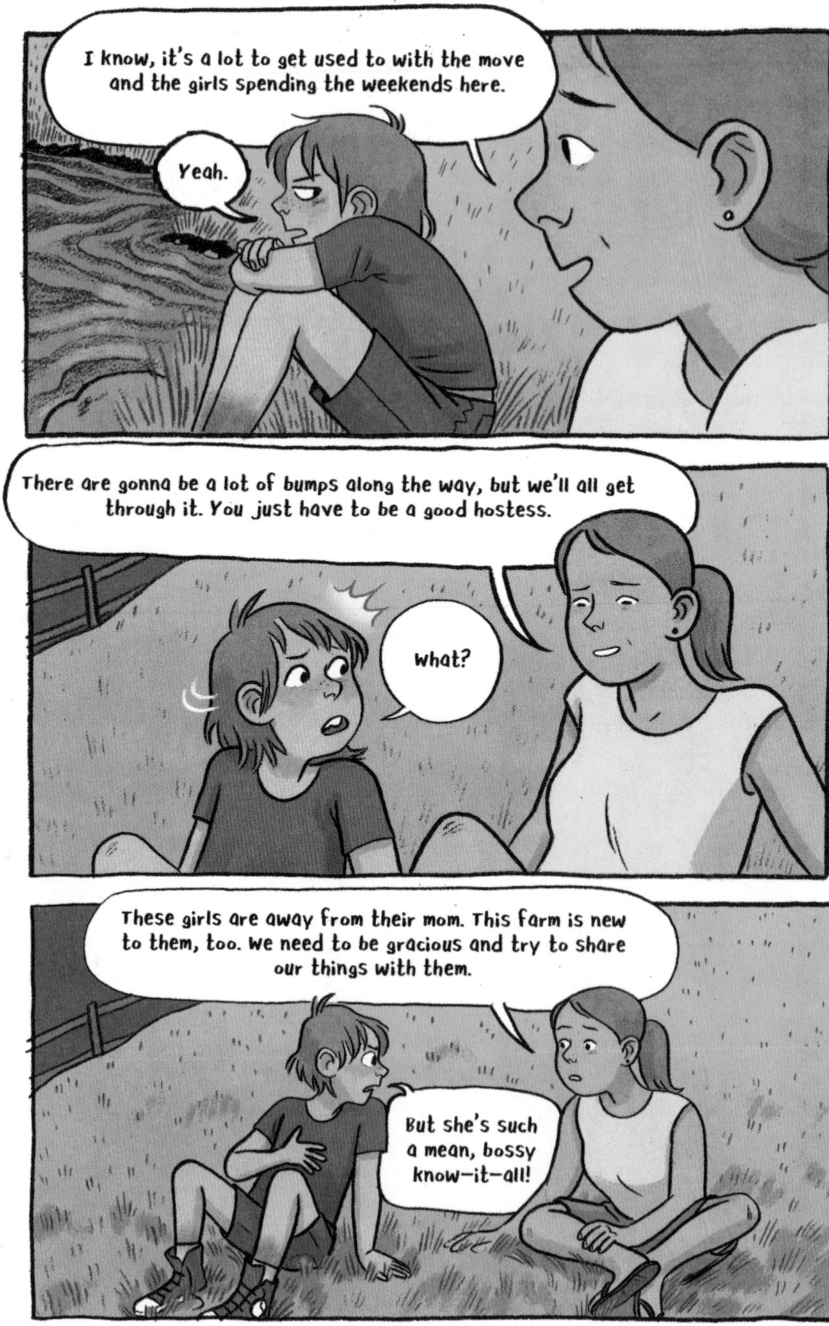
I know, it's a lot to get used to with the move and the girls spending the weekends here.
Yeah.
There are gonna be a lot of bumps along the way, but we'll all get through it. You just have to be a good hostess.
What?
These girls are away from their mom. This farm is new to them, too. We need to be gracious and try to share our things with them.
But she's such a mean, bossy know-it-all!

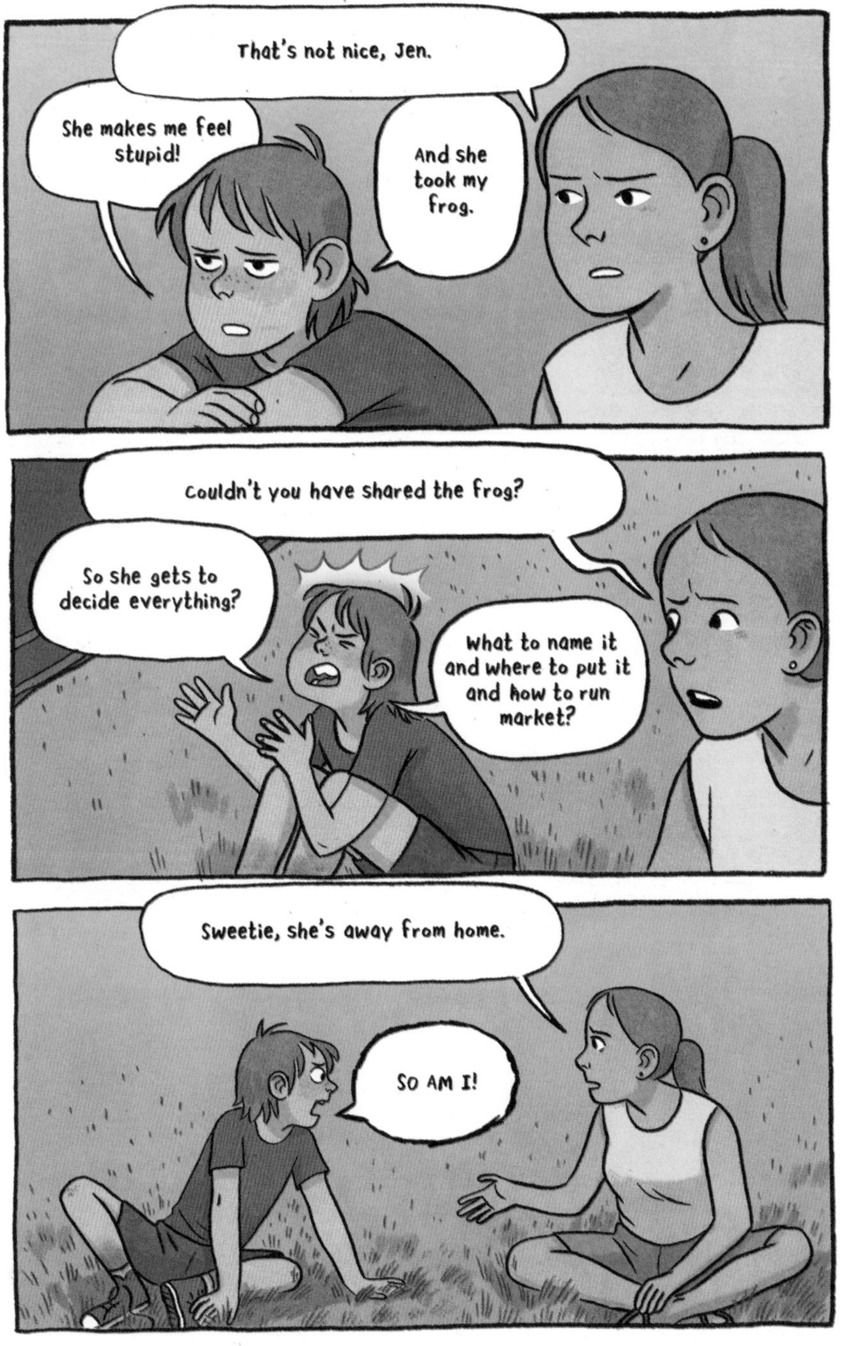
That's not nice, Jen.
She makes me feel stupid!
And she took my frog.
Couldn't you have shared the frog?
So she gets to decide everything?
What to name it and where to put it and how to run market?
Sweetie, she's away from home.
SO AM I!

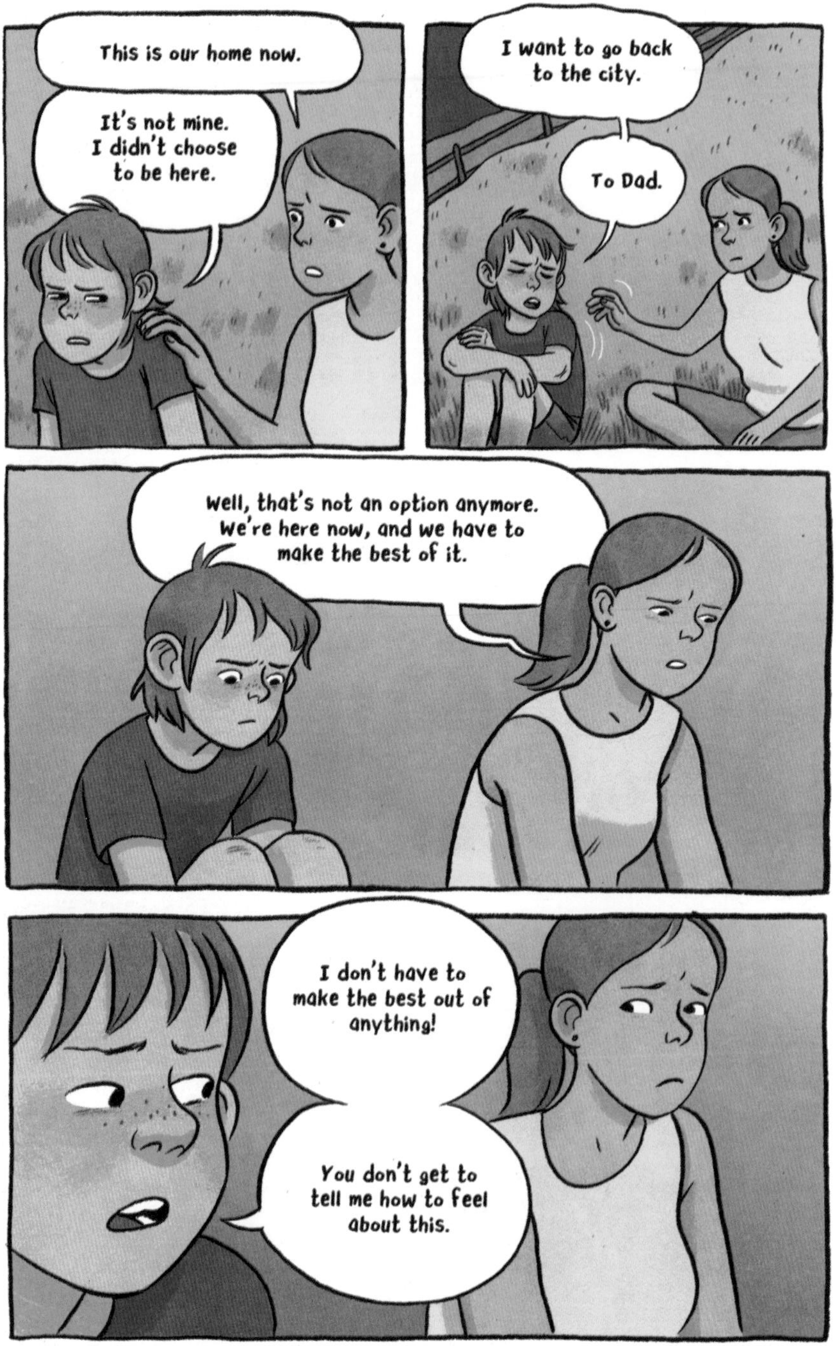
This is our home now.
It's not mine. I didn't choose to be here.
I want to go back to the city.
To Dad.
Well, that's not an option anymore. We're here now, and we have to make the best of it.
I don't have to make the best out of anything!
You don't get to tell me how to feel about this.

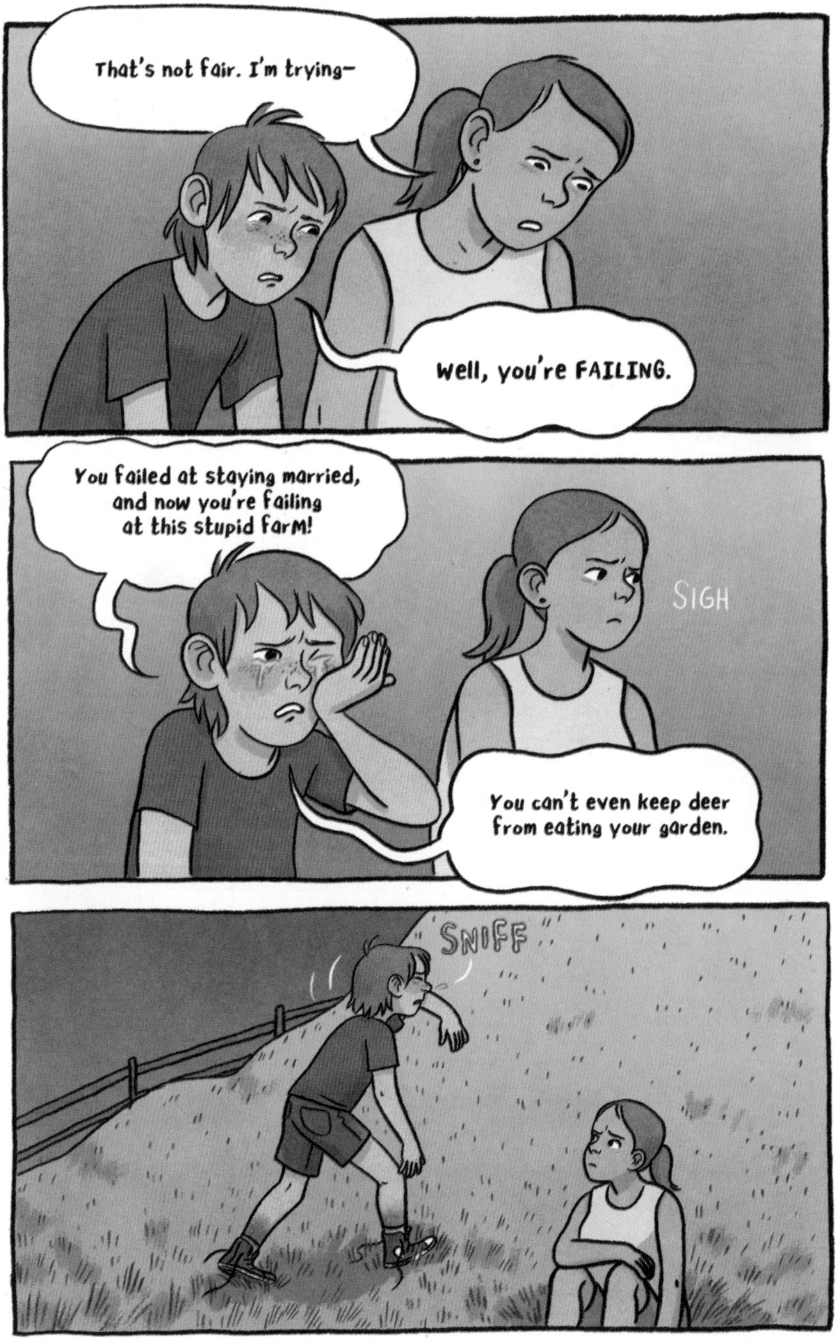
That's not fair. I'm trying—
Well, you're FAILING.
You failed at staying married, and now you're failing at this stupid farm!
SIGH
You can't even keep deer from eating your garden.
SNIFF

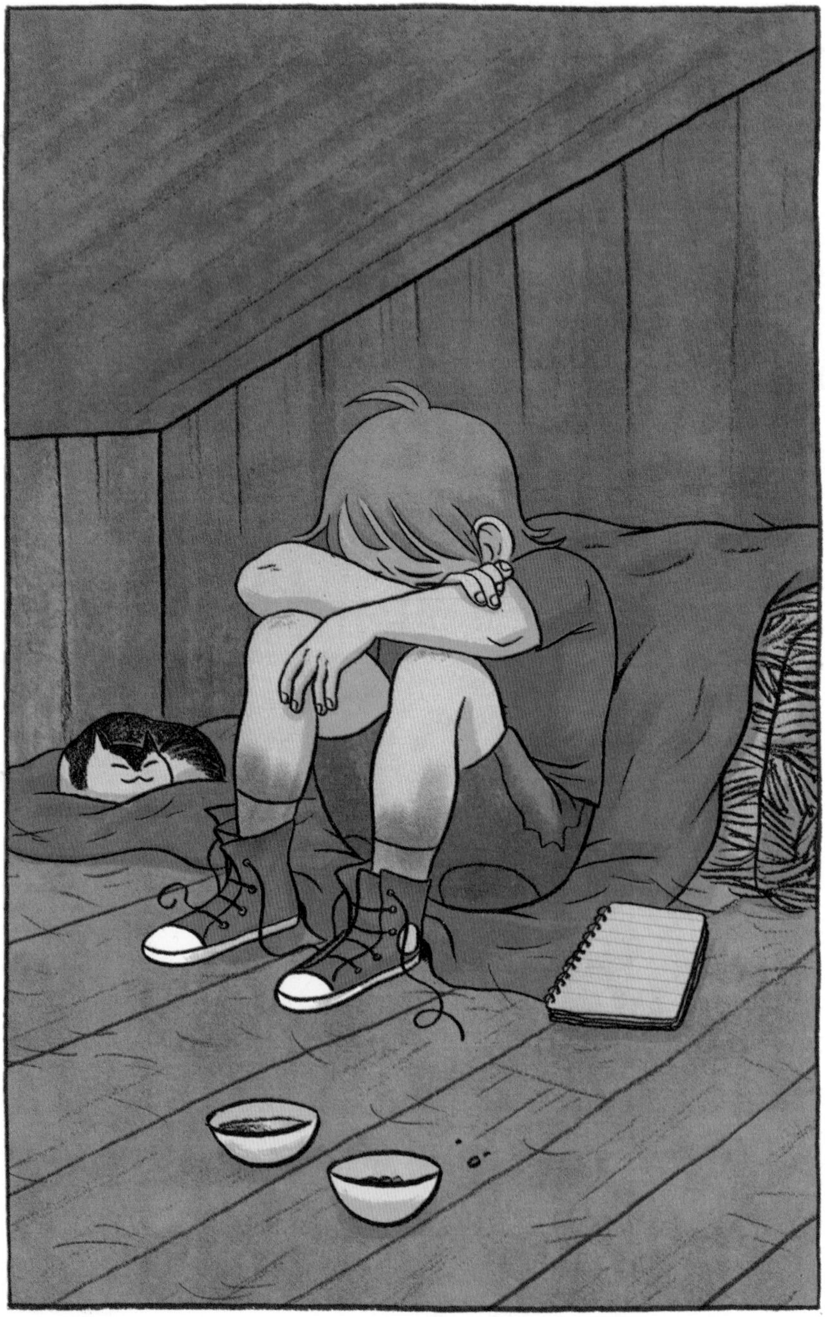

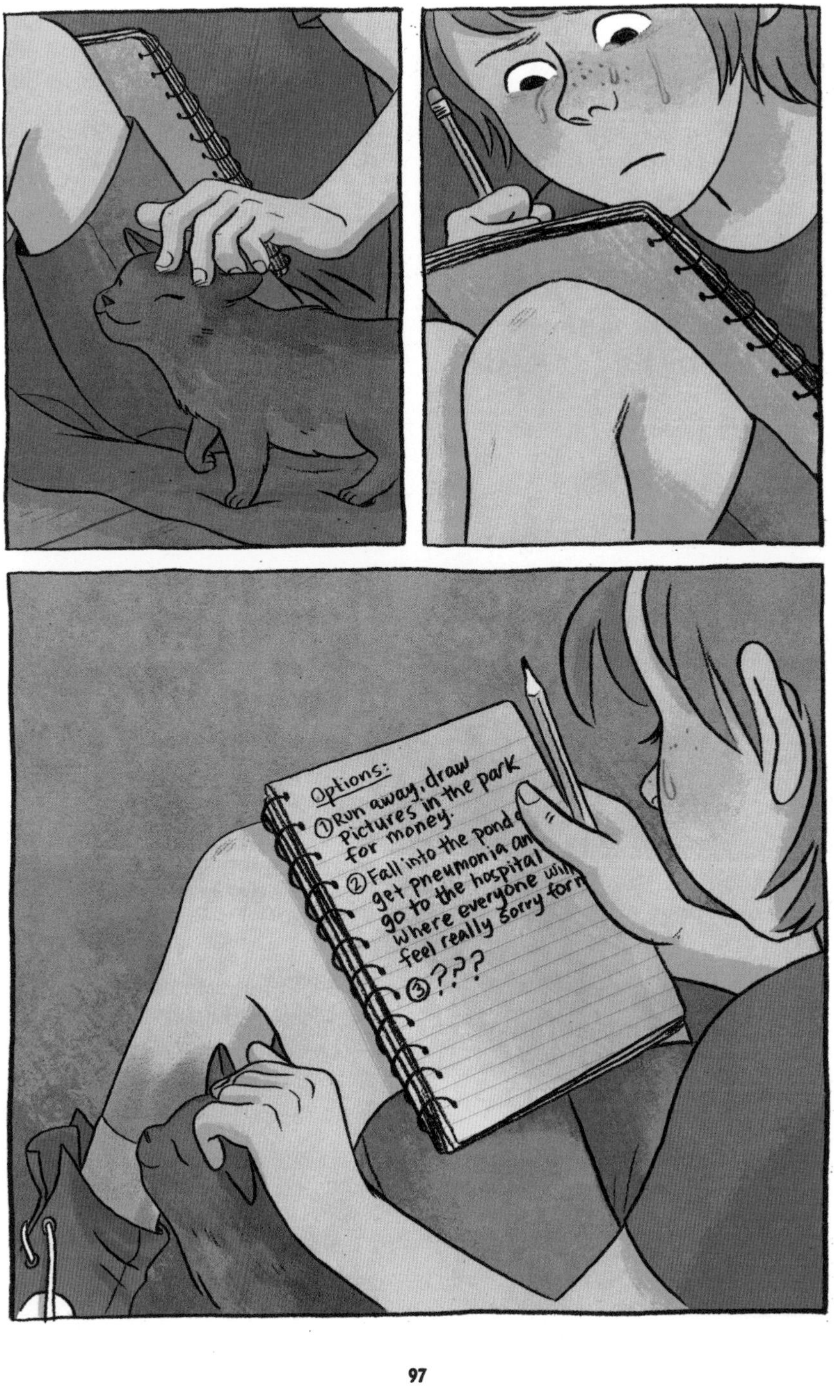
Options:
① Run away, draw pictures in the park for money.
② Fall into the pond
get pneumonia an
go to the hospital
where everyone wil
feel really sorry for
③ ???

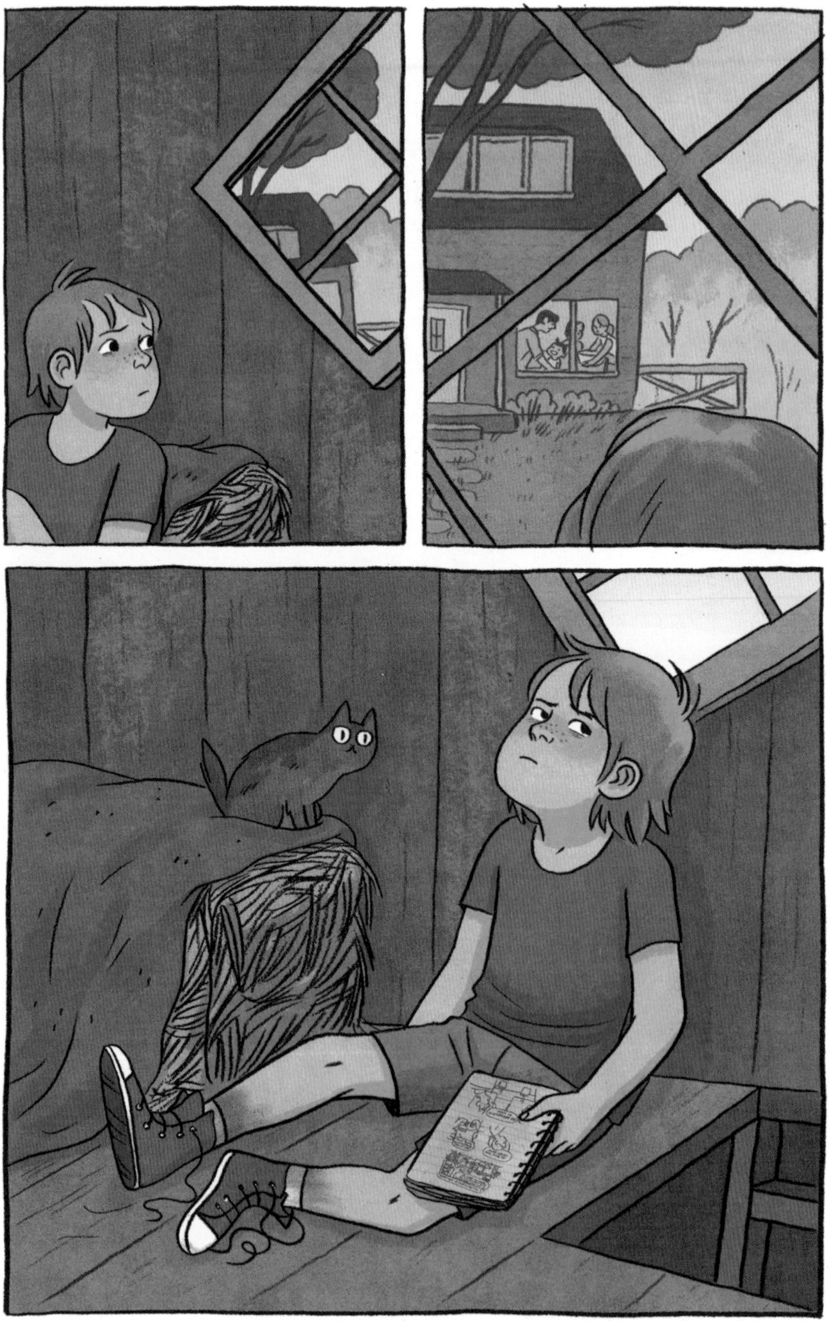

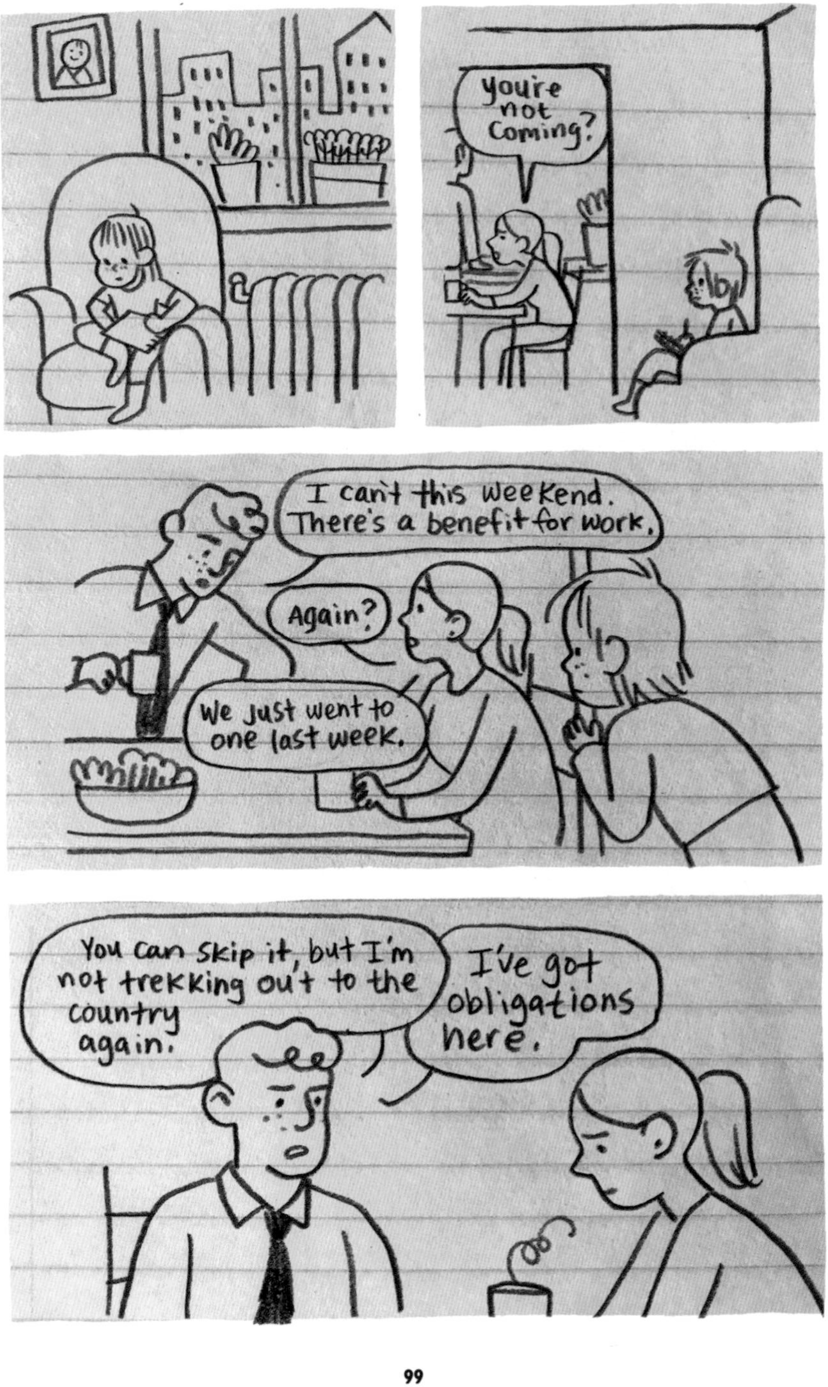
you're not Coming?
I can't this weekend. There's a benefit for work.
Again?
We just went to one last week.
You can skip it, but I'm not trekking out to the country again.
I've got obligations here.

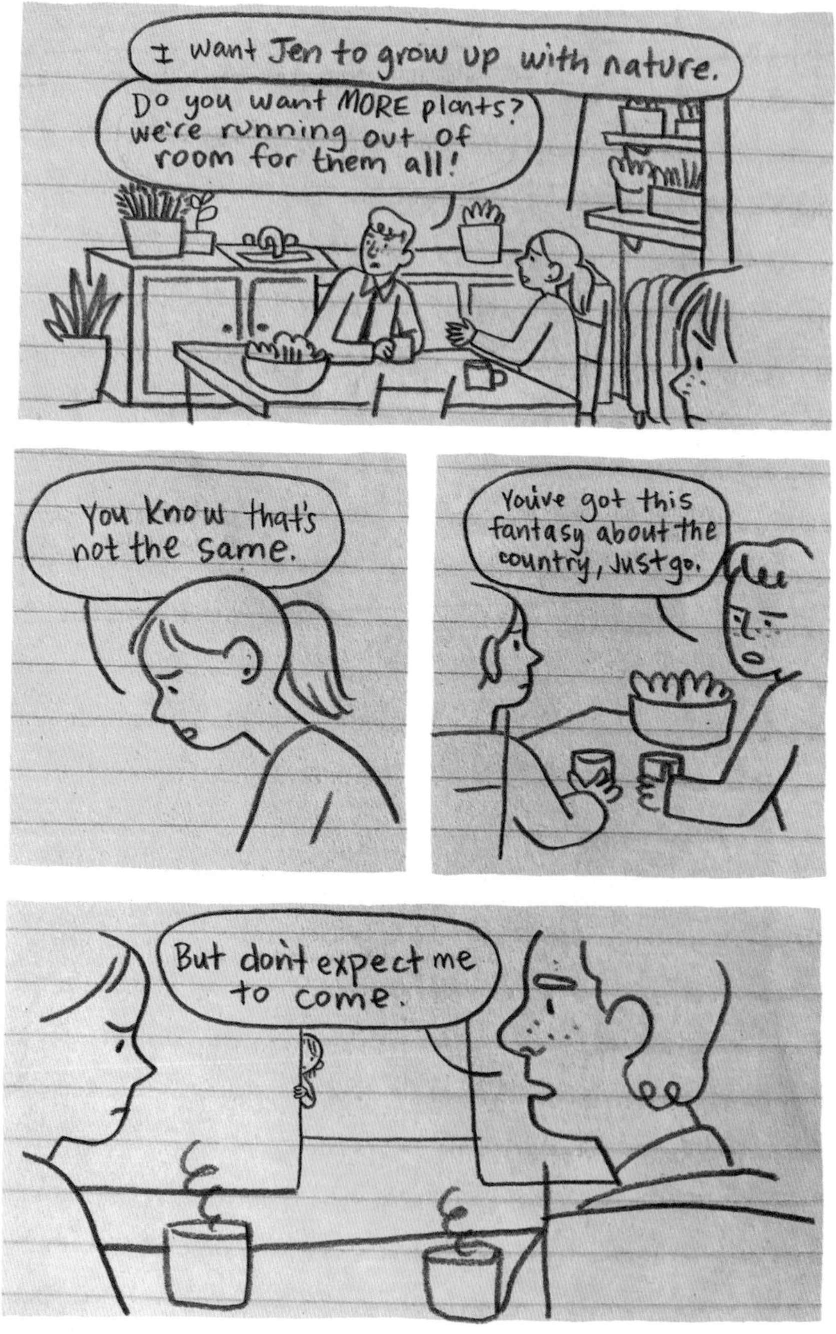
I want Jen to grow up with nature.
Do you want MORE plants? we're running out of room for them all!
You know that's not the same.
You've got this fantasy about the country, just go.
But don't expect me to come.

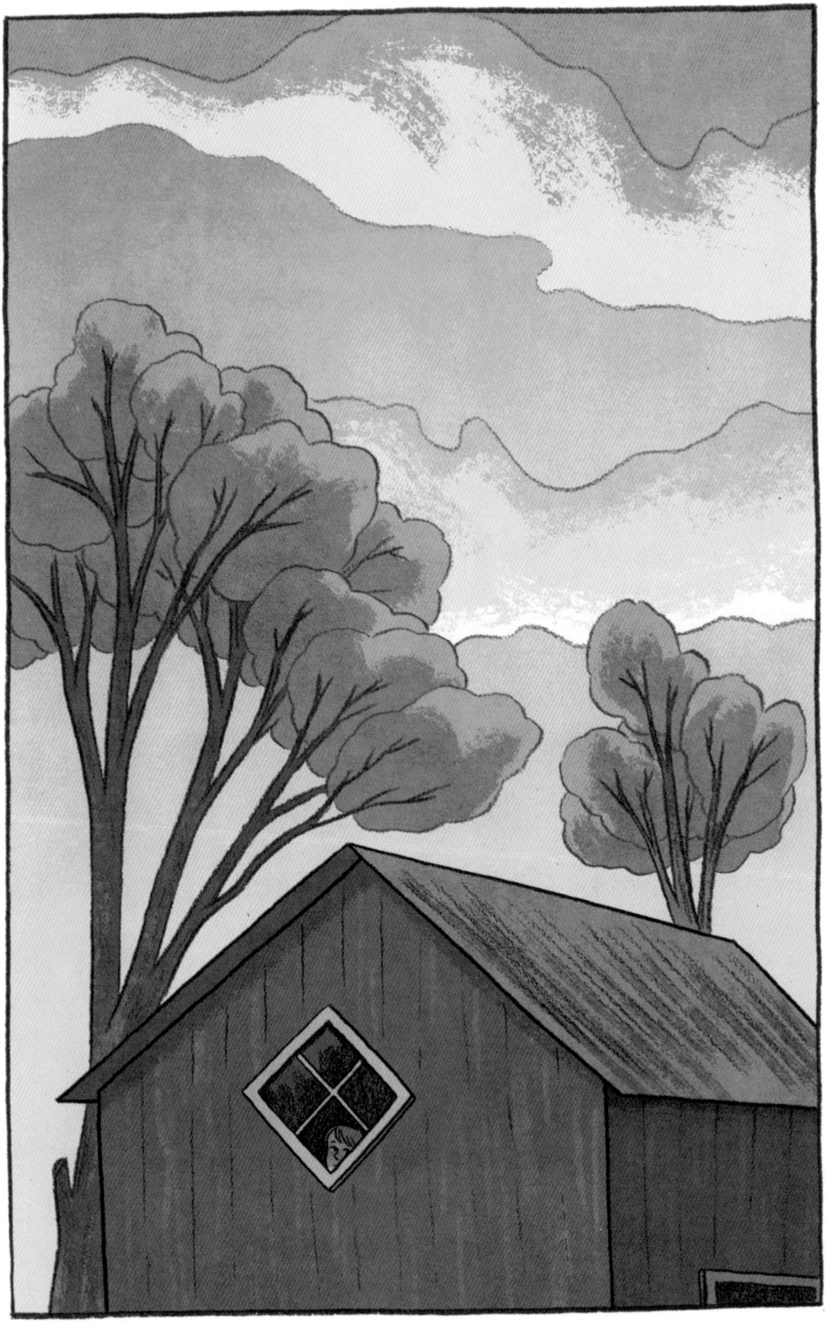

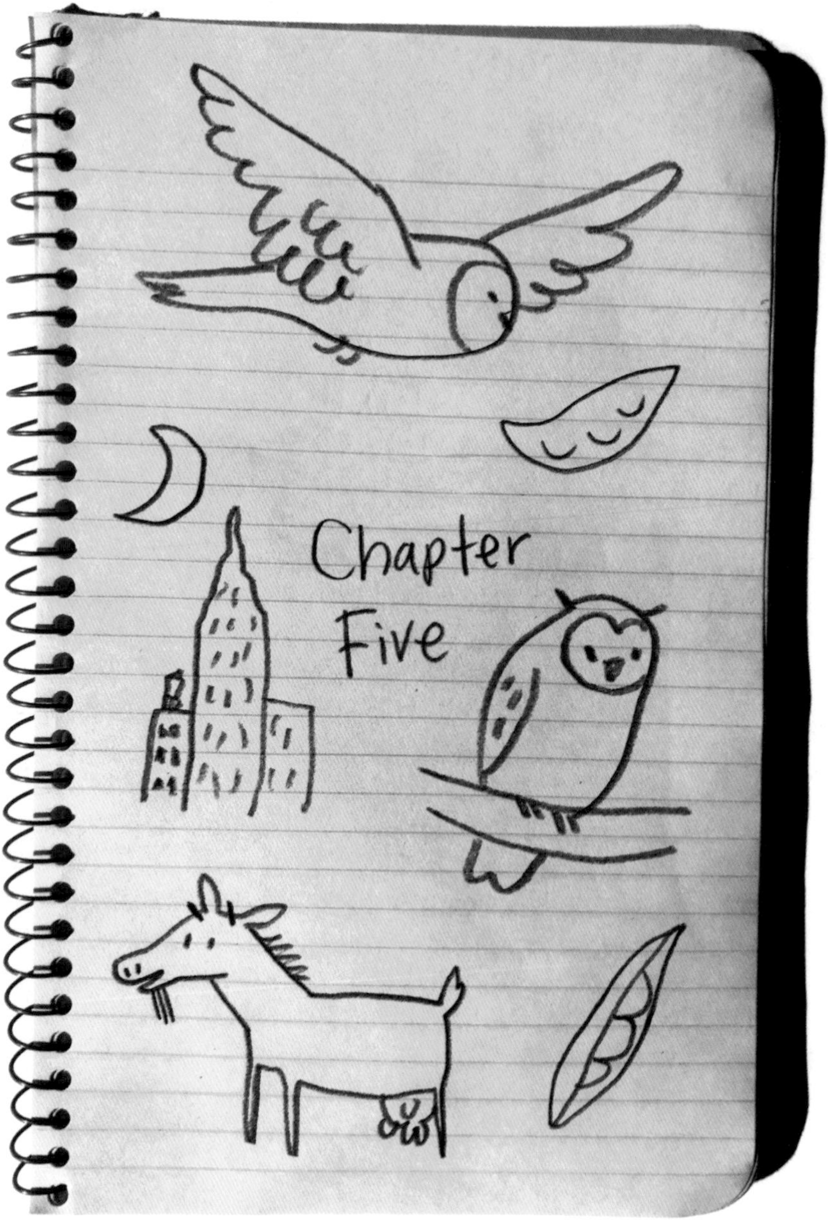
Chapter
Five

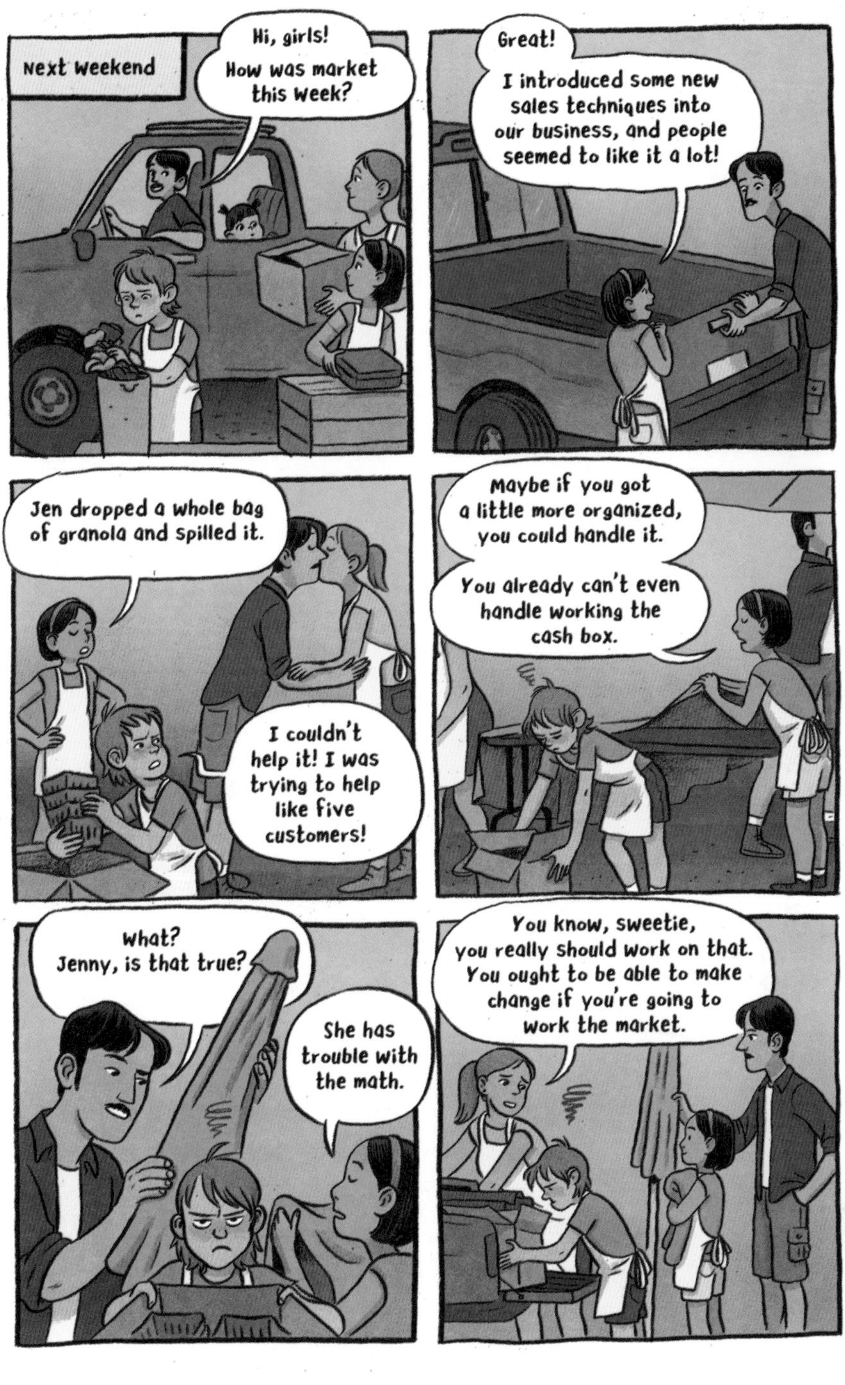
Next Weekend
Hi, girls!
How was market this week?
Great!
I introduced some new sales techniques into our business, and people seemed to like it a lot!
Jen dropped a whole bag of granola and spilled it.
I couldn't help it! I was trying to help like five customers!
Maybe if you got a little more organized, you could handle it.
You already can't even handle working the cash box.
What?
Jenny, is that true?
She has trouble with the math.
You know, sweetie, you really should work on that. You ought to be able to make change if you're going to work the market.

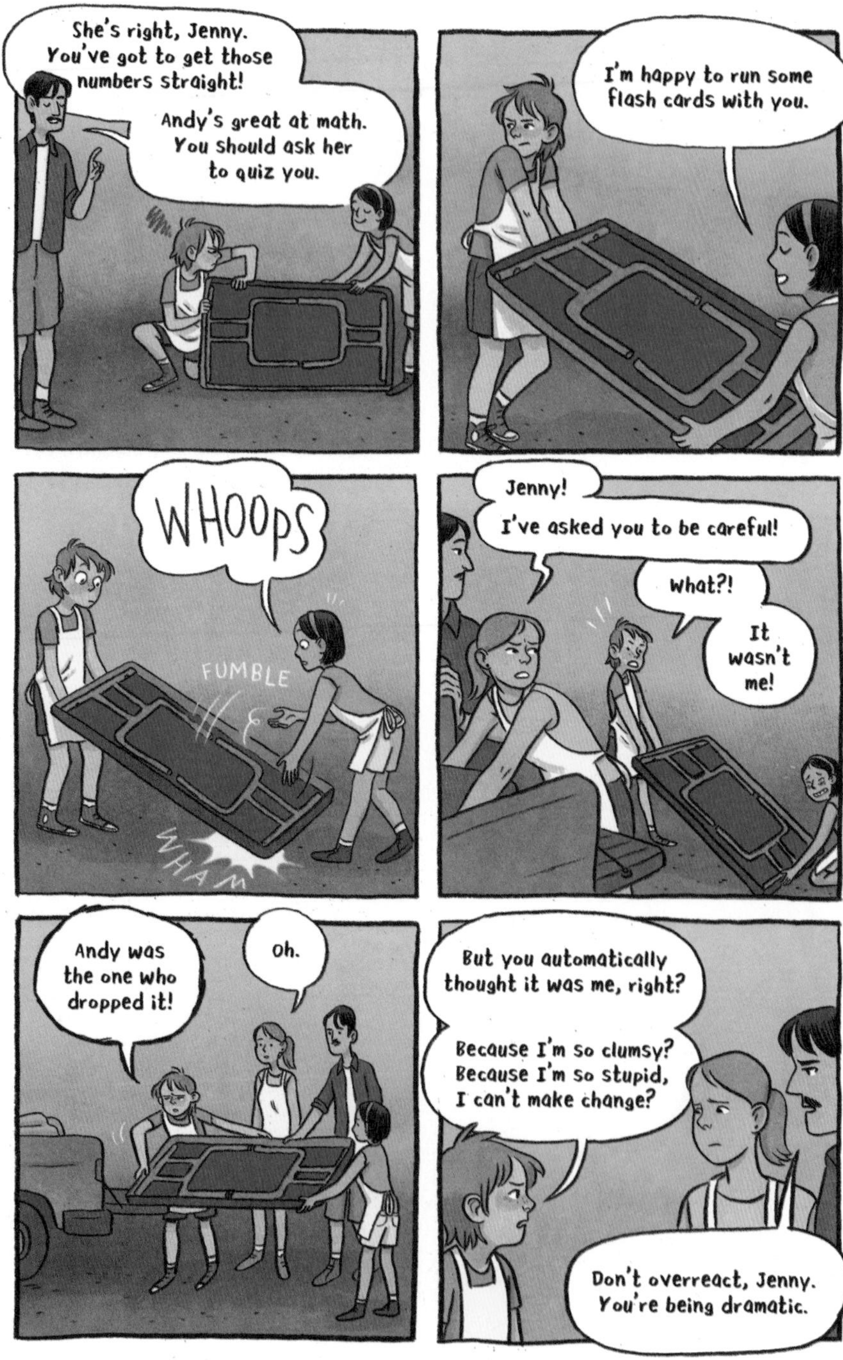
She's right, Jenny. You've got to get those numbers straight!
Andy's great at math. You should ask her to quiz you.
I'm happy to run some flash cards with you.
WHOOPS
FUMBLE
WHAM
Jenny!
I've asked you to be careful!
What?!
It wasn't me!
Andy was the one who dropped it!
Oh.
But you automatically thought it was me, right?
Because I'm so clumsy? Because I'm so stupid, I can't make change?
Don't overreact, Jenny. You're being dramatic.

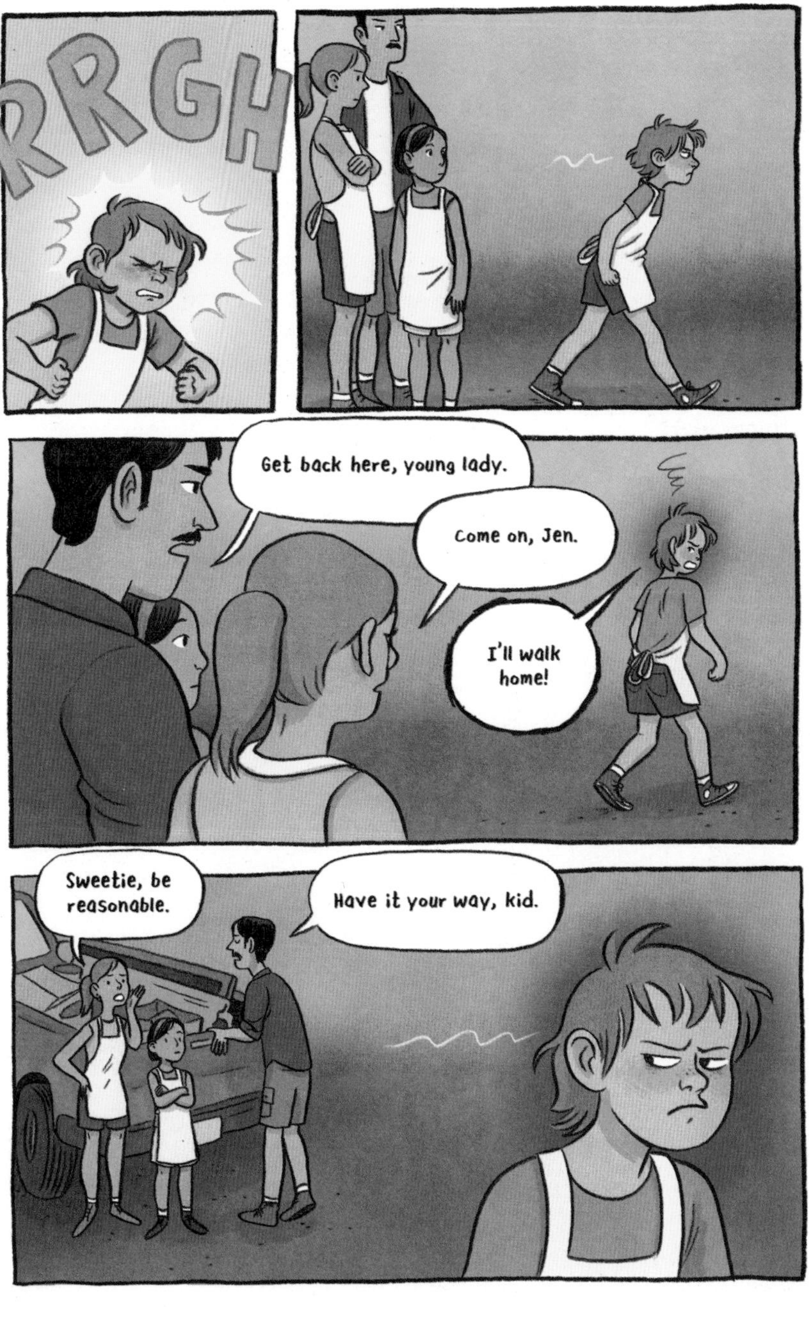
RRGH
Get back here, young lady.
Come on, Jen.
I'll walk home!
Sweetie, be reasonable.
Have it your way, kid.

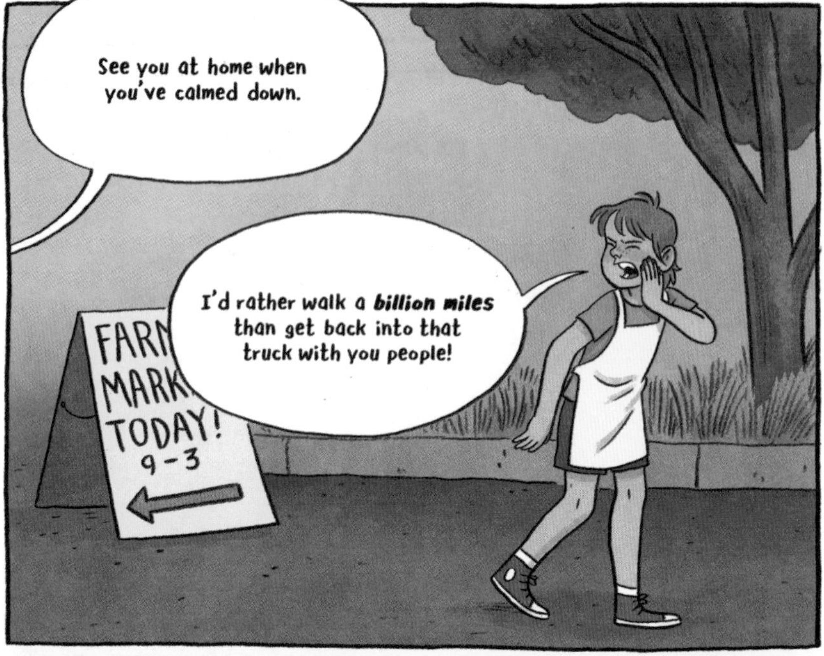
See you at home when you've calmed down.
I'd rather walk a **billion miles** than get back into that truck with you people!
FARM MARK TODAY! 9-3

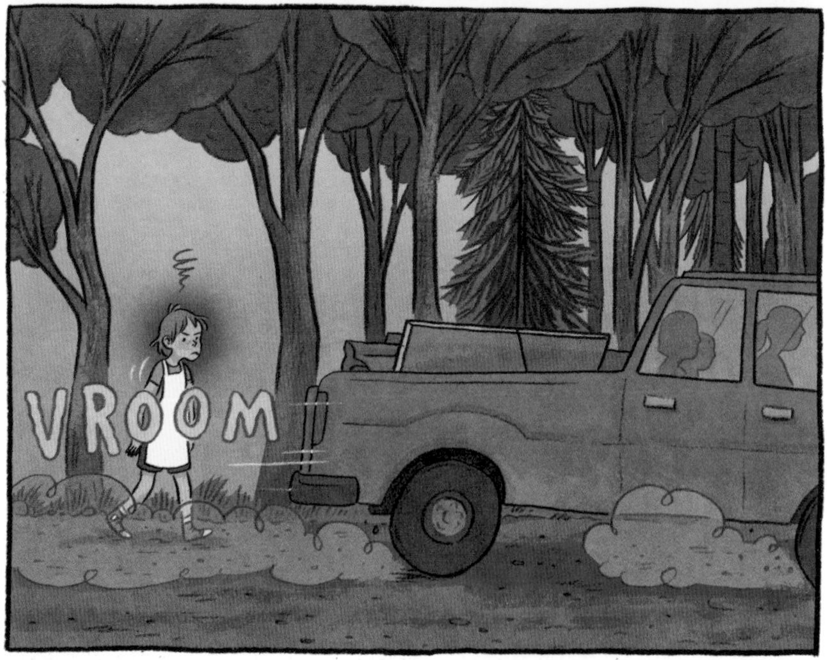
VROOM

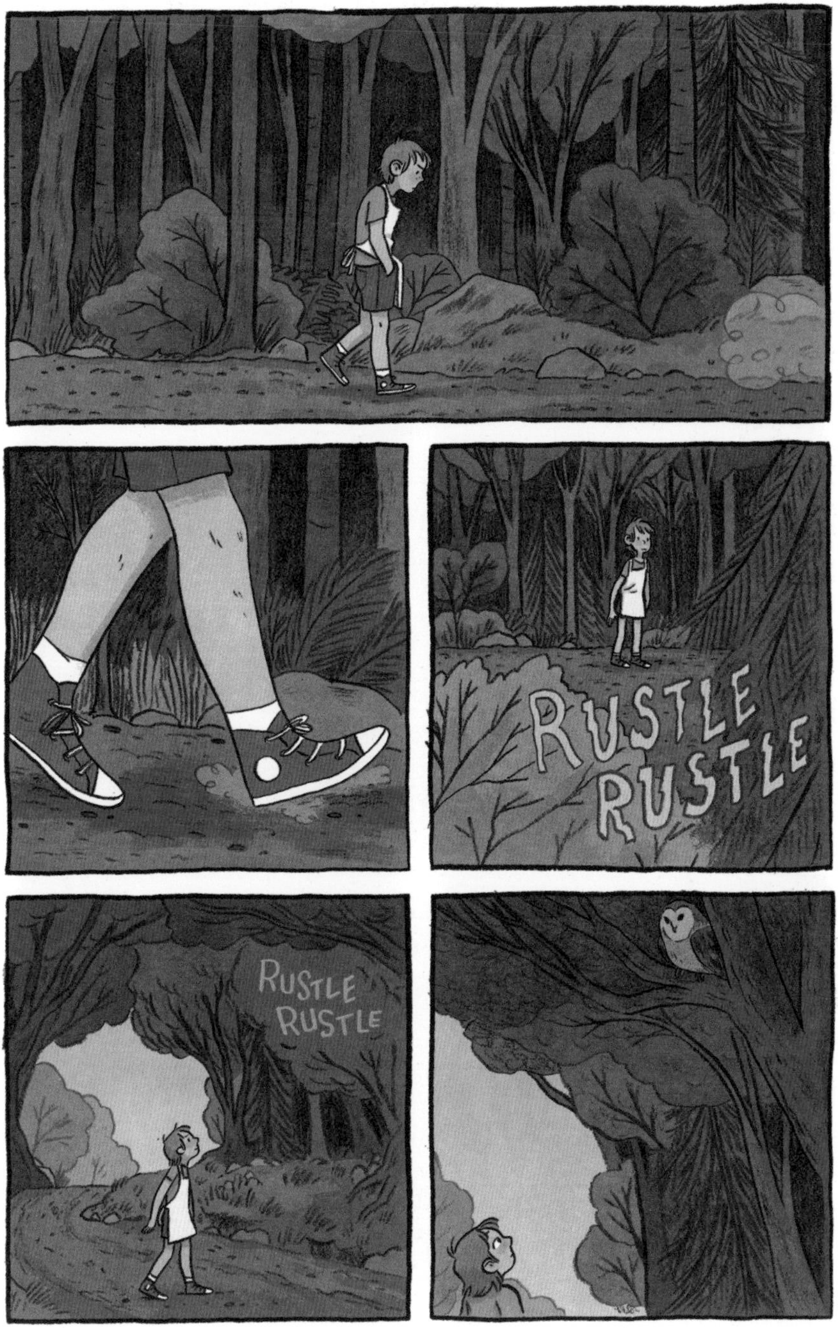
RUSTLE
RUSTLE
RUSTLE
RUSTLE

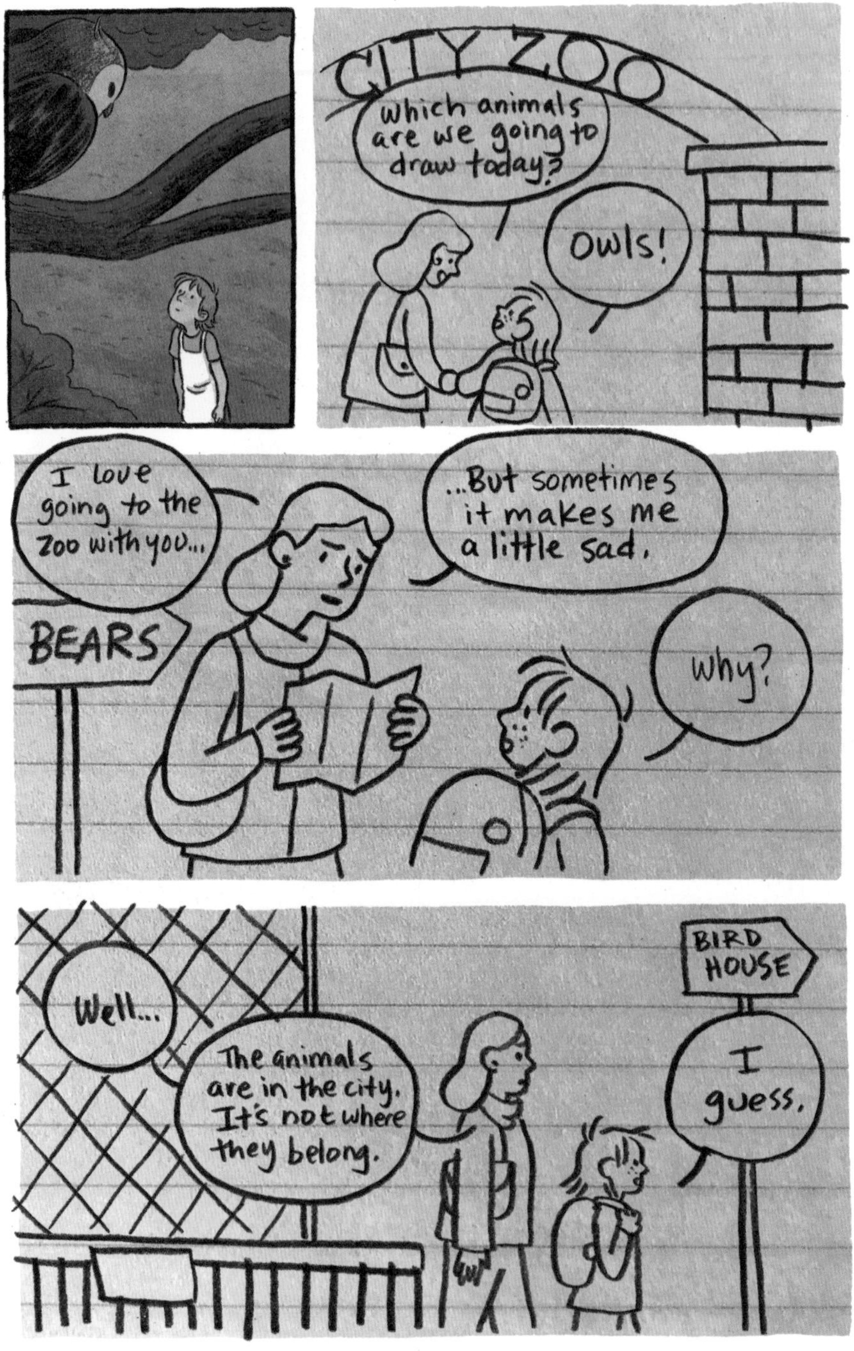
CITY ZOO
Which animals are we going to draw today?
Owls!
I love going to the zoo with you...
...But sometimes it makes me a little sad.
BEARS
Why?
Well...
The animals are in the city. It's not where they belong.
BIRD HOUSE
I guess.

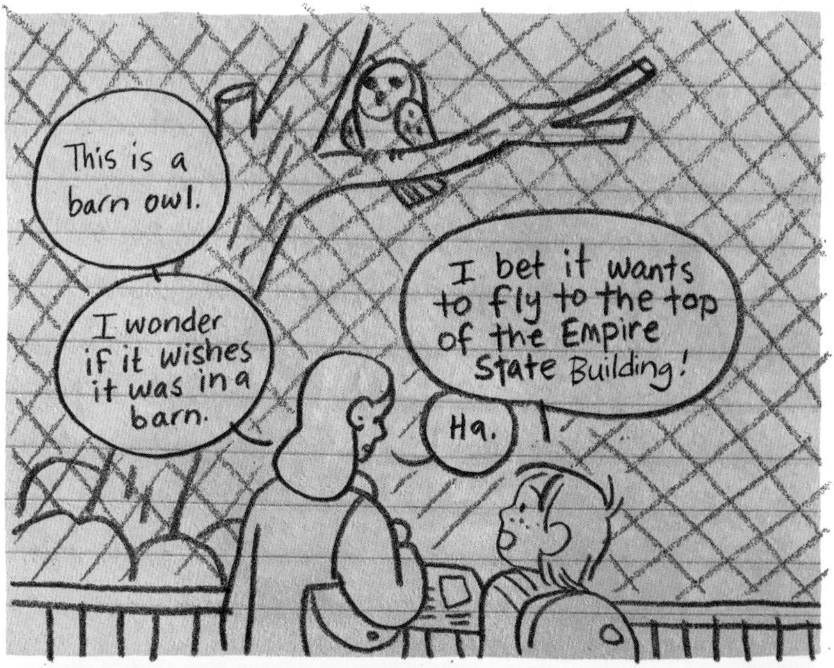
This is a barn owl.
I wonder if it wishes it was in a barn.
I bet it wants to fly to the top of the Empire State Building!
Ha.

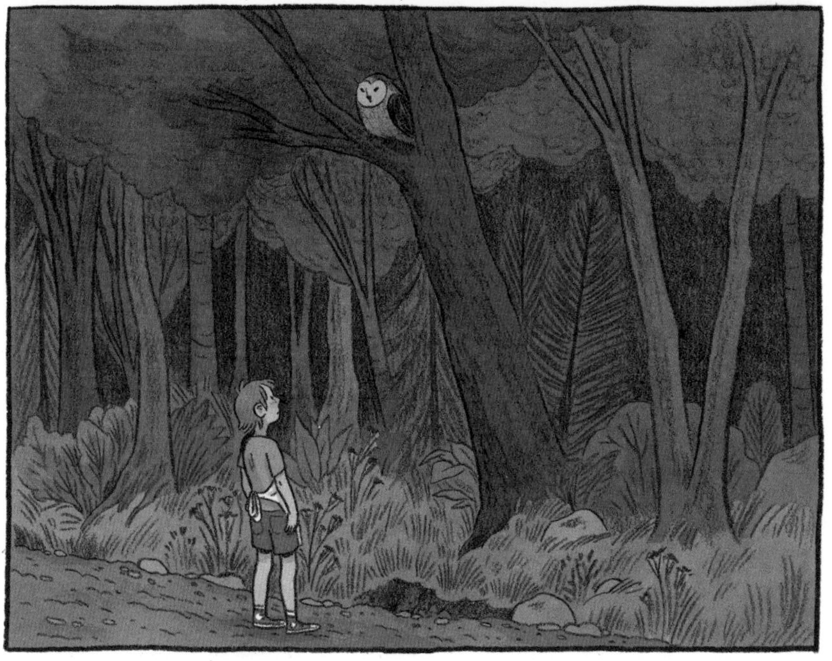

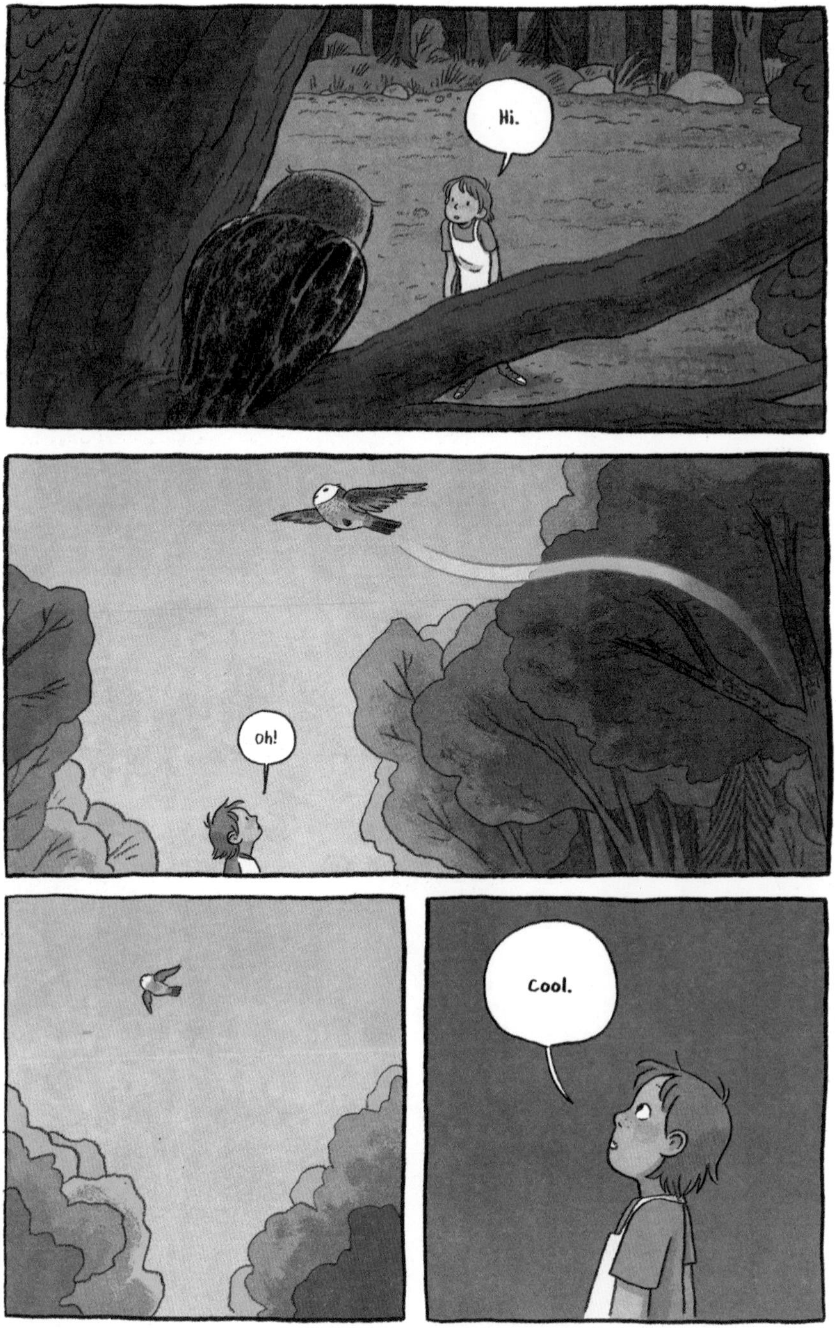
Hi.
Oh!
Cool.

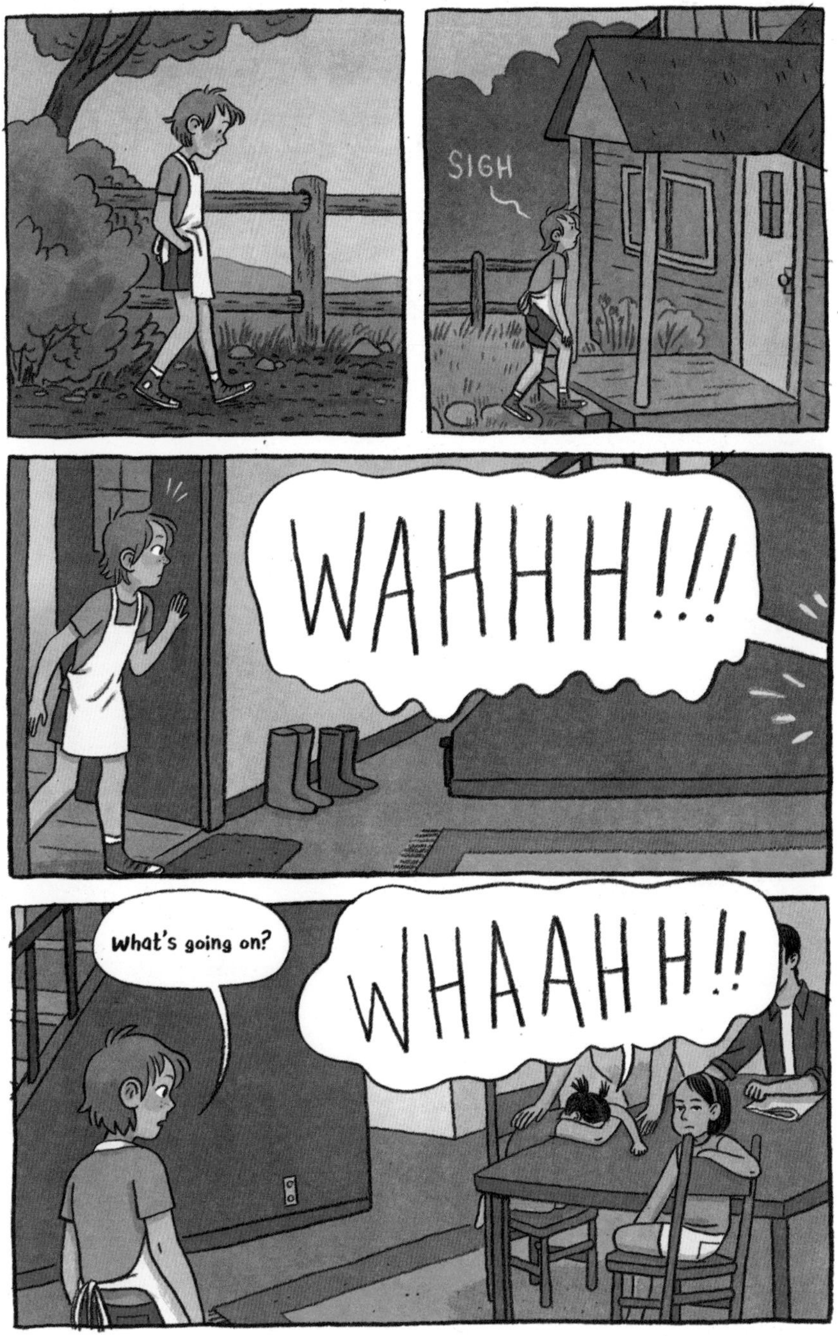
SIGH
WAHHH!!!
What's going on?
WHAAHH!!

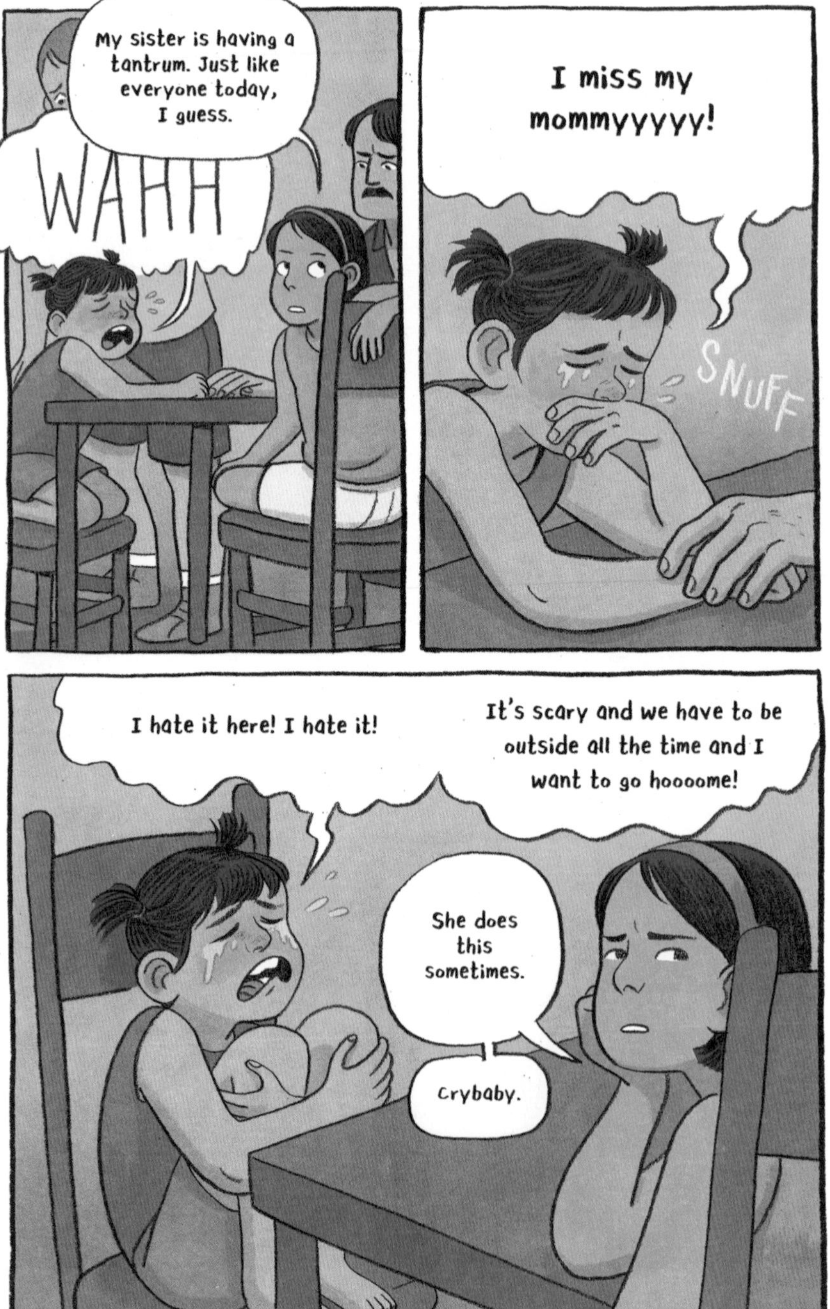
My sister is having a tantrum. Just like everyone today, I guess.
WAHH
I miss my mommyyyyy!
SNUFF
I hate it here! I hate it!
It's scary and we have to be outside all the time and I want to go hoooome!
She does this sometimes.
Crybaby.

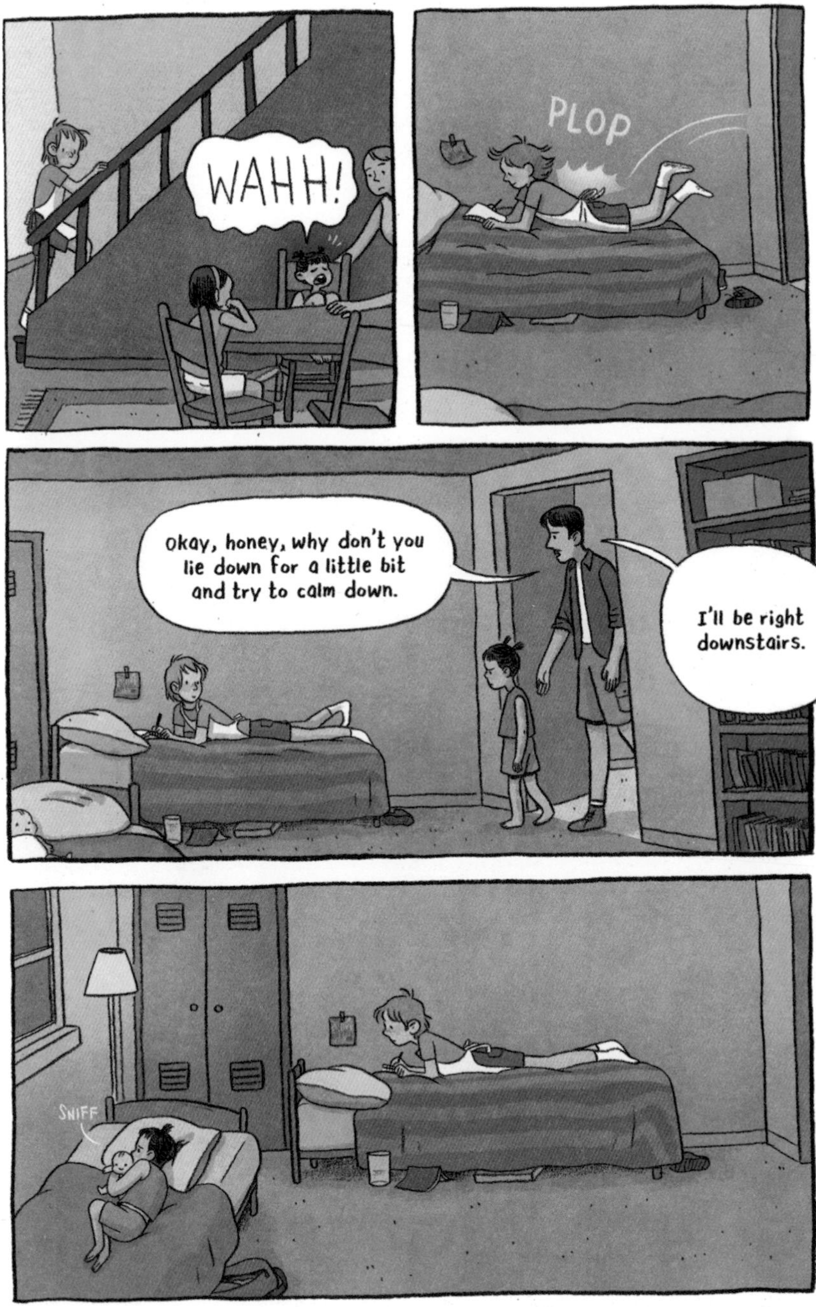
WAHH!
PLOP
Okay, honey, why don't you lie down for a little bit and try to calm down.
I'll be right downstairs.
SNIFF

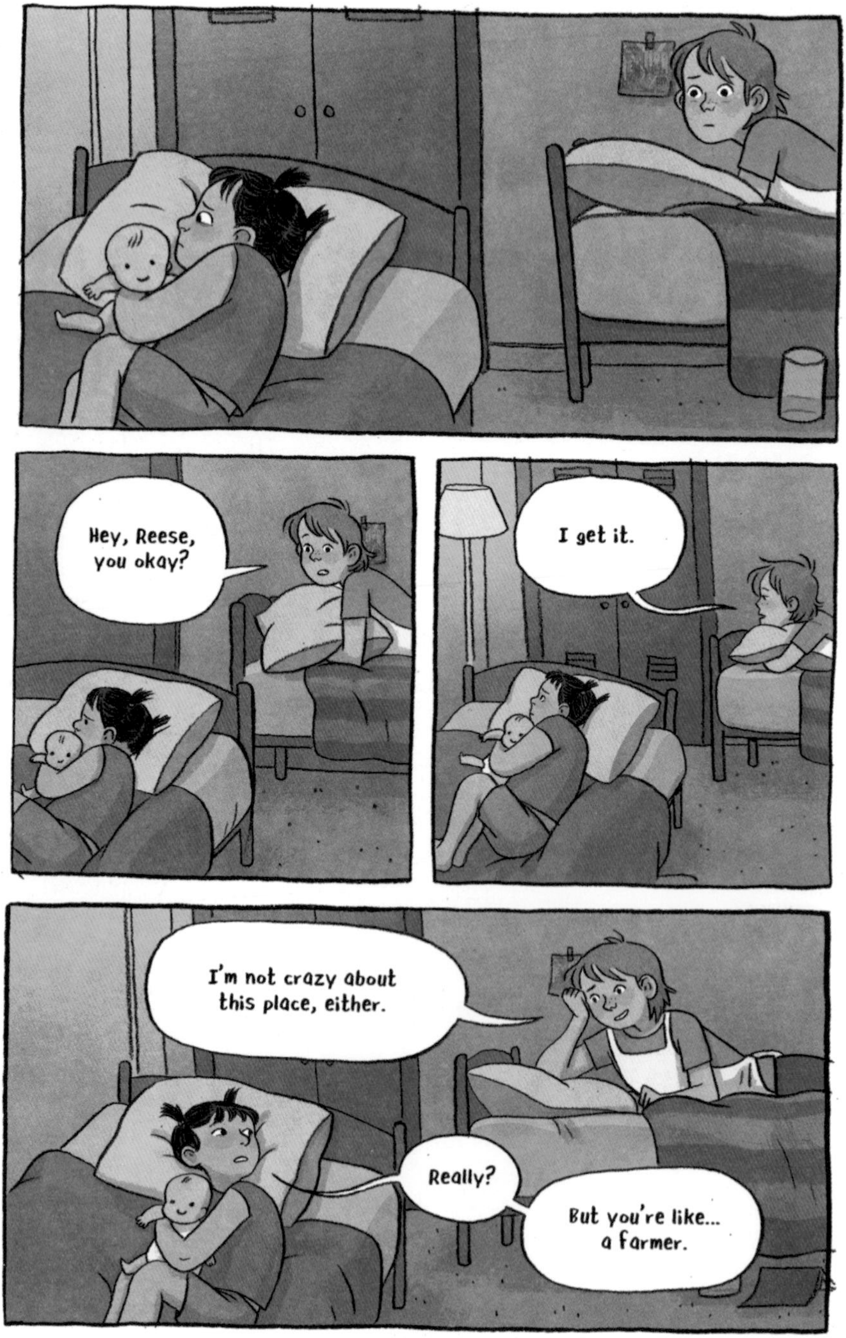
Hey, Reese, you okay?
I get it.
I'm not crazy about this place, either.
Really?
But you're like... a farmer.

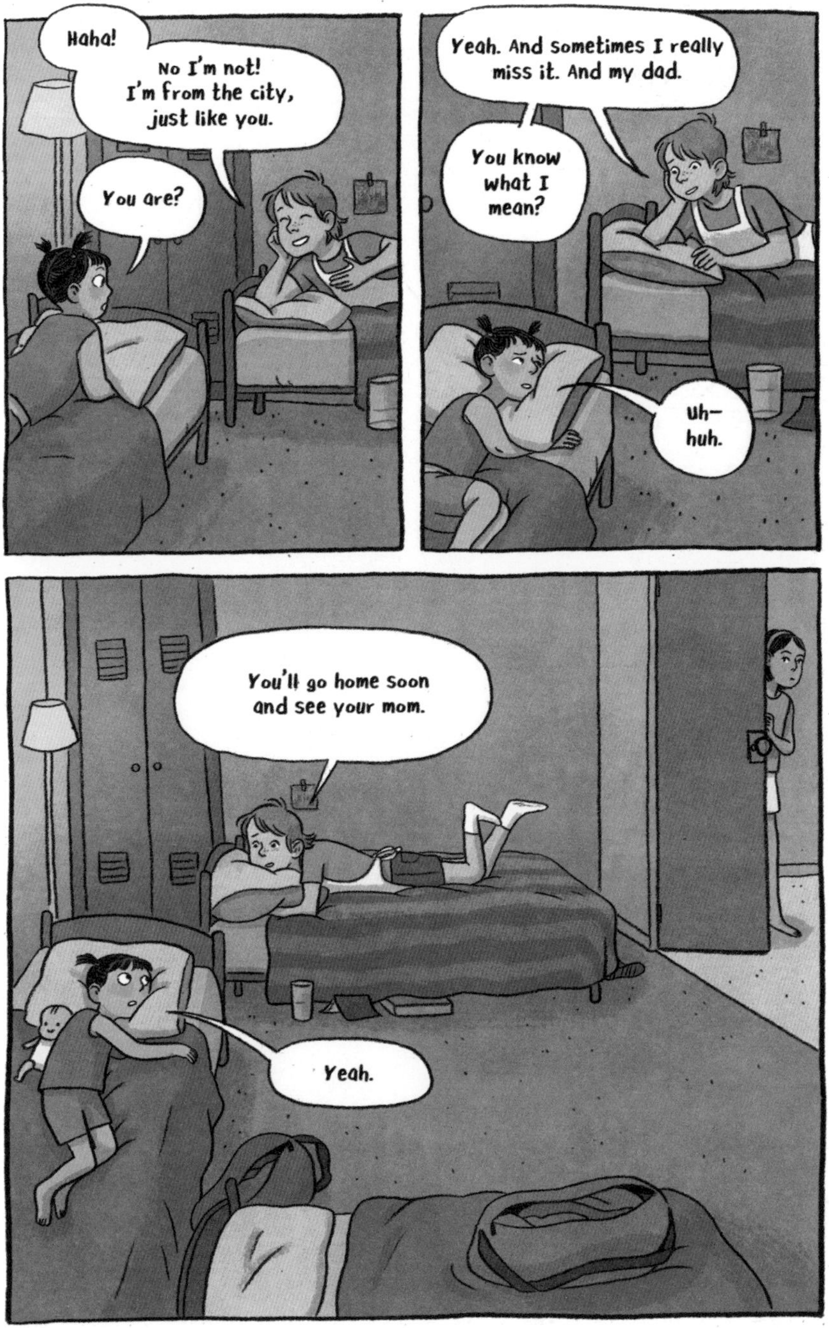
Haha!
No I'm not! I'm from the city, just like you.
You are?
Yeah. And sometimes I really miss it. And my dad.
You know what I mean?
Uh-huh.
You'll go home soon and see your mom.
Yeah.

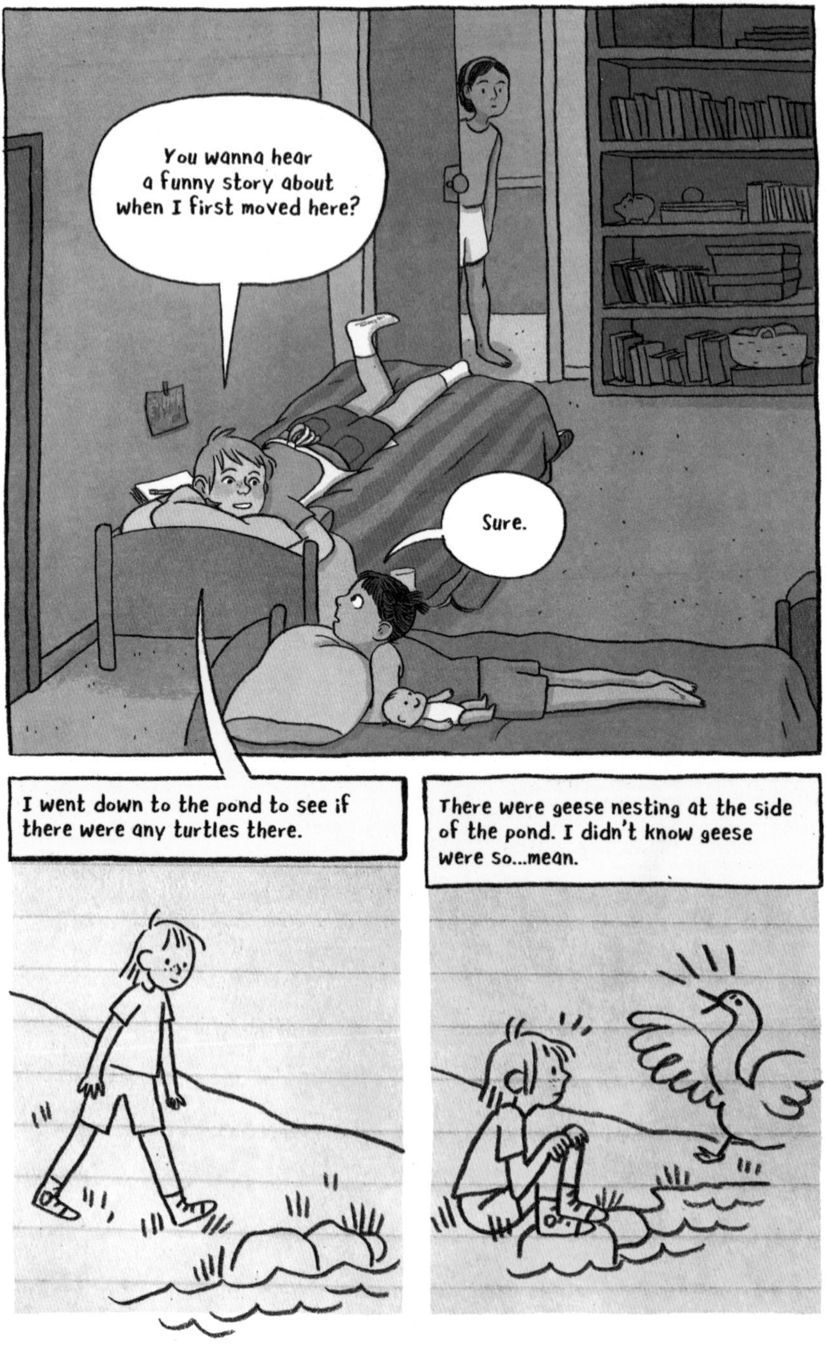
You wanna hear a funny story about when I first moved here?
Sure.
I went down to the pond to see if there were any turtles there.
There were geese nesting at the side of the pond. I didn't know geese were so...mean.

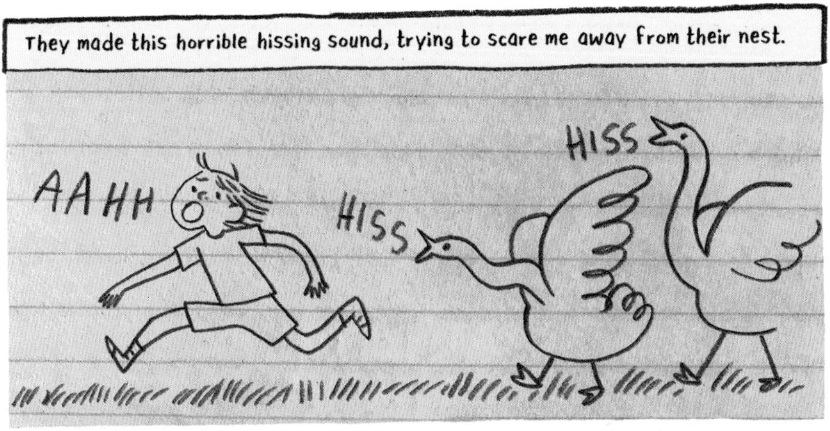
They made this horrible hissing sound, trying to scare me away from their nest.
AAHH
HISS
HISS

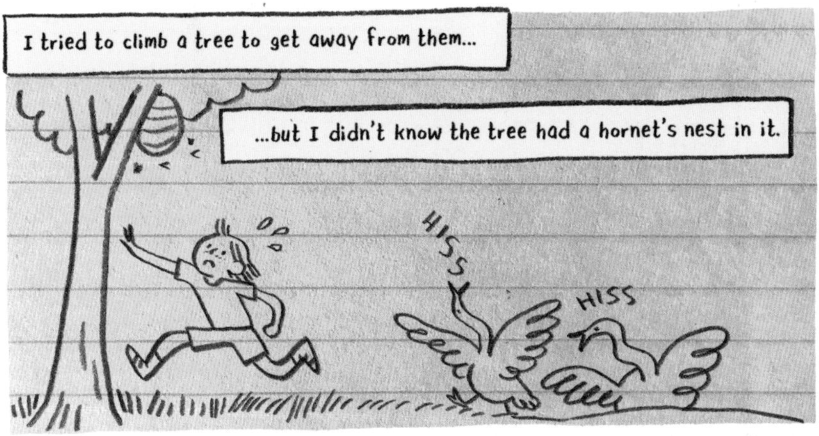
I tried to climb a tree to get away from them...
...but I didn't know the tree had a hornet's nest in it.
HISS
HISS

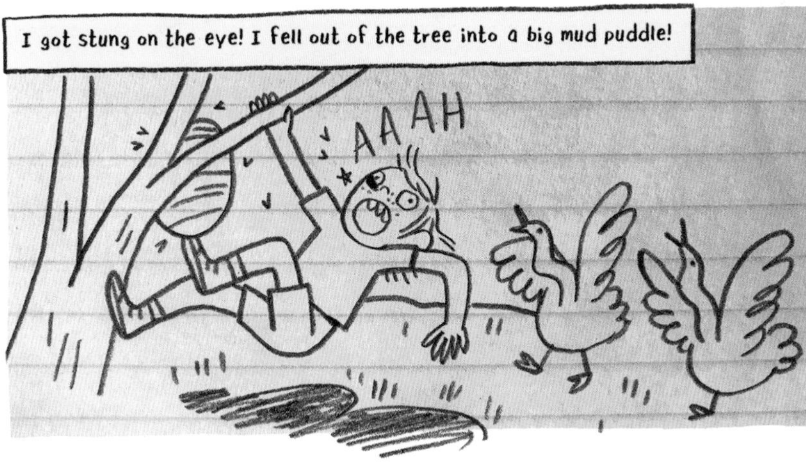
I got stung on the eye! I fell out of the tree into a big mud puddle!
AAAH

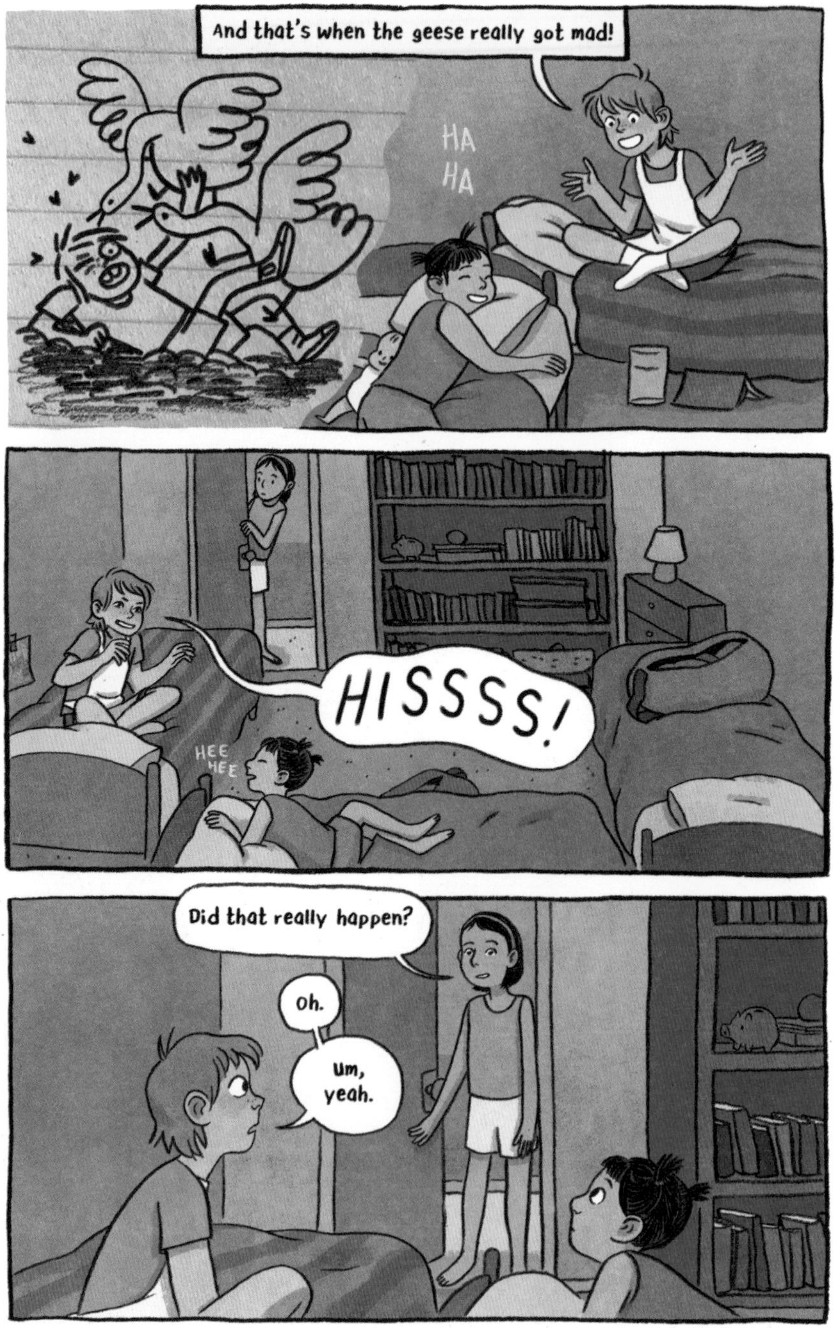
And that's when the geese really got mad!
HA
HA
HISSSS!
HEE
HEE
Did that really happen?
Oh.
Um,
yeah.

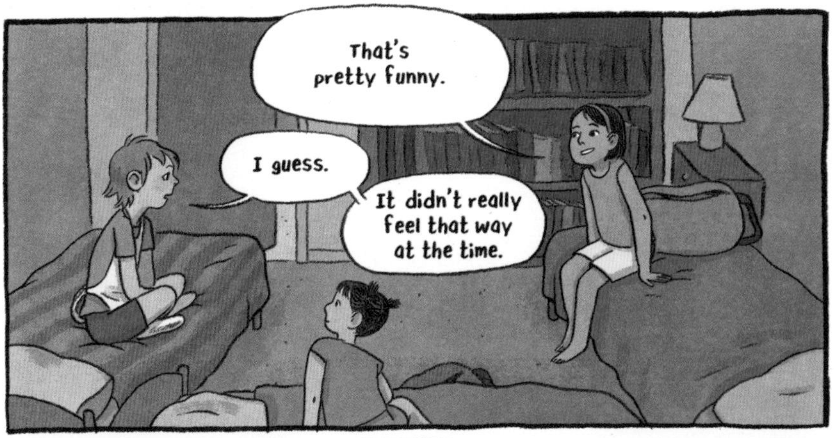
That's pretty funny.
I guess.
It didn't really feel that way at the time.

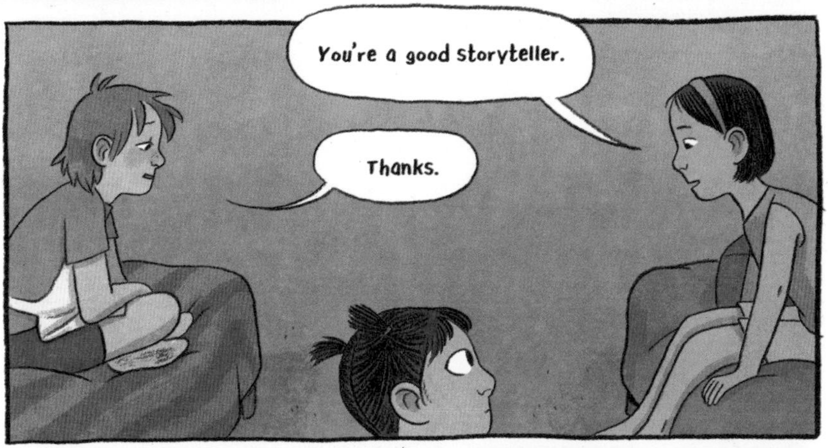
You're a good storyteller.
Thanks.

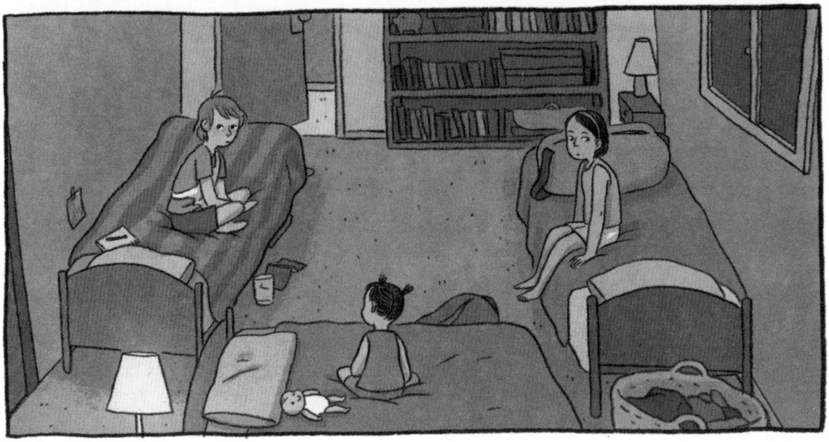

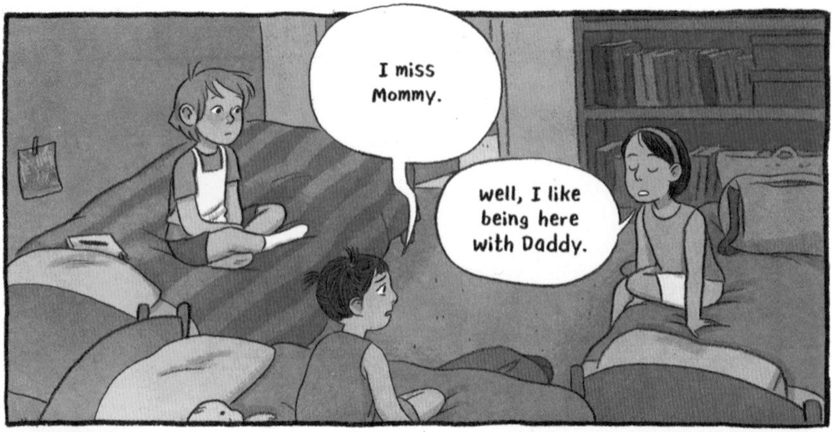
I miss Mommy.
Well, I like being here with Daddy.

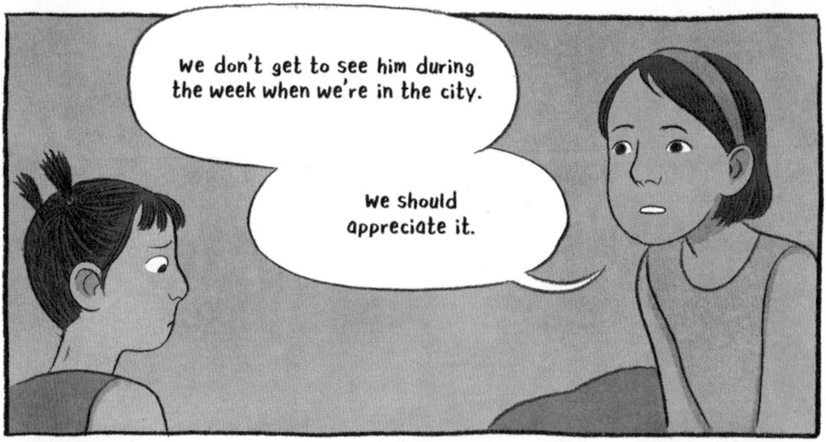
We don't get to see him during the week when we're in the city.
We should appreciate it.

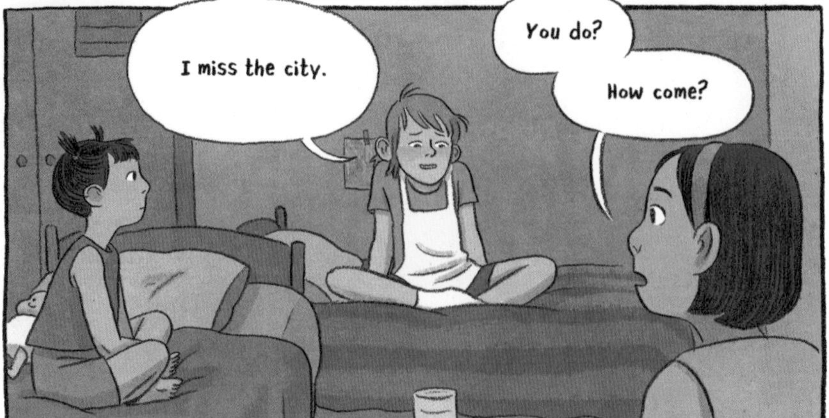
I miss the city.
You do?
How come?

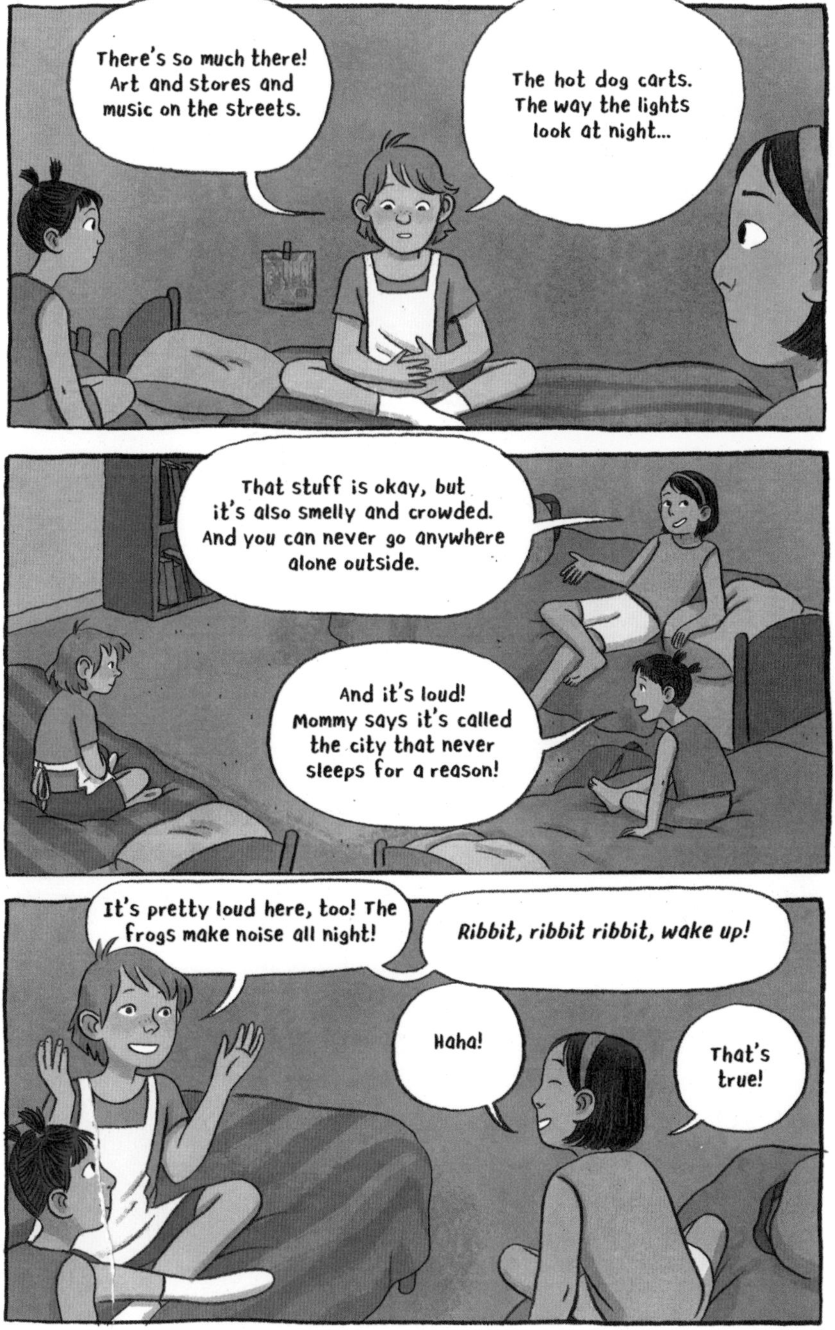
There's so much there! Art and stores and music on the streets.
The hot dog carts. The way the lights look at night...
That stuff is okay, but it's also smelly and crowded. And you can never go anywhere alone outside.
And it's loud! Mommy says it's called the city that never sleeps for a reason!
It's pretty loud here, too! The frogs make noise all night!
Ribbit, ribbit ribbit, wake up!
Haha!
That's true!

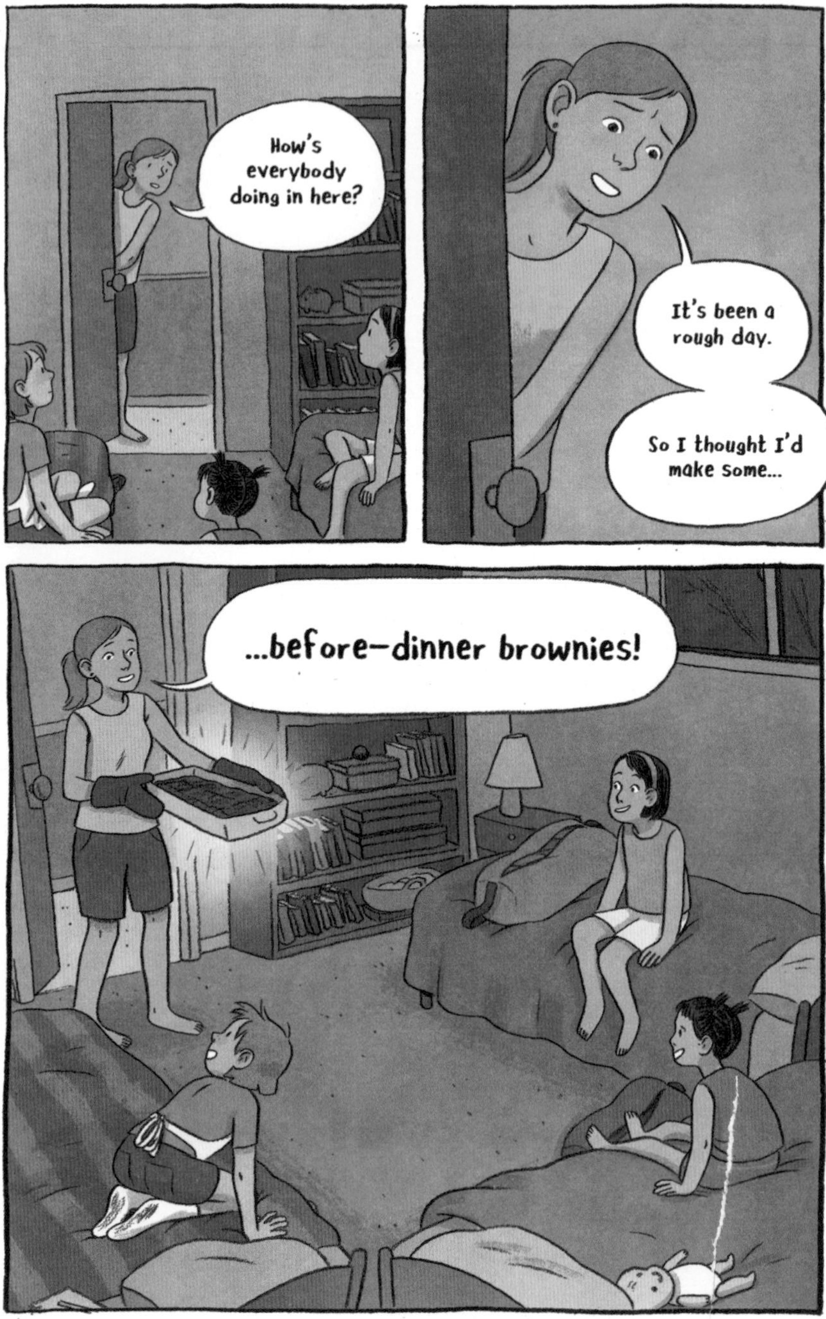
How's everybody doing in here?
It's been a rough day.
So I thought I'd make some...
...before-dinner brownies!

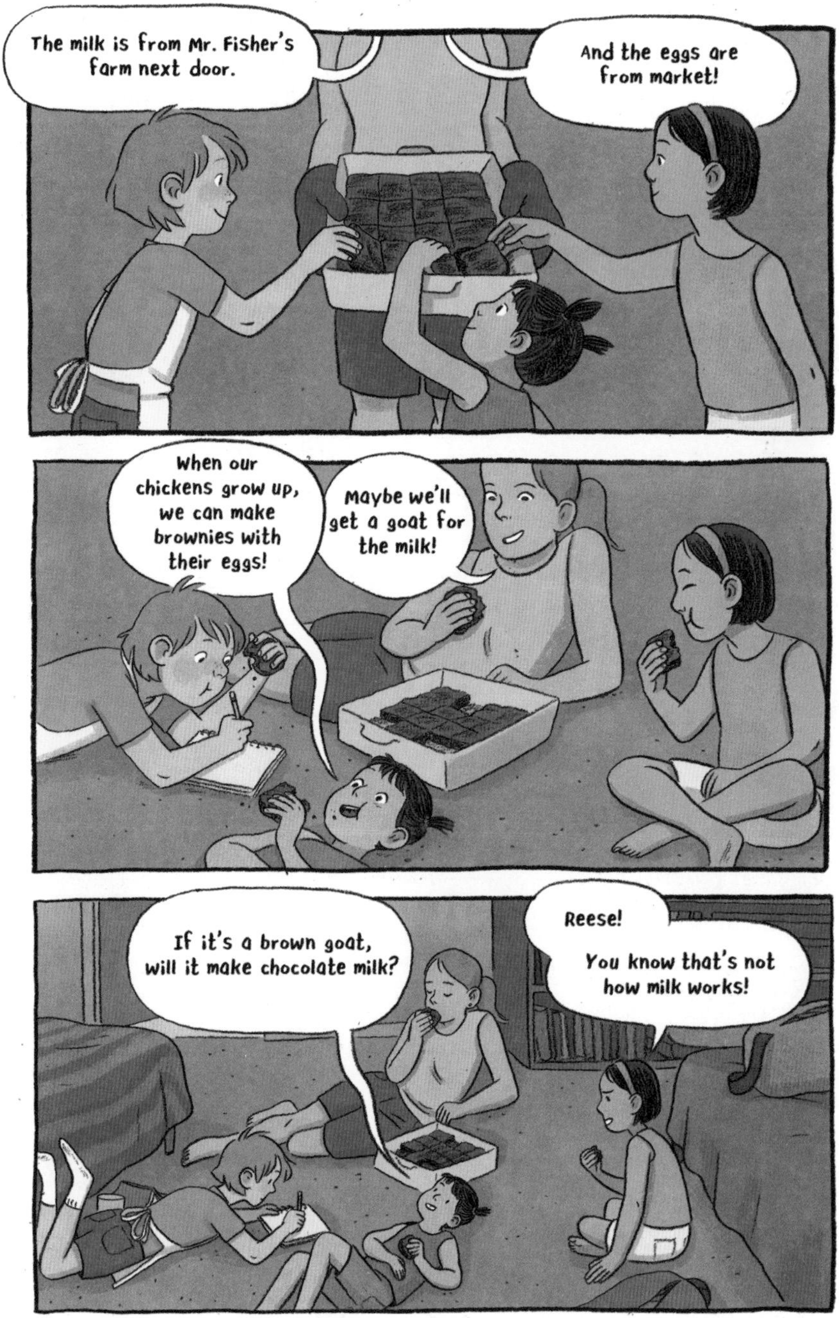
The milk is from Mr. Fisher's farm next door.
And the eggs are from market!
When our chickens grow up, we can make brownies with their eggs!
Maybe we'll get a goat for the milk!
If it's a brown goat, will it make chocolate milk?
Reese!
You know that's not how milk works!

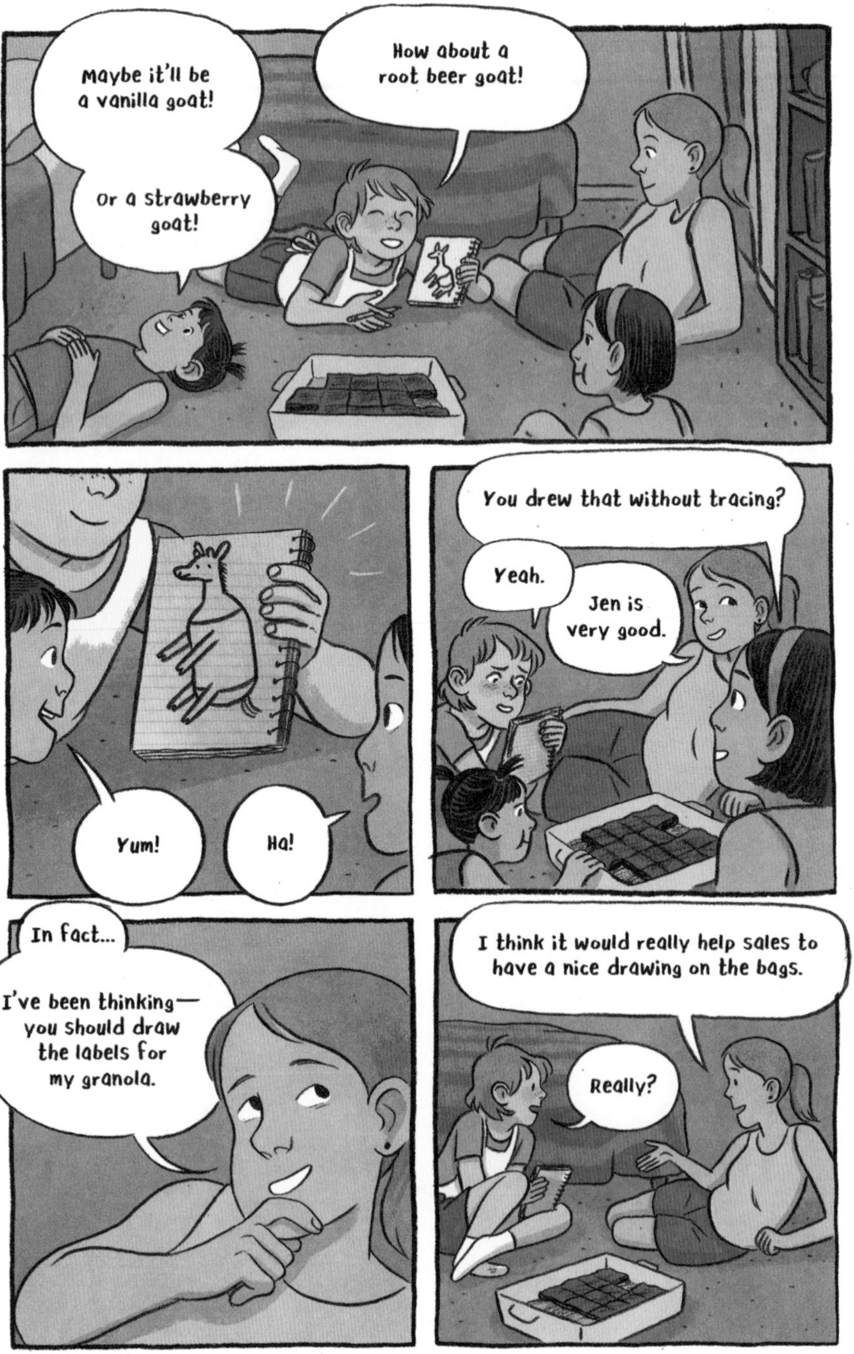
Maybe it'll be a vanilla goat!
Or a strawberry goat!
How about a root beer goat!
Yum!
Ha!
You drew that without tracing?
Yeah.
Jen is very good.
In fact...
I've been thinking— you should draw the labels for my granola.
I think it would really help sales to have a nice drawing on the bags.
Really?

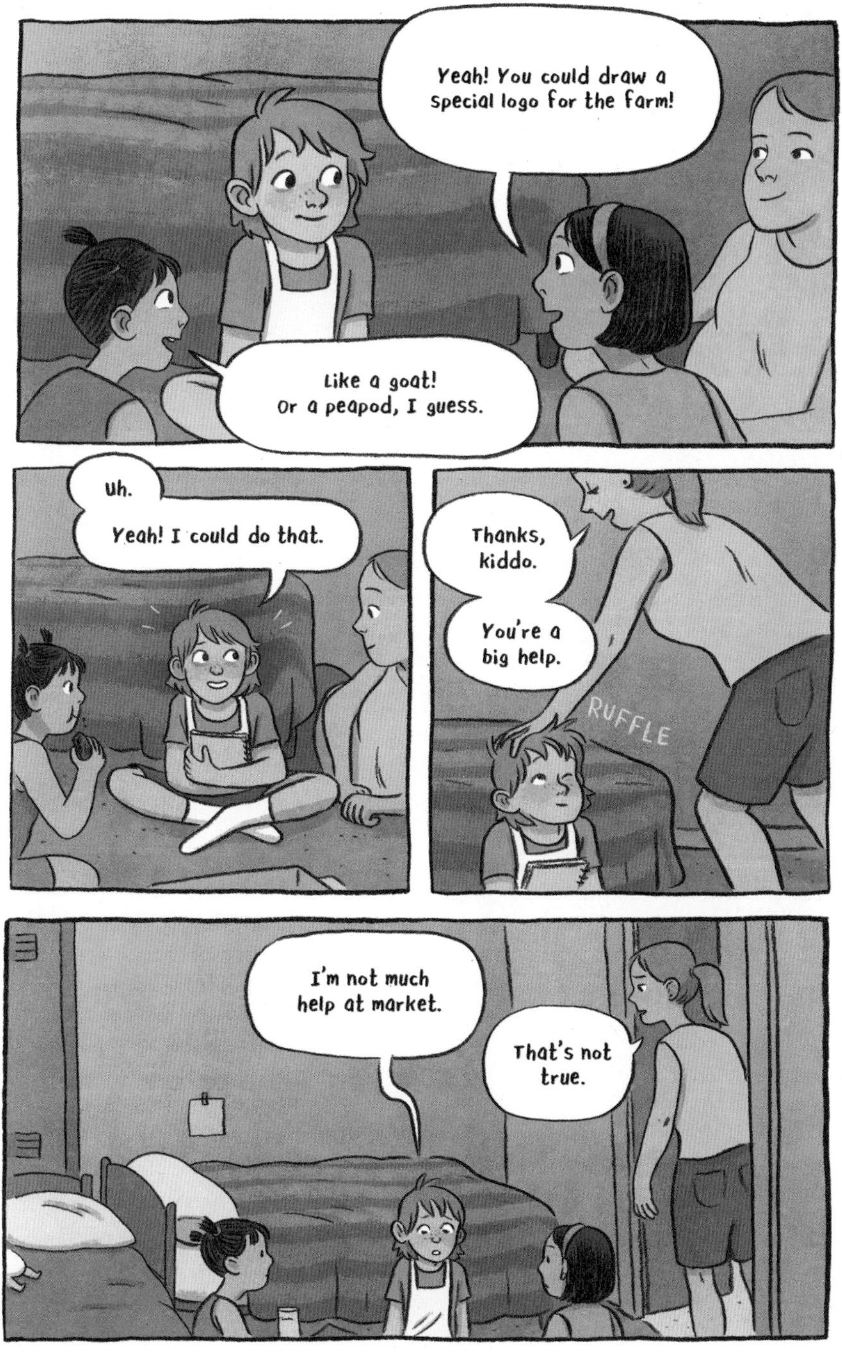
Yeah! You could draw a special logo for the farm!
Like a goat! Or a peapod, I guess.
Uh.
Yeah! I could do that.
Thanks, kiddo.
You're a big help.
RUFFLE
I'm not much help at market.
That's not true.

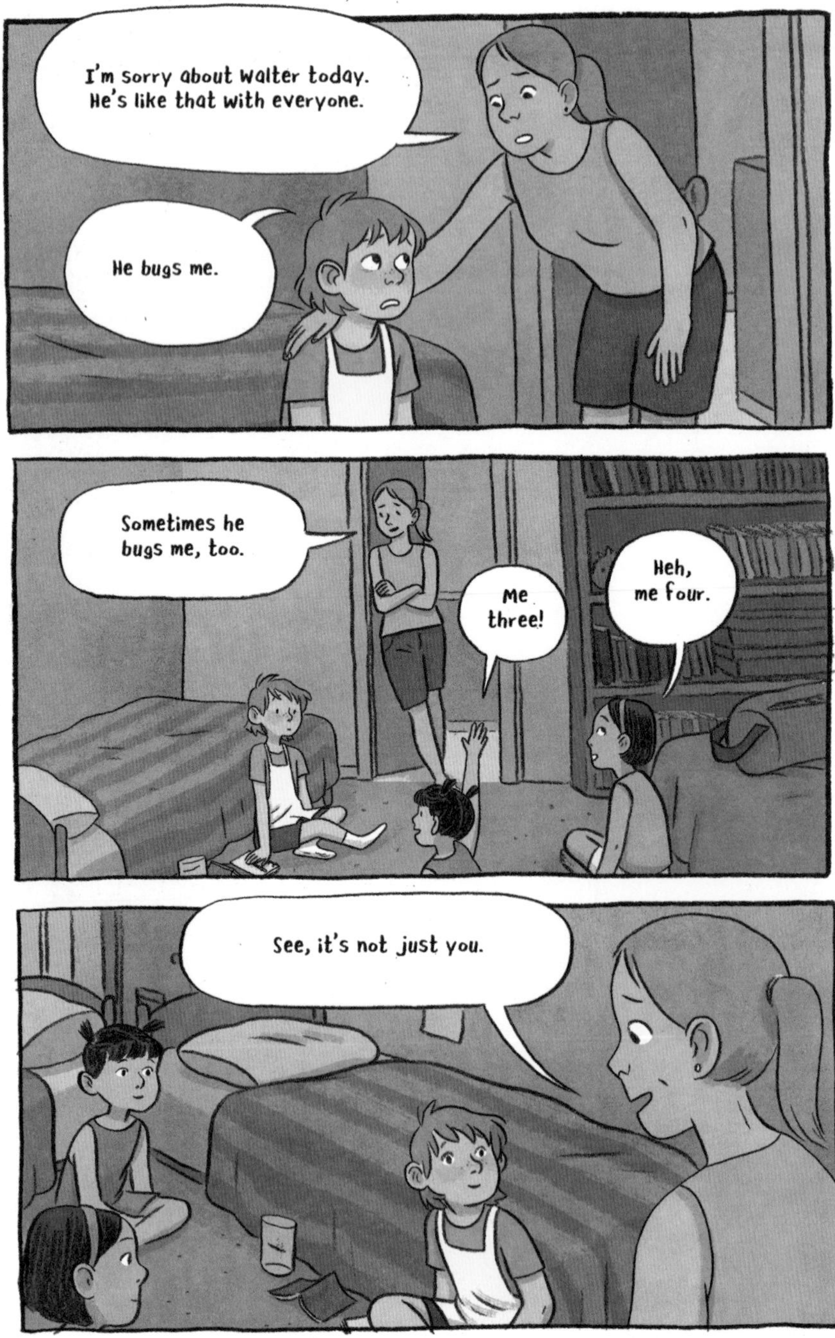
I'm sorry about Walter today. He's like that with everyone.
He bugs me.
Sometimes he bugs me, too.
Me three!
Heh, me four.
See, it's not just you.

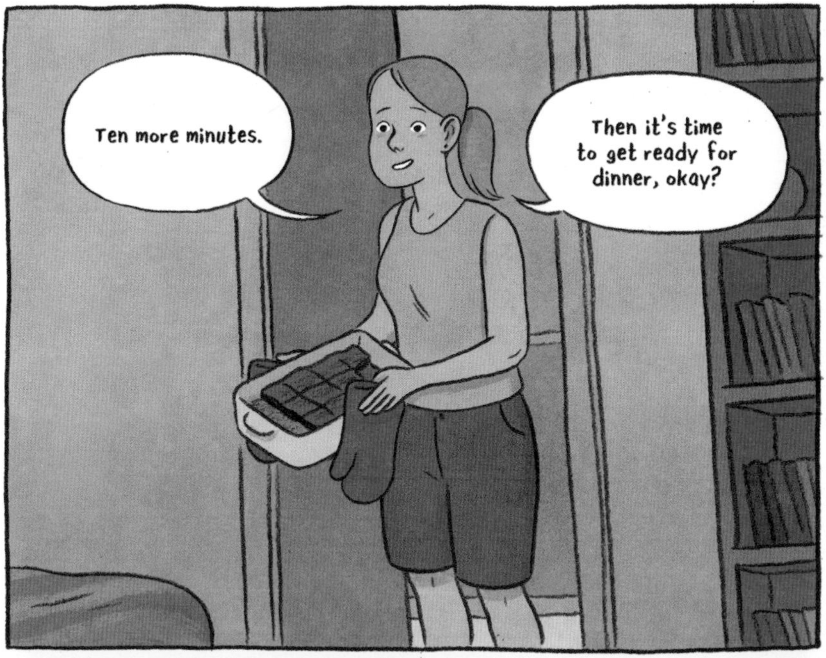
Ten more minutes.
Then it's time to get ready for dinner, okay?

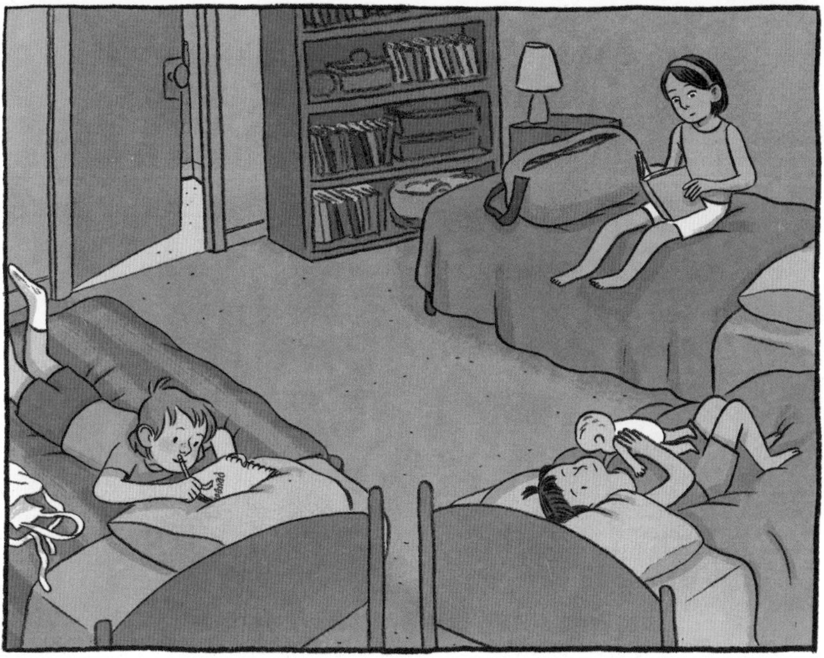

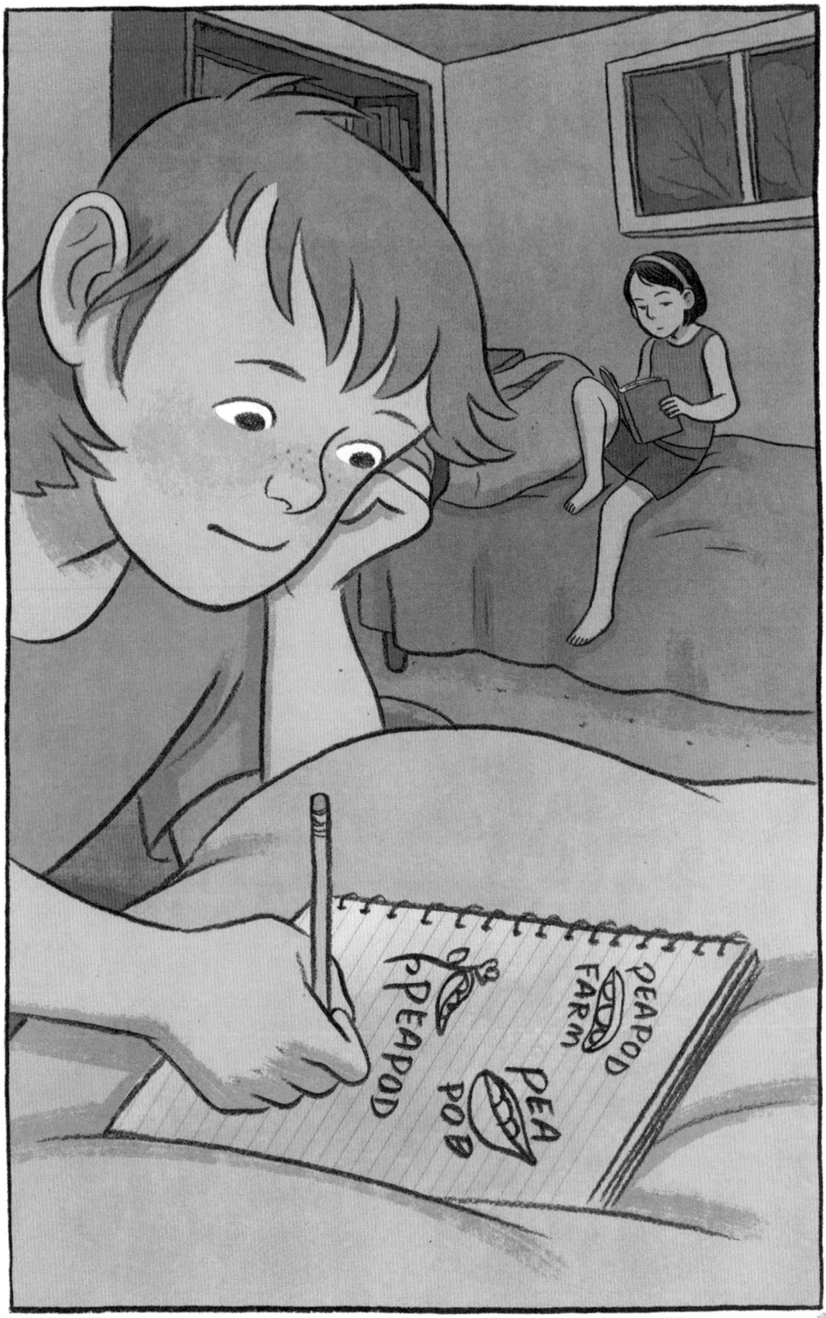
PEAPOD
PEAPOD FARM
PEA POD

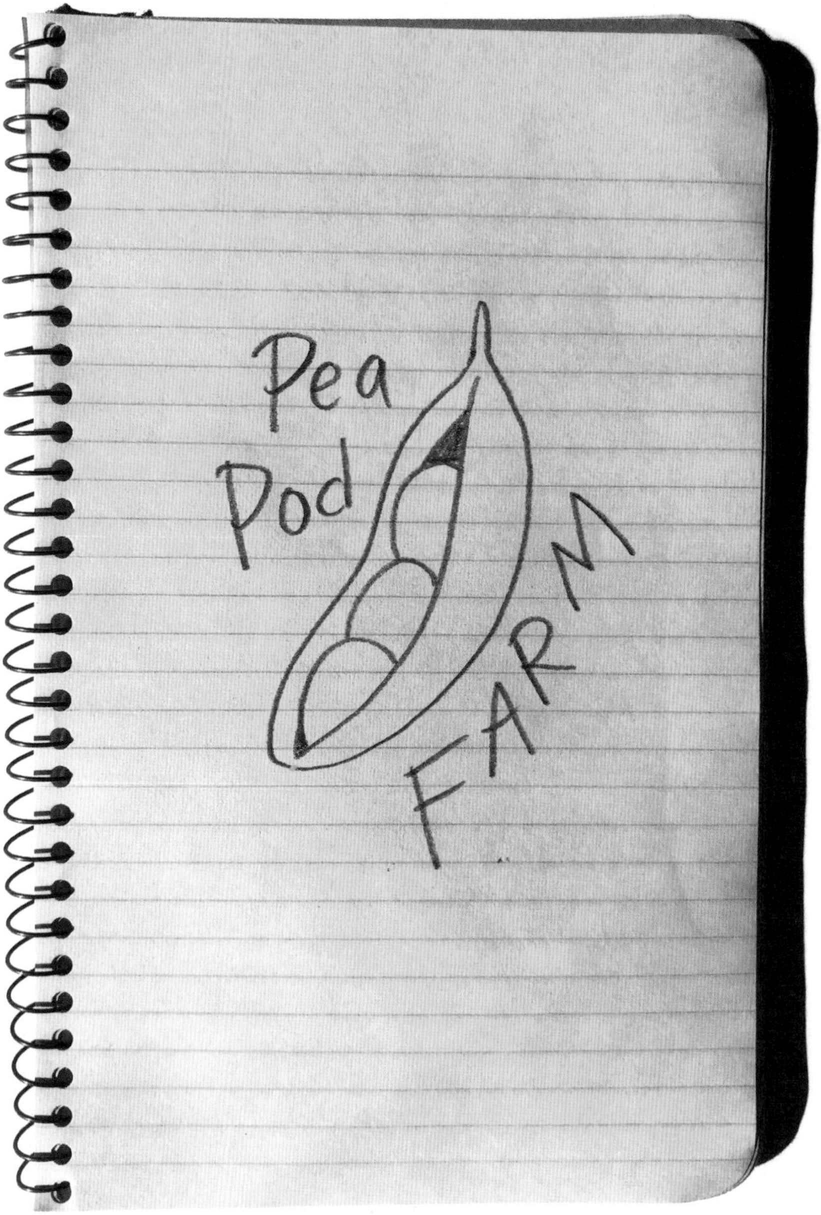
Pea
Pod
FARM

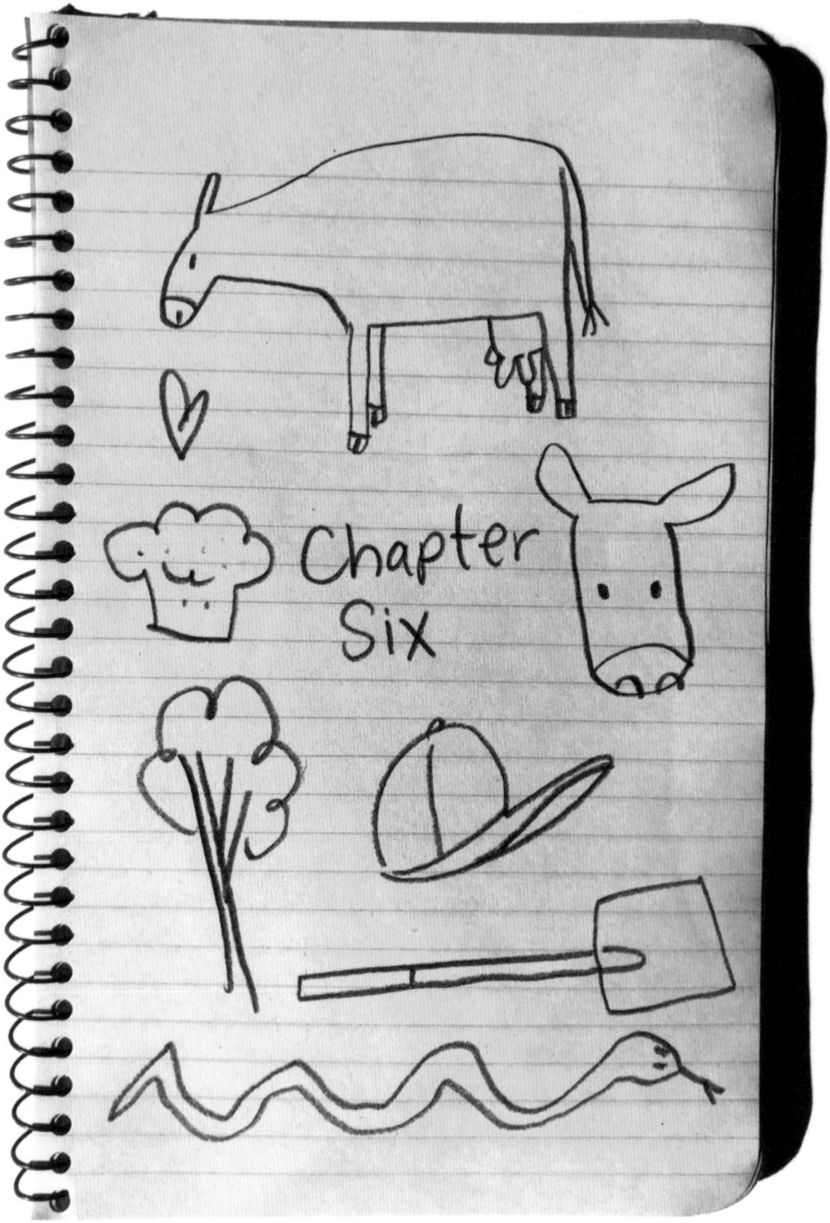
Chapter
Six

next weekend

Ya don't just wanna yank on it.

You gotta be gentle.

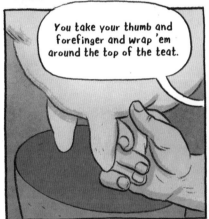

You take your thumb and forefinger and wrap 'em around the top of the teat.

Then you close your fist toward your palm, like so.

So! Who wants to go first?

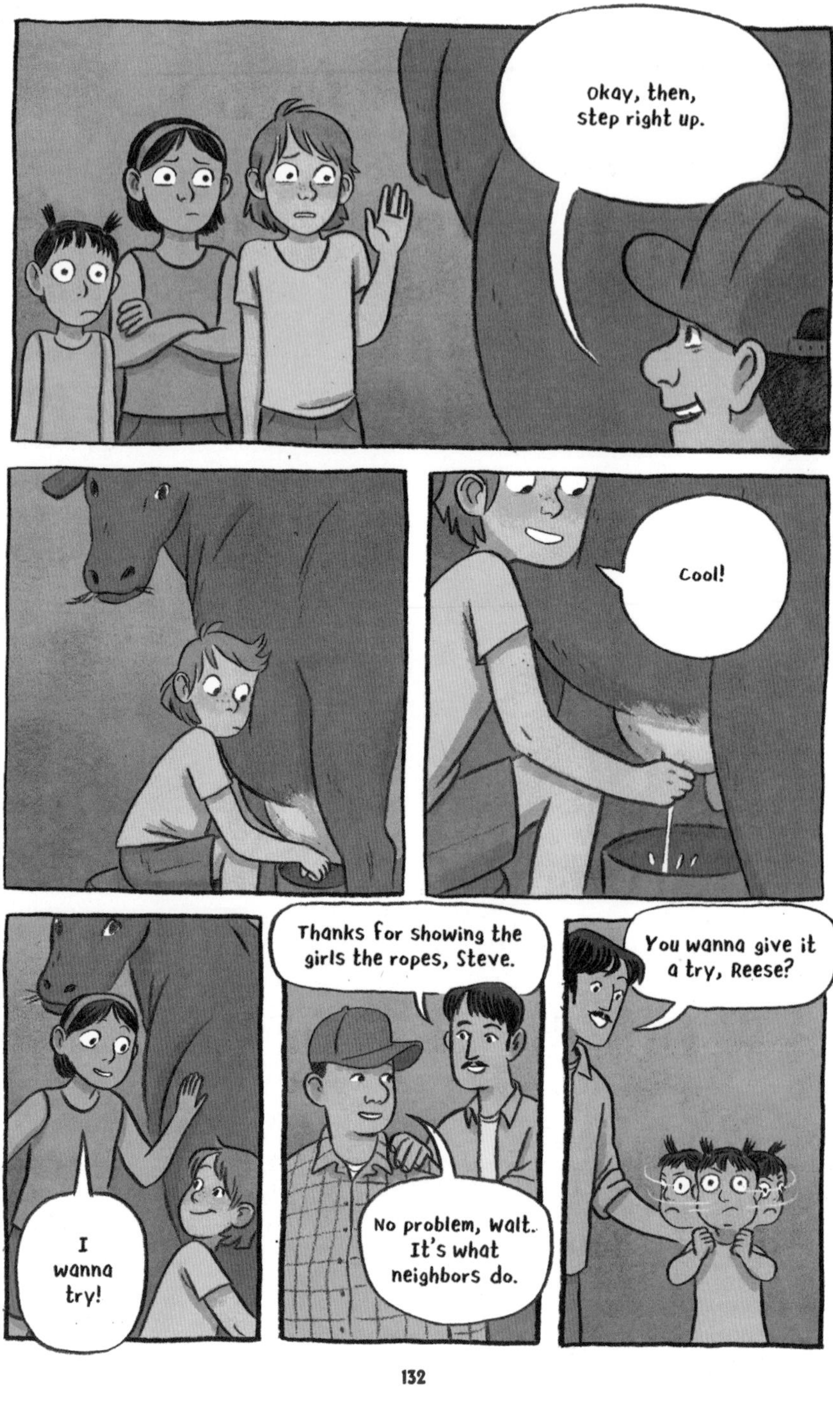
Okay, then, step right up.
Cool!
I wanna try!
Thanks for showing the girls the ropes, Steve.
No problem, Walt. It's what neighbors do.
You wanna give it a try, Reese?

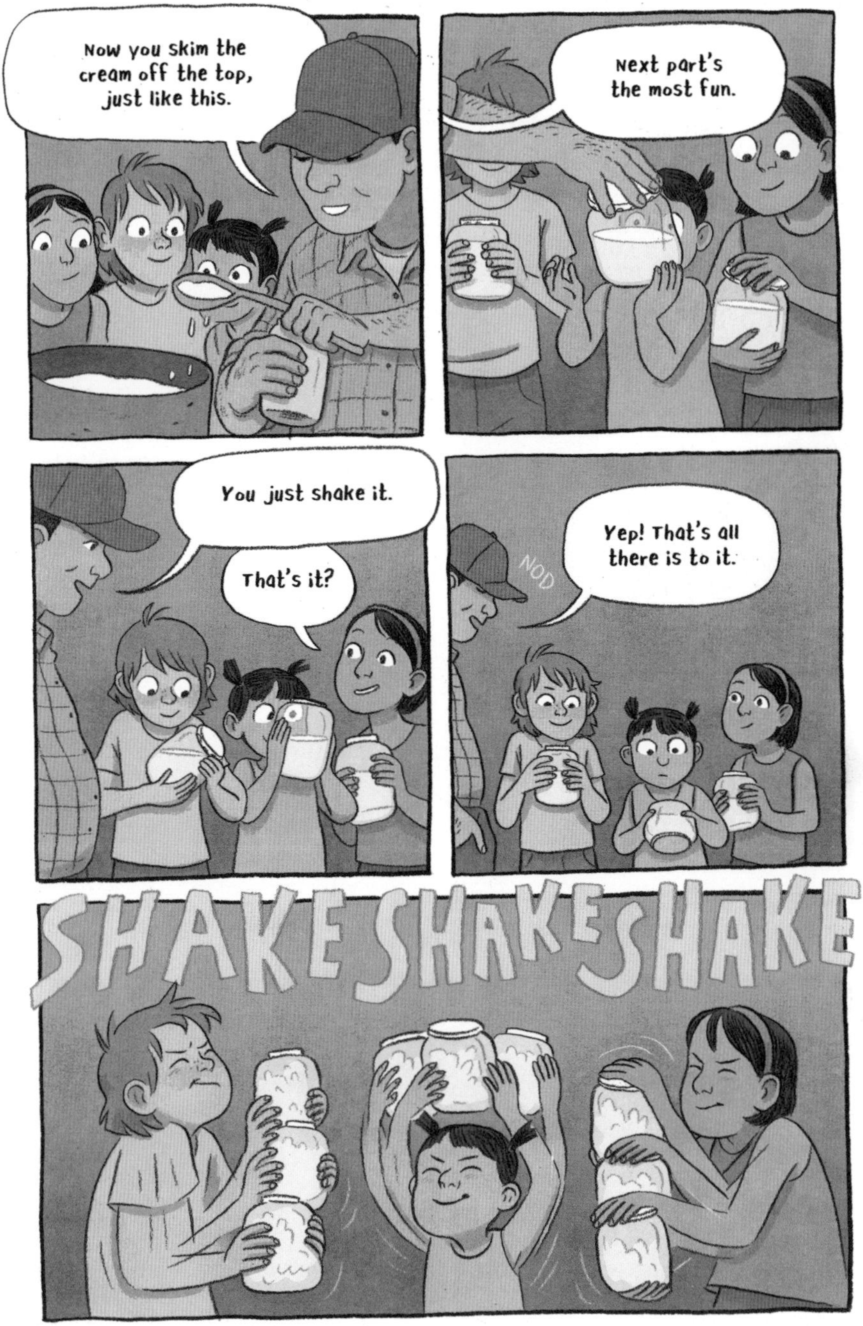
Now you skim the cream off the top, just like this.
Next part's the most fun.
You just shake it.
That's it?
NOD
Yep! That's all there is to it.
SHAKE SHAKE SHAKE

Ten shaky minutes later...

Okay, let's see how it tastes on one of Mike's blueberry muffins.

You girls are in for a treat!

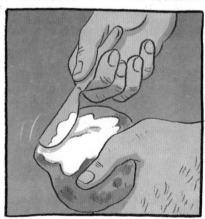

And there you have it! Fresh churned butter, straight from the cow.

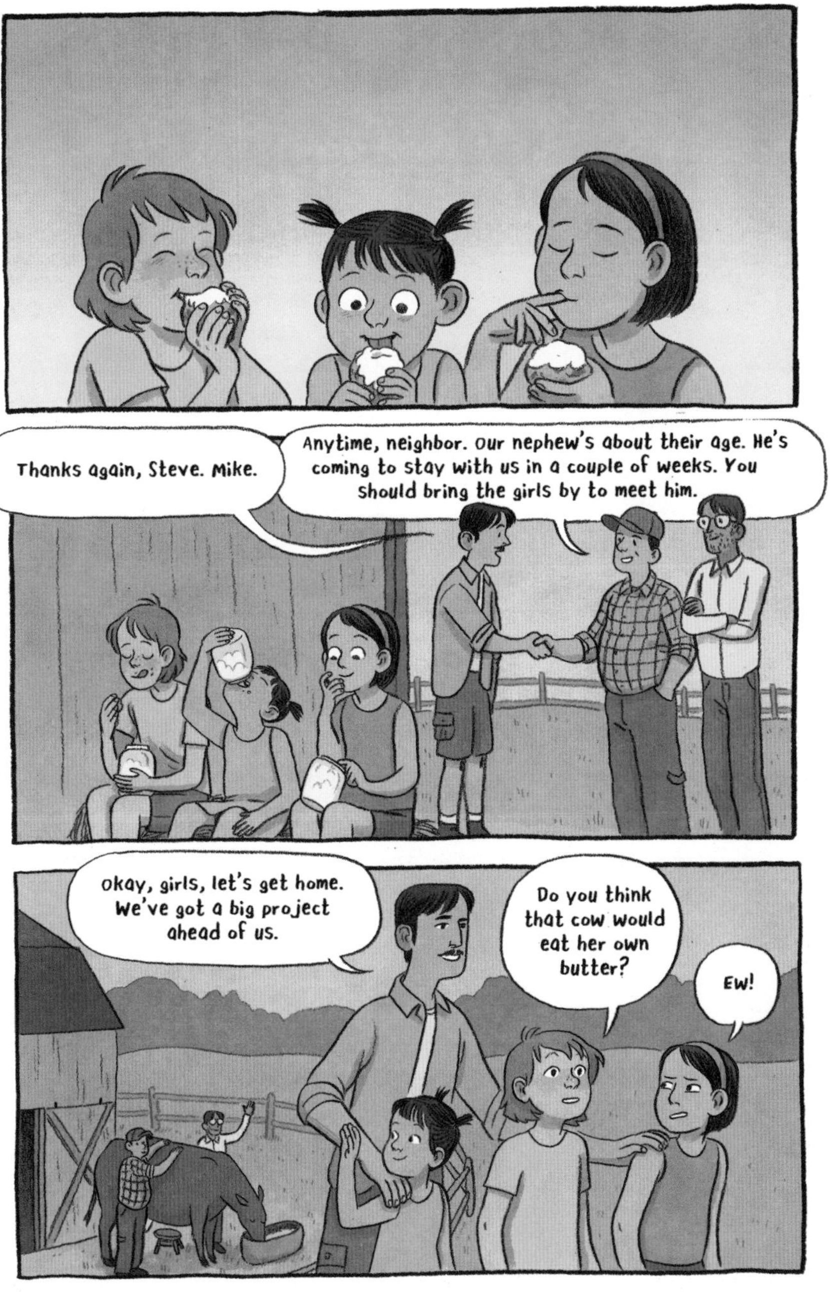
Thanks again, Steve. Mike.
Anytime, neighbor. Our nephew's about their age. He's coming to stay with us in a couple of weeks. You should bring the girls by to meet him.
Okay, girls, let's get home. We've got a big project ahead of us.
Do you think that cow would eat her own butter?
Ew!

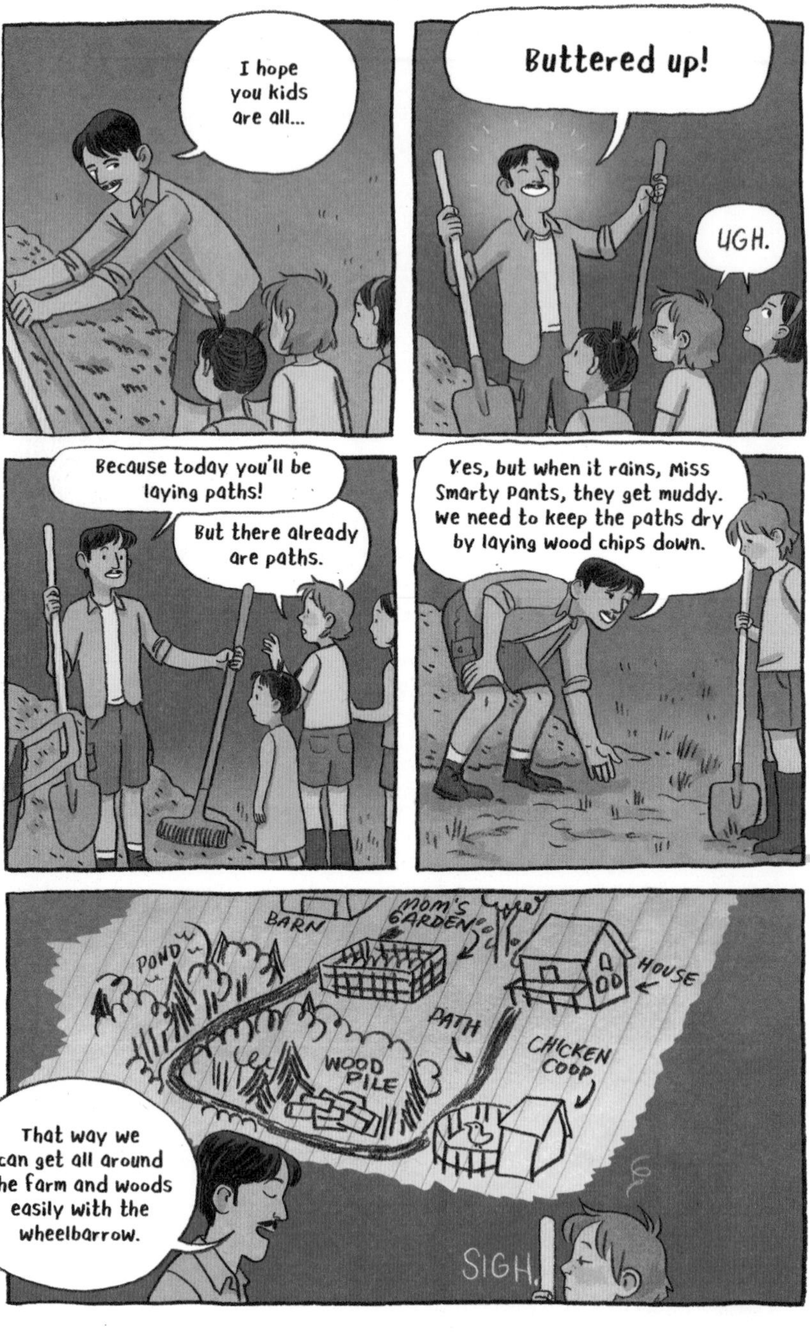

I hope you kids are all...
Buttered up!
UGH.
Because today you'll be laying paths!
But there already are paths.
Yes, but when it rains, Miss Smarty Pants, they get muddy. We need to keep the paths dry by laying wood chips down.
BARN
MOM'S GARDEN
POND
HOUSE
PATH
CHICKEN COOP
WOOD PILE
That way we can get all around the farm and woods easily with the wheelbarrow.
SIGH.

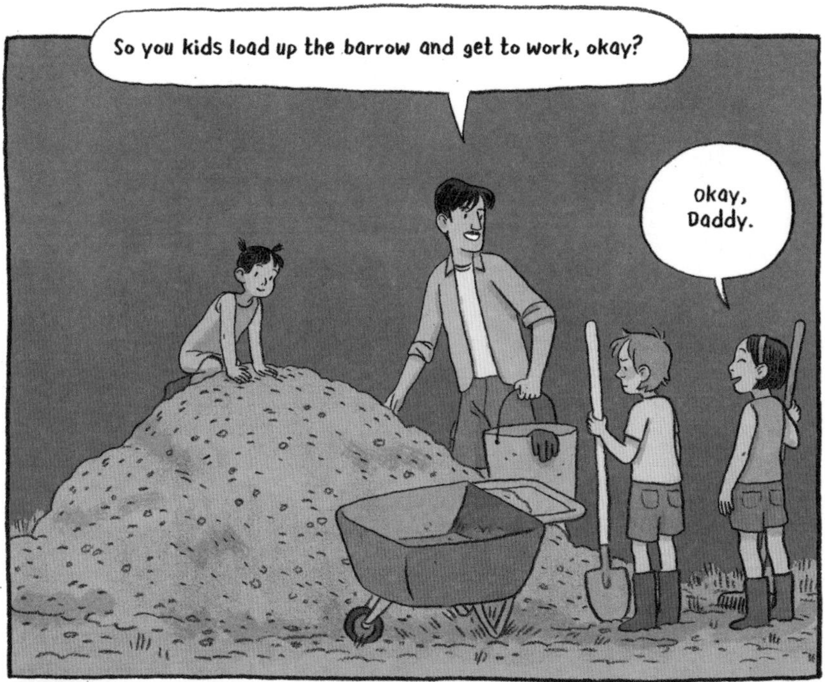
So you kids load up the barrow and get to work, okay?
Okay, Daddy.

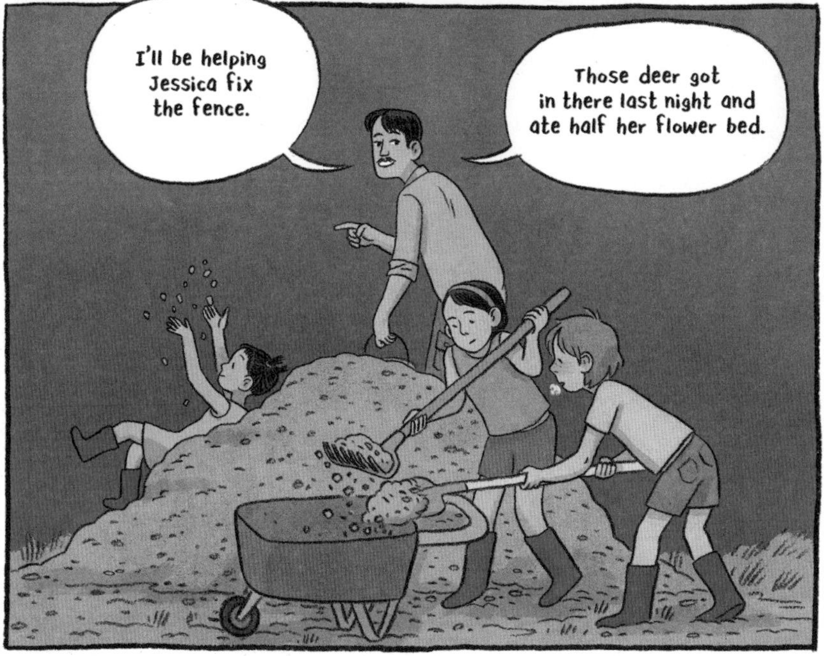
I'll be helping Jessica fix the fence.
Those deer got in there last night and ate half her flower bed.

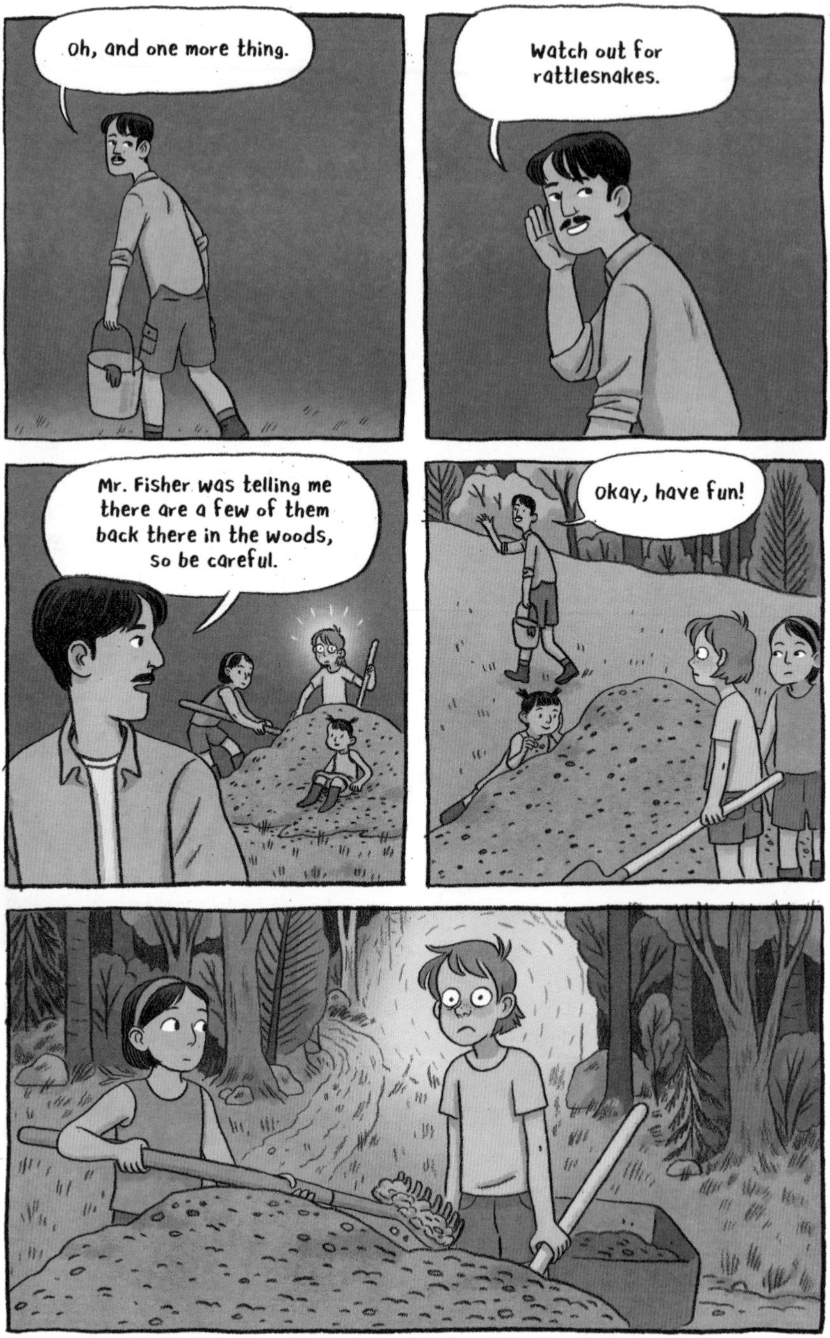
Oh, and one more thing.
Watch out for rattlesnakes.
Mr. Fisher was telling me there are a few of them back there in the woods, so be careful.
Okay, have fun!

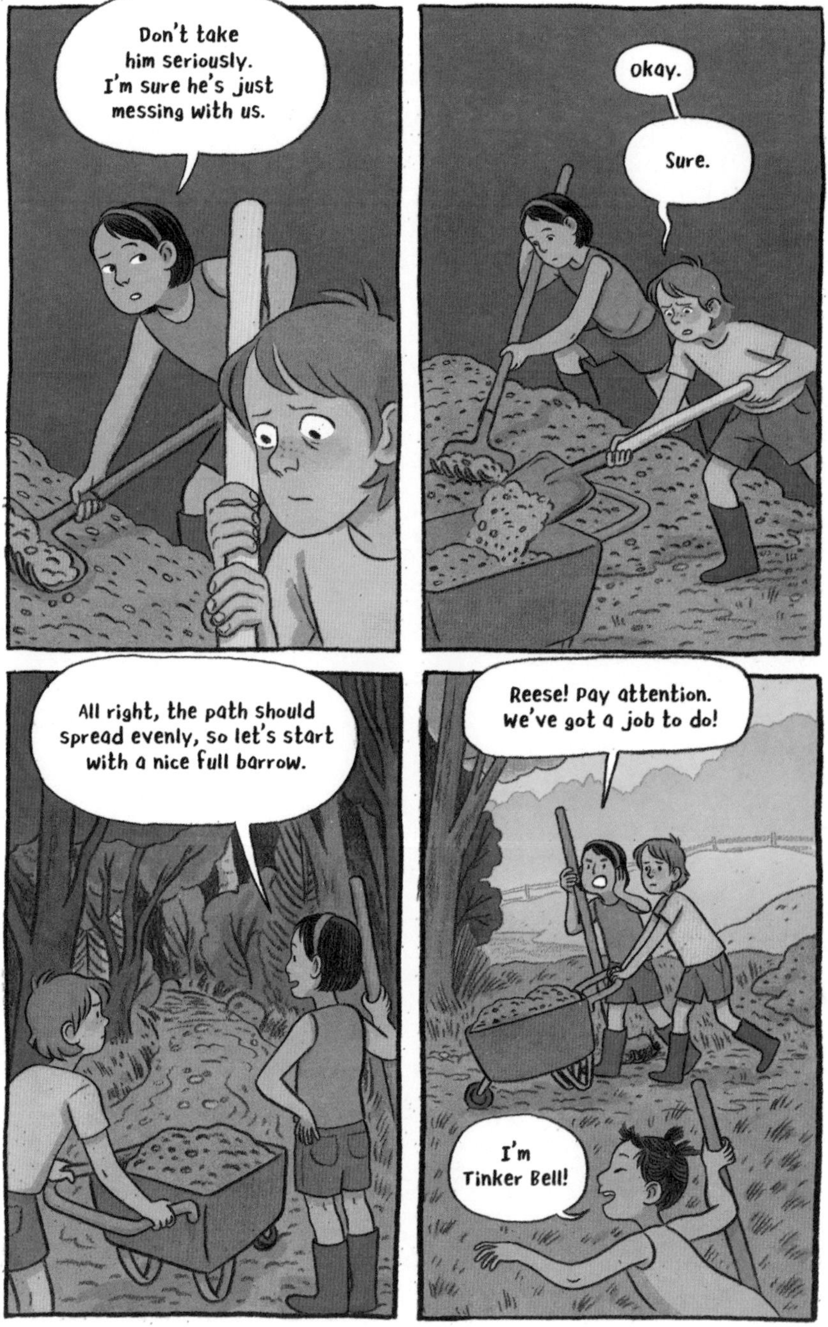
Don't take him seriously. I'm sure he's just messing with us.
Okay.
Sure.
All right, the path should spread evenly, so let's start with a nice full barrow.
Reese! Pay attention. We've got a job to do!
I'm Tinker Bell!

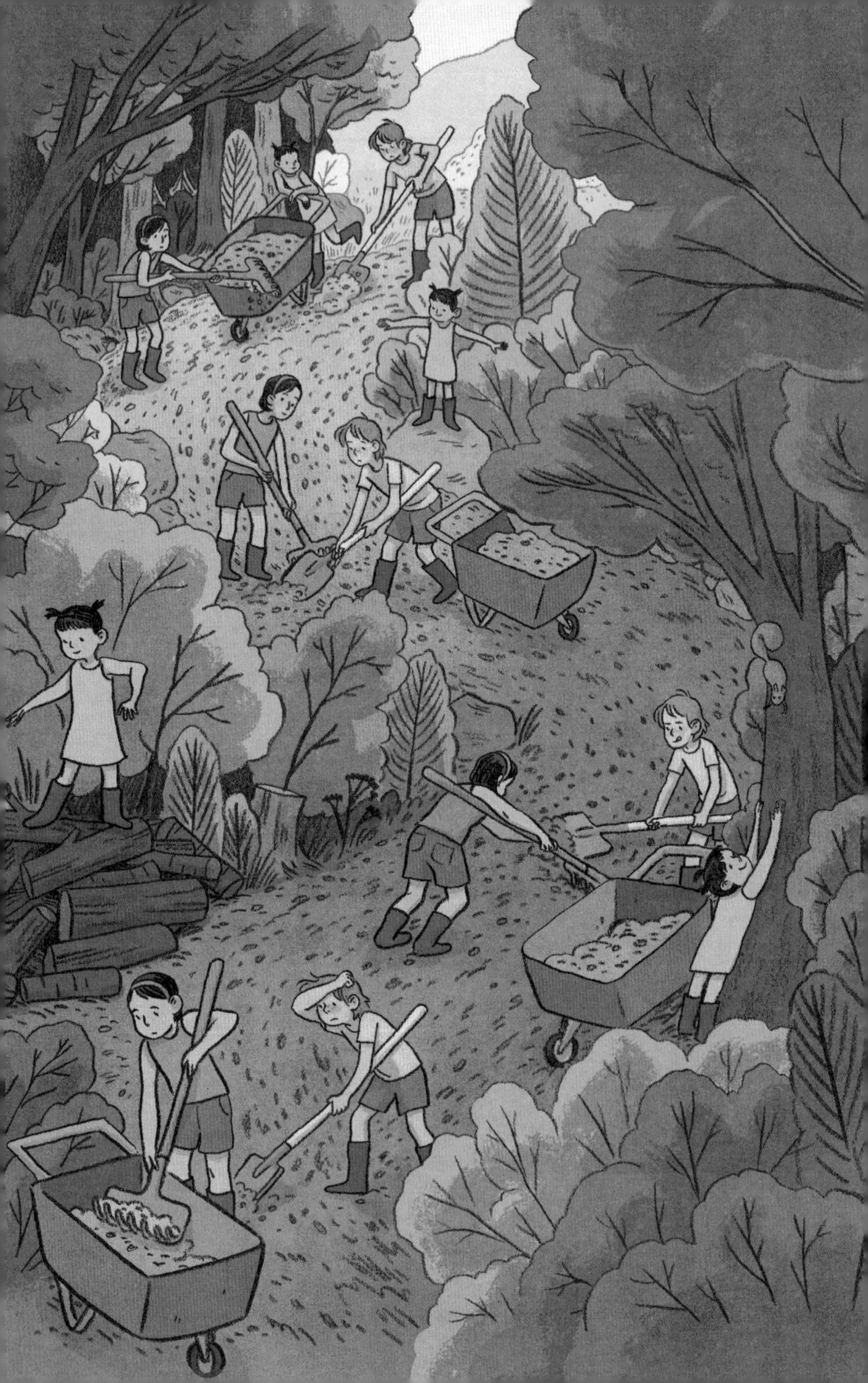

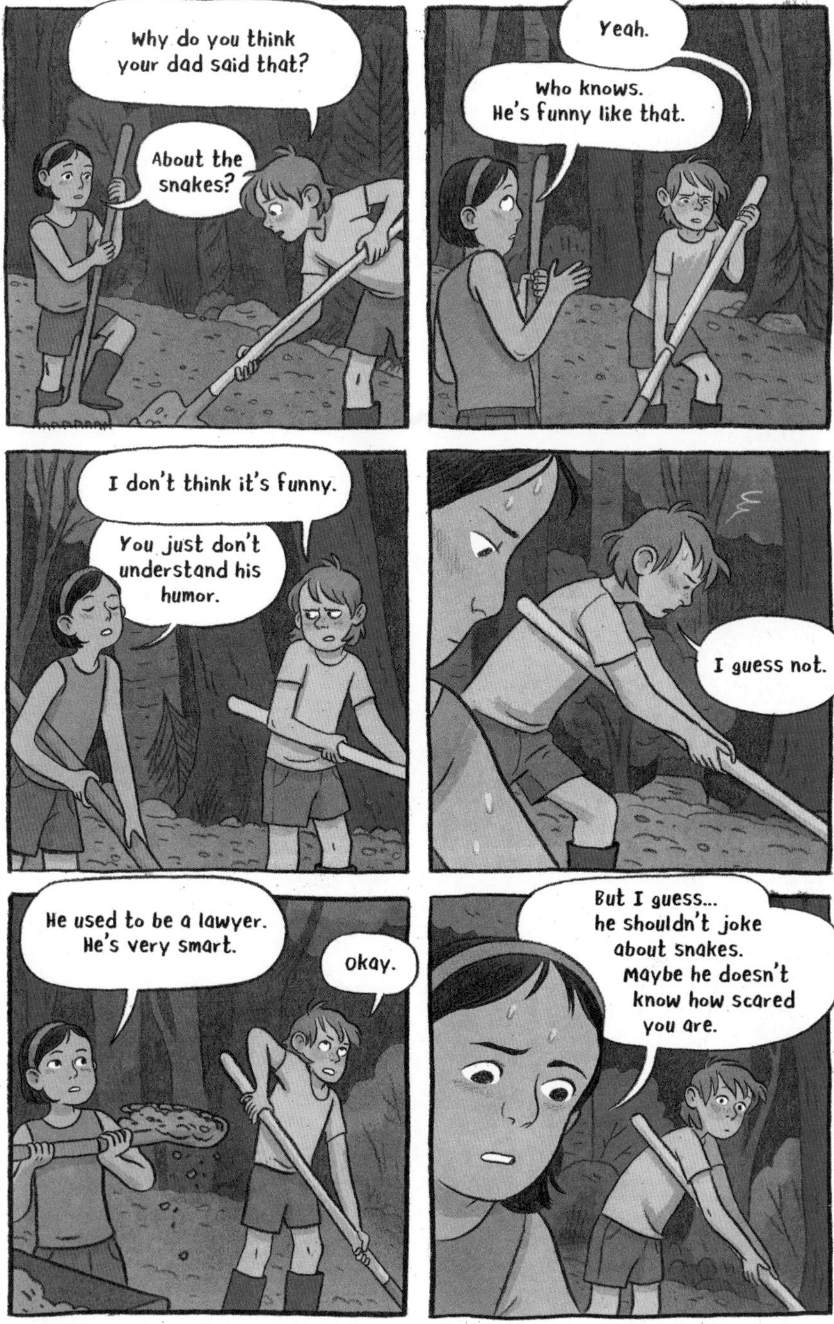
Why do you think your dad said that?
About the snakes?
Yeah.
Who knows. He's funny like that.
I don't think it's funny.
You just don't understand his humor.
I guess not.
He used to be a lawyer. He's very smart.
Okay.
But I guess... he shouldn't joke about snakes. Maybe he doesn't know how scared you are.

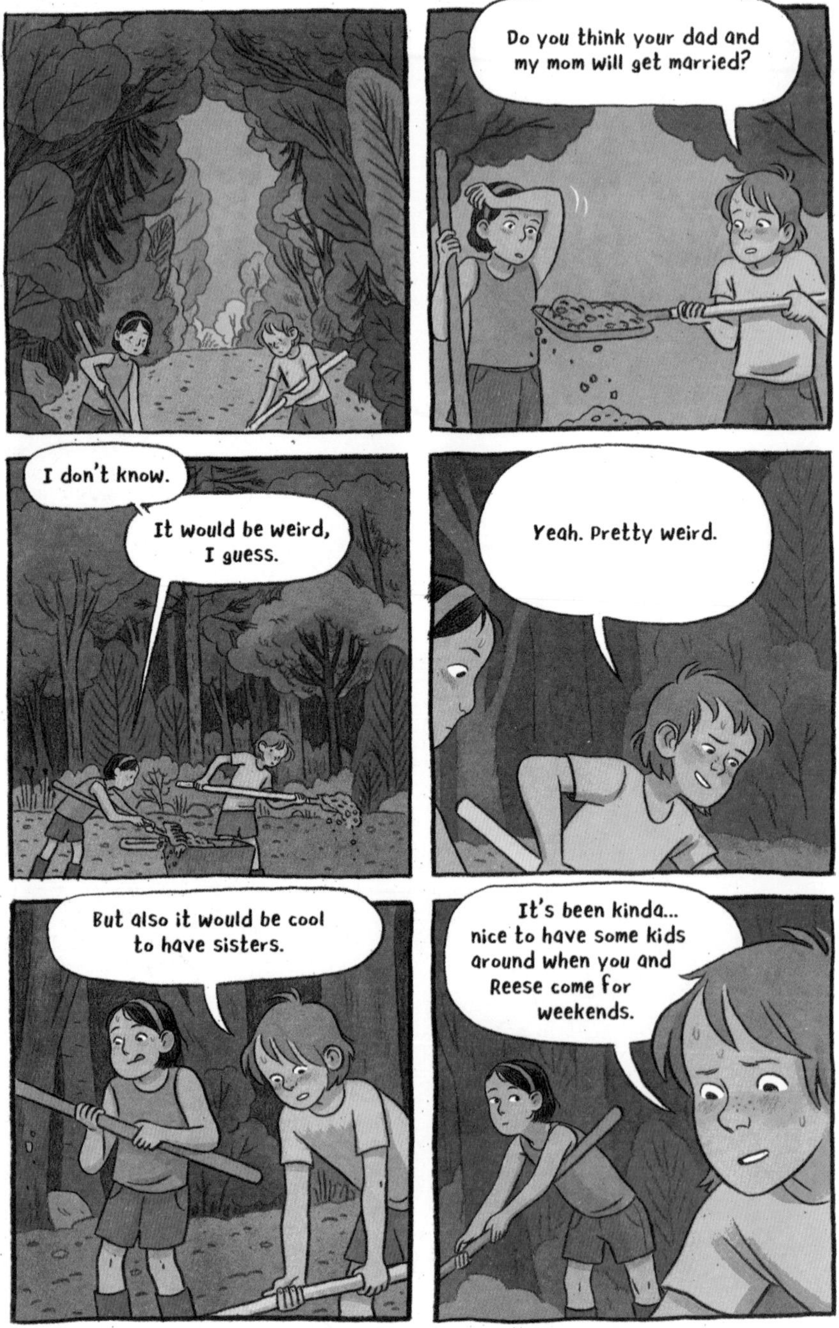
Do you think your dad and my mom will get married?
I don't know.
It would be weird, I guess.
Yeah. Pretty weird.
But also it would be cool to have sisters.
It's been kinda... nice to have some kids around when you and Reese come for weekends.

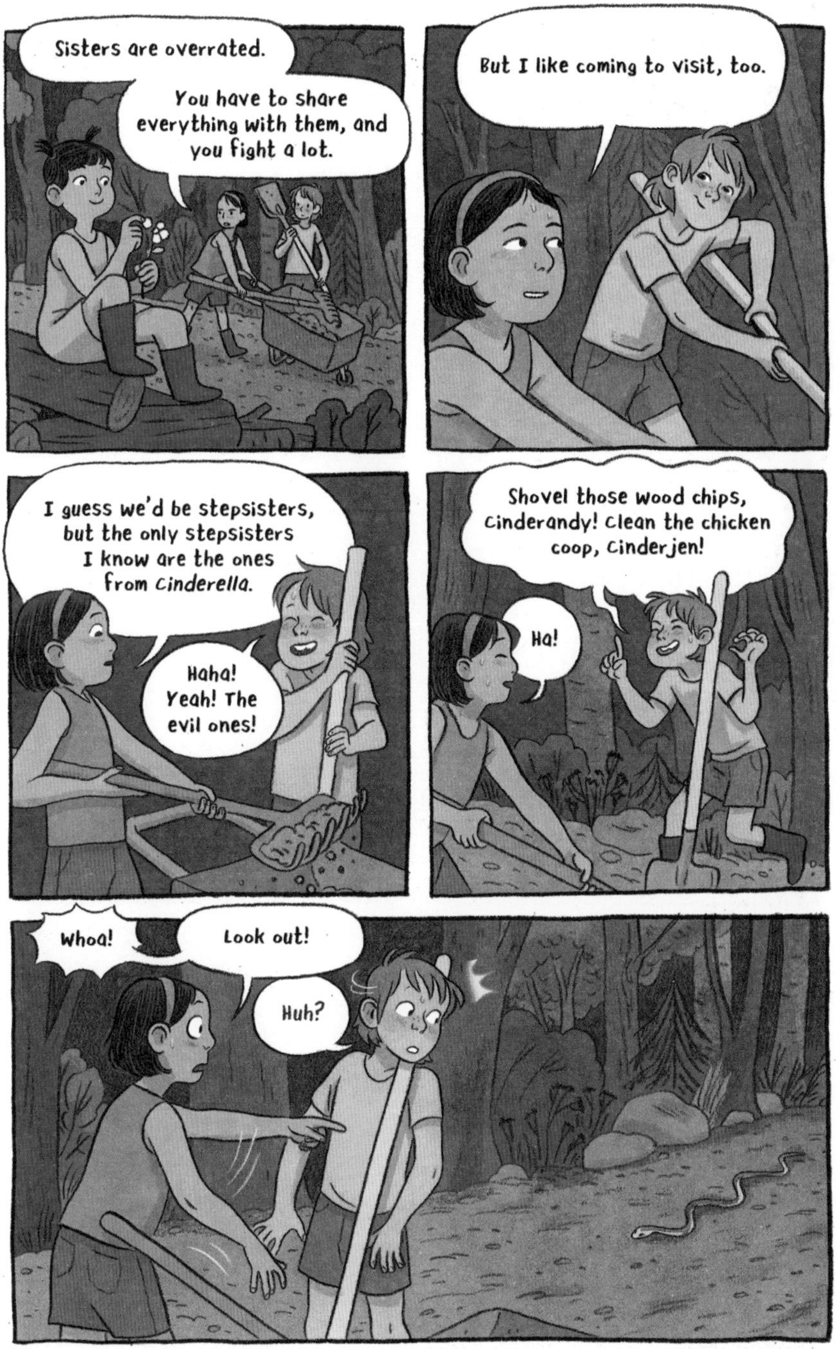
Sisters are overrated.
You have to share everything with them, and you fight a lot.
But I like coming to visit, too.
I guess we'd be stepsisters, but the only stepsisters I know are the ones from Cinderella.
Haha! Yeah! The evil ones!
Shovel those wood chips, Cinderandy! Clean the chicken coop, Cinderjen!
Ha!
Whoa!
Look out!
Huh?

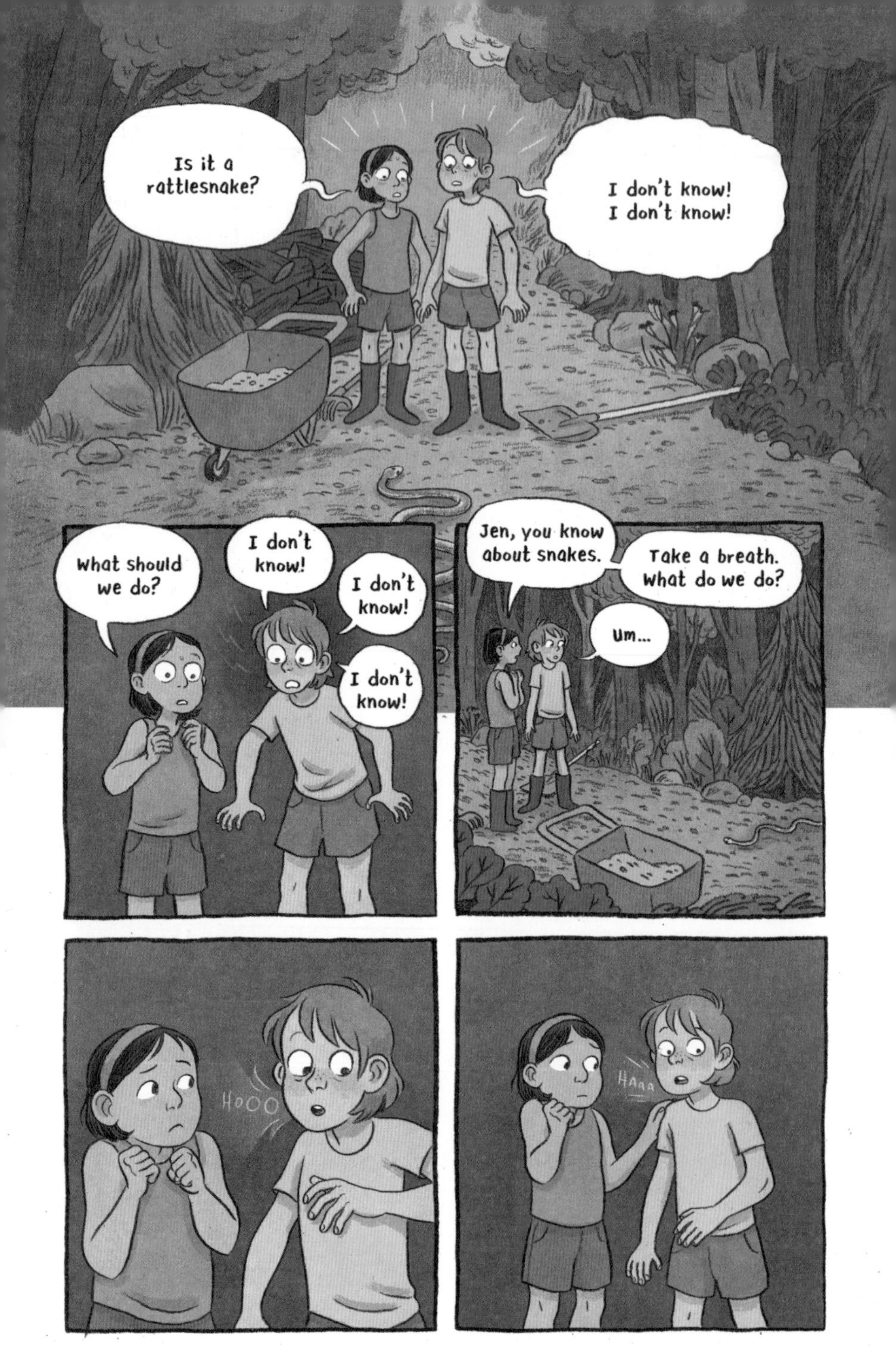
Is it a rattlesnake?
I don't know! I don't know!
What should we do?
I don't know!
I don't know!
I don't know!
Jen, you know about snakes.
Take a breath. What do we do?
Um...
HOOO
Haaa

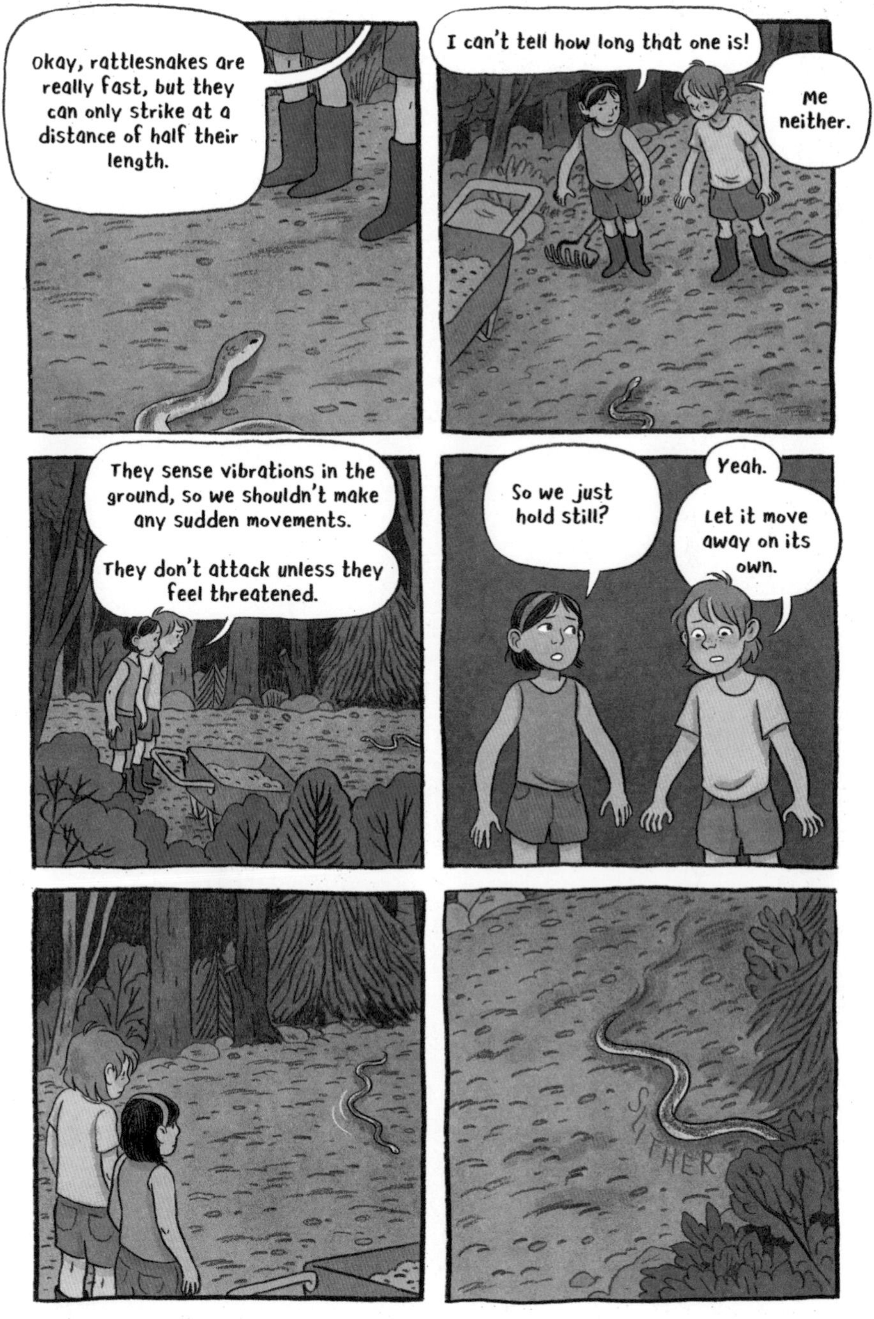
Okay, rattlesnakes are really fast, but they can only strike at a distance of half their length.
I can't tell how long that one is!
Me neither.
They sense vibrations in the ground, so we shouldn't make any sudden movements.
They don't attack unless they feel threatened.
So we just hold still?
Yeah.
Let it move away on its own.
SLITHER

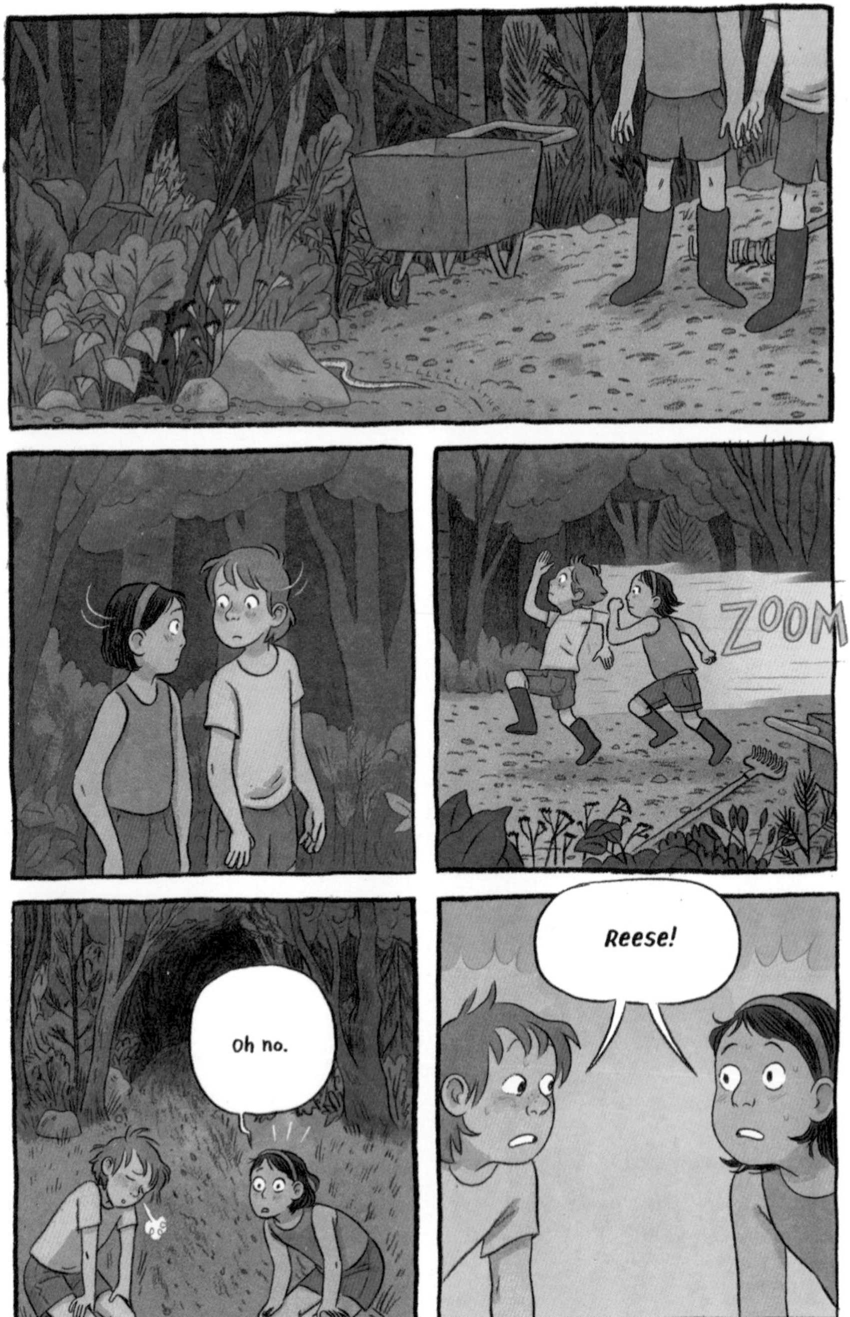
SLLLLL
ZOOM
Oh no.
Reese!

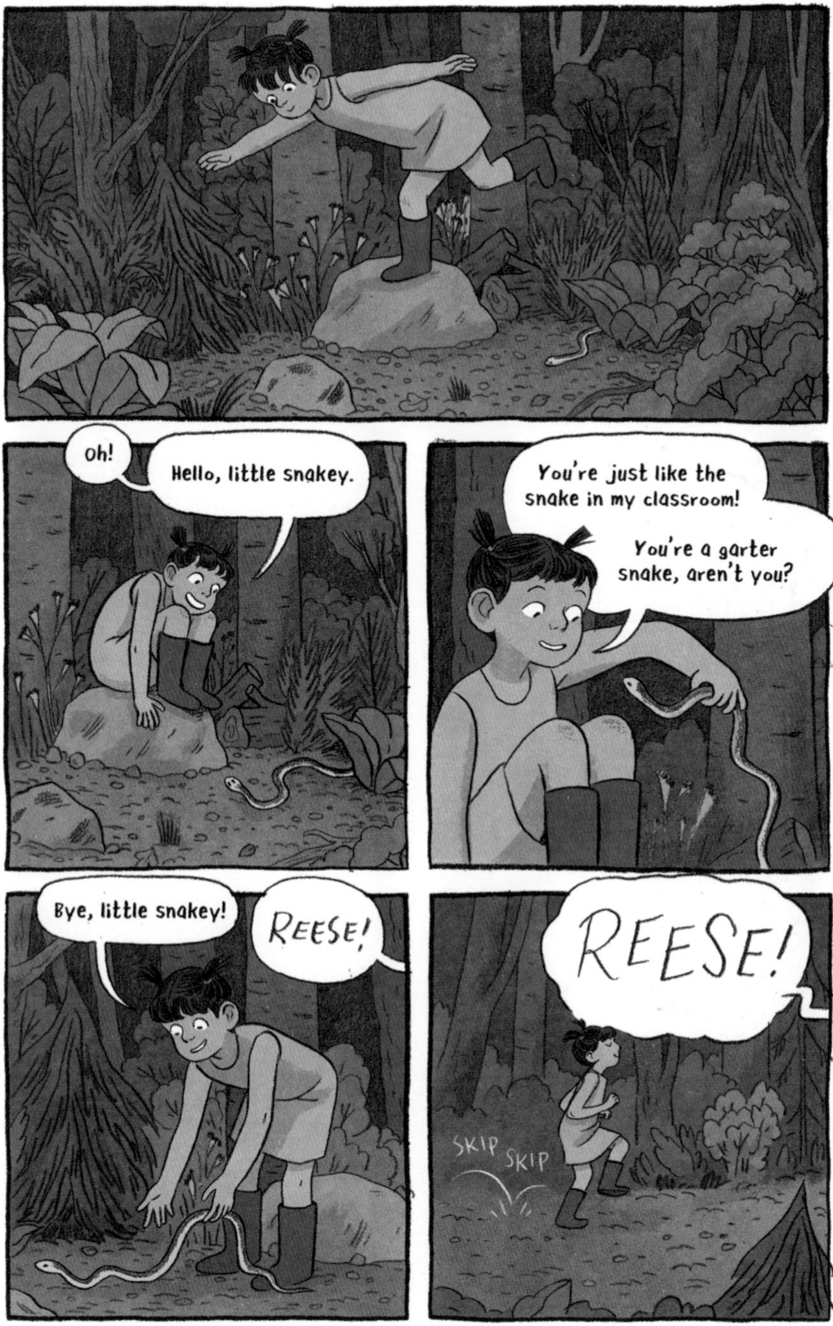
Oh!
Hello, little snakey.
You're just like the snake in my classroom!
You're a garter snake, aren't you?
Bye, little snakey!
REESE!
REESE!
SKIP SKIP

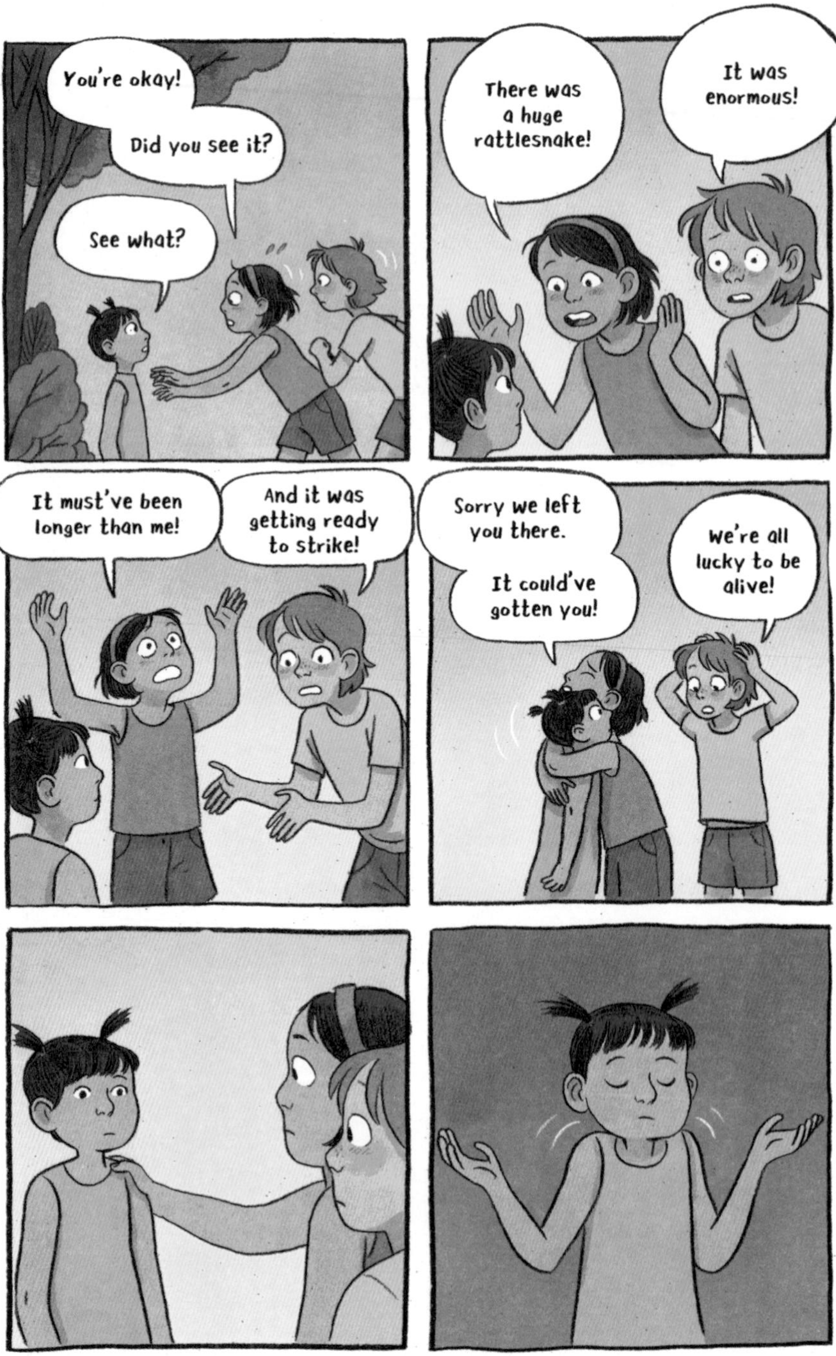
You're okay!
Did you see it?
See what?
There was a huge rattlesnake!
It was enormous!
It must've been longer than me!
And it was getting ready to strike!
Sorry we left you there.
It could've gotten you!
We're all lucky to be alive!

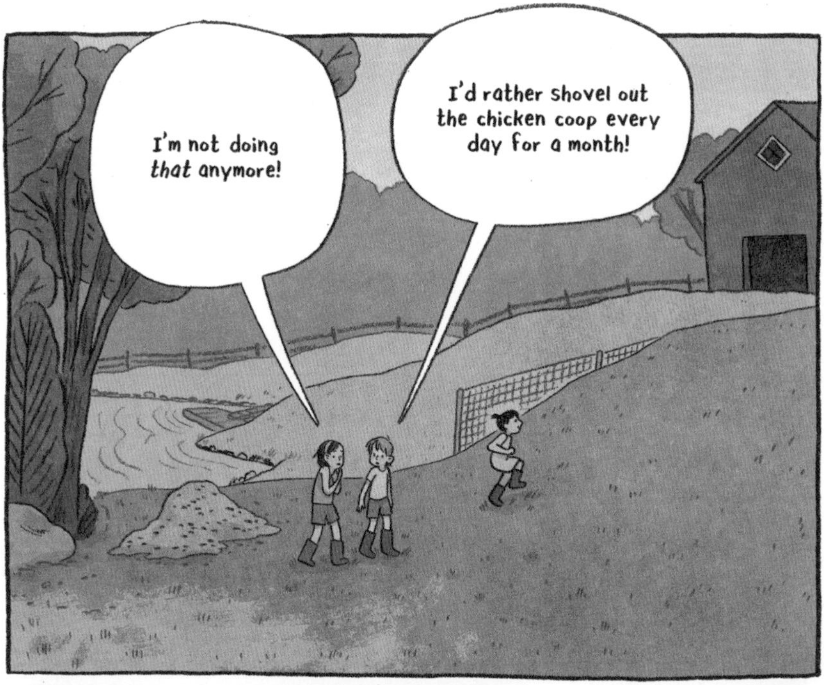
I'm not doing *that* anymore!
I'd rather shovel out the chicken coop every day for a month!

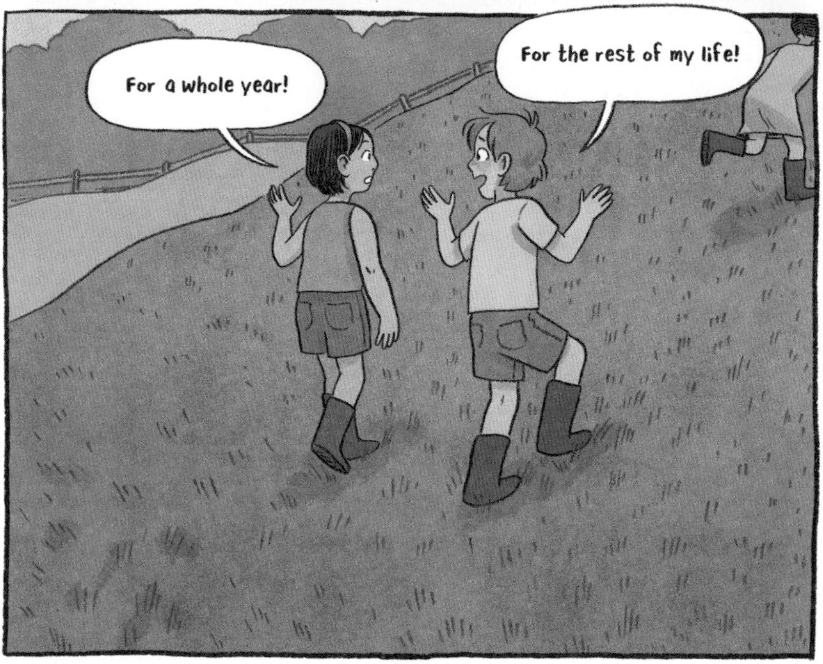
For a whole year!
For the rest of my life!

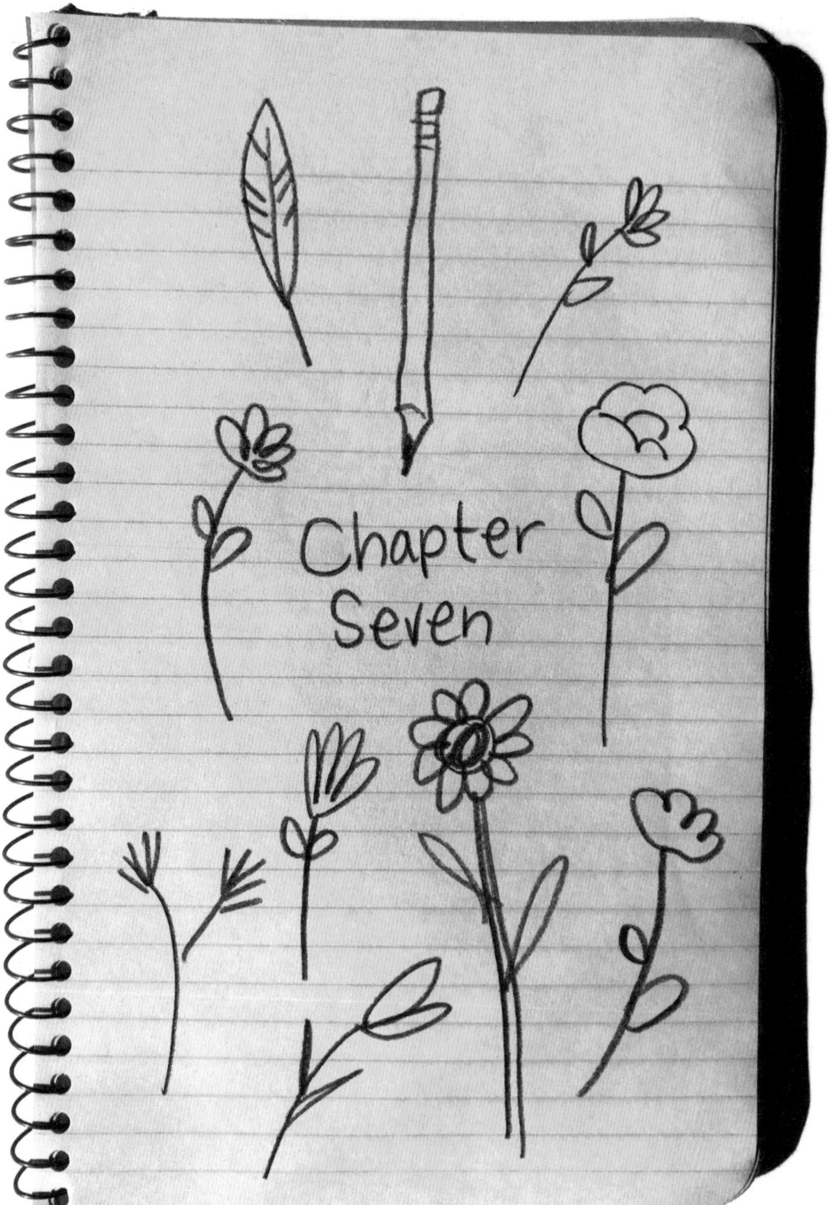
Chapter
Seven

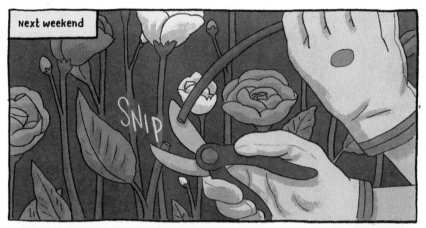

next weekend

SNIP

Are the chickens supposed to be in here?

Yes!

They're helping by eating the bad bugs that try to eat the flowers and veggies.

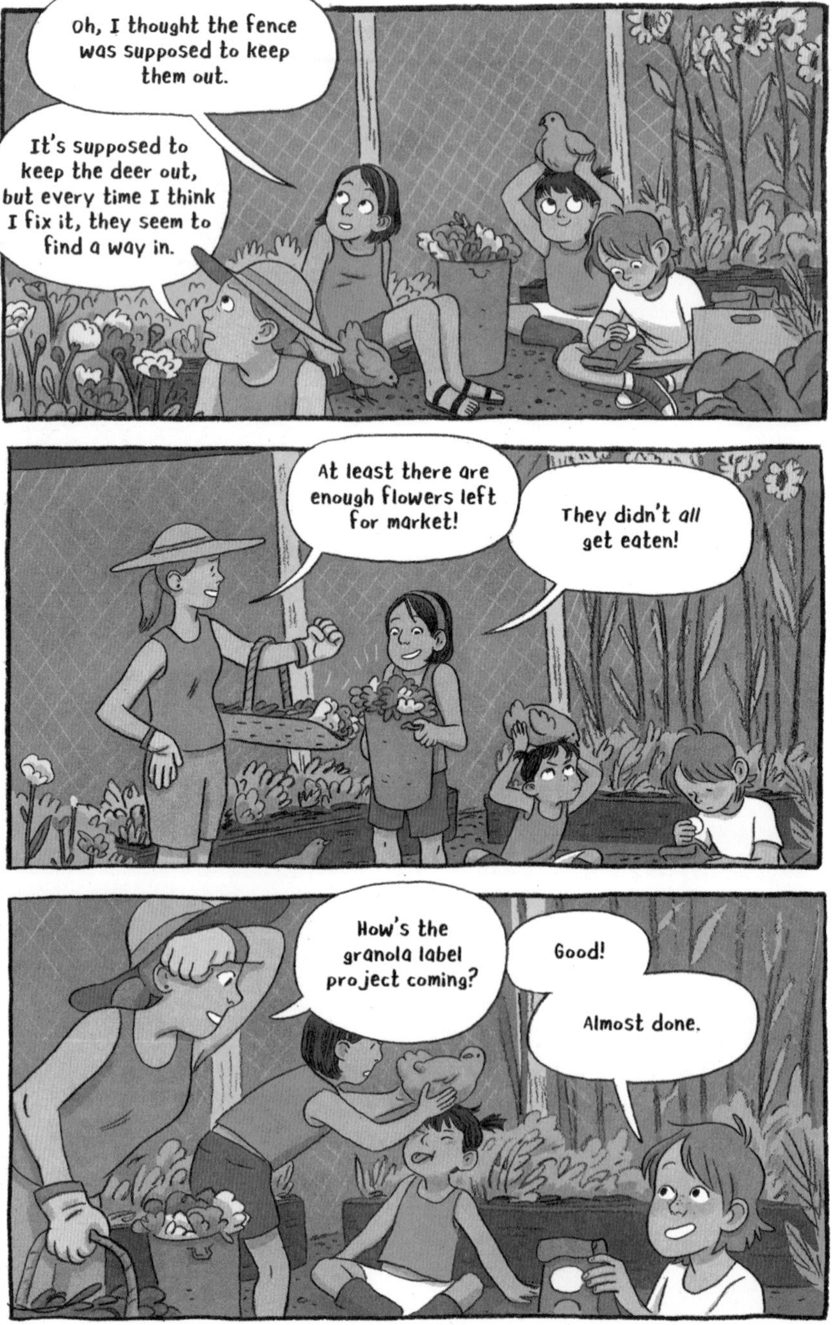
Oh, I thought the fence was supposed to keep them out.
It's supposed to keep the deer out, but every time I think I fix it, they seem to find a way in.
At least there are enough flowers left for market!
They didn't all get eaten!
How's the granola label project coming?
Good!
Almost done.

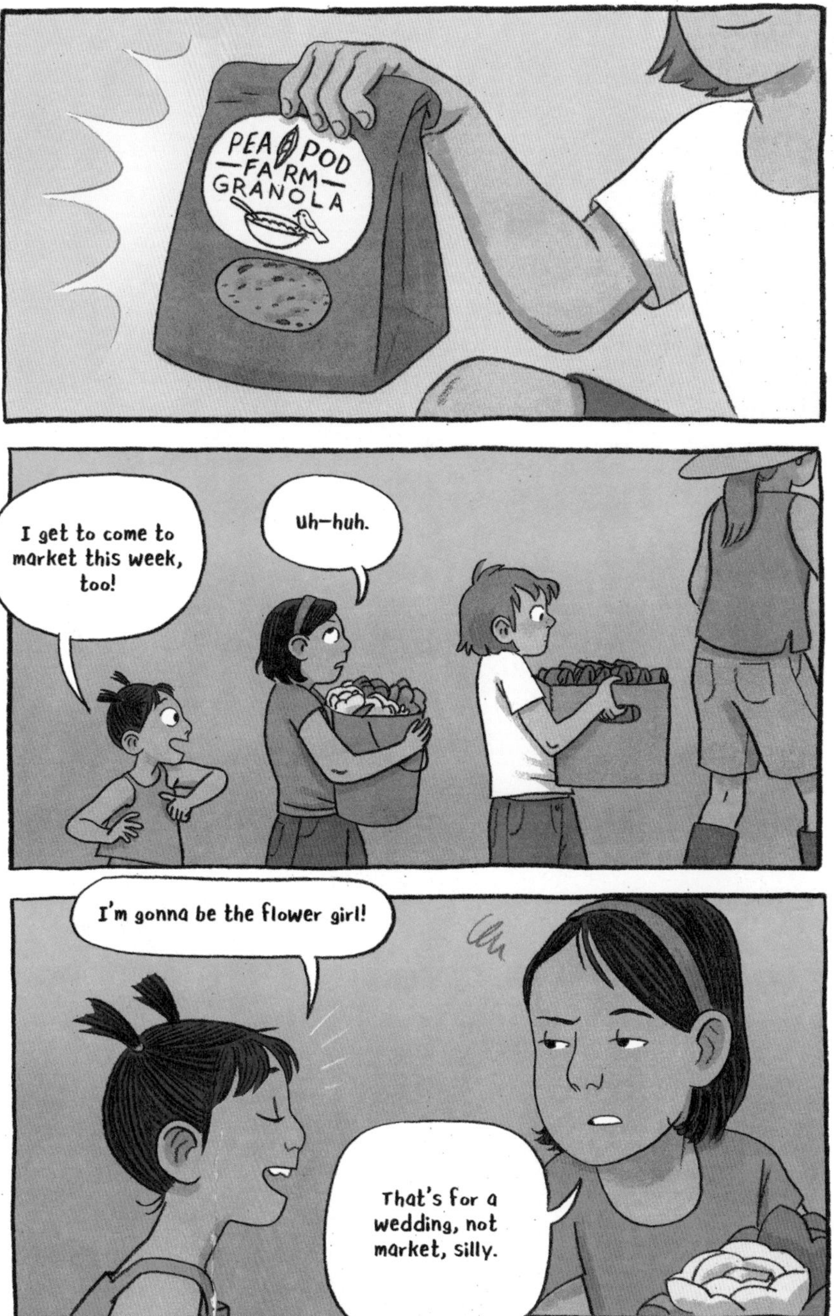
PEA POD FARM GRANOLA
I get to come to market this week, too!
Uh-huh.
I'm gonna be the flower girl!
That's for a wedding, not market, silly.

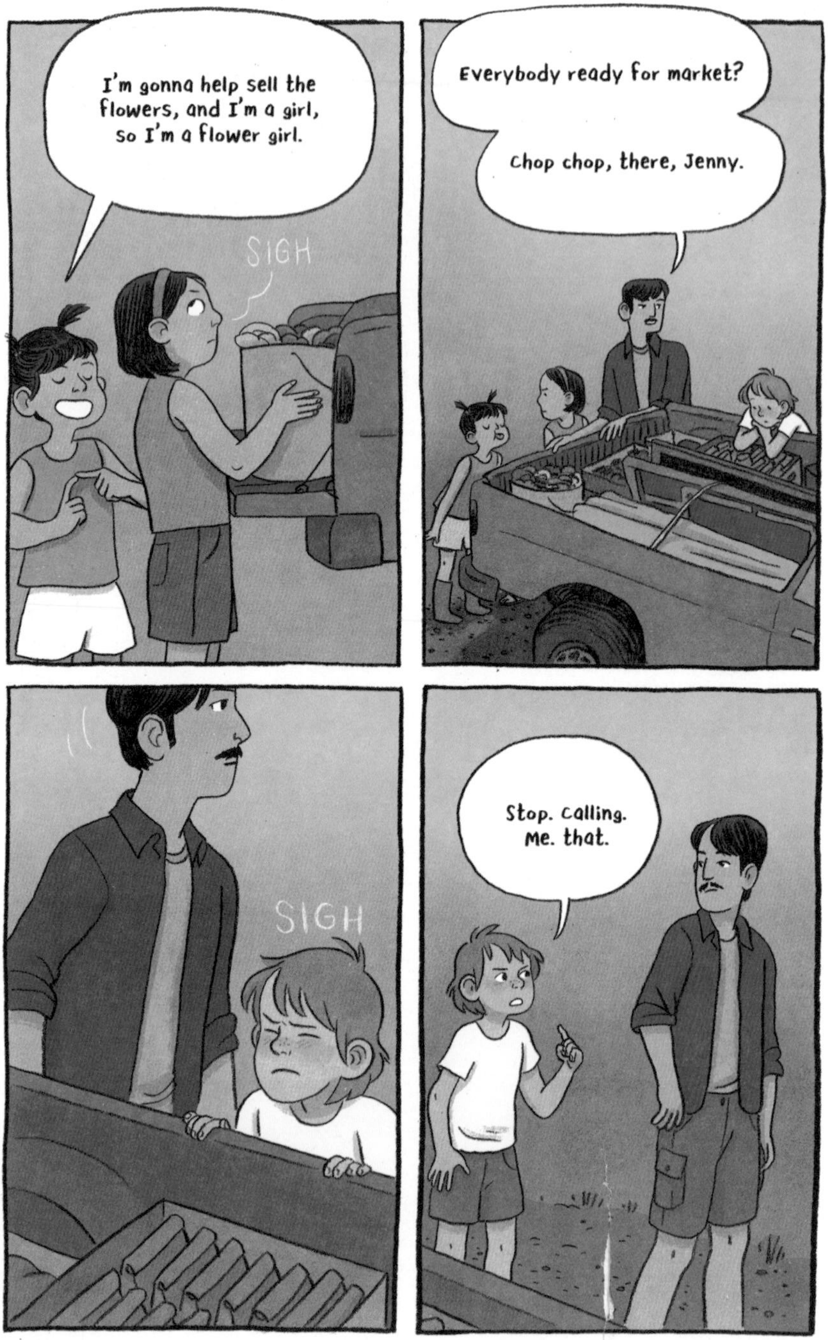
I'm gonna help sell the flowers, and I'm a girl, so I'm a flower girl.
SIGH
Everybody ready for market?
Chop chop, there, Jenny.
SIGH
Stop. Calling. Me. that.

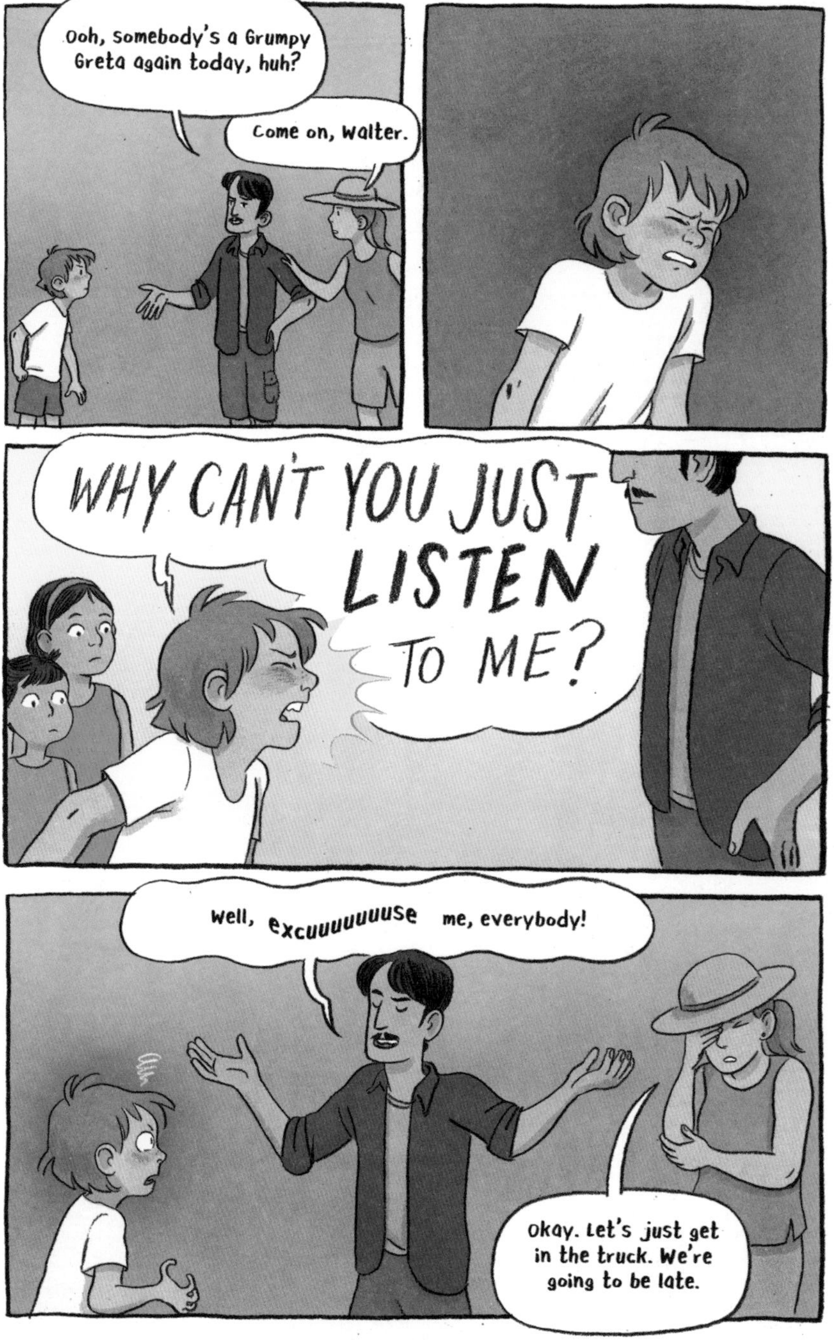
Ooh, somebody's a Grumpy Greta again today, huh?
Come on, Walter.
WHY CAN'T YOU JUST LISTEN TO ME?
Well, excuuuuuuuse me, everybody!
Okay. Let's just get in the truck. We're going to be late.

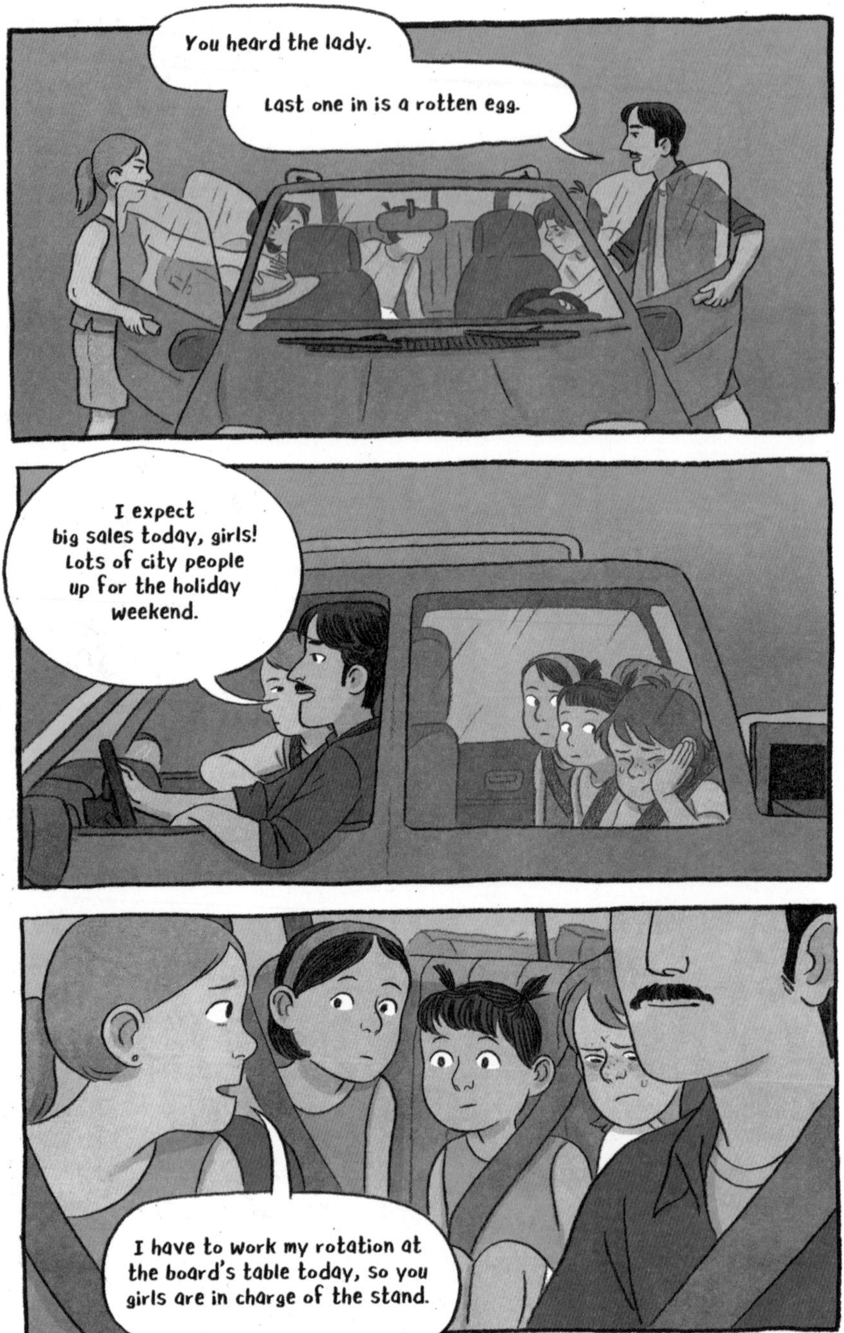
You heard the lady.
Last one in is a rotten egg.
I expect big sales today, girls! Lots of city people up for the holiday weekend.
I have to work my rotation at the board's table today, so you girls are in charge of the stand.

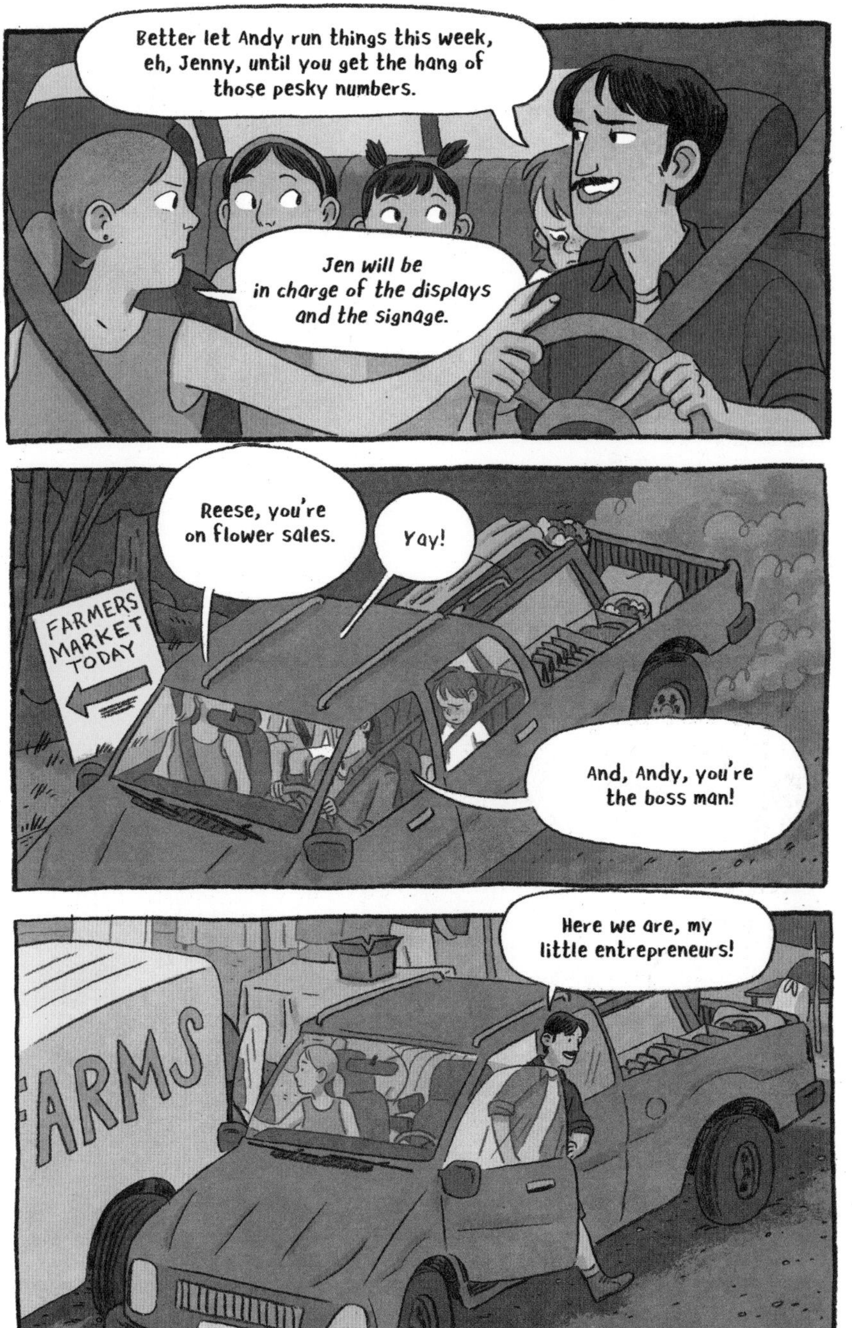
Better let Andy run things this week, eh, Jenny, until you get the hang of those pesky numbers.
Jen will be in charge of the displays and the signage.
FARMERS MARKET TODAY
Reese, you're on flower sales.
Yay!
And, Andy, you're the boss man!
FARMS
Here we are, my little entrepreneurs!

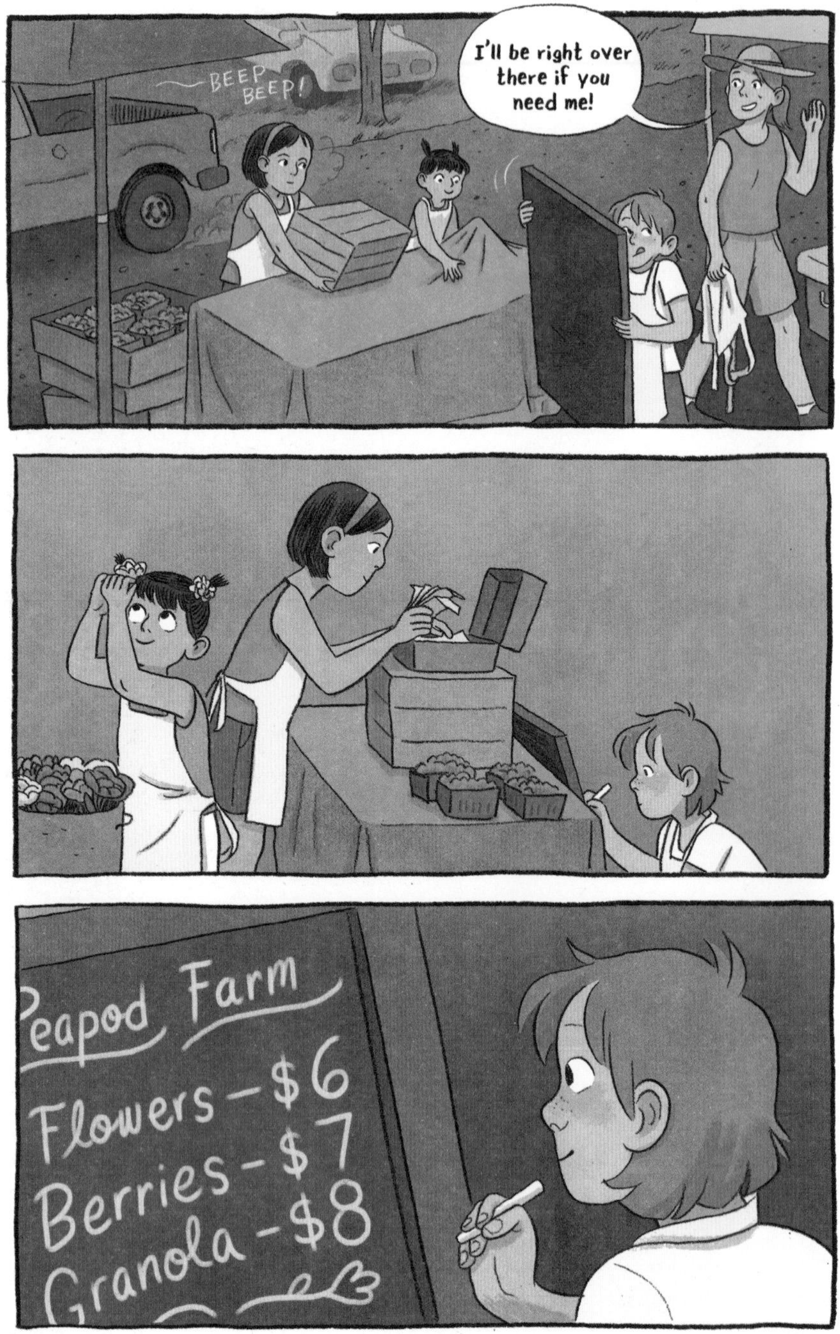

BEEP BEEP!
I'll be right over there if you need me!
Peapod Farm
Flowers - $6
Berries - $7
Granola - $8

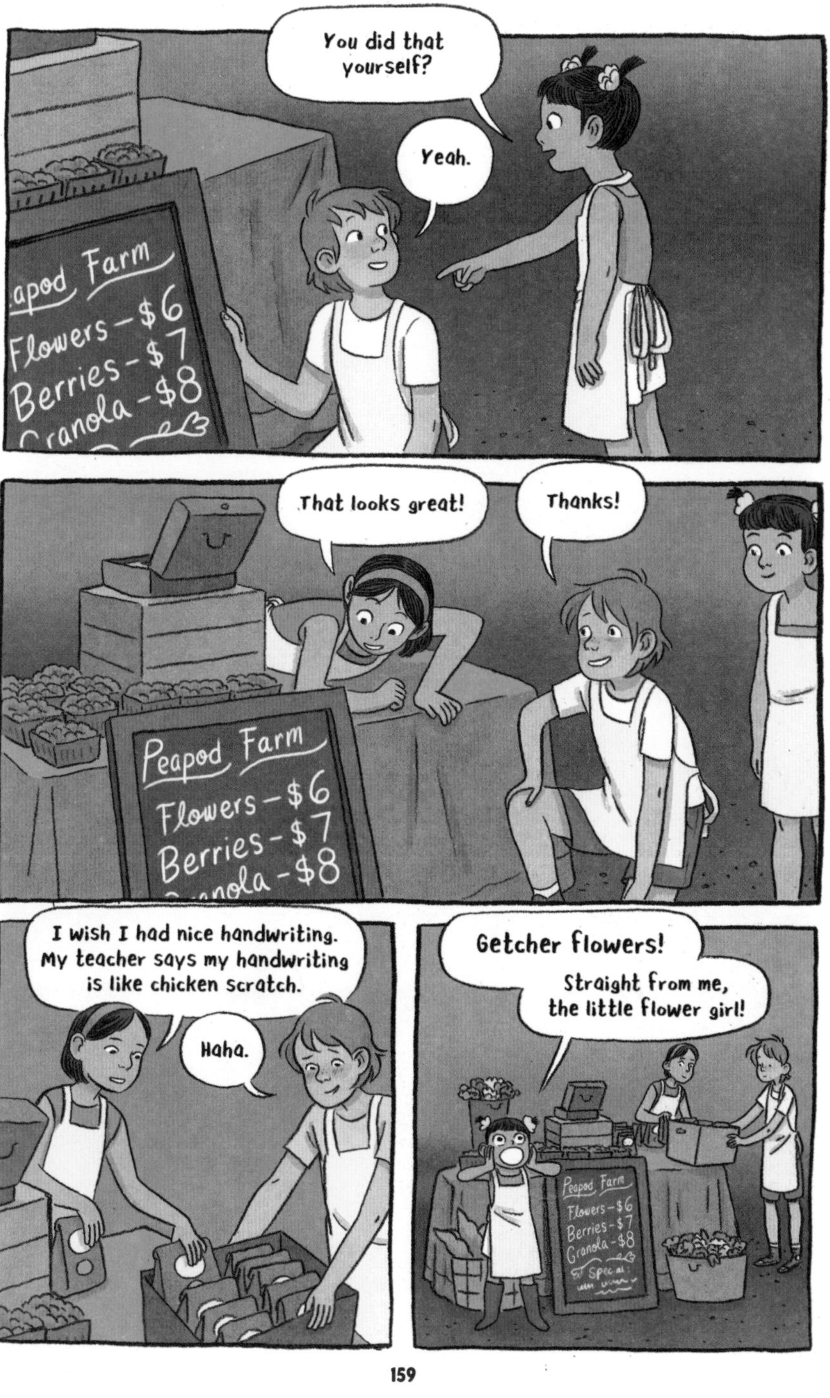
You did that yourself?
Yeah.
Flowers-$6
Berries-$7
That looks great!
Thanks!
Peapod Farm
Flowers-$6
Berries-$7
I wish I had nice handwriting. My teacher says my handwriting is like chicken scratch.
Haha.
Getcher flowers!
Straight from me, the little flower girl!
Peapod Farm
Flowers-$6
Berries-$7
Granola-$8

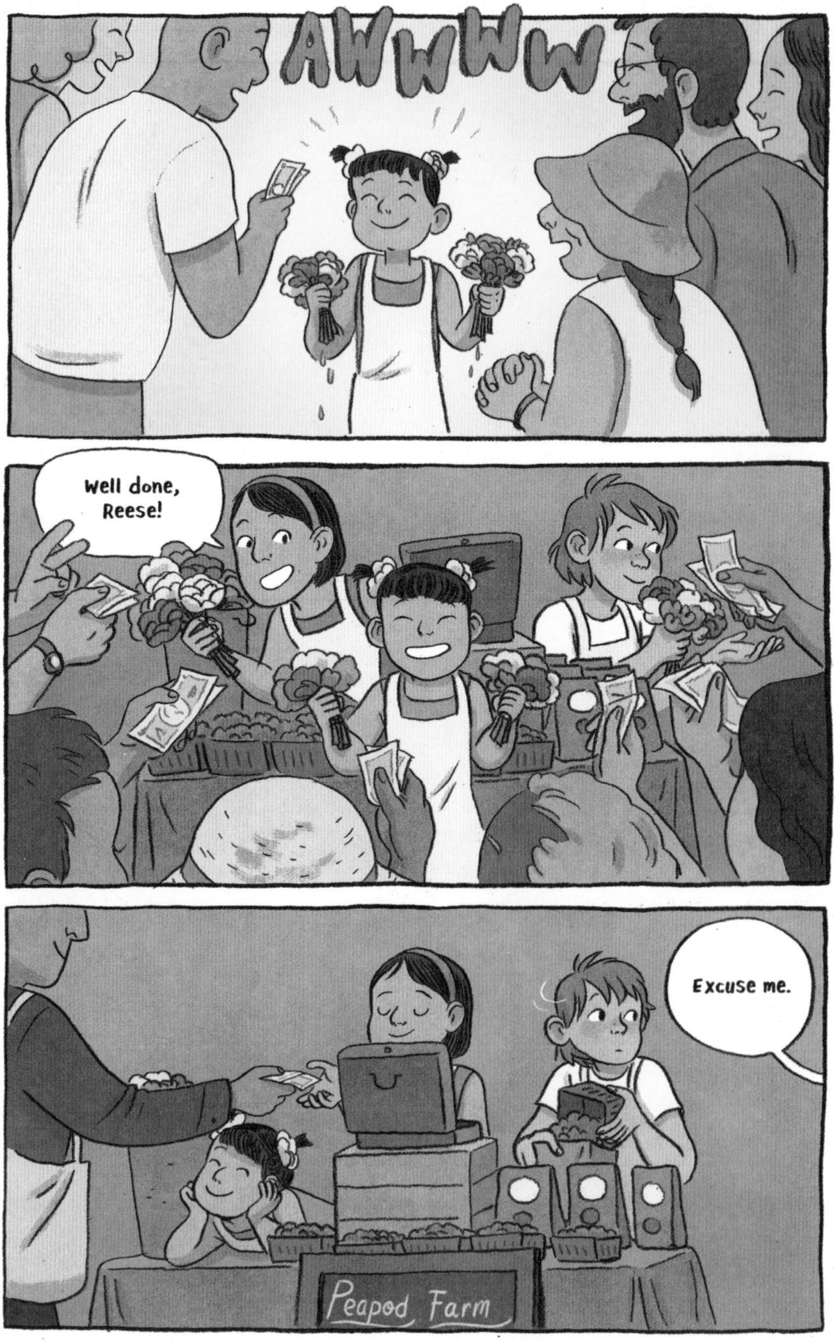
AWWWW
Well done, Reese!
Excuse me.
Peapod Farm

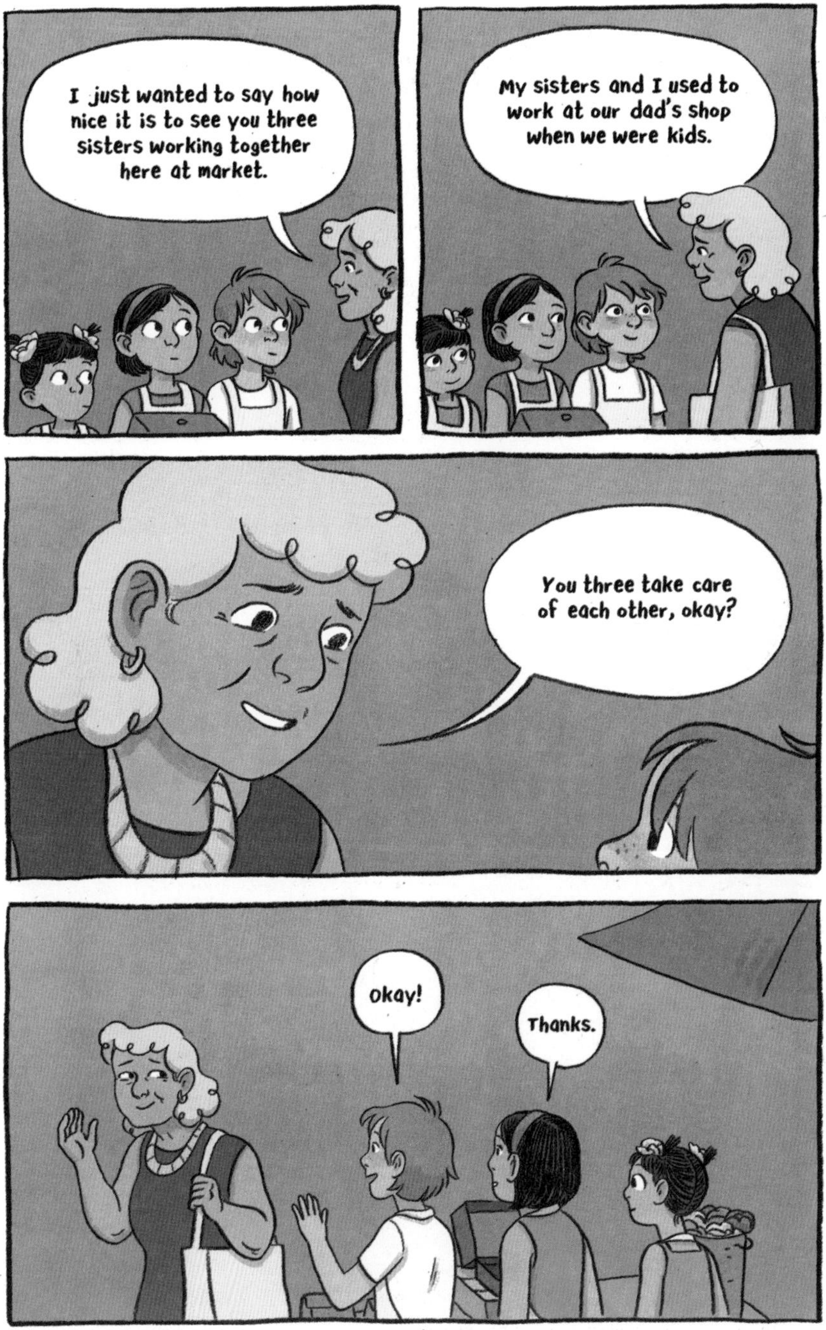
I just wanted to say how nice it is to see you three sisters working together here at market.
My sisters and I used to work at our dad's shop when we were kids.
You three take care of each other, okay?
Okay!
Thanks.

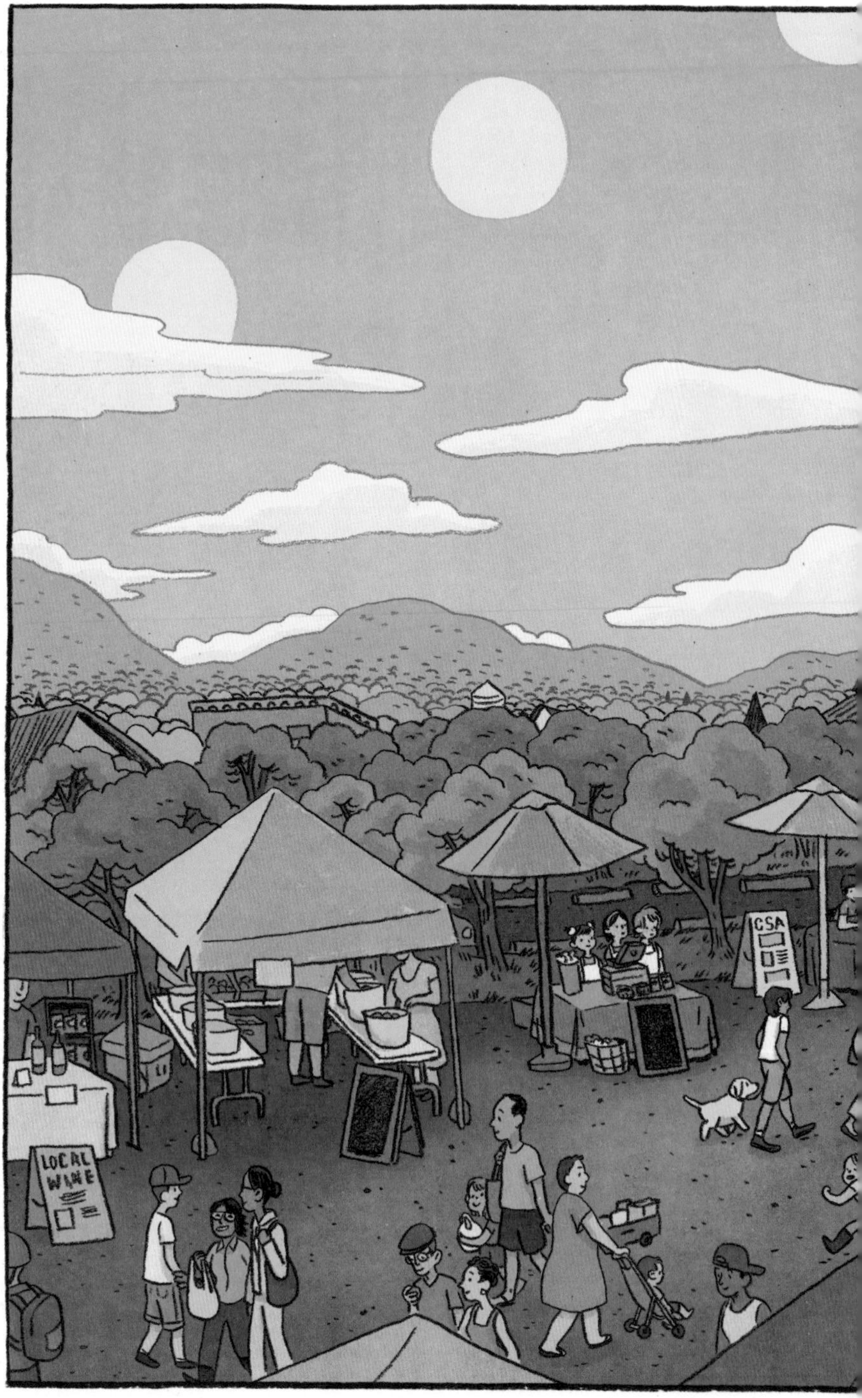
CSA
LOCAL WINE

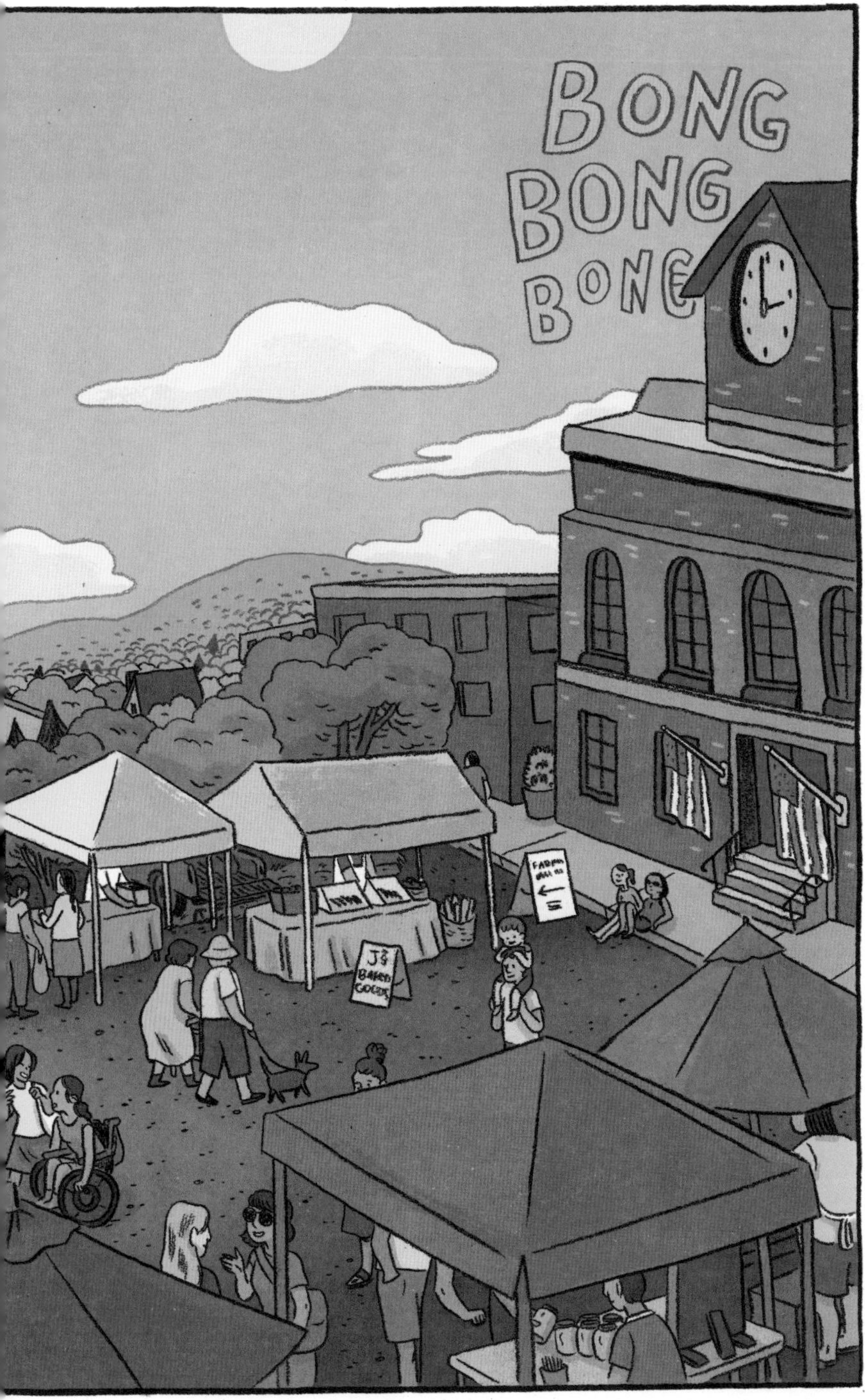
BONG
BONG
BONG
FARM
J's
BAKED
GOODS

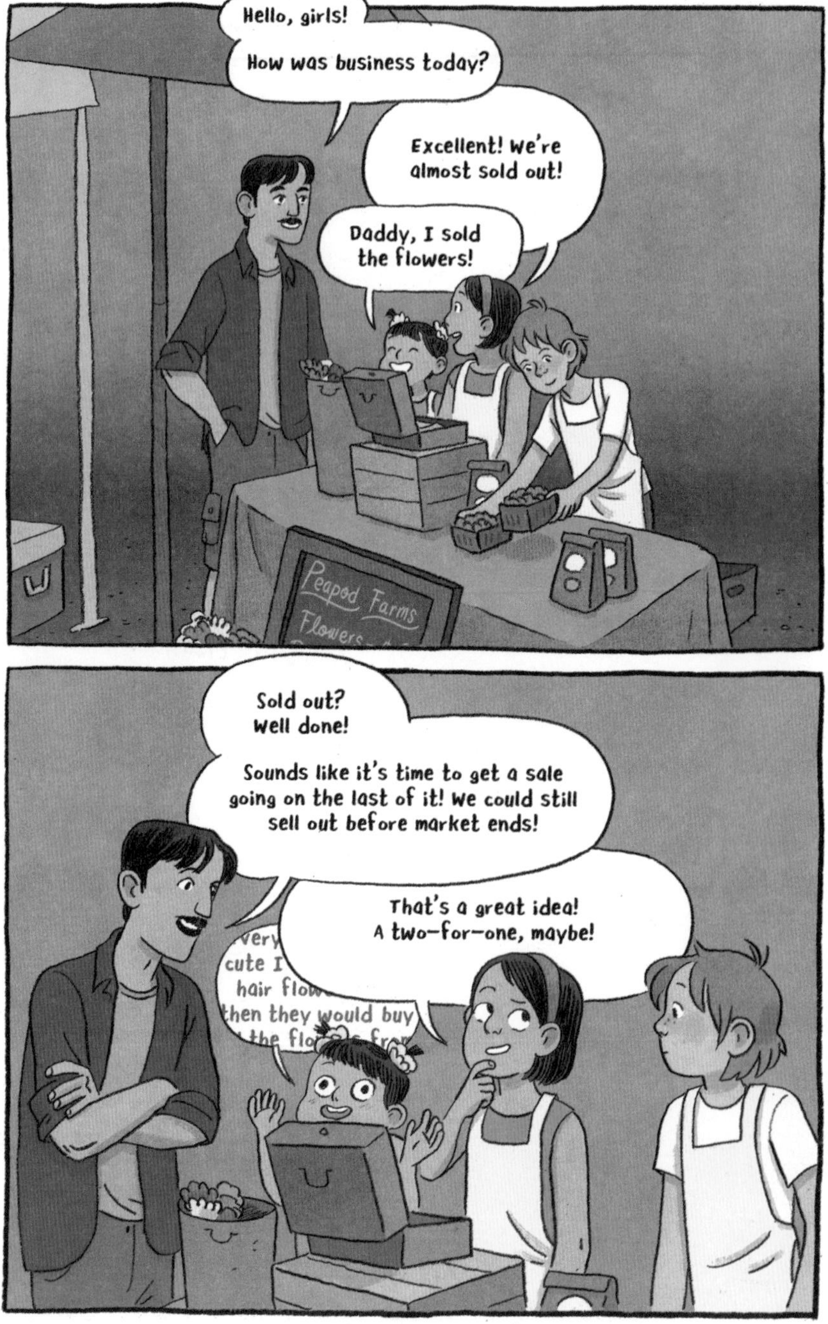
Hello, girls!
How was business today?
Excellent! We're almost sold out!
Daddy, I sold the flowers!
Peapod Farms
Sold out? Well done!
Sounds like it's time to get a sale going on the last of it! We could still sell out before market ends!
That's a great idea! A two-for-one, maybe!

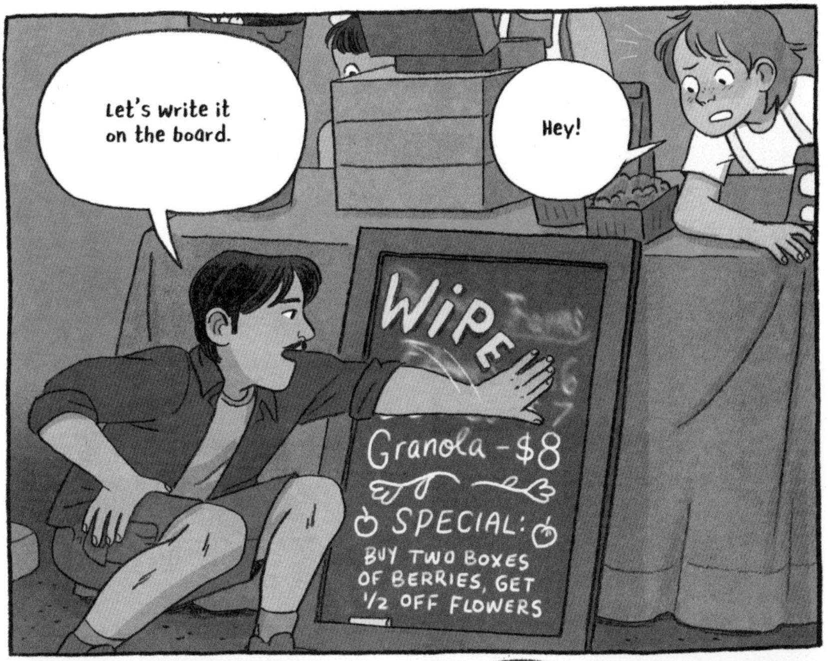
Let's write it on the board.
Hey!
WIPE
Granola - $8
SPECIAL:
BUY TWO BOXES OF BERRIES, GET 1/2 OFF FLOWERS

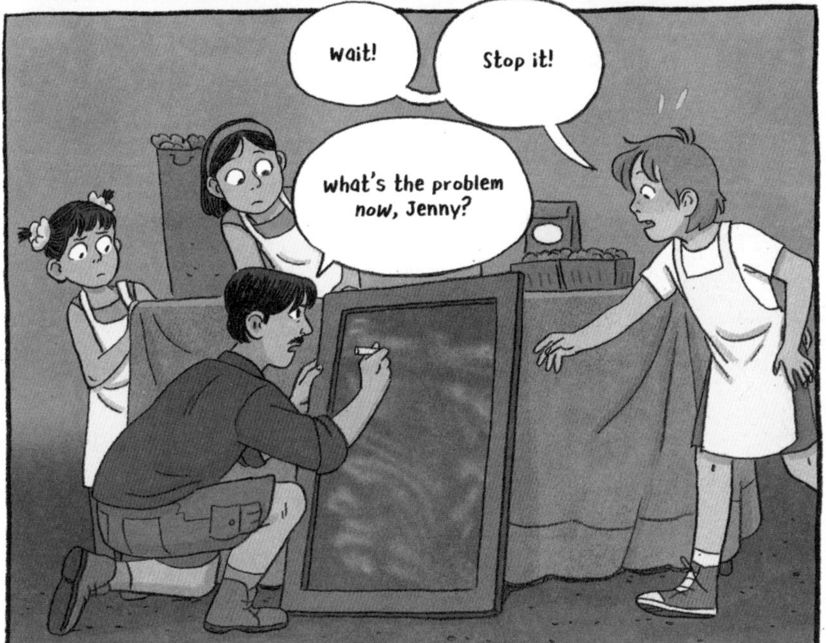
Wait!
Stop it!
What's the problem now, Jenny?

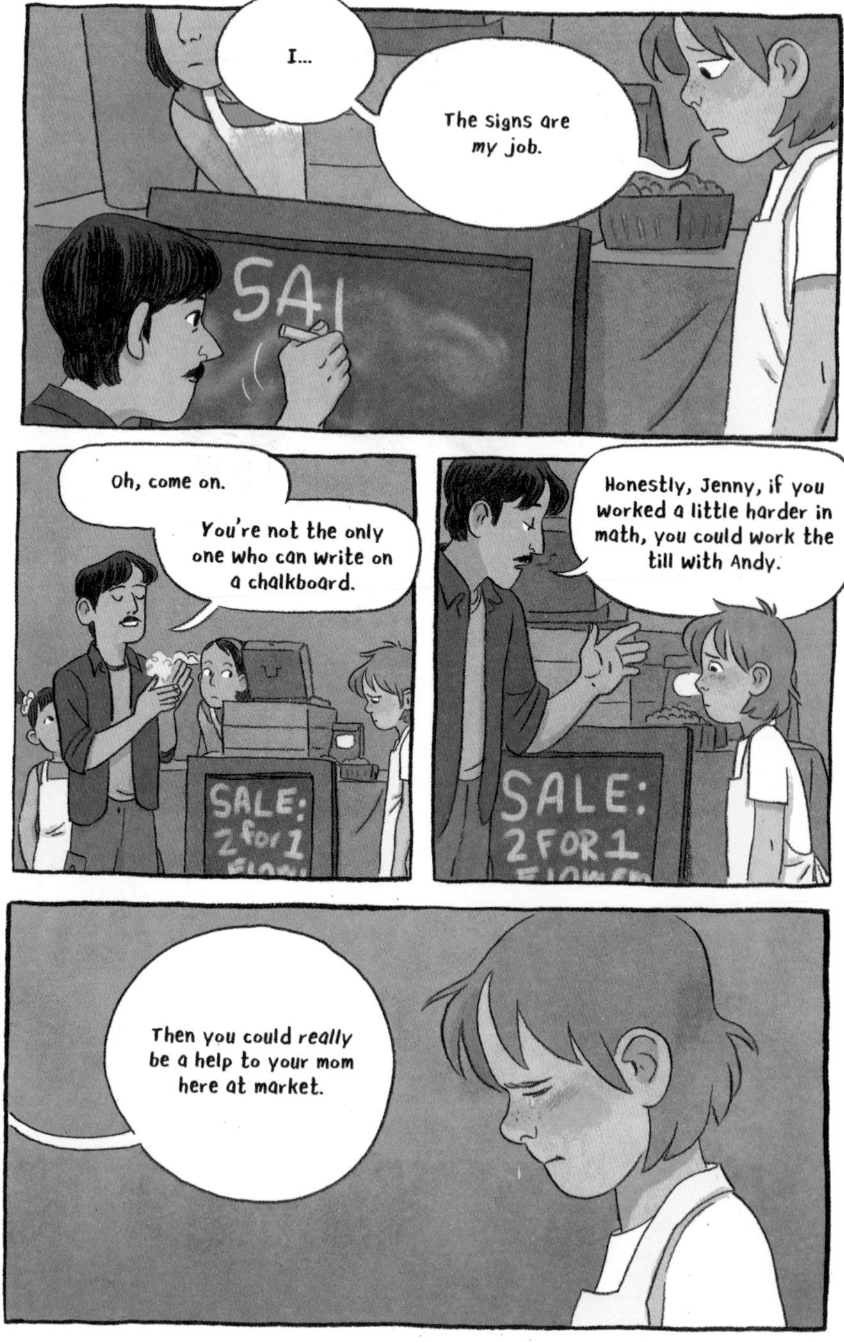
I...
The signs are my job.
SAI
Oh, come on.
You're not the only one who can write on a chalkboard.
SALE: 2 for 1
Honestly, Jenny, if you worked a little harder in math, you could work the till with Andy.
SALE: 2 FOR 1
Then you could *really* be a help to your mom here at market.

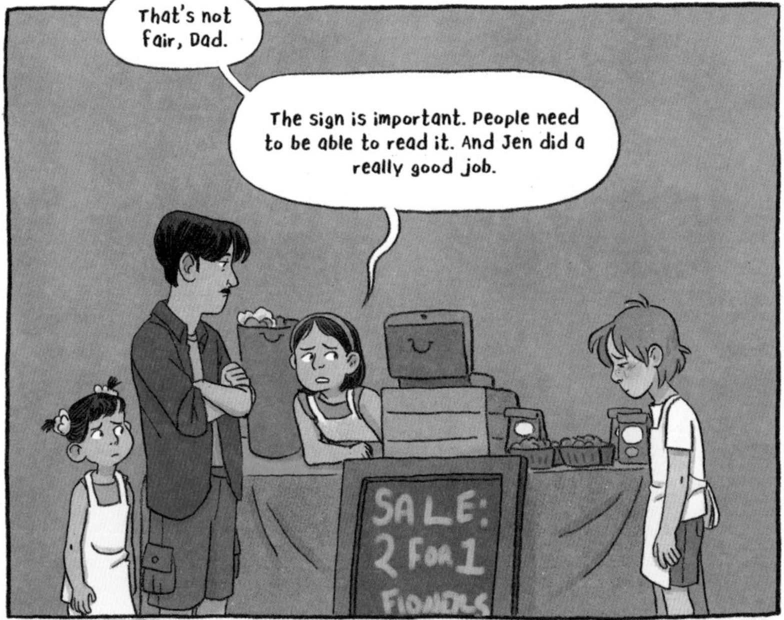
That's not fair, Dad.
The sign is important. People need to be able to read it. And Jen did a really good job.
SALE: 2 FOR 1 FLOWERS

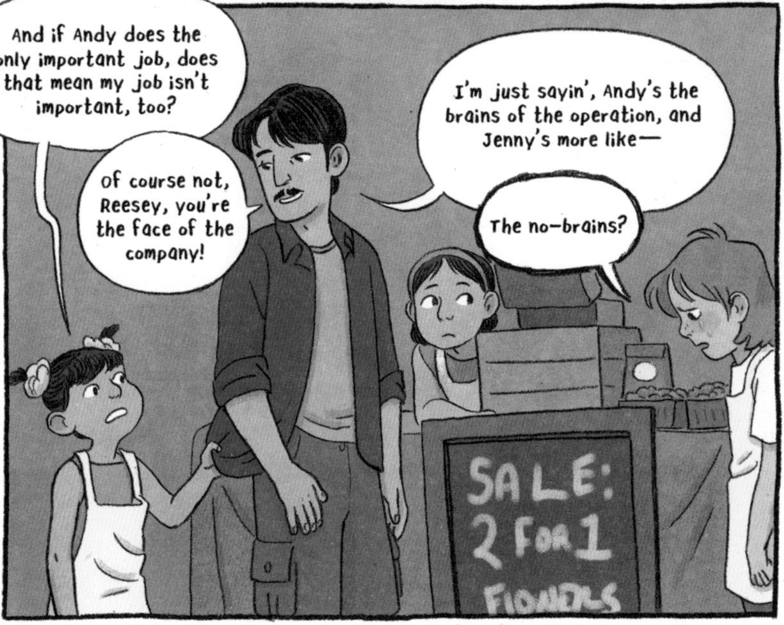
And if Andy does the only important job, does that mean my job isn't important, too?
Of course not, Reesey, you're the face of the company!
I'm just sayin', Andy's the brains of the operation, and Jenny's more like—
The no-brains?
SALE: 2 FOR 1 FLOWERS

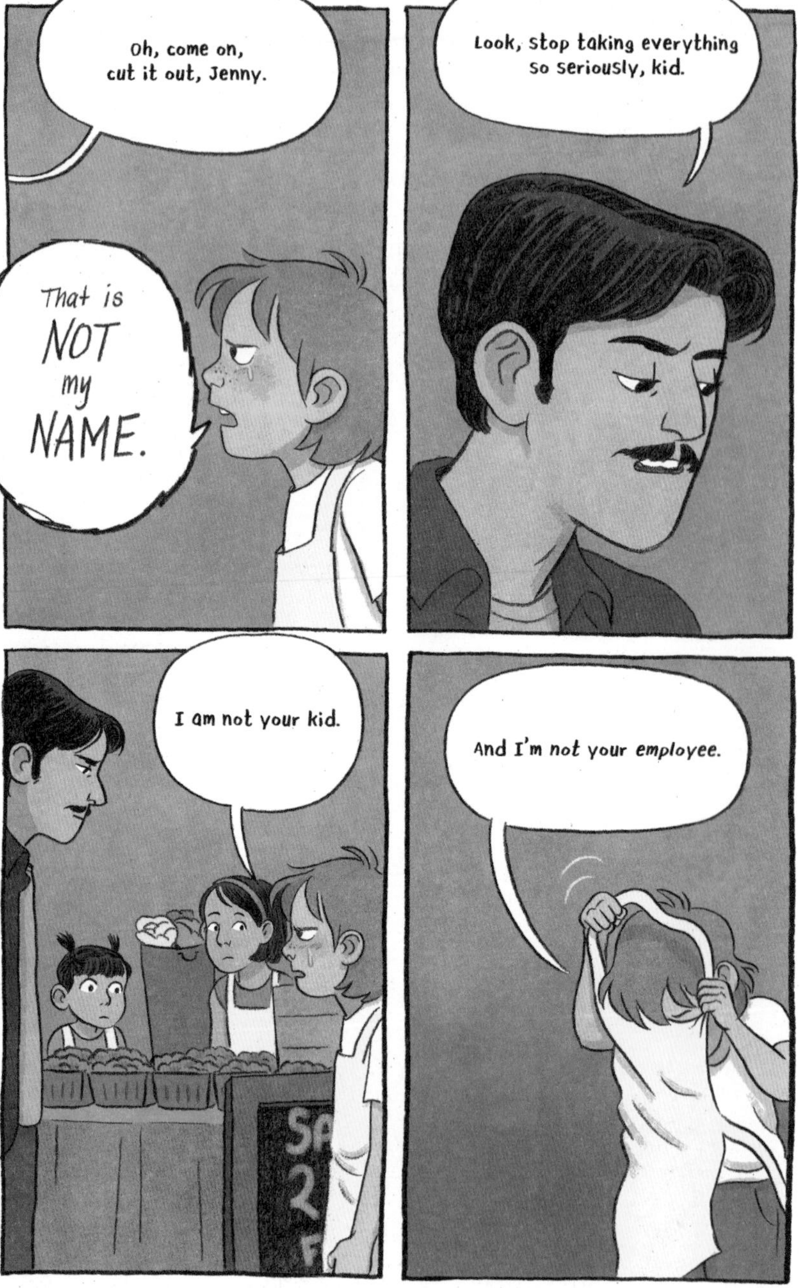
Oh, come on, cut it out, Jenny.
That is NOT my NAME.
Look, stop taking everything so seriously, kid.
I am not your kid.
And I'm *not* your *employee.*

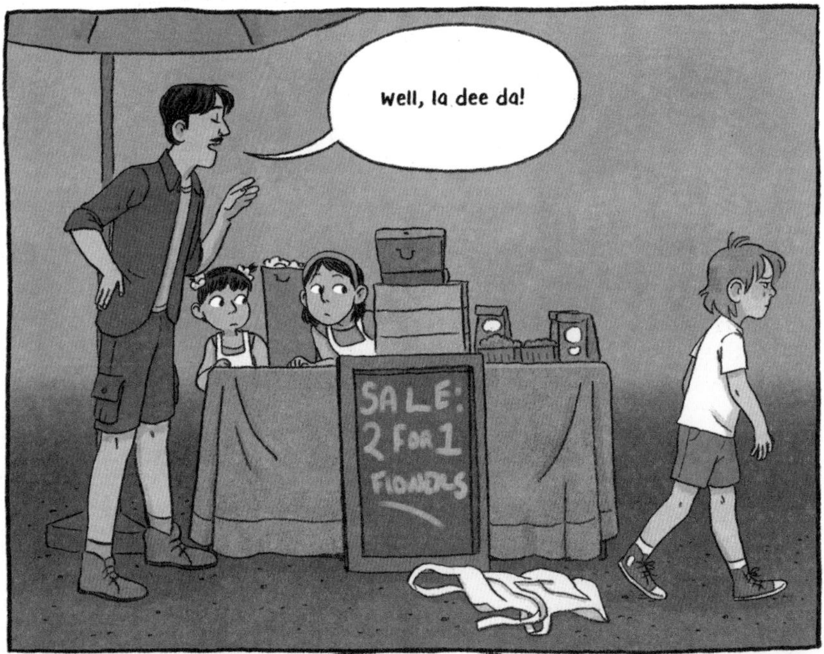
Well, la dee da!
SALE: 2 FOR 1 FLOWERS

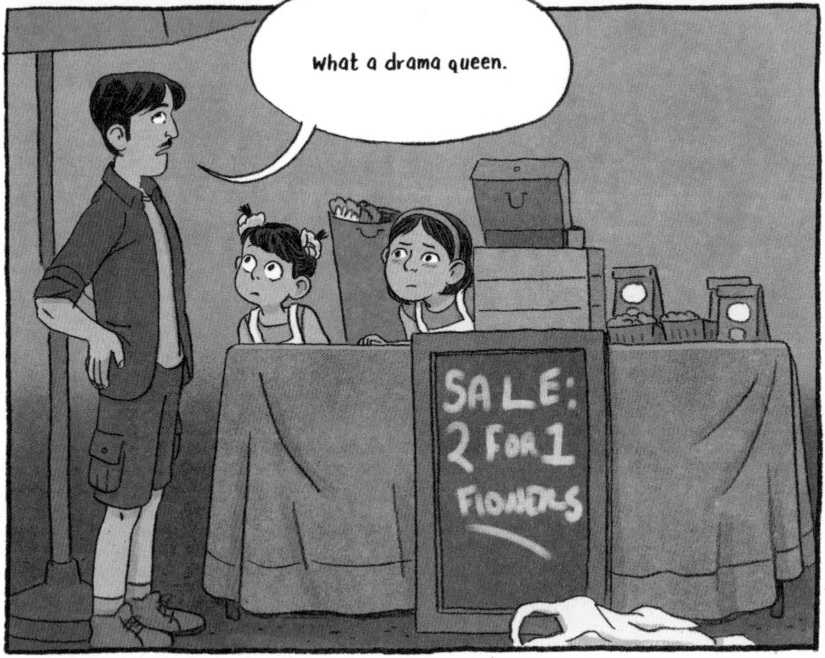
What a drama queen.
SALE: 2 FOR 1 FLOWERS

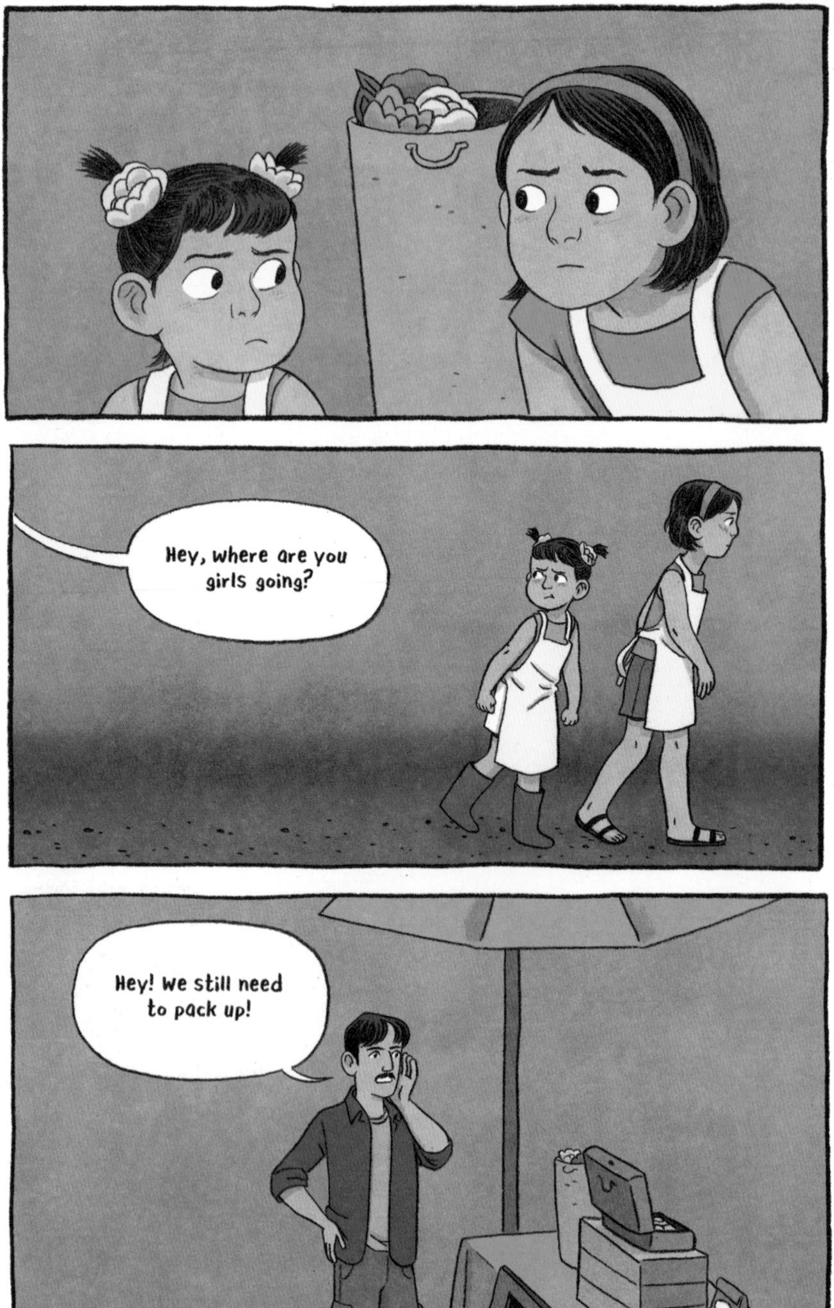
Hey, where are you girls going?
Hey! We still need to pack up!

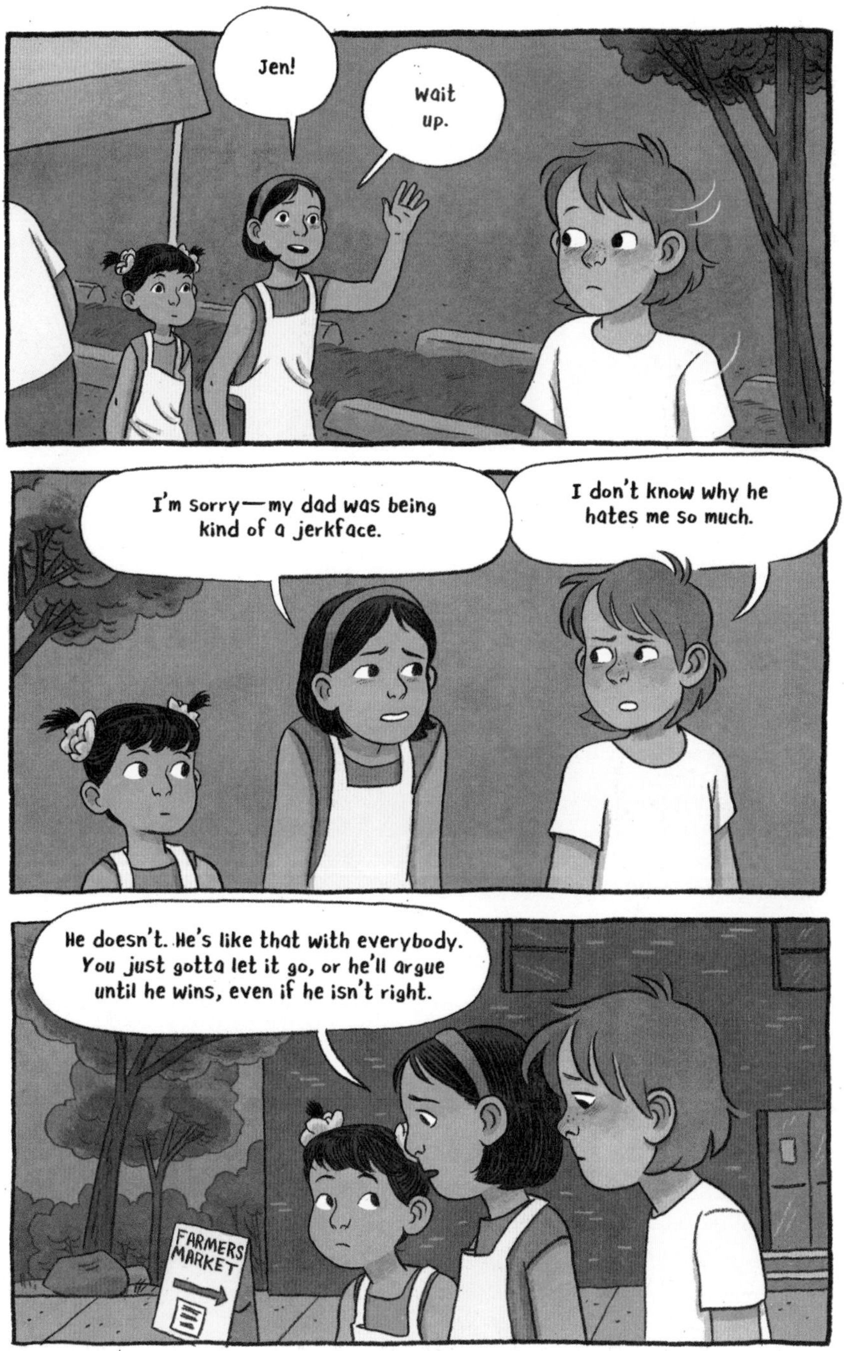
Jen!
Wait up.
I'm sorry—my dad was being kind of a jerkface.
I don't know why he hates me so much.
He doesn't. He's like that with everybody. You just gotta let it go, or he'll argue until he wins, even if he isn't right.
FARMERS MARKET

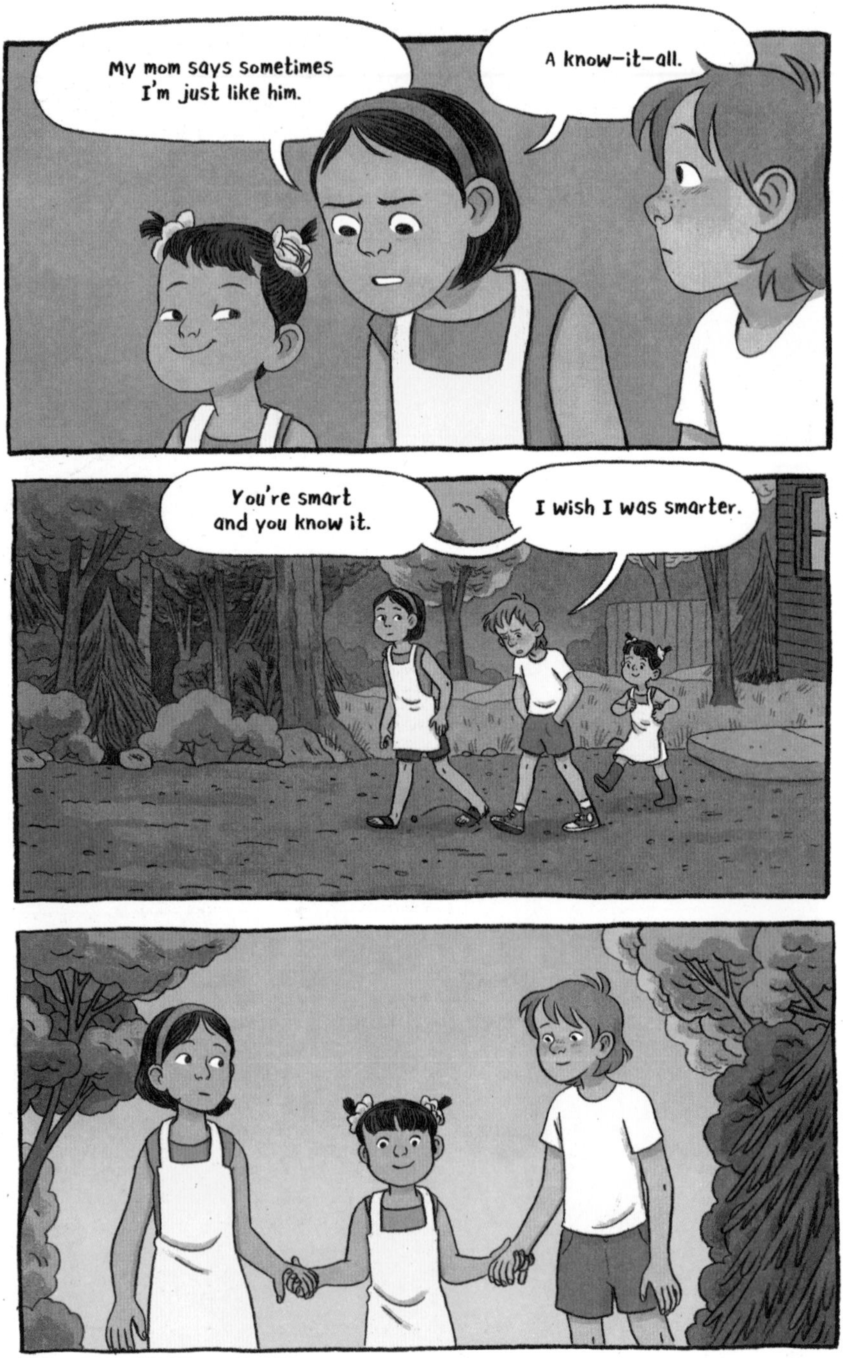
My mom says sometimes I'm just like him.
A know-it-all.
You're smart and you know it.
I wish I was smarter.

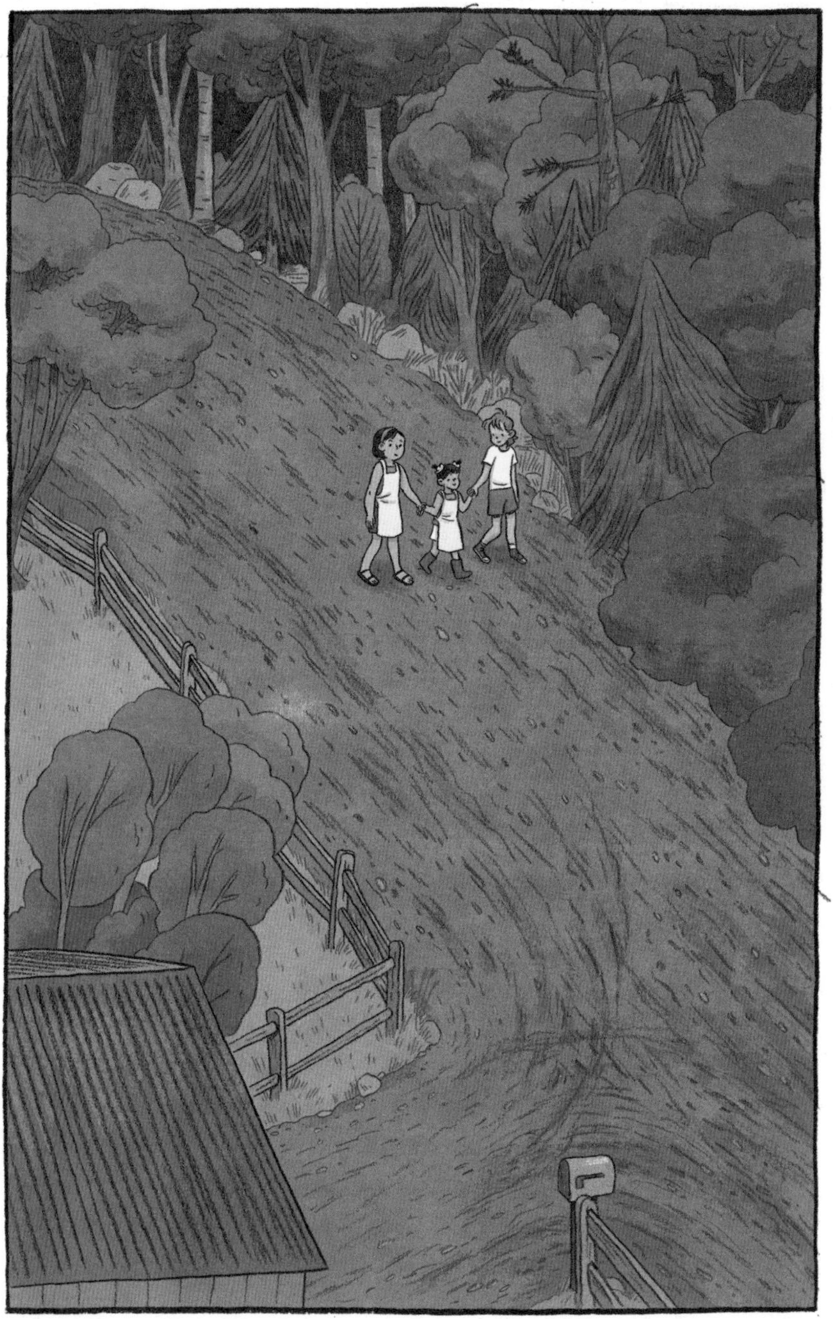

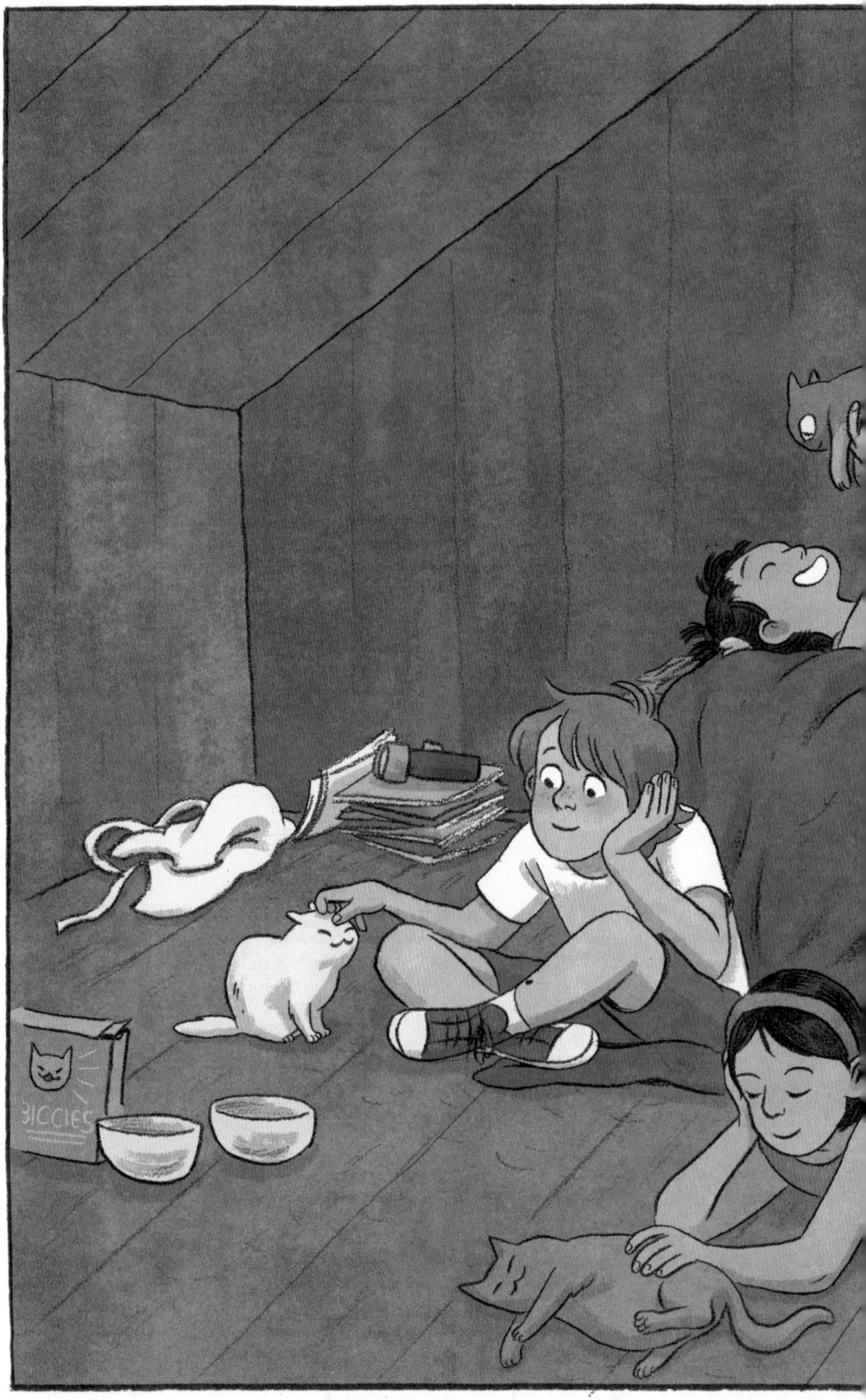
BICCIES

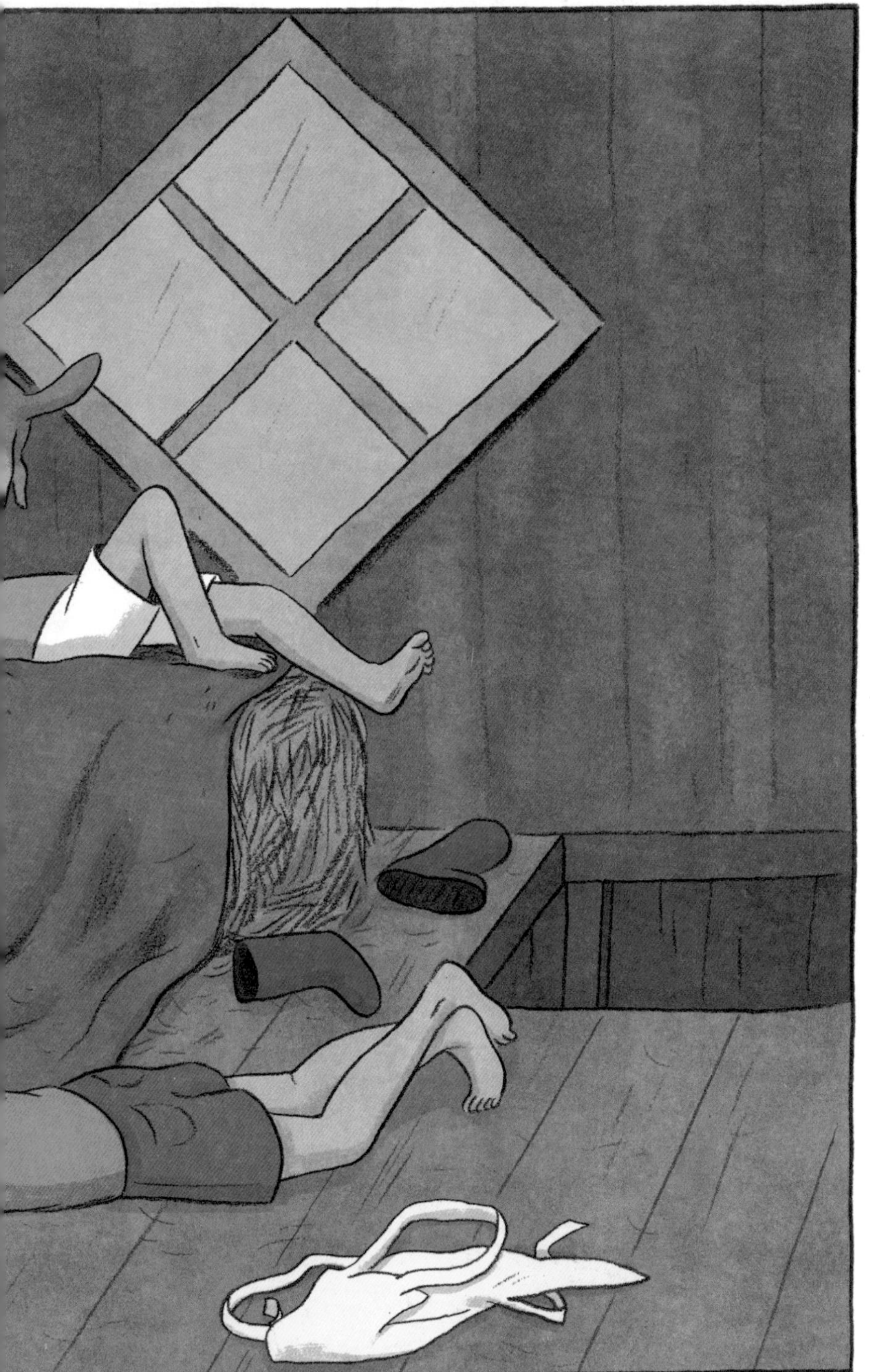

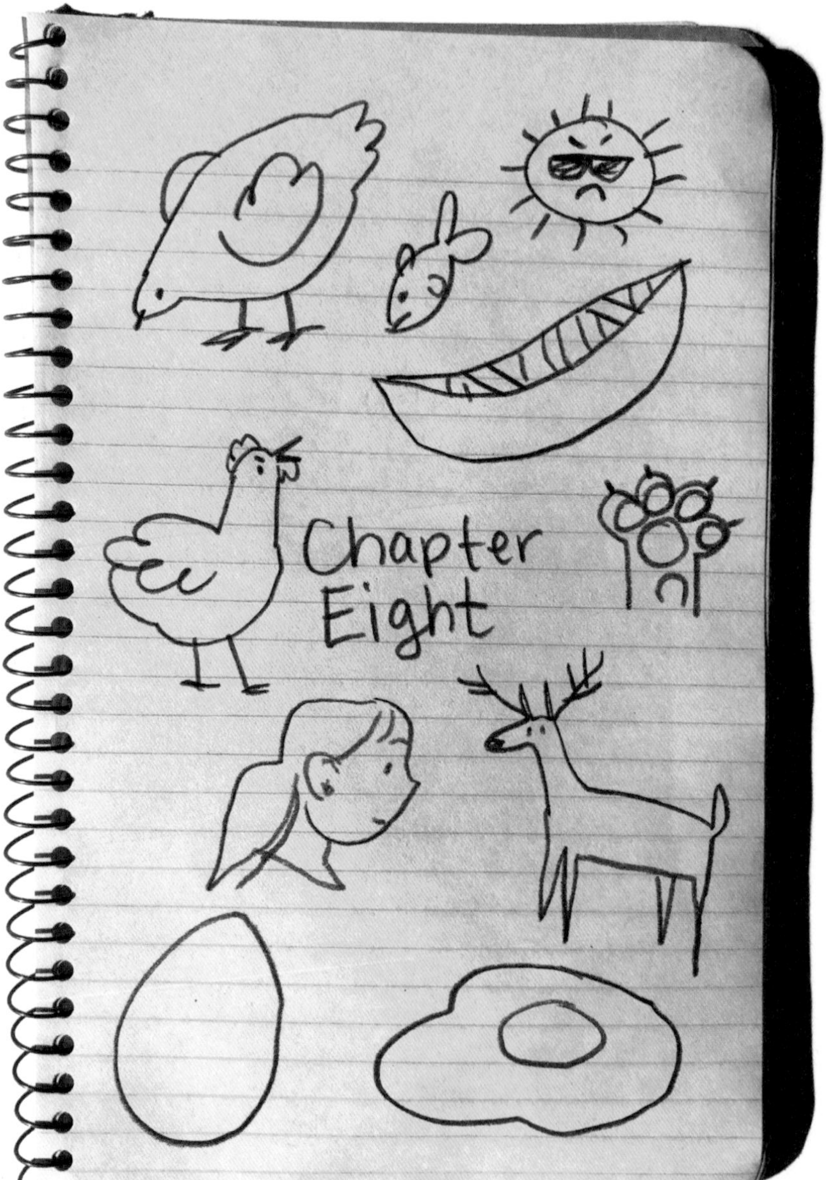
Chapter
Eight

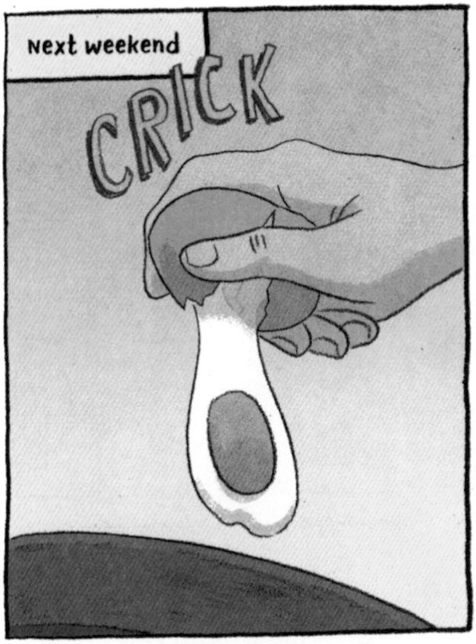
Next weekend
CRICK

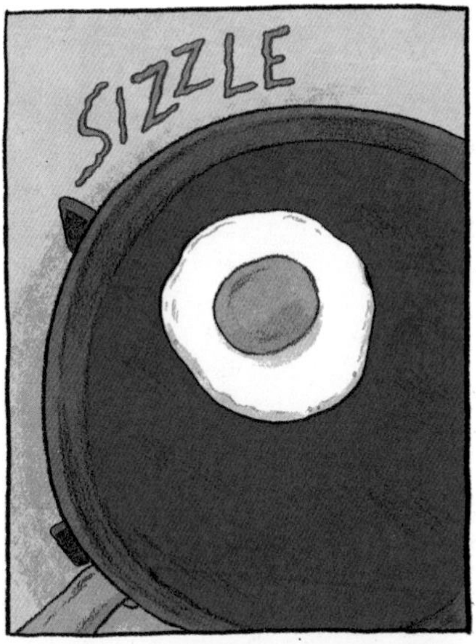
SIZZLE

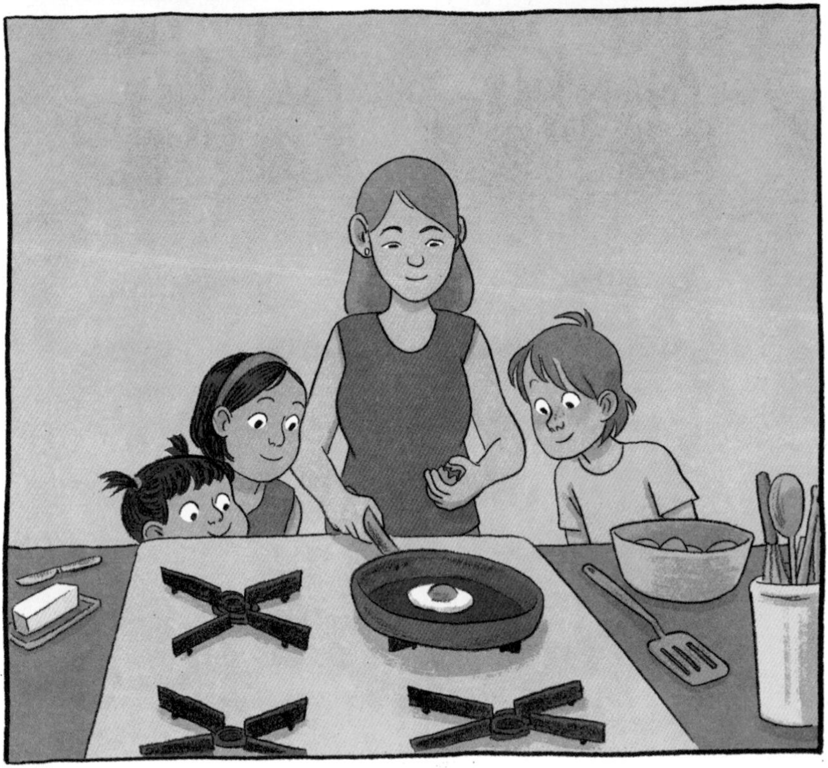

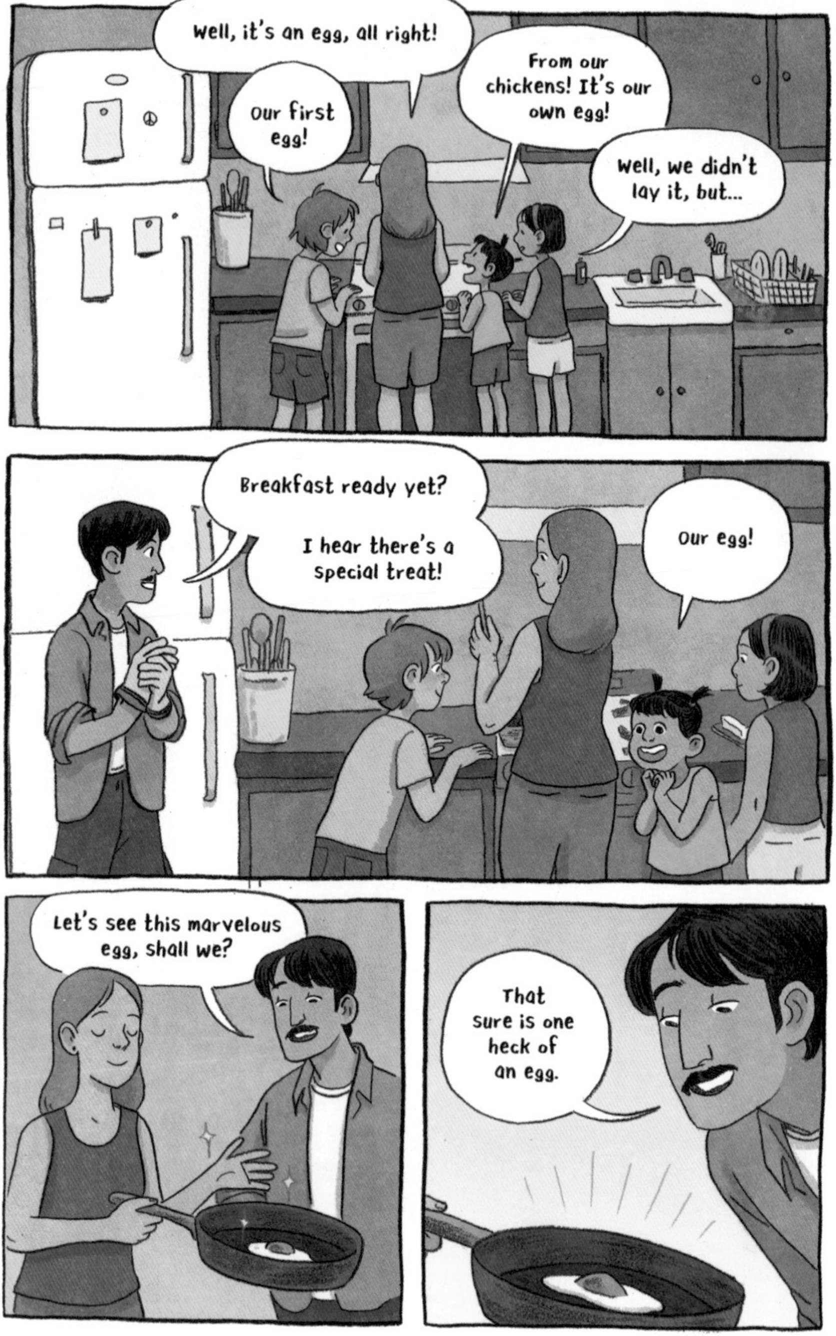
Well, it's an egg, all right!
Our first egg!
From our chickens! It's our own egg!
Well, we didn't lay it, but...
Breakfast ready yet?
I hear there's a special treat!
Our egg!
Let's see this marvelous egg, shall we?
That sure is one heck of an egg.

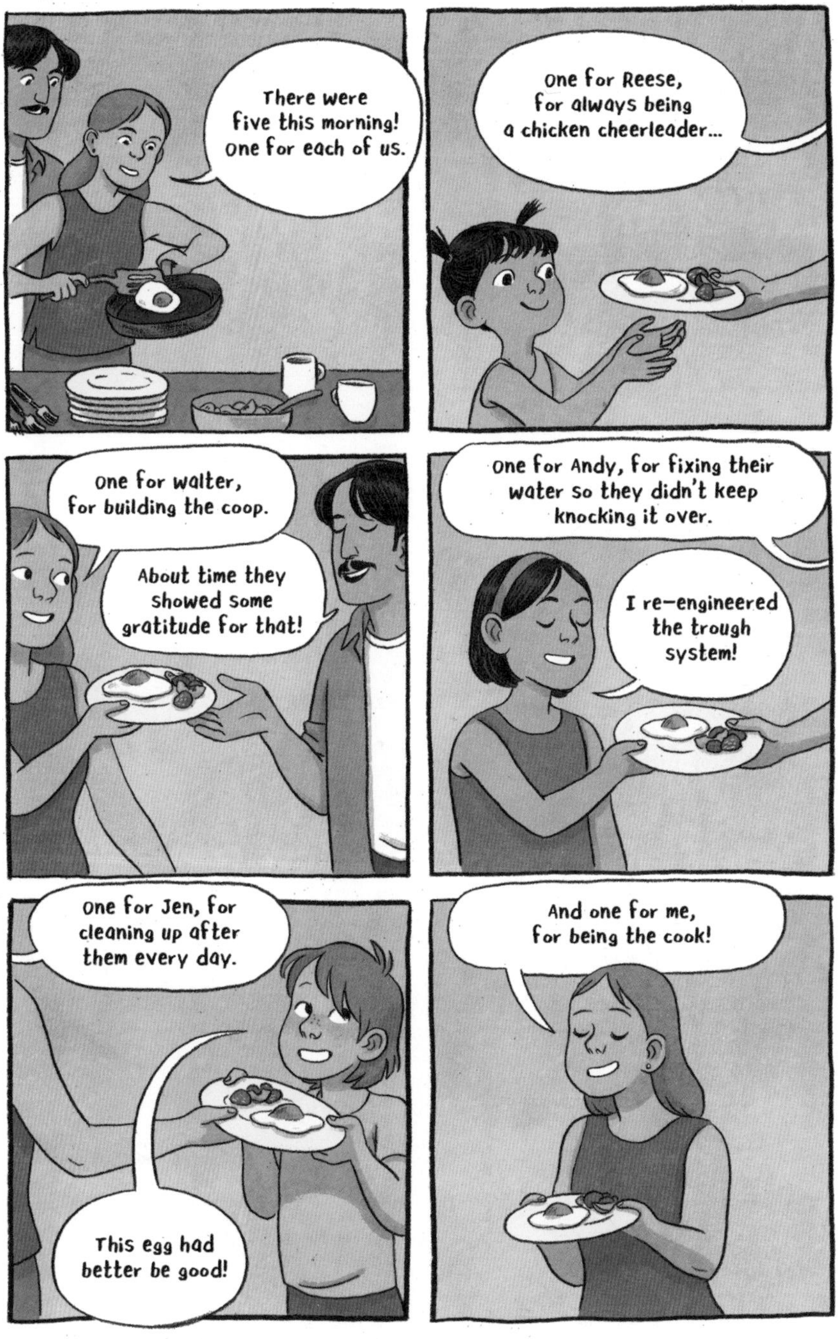

There were five this morning! One for each of us.
One for Reese, for always being a chicken cheerleader...
One for Walter, for building the coop.
About time they showed some gratitude for that!
One for Andy, for fixing their water so they didn't keep knocking it over.
I re-engineered the trough system!
One for Jen, for cleaning up after them every day.
This egg had better be good!
And one for me, for being the cook!

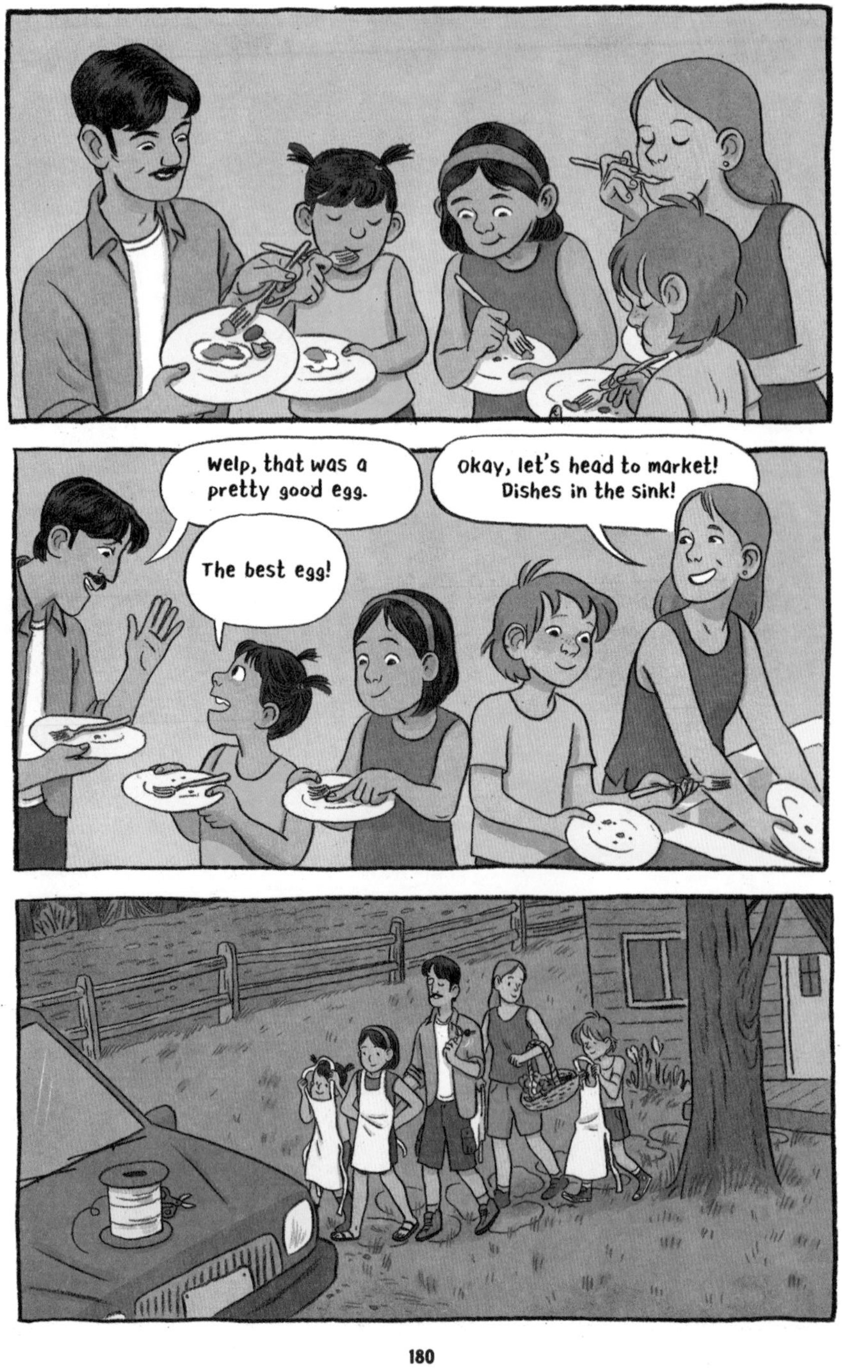
Welp, that was a pretty good egg.
The best egg!
Okay, let's head to market! Dishes in the sink!

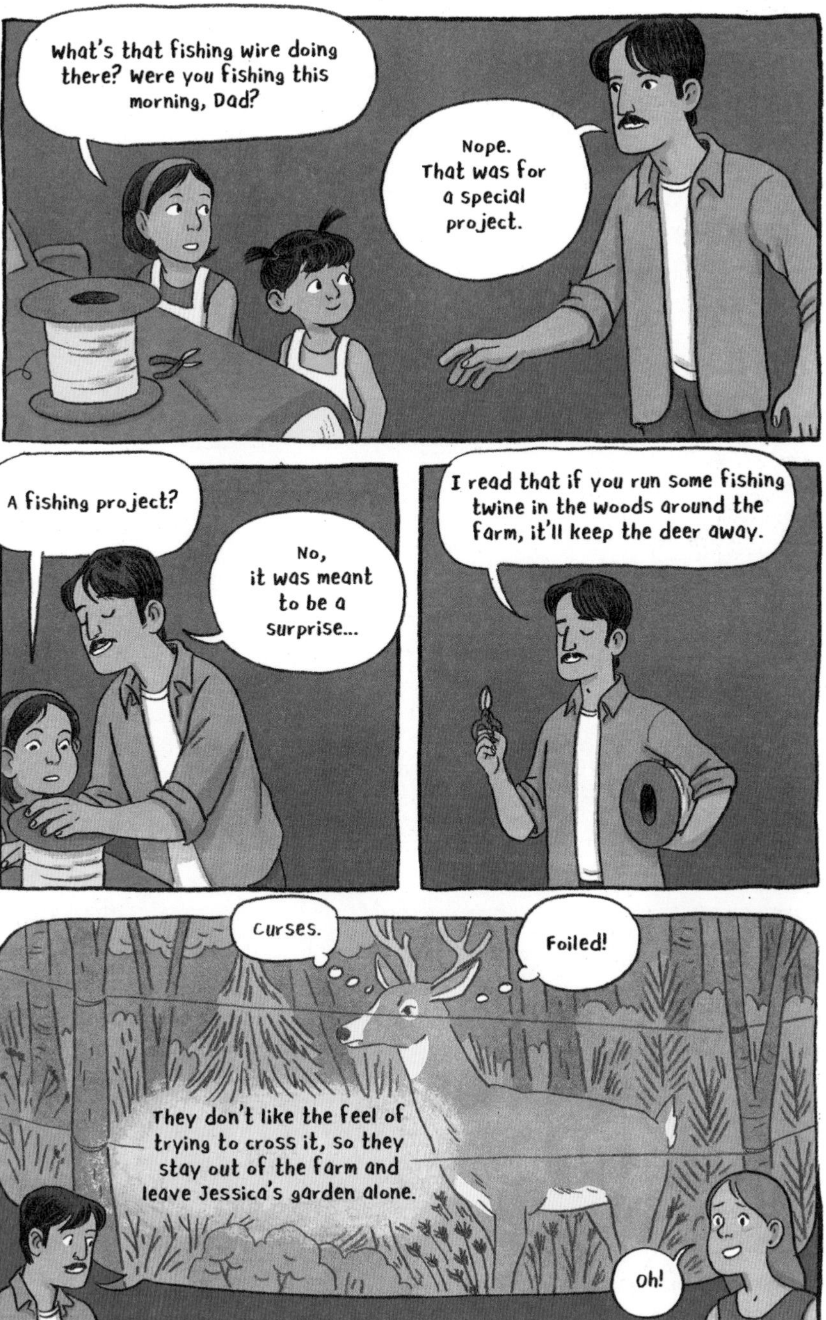
What's that fishing wire doing there? Were you fishing this morning, Dad?
Nope. That was for a special project.
A fishing project?
No, it was meant to be a surprise...
I read that if you run some fishing twine in the woods around the farm, it'll keep the deer away.
Curses.
Foiled!
They don't like the feel of trying to cross it, so they stay out of the farm and leave Jessica's garden alone.
Oh!

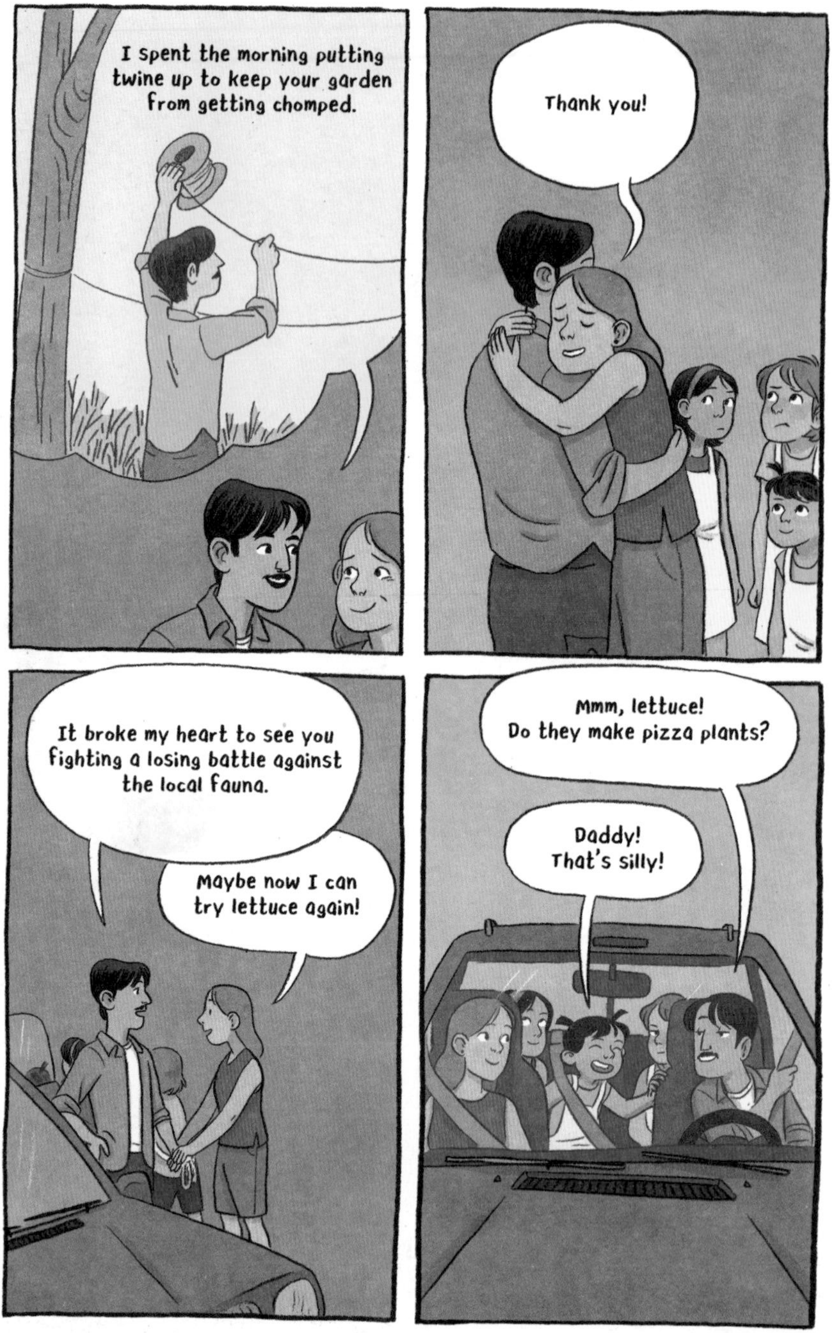
I spent the morning putting twine up to keep your garden from getting chomped.
Thank you!
It broke my heart to see you fighting a losing battle against the local fauna.
Maybe now I can try lettuce again!
Mmm, lettuce! Do they make pizza plants?
Daddy! That's silly!

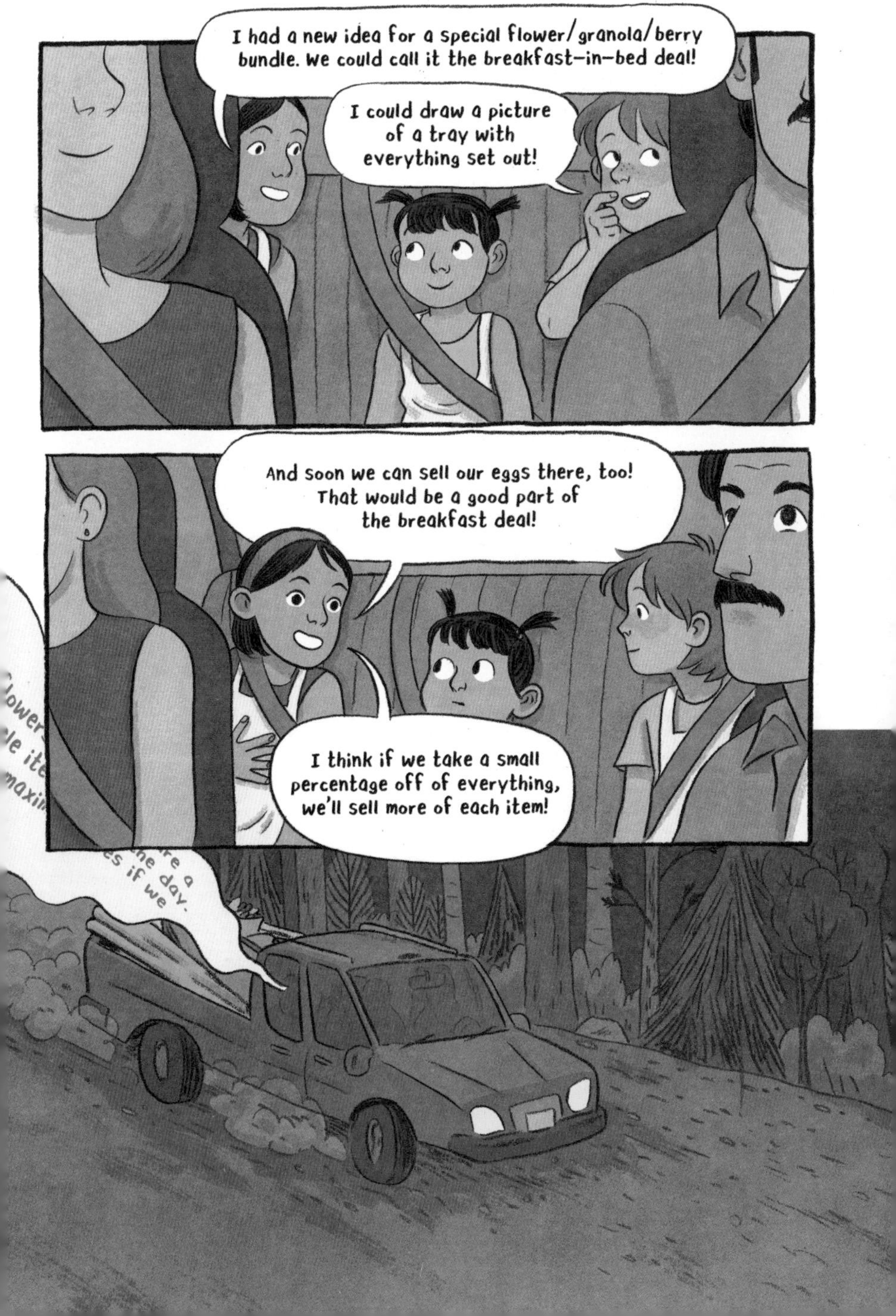
I had a new idea for a special flower/granola/berry bundle. We could call it the breakfast-in-bed deal!
I could draw a picture of a tray with everything set out!
And soon we can sell our eggs there, too! That would be a good part of the breakfast deal!
I think if we take a small percentage off of everything, we'll sell more of each item!

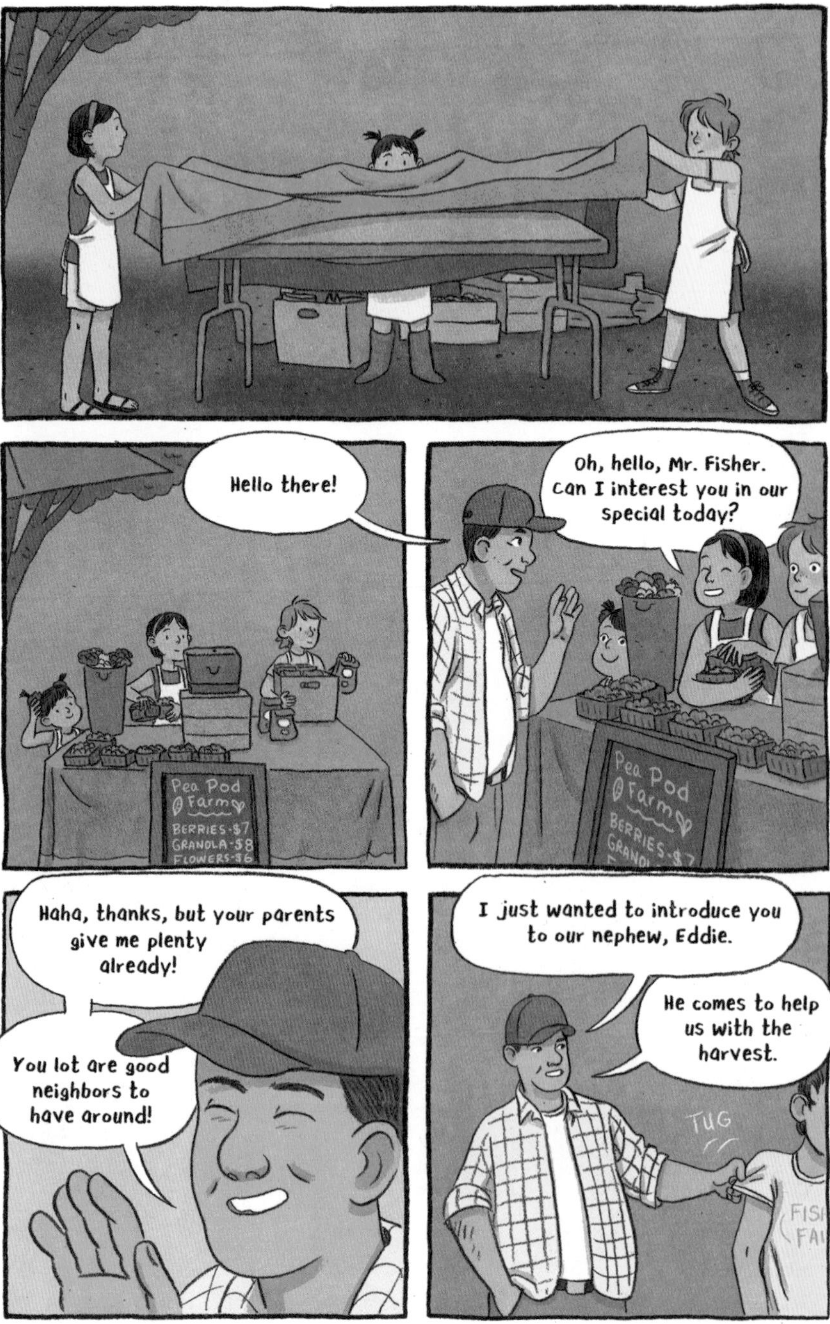
Hello there!
Oh, hello, Mr. Fisher. Can I interest you in our special today?
Pea Pod Farm
BERRIES-$7
GRANOLA-$8
FLOWERS-$6
Haha, thanks, but your parents give me plenty already!
You lot are good neighbors to have around!
I just wanted to introduce you to our nephew, Eddie.
He comes to help us with the harvest.
TUG

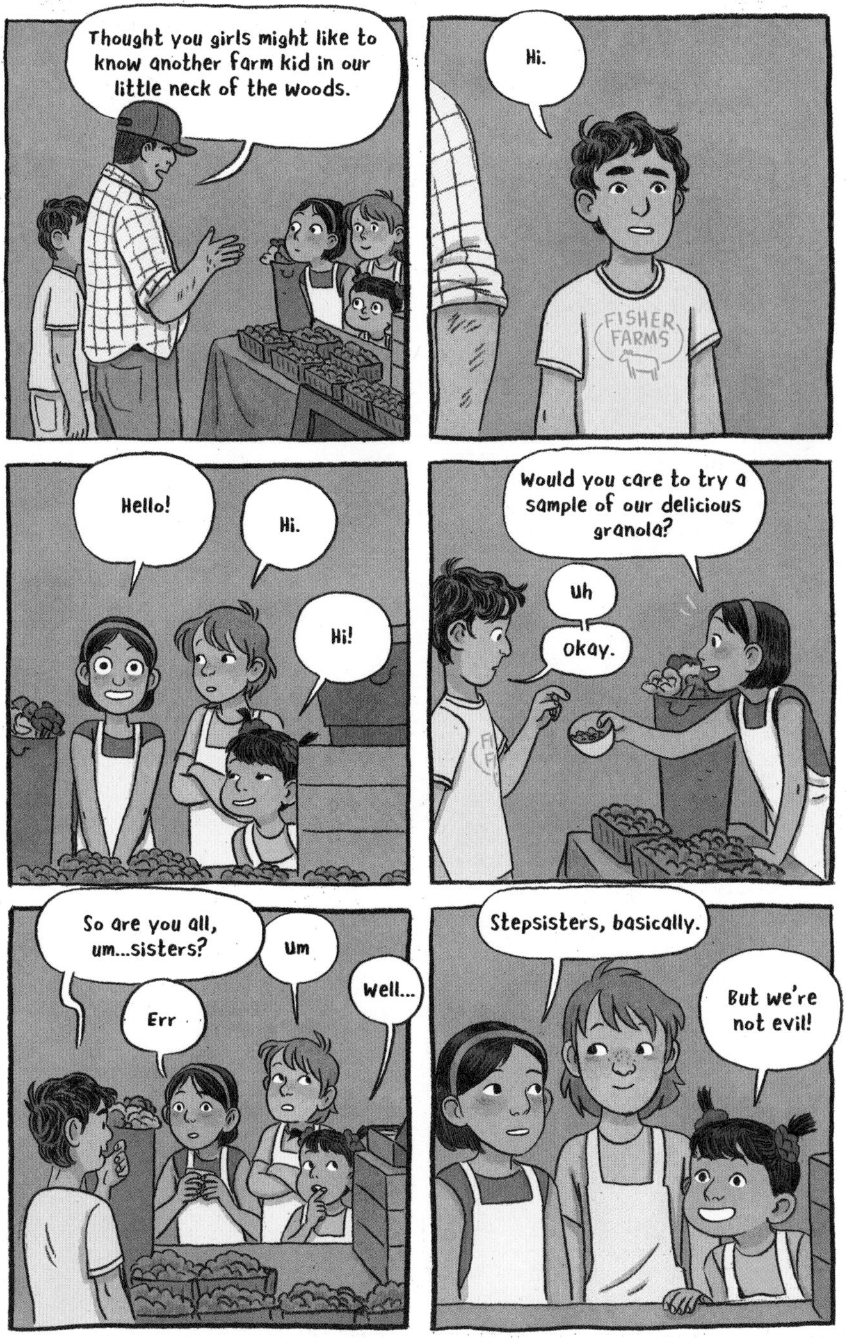
Thought you girls might like to know another farm kid in our little neck of the woods.
Hi.
FISHER FARMS
Hello!
Hi.
Hi!
Would you care to try a sample of our delicious granola?
Uh
okay.
So are you all, um...sisters?
Err
Um
Well...
Stepsisters, basically.
But we're not evil!

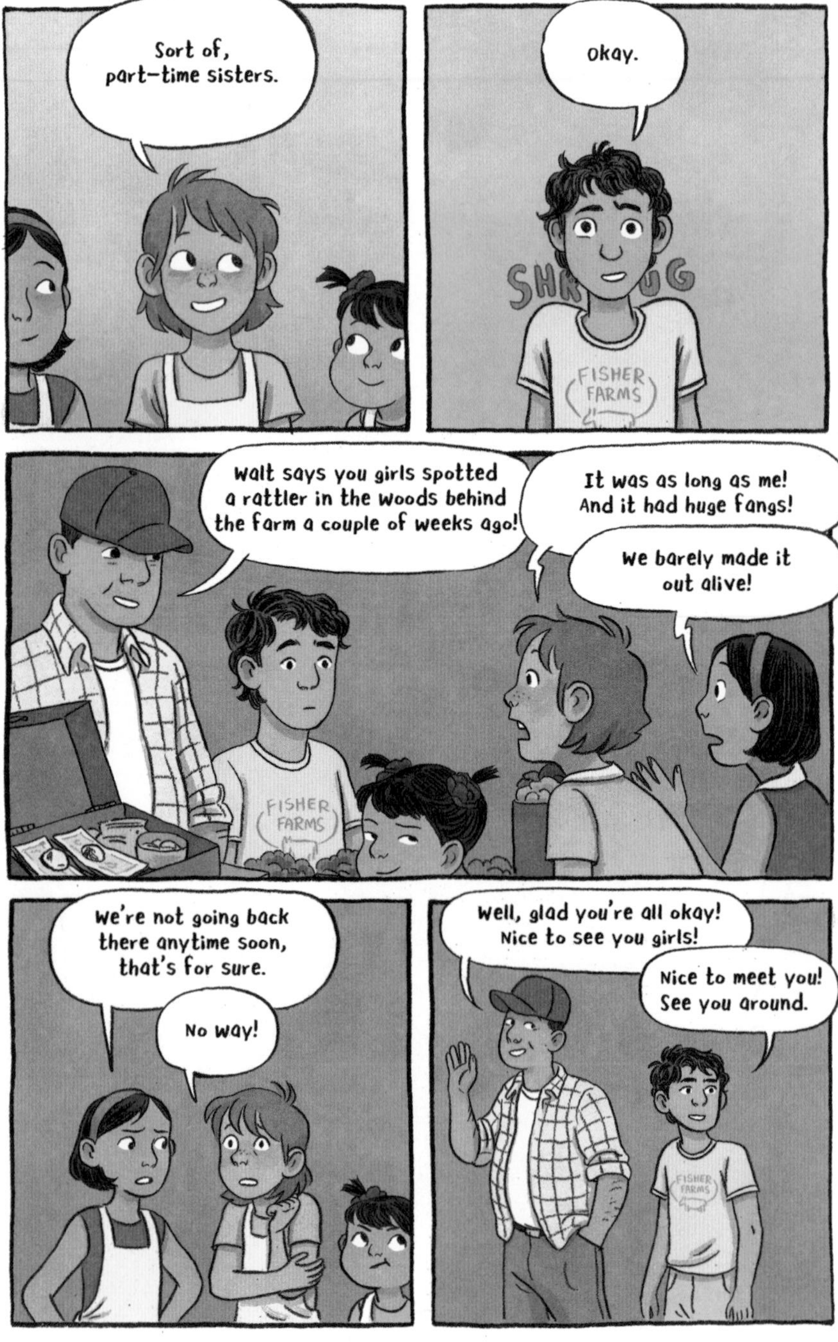
Sort of, part-time sisters.
Okay.
SHRUG
FISHER FARMS
Walt says you girls spotted a rattler in the woods behind the farm a couple of weeks ago!
It was as long as me! And it had huge fangs!
We barely made it out alive!
FISHER FARMS
We're not going back there anytime soon, that's for sure.
No way!
Well, glad you're all okay! Nice to see you girls!
Nice to meet you! See you around.
FISHER FARMS

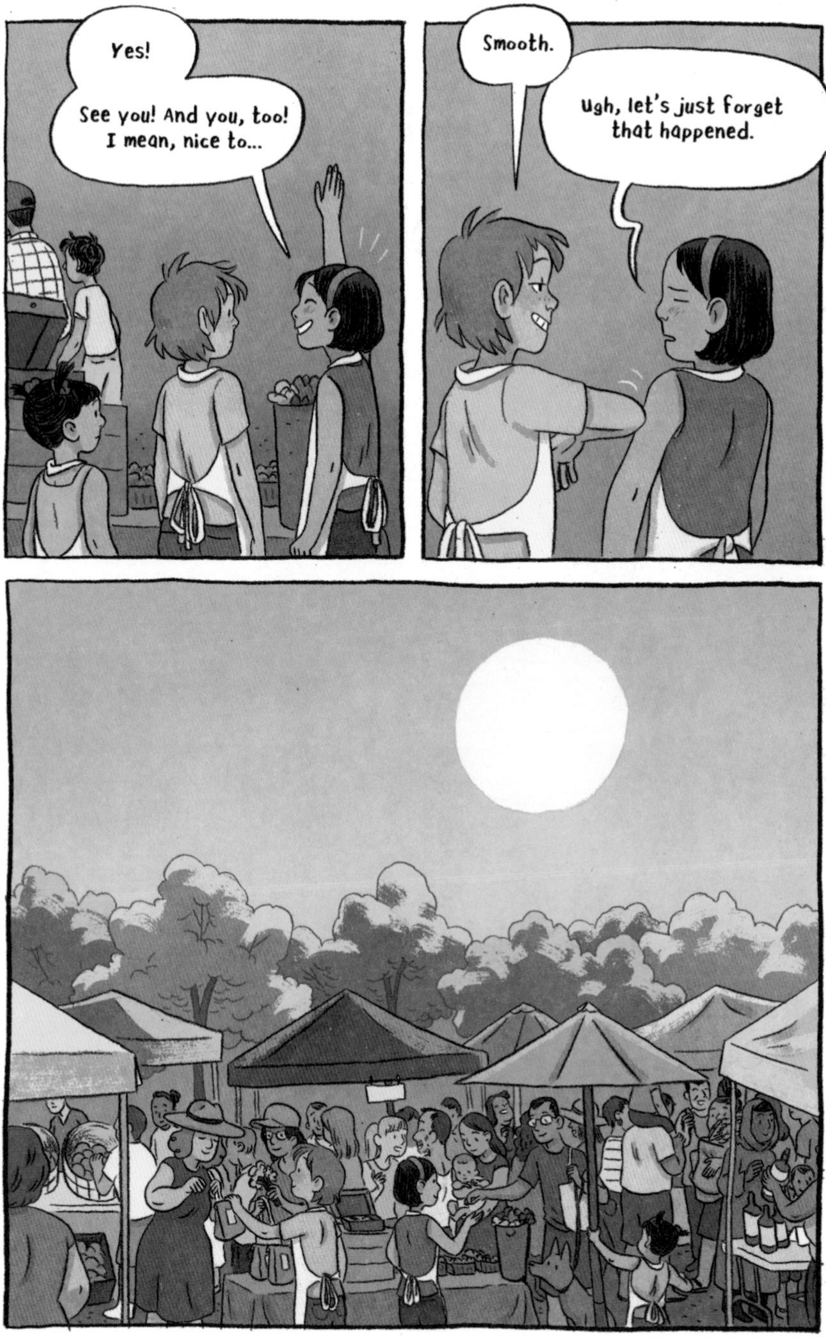
Yes!
See you! And you, too! I mean, nice to...
Smooth.
Ugh, let's just forget that happened.

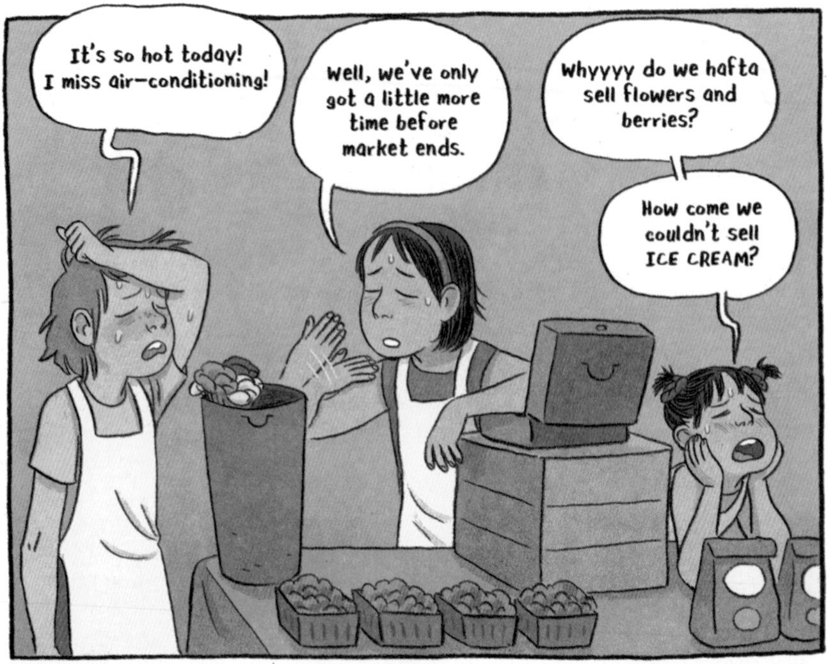
It's so hot today! I miss air-conditioning!
Well, we've only got a little more time before market ends.
Whyyyy do we hafta sell flowers and berries?
How come we couldn't sell ICE CREAM?

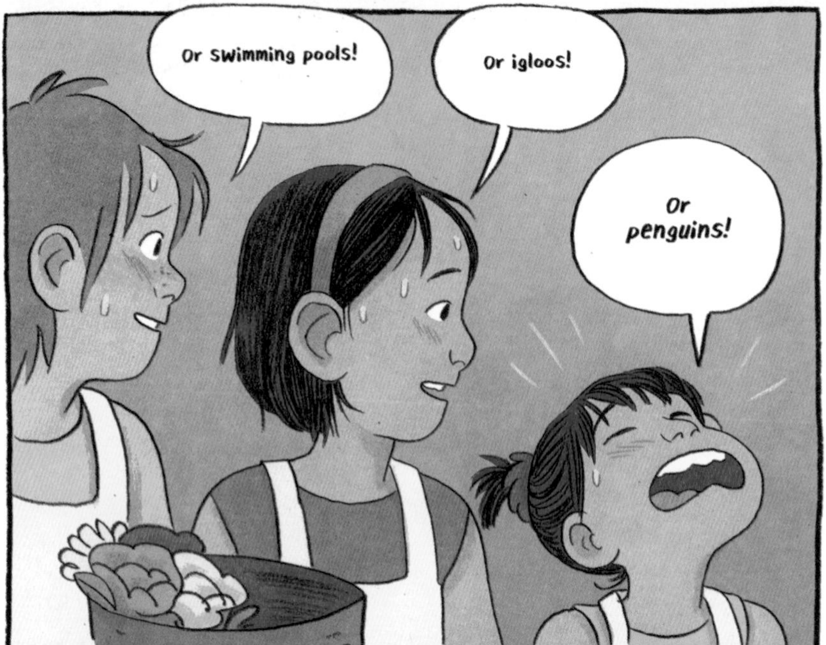
Or swimming pools!
Or igloos!
Or penguins!

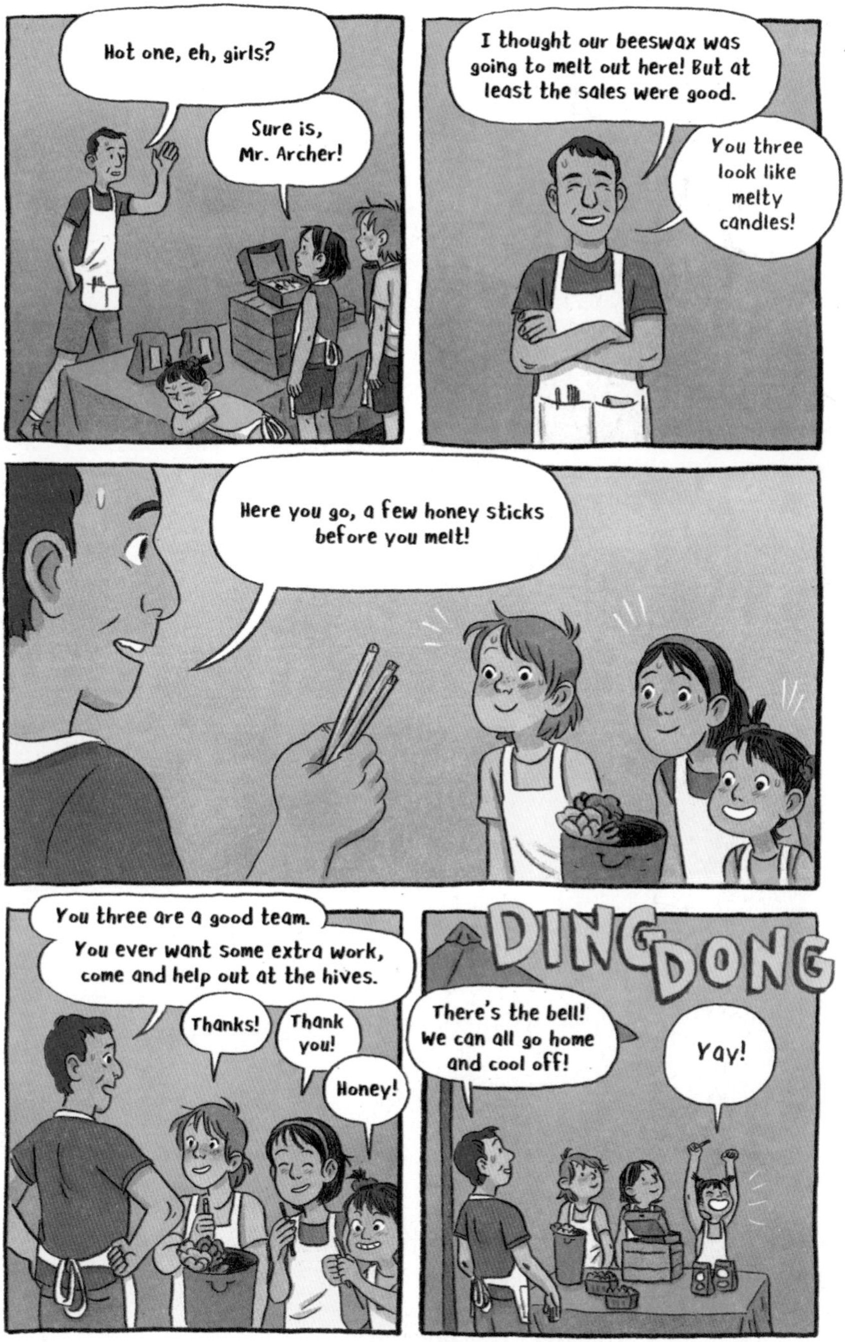
Hot one, eh, girls?
Sure is, Mr. Archer!
I thought our beeswax was going to melt out here! But at least the sales were good.
You three look like melty candles!
Here you go, a few honey sticks before you melt!
You three are a good team.
You ever want some extra work, come and help out at the hives.
Thanks!
Thank you!
Honey!
DING DONG
There's the bell! We can all go home and cool off!
Yay!

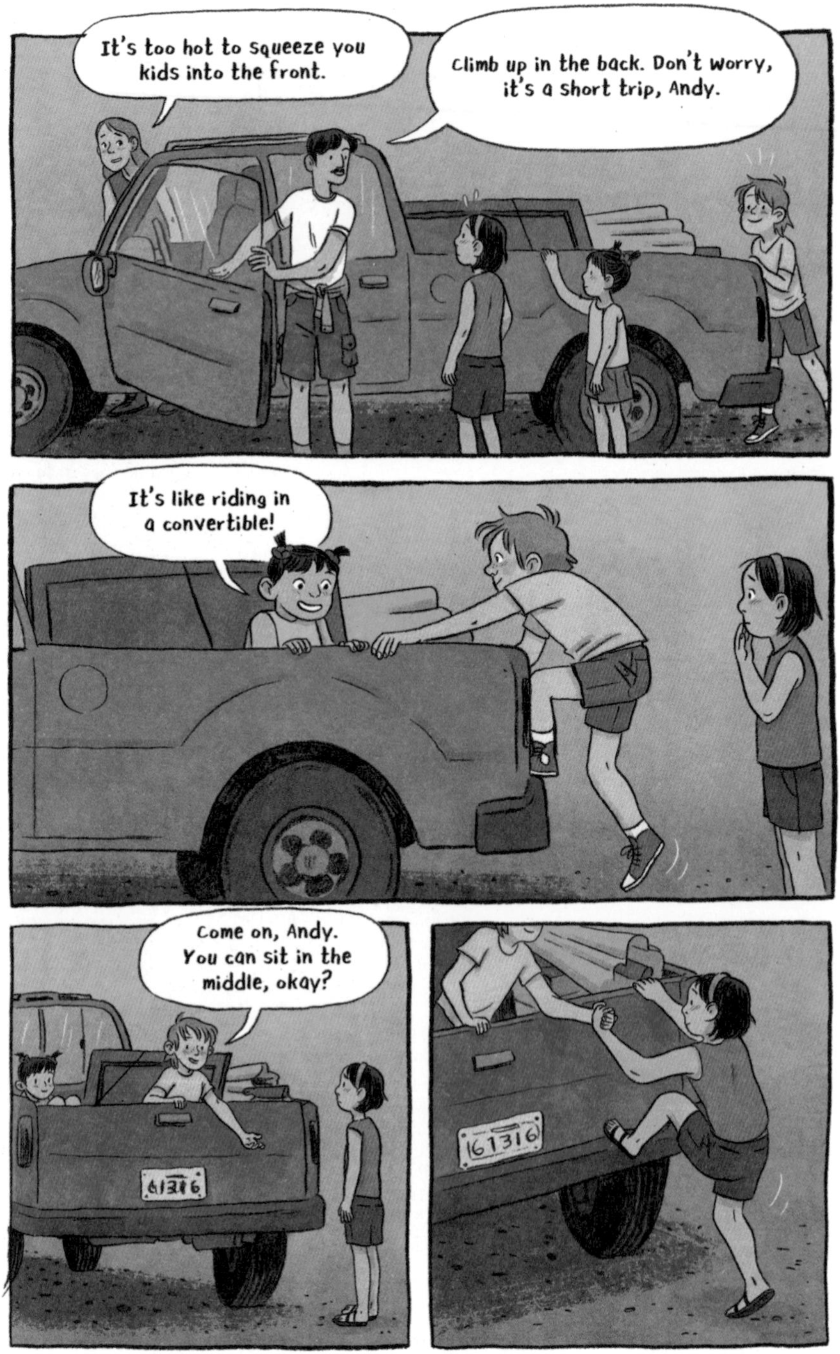
It's too hot to squeeze you kids into the front.
Climb up in the back. Don't worry, it's a short trip, Andy.
It's like riding in a convertible!
Come on, Andy. You can sit in the middle, okay?
61316
61316

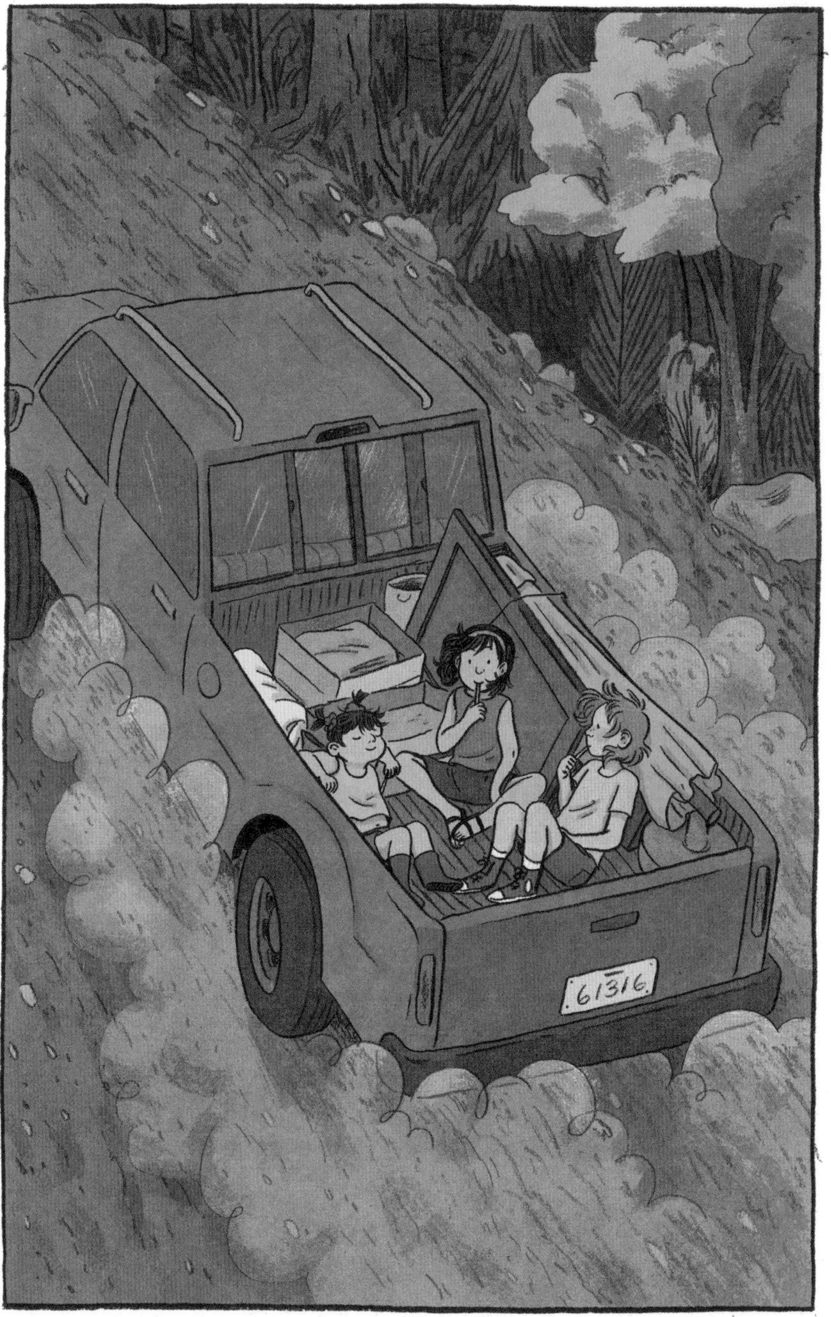
61316

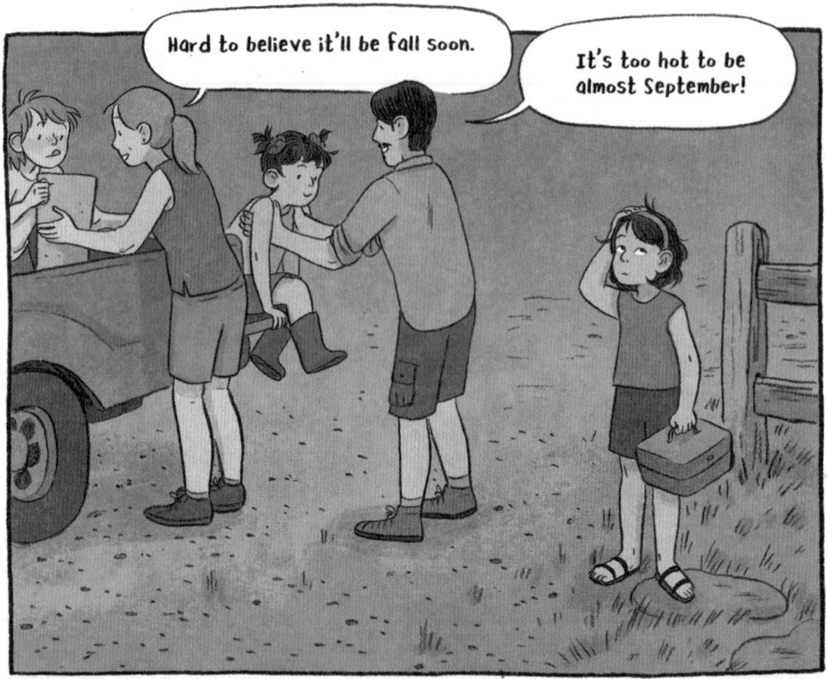
Hard to believe it'll be fall soon.
It's too hot to be almost September!

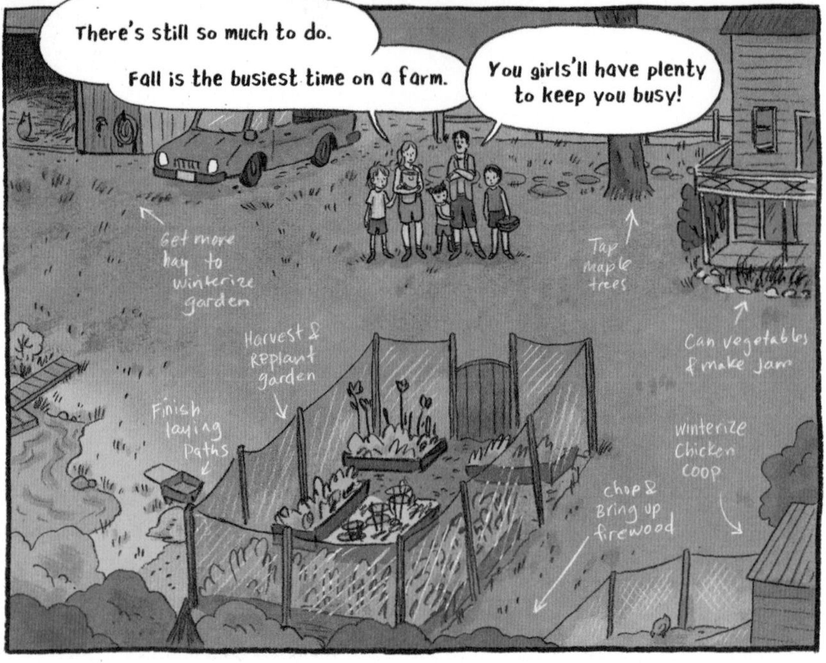
There's still so much to do.
Fall is the busiest time on a farm.
You girls'll have plenty to keep you busy!
Get more hay to winterize garden
Tap maple trees
Can vegetables & make jam
Harvest & Replant garden
Finish laying paths
Winterize chicken coop
Chop & Bring up firewood

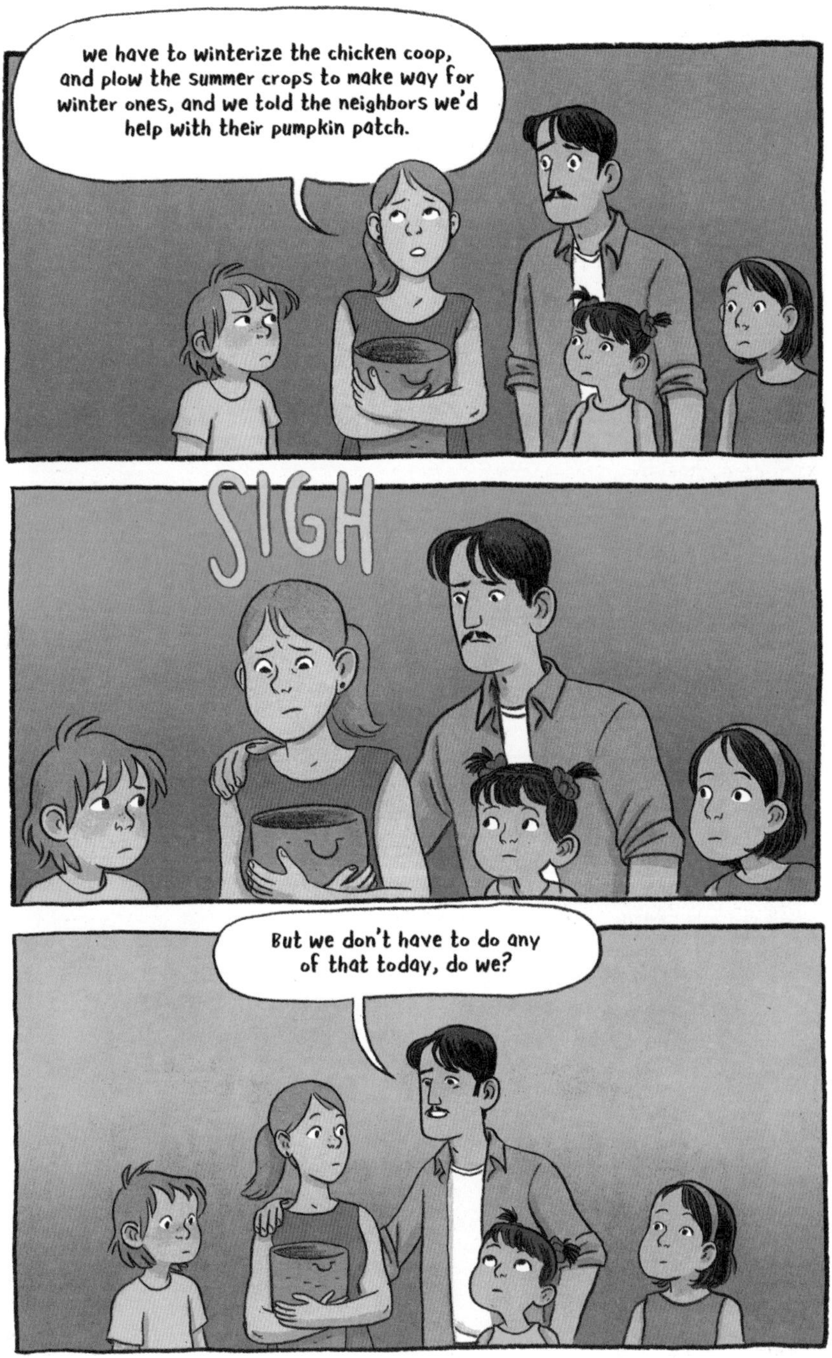
we have to winterize the chicken coop, and plow the summer crops to make way for winter ones, and we told the neighbors we'd help with their pumpkin patch.
SIGH
But we don't have to do any of that today, do we?

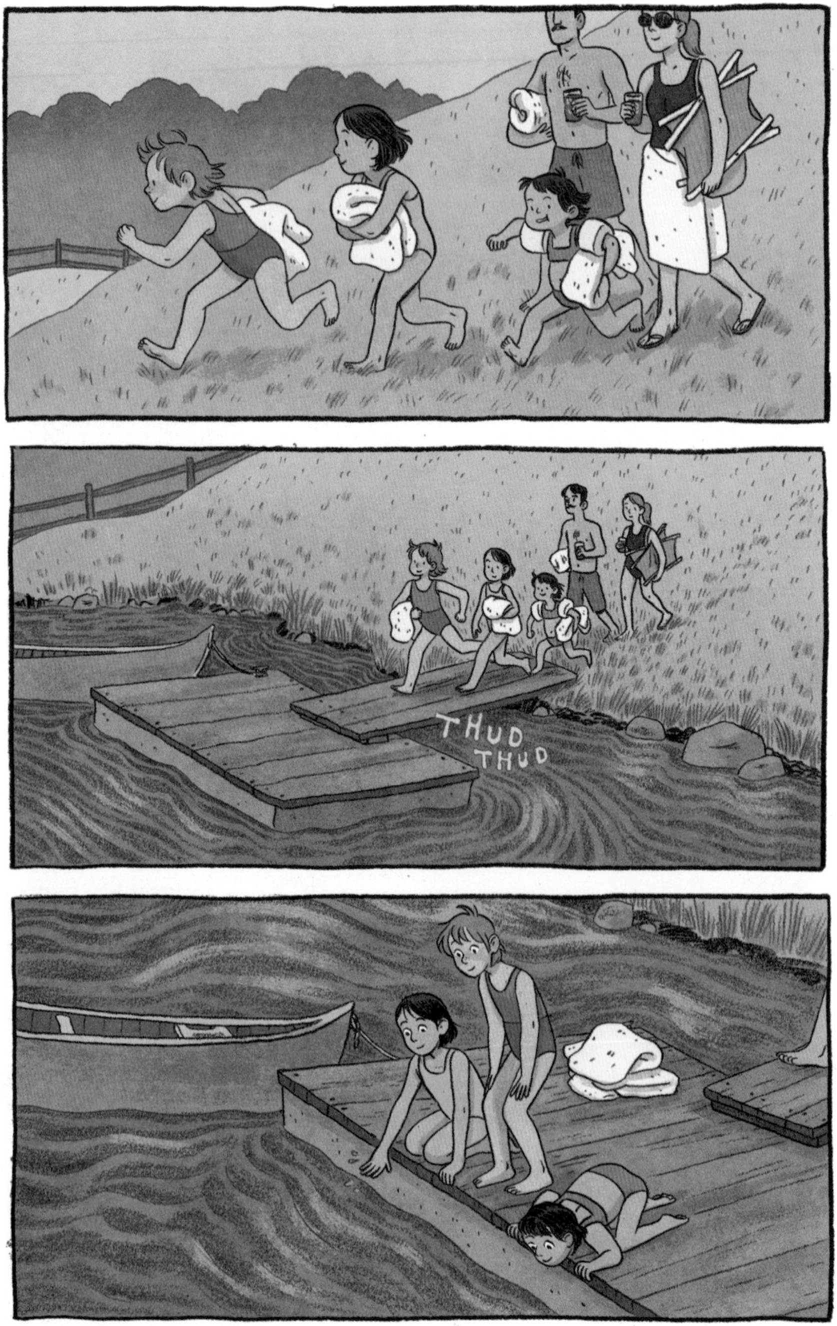
THUD
THUD

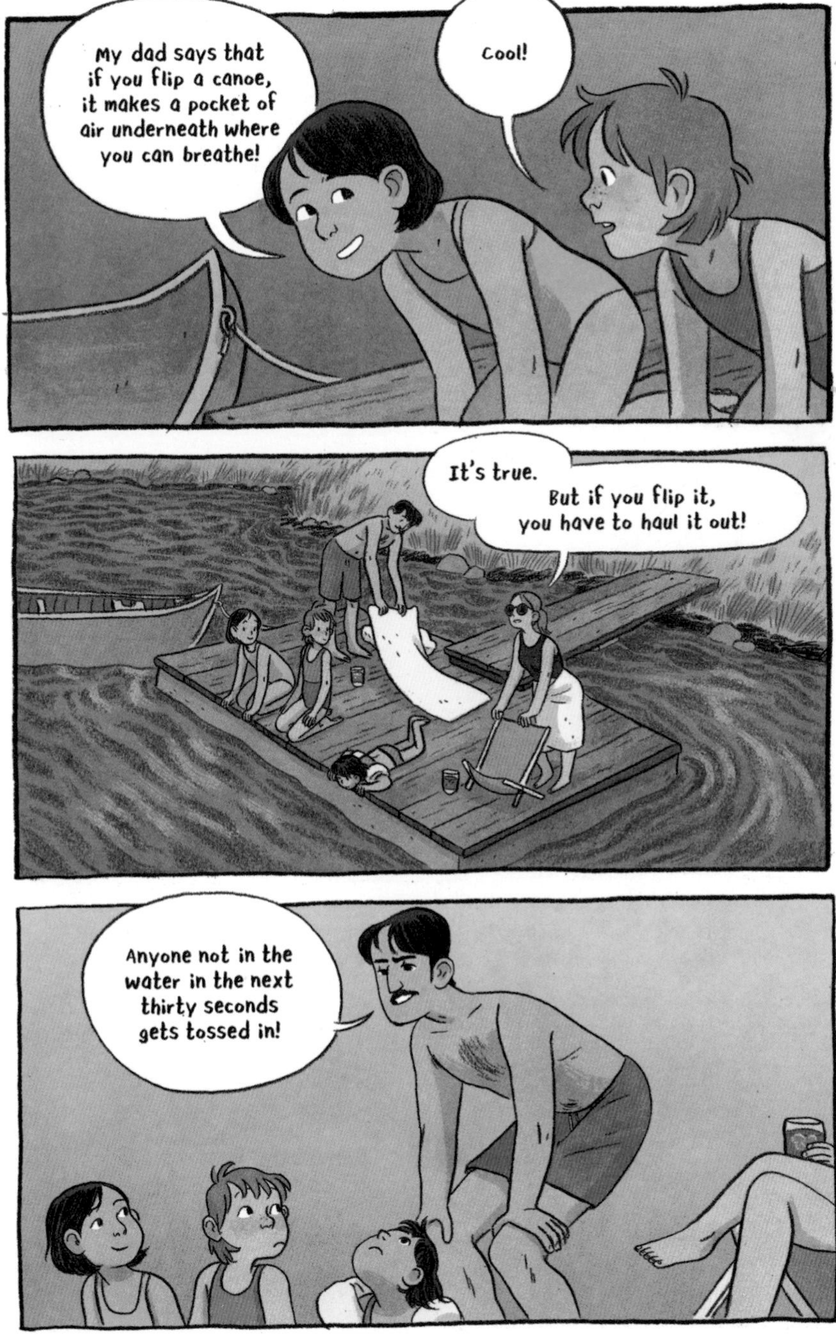
My dad says that if you flip a canoe, it makes a pocket of air underneath where you can breathe!
Cool!
It's true.
But if you flip it, you have to haul it out!
Anyone not in the water in the next thirty seconds gets tossed in!

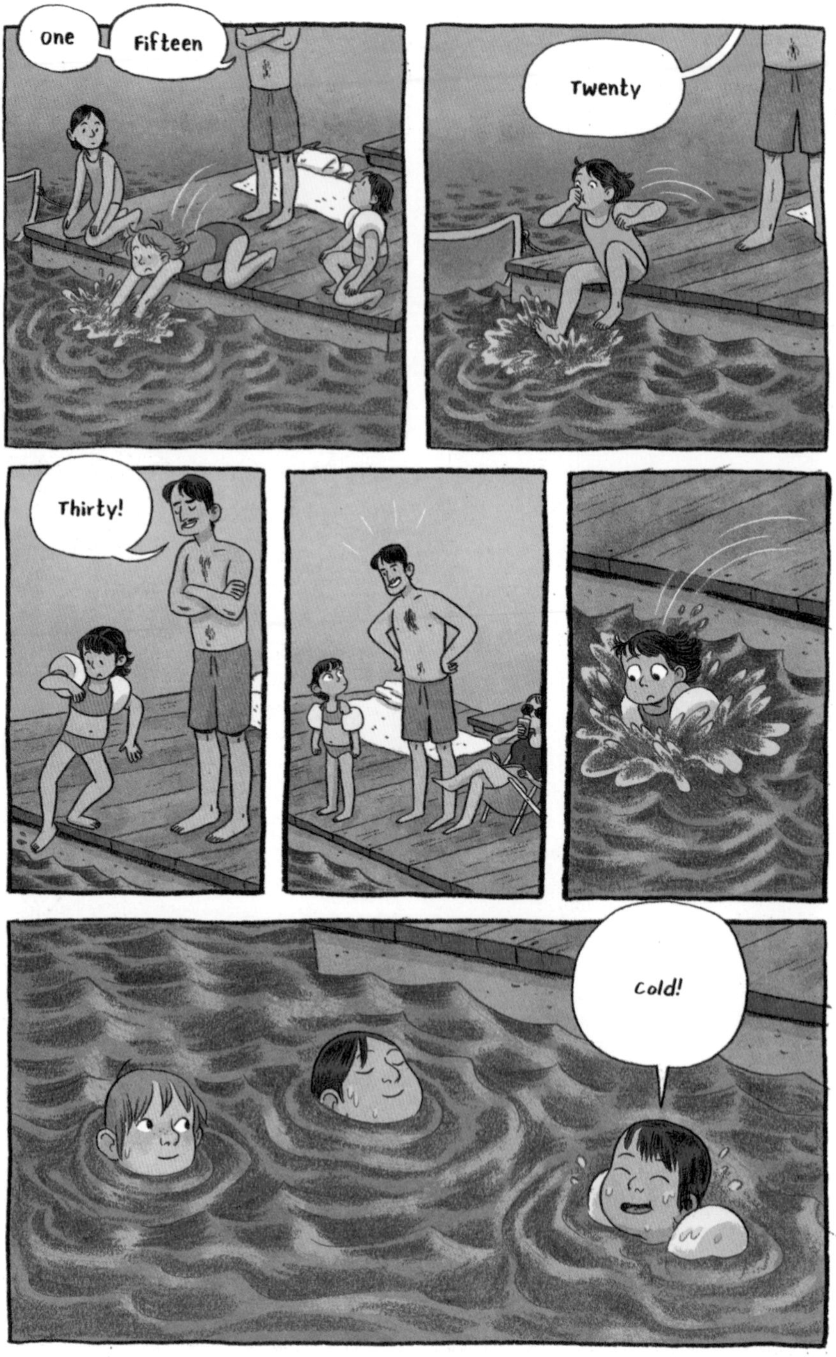
One
Fifteen
Twenty
Thirty!
Cold!

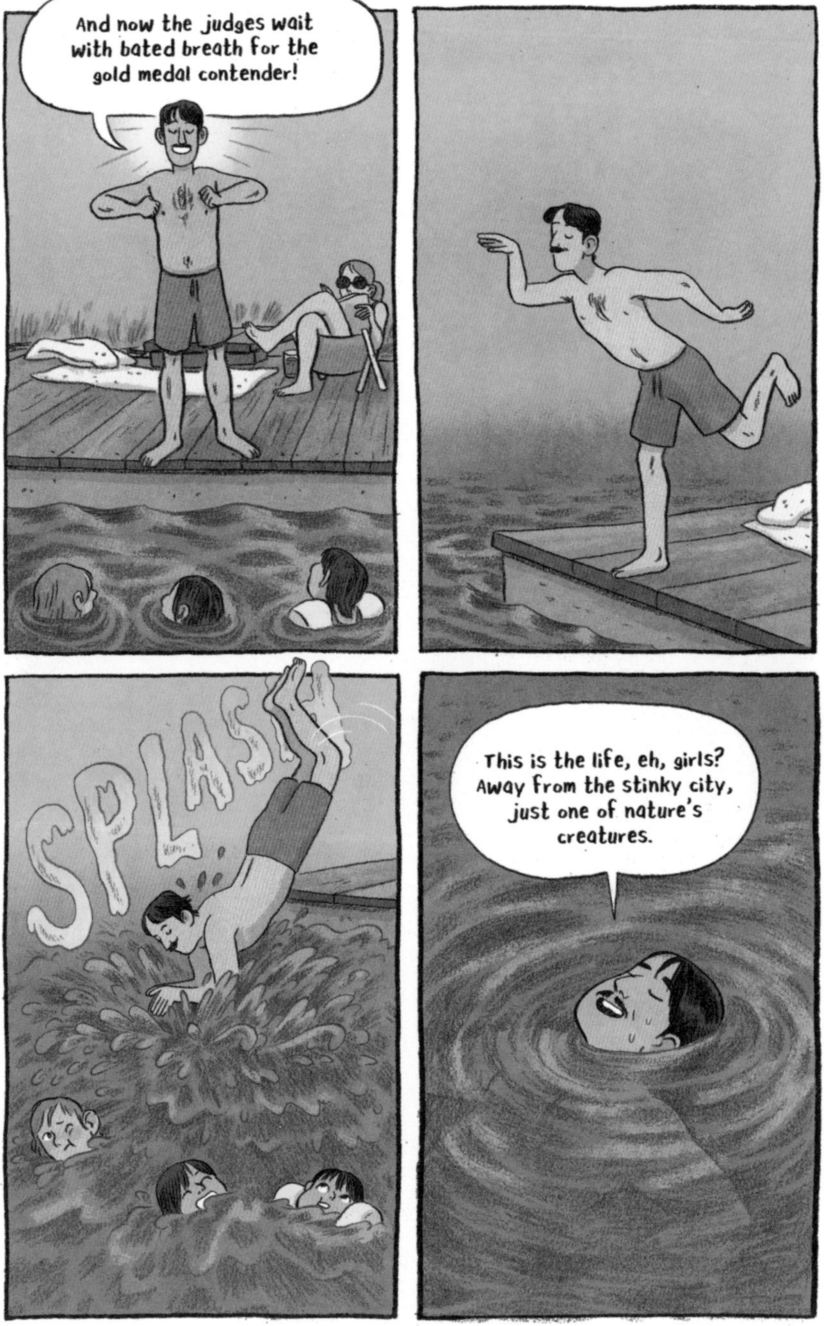
And now the judges wait with bated breath for the gold medal contender!
SPLASH
This is the life, eh, girls? Away from the stinky city, just one of nature's creatures.

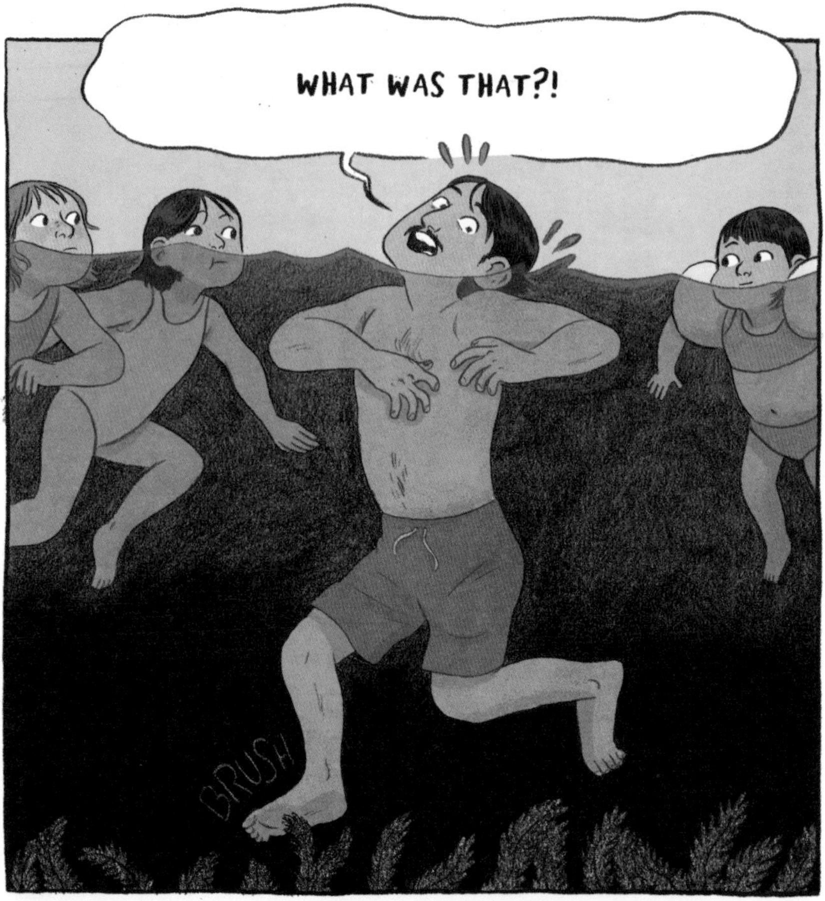
WHAT WAS THAT?!
BRUSH

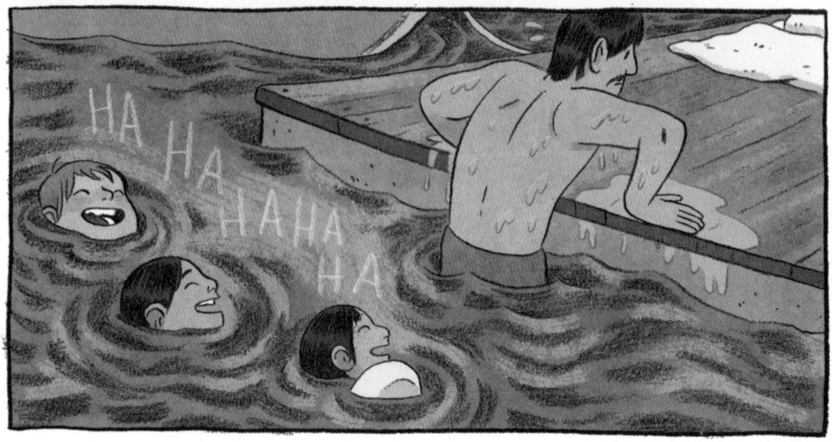
HA HA HAHA HA

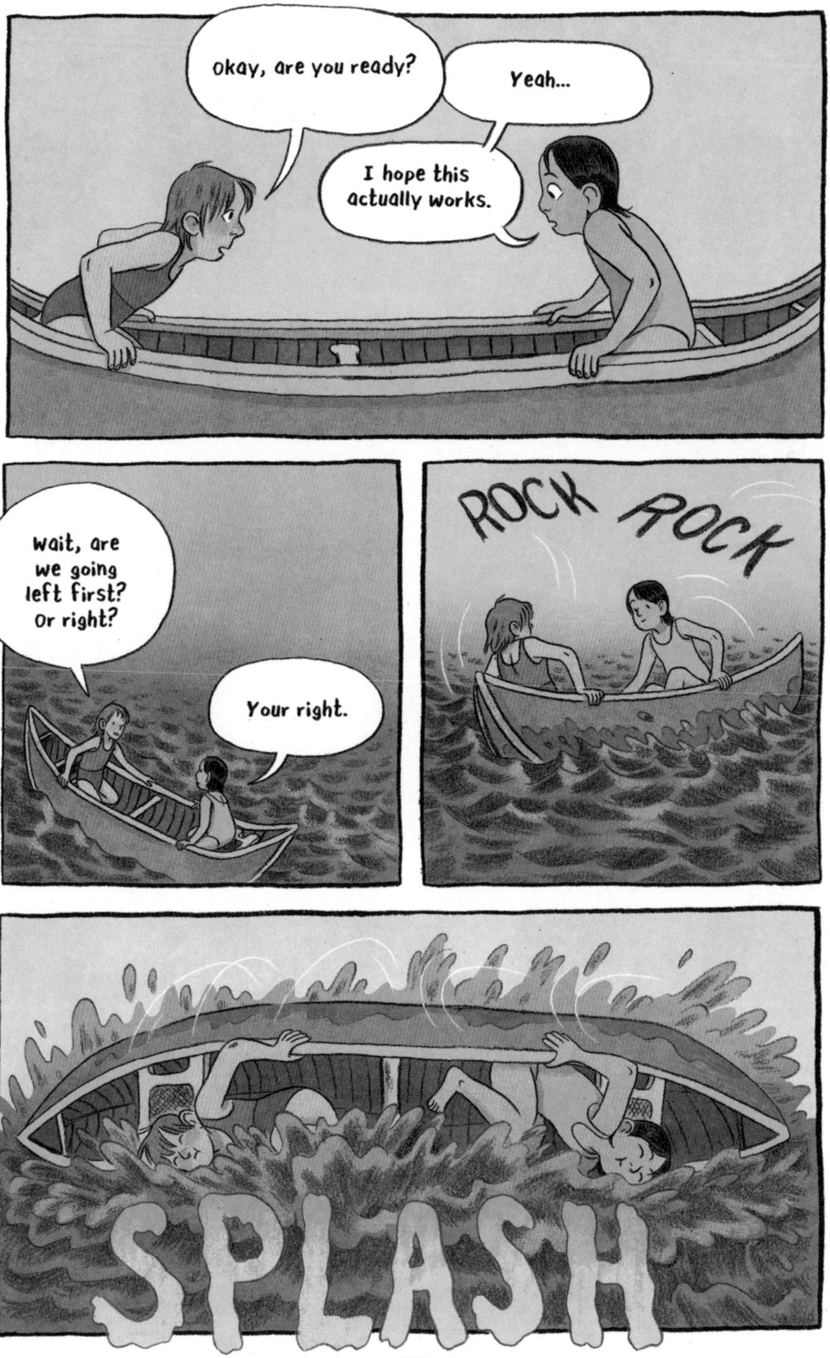
Okay, are you ready?
Yeah...
I hope this actually works.
Wait, are we going left first? Or right?
Your right.
ROCK ROCK
SPLASH

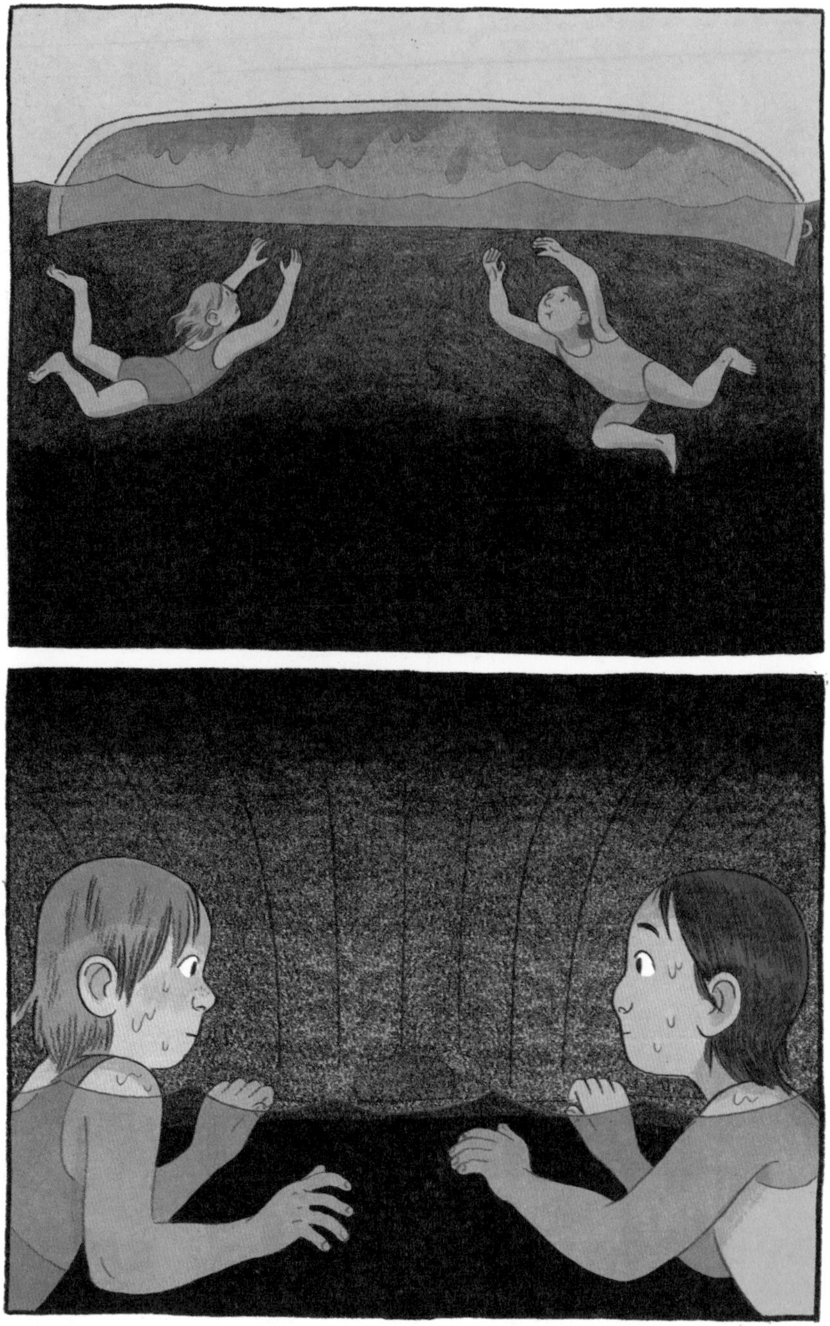

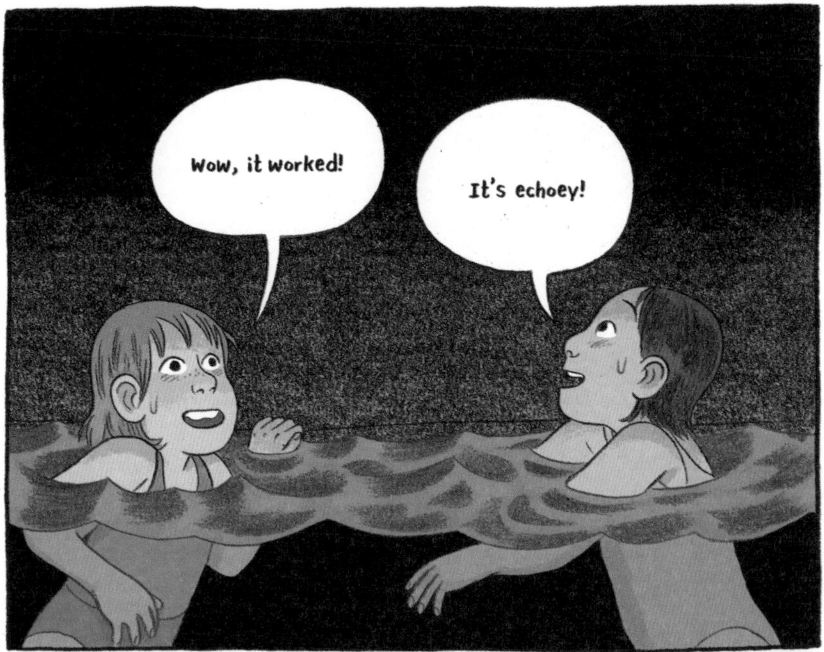
Wow, it worked!
It's echoey!

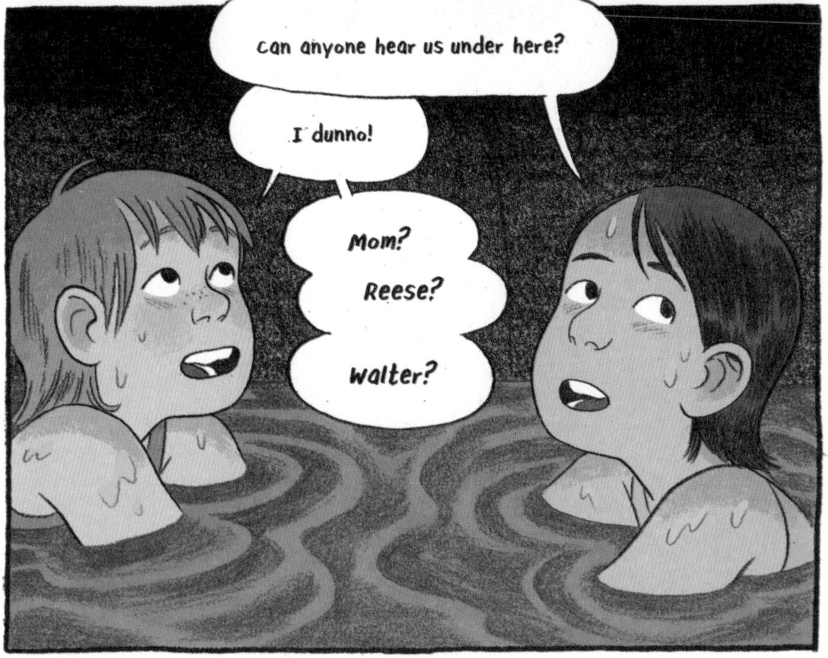
can anyone hear us under here?
I dunno!
Mom?
Reese?
walter?

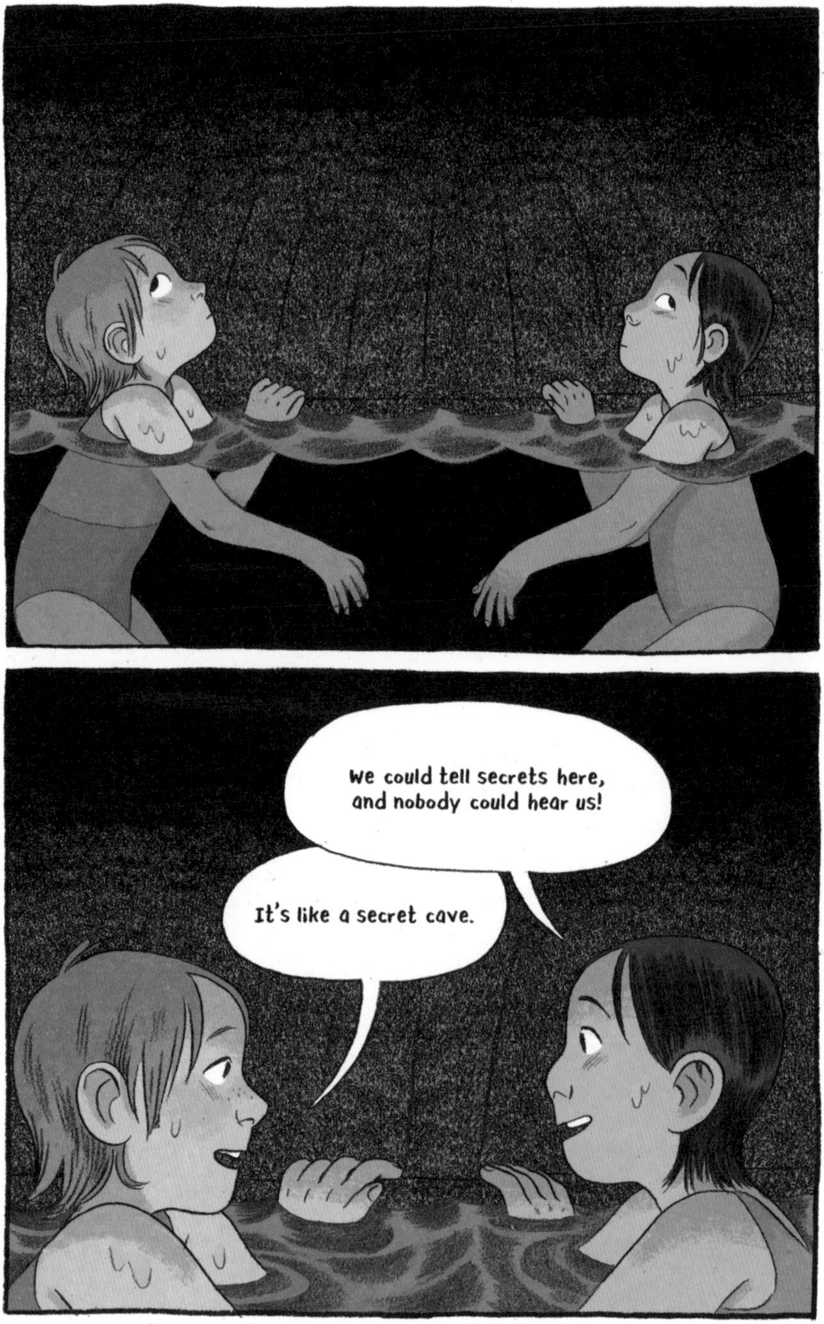
We could tell secrets here, and nobody could hear us!
It's like a secret cave.

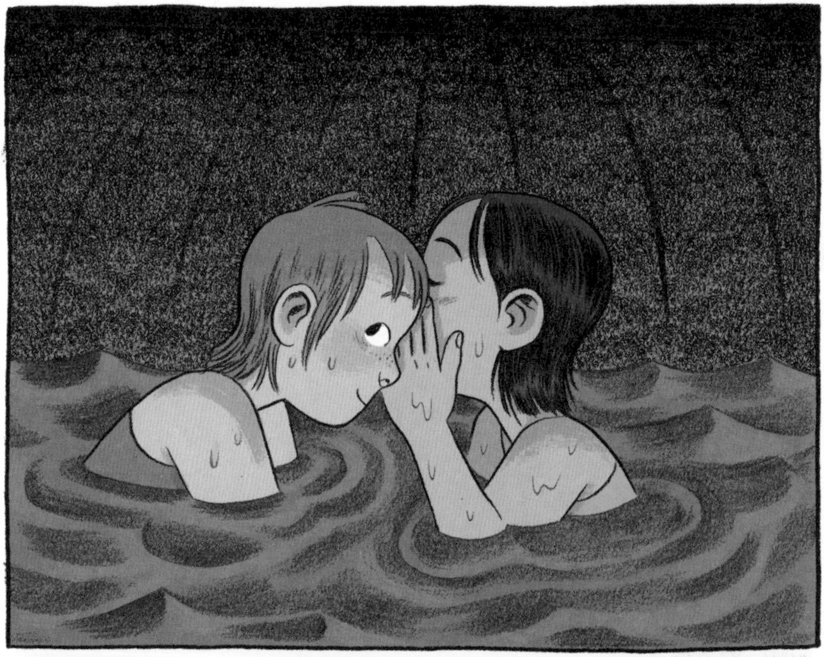

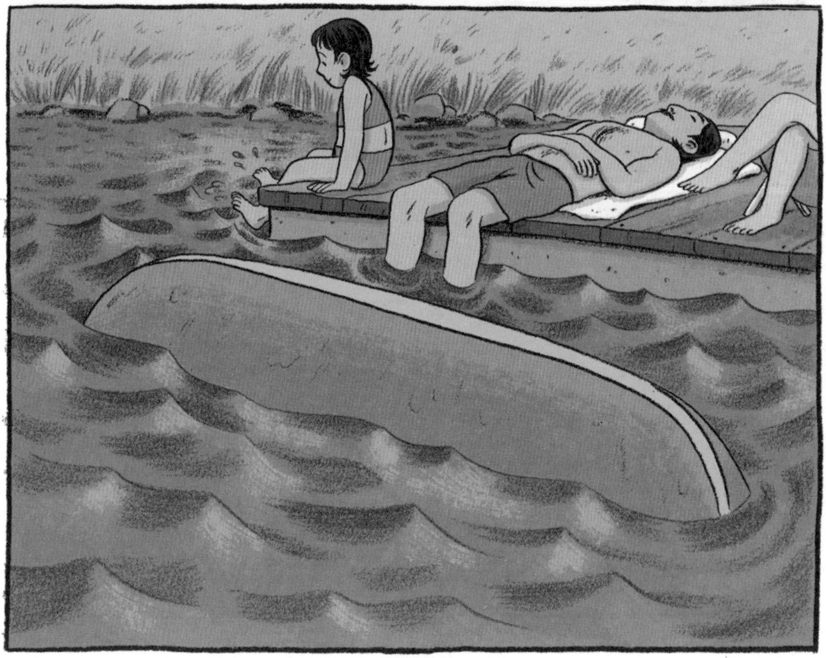

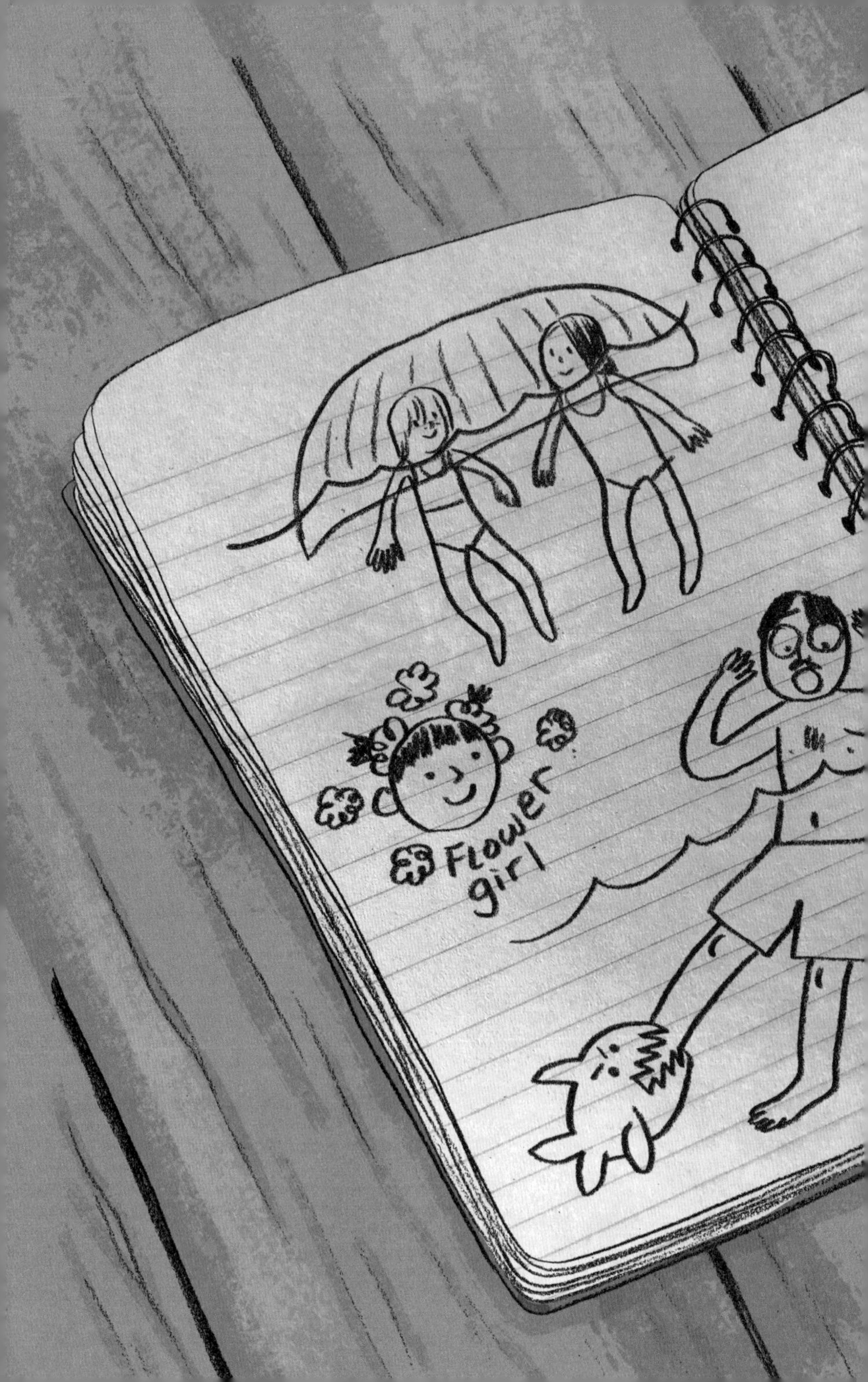
Flower
girl

...hings that are O.K. about the country:
1. Swimming!
2. The food
3. Riding in the truck
4. Mom is happy
5. My part-time sisters

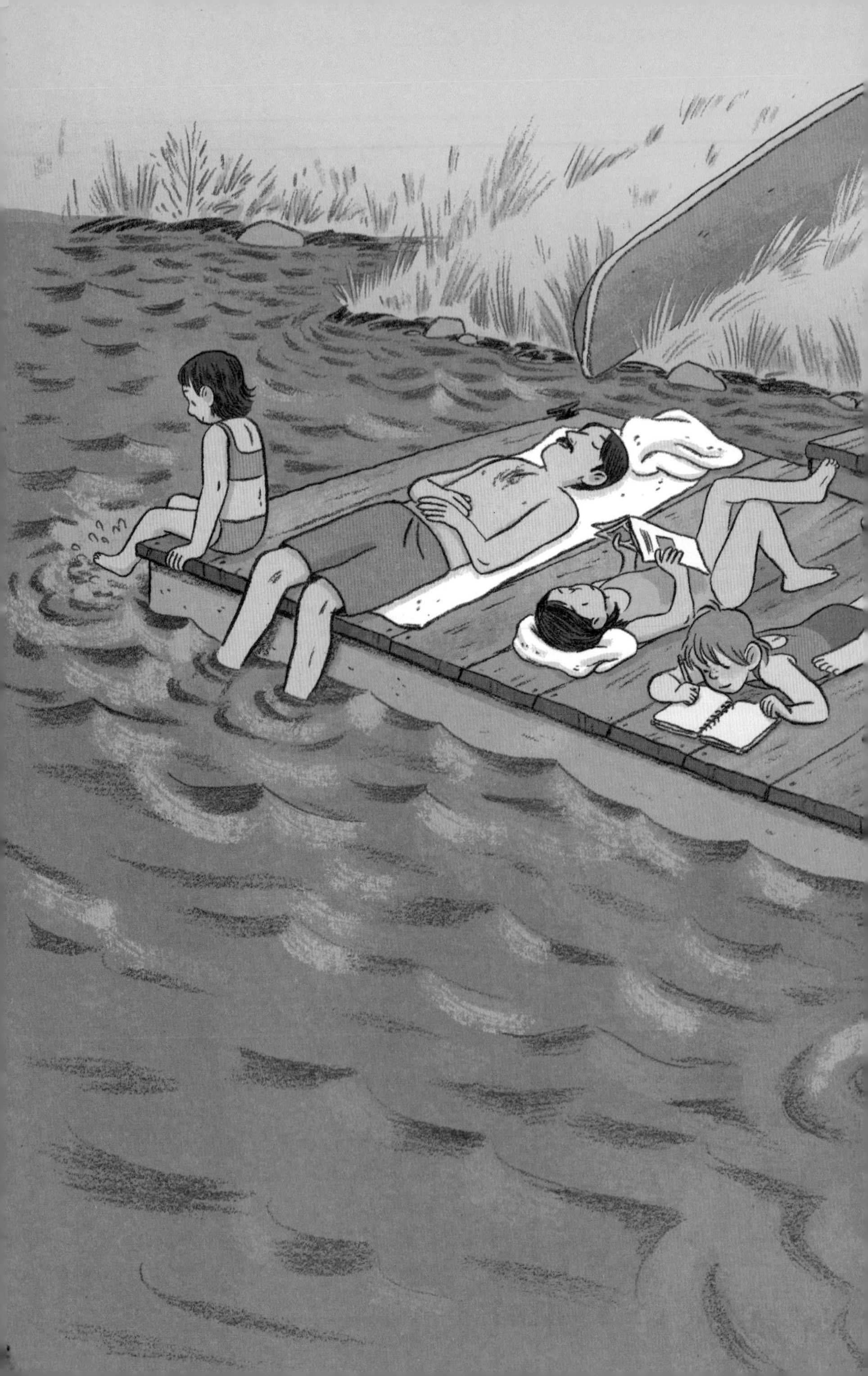

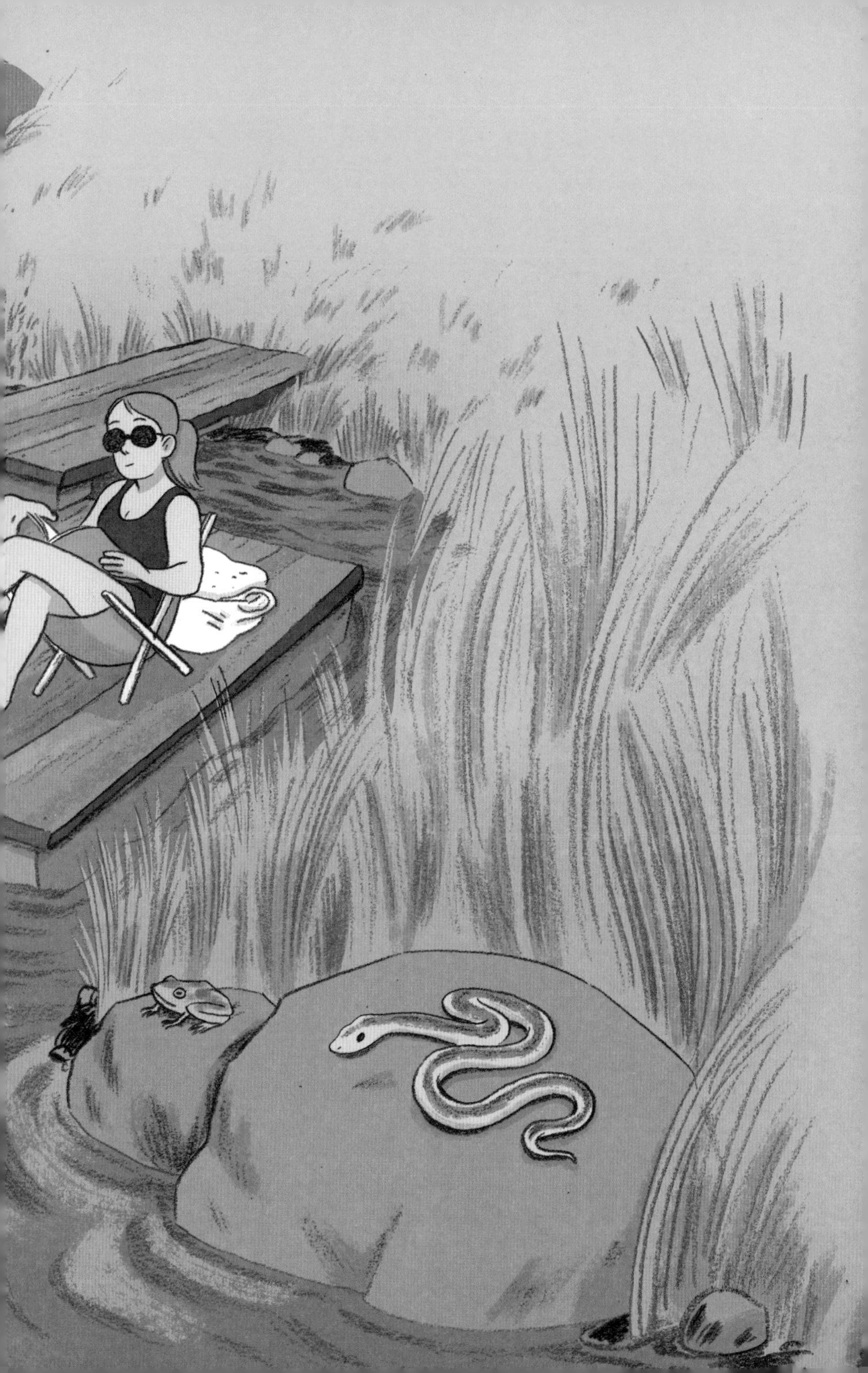

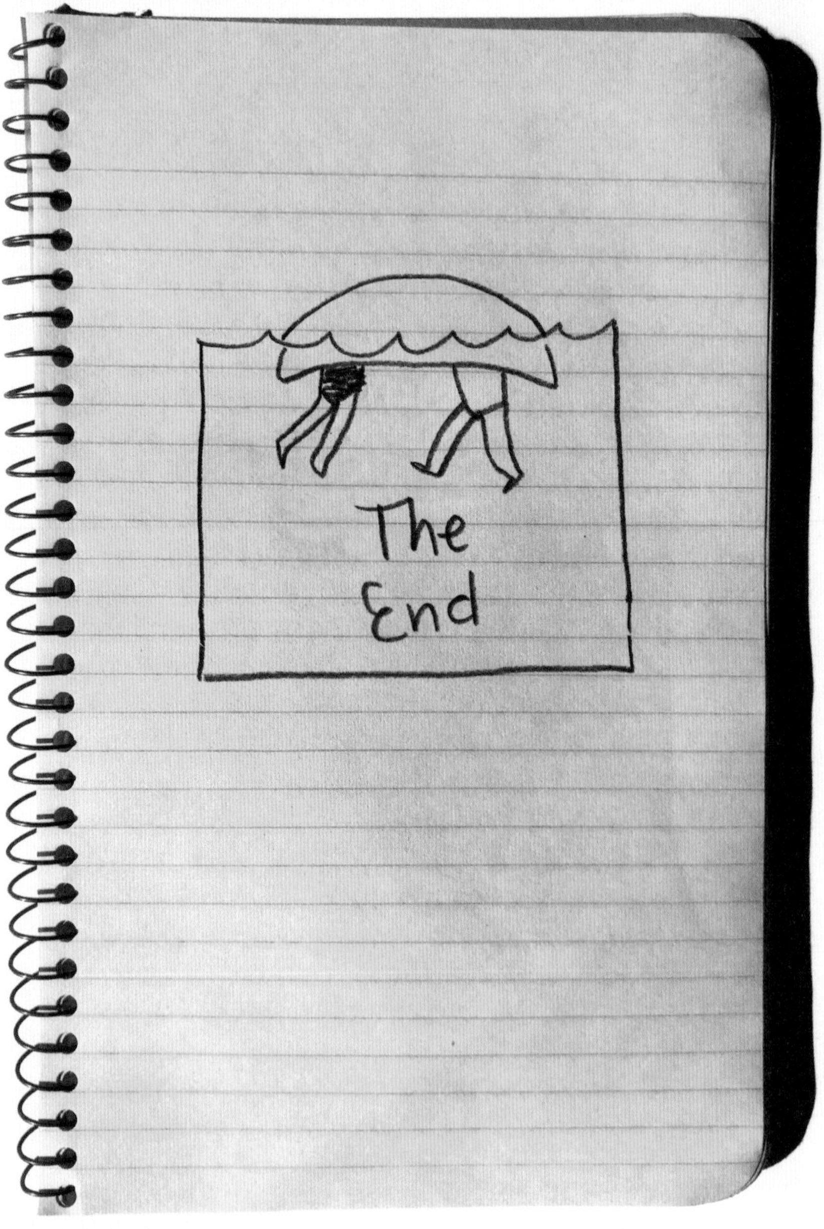
The
End

A Note From The Author

When I was a kid, my parents split up and my mom and I moved from New York City to a little farm in the country.

She wanted to grow flowers and berries and get her hands dirty. I wanted to read comic books INSIDE where it was CLEAN, but sometimes when you're a kid, you're just along for the ride.

Mom →

← Me

I wasn't always thrilled with my mom's decision to become a super farmer lady, but I didn't have much of a choice about becoming a not-so-super farm kid.

Then my mom got a boyfriend. He was loud, bossy, and annoying. I'd never met such an annoying grown-up! And his daughters! A loud, bossy kid and her whiny little sister! Suddenly, I was sharing my room every weekend with these total strangers.

One of the worst things about being a kid is finding yourself in these situations where you have no control over the decisions the adults are making that affect you. But sometimes it's also one of the best things— to find yourself in a situation you couldn't possibly have chosen for yourself, totally at sea. It can sometimes bring unexpected beauty, and introduce strangers that become family.

My "Andy" is still loud and bossy, but she's also brilliant and funny. My "Reese" is much less whiney now, and much cooler than all of us, as she has always been.

My "Walter" was both annoying and beloved until his dying day.

My mom is still getting her hands dirty and loving her life in the country, and I am so thankful to her for forcing me to endure such a beautiful childhood full of rattlesnakes and ponds and lots more stories to tell.

(Another little note)

Big Shocker: I am bad at math.

$$\begin{array}{r} 4 \\ \times 7 \\ \hline 28 \end{array}$$

I'm not just BAD at math, though; I'm dyscalculiac! It's a little like dyslexia, but rather than reading, this one impairs your ability to process numbers and magnitude.

When I graduated, I breathed a sigh of relief that I'd never have to do math again, but then I became a comic artist and had to learn how to measure and divide a page of panels! It was like algebra RETURNING FROM THE GRAVE TO HAUNT ME.

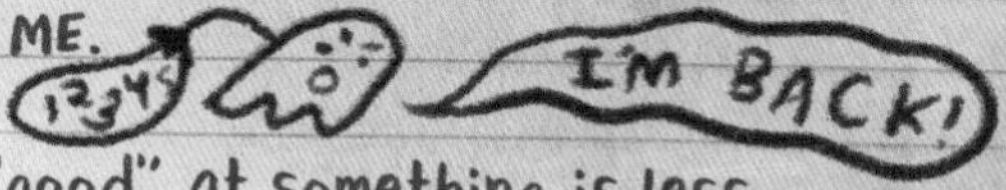
I'M BACK!

Being "good" at something is less important than trying or practicing. After all, I became a comic artist after years and YEARS of practicing my drawing and writing. And I'm much better at math than I used to be! My "Andy," of course, is an engineer, and sometimes she has to draw diagrams and she's rotten at it, but she's getting better, too. Who'da thunk it?

Acknowledgments:

Thank you to Taylor, Chelsea, and Georgia.
Thank you to the Rhinebeck Farmers' Market.
Thank you to my fellow children of divorce.

Thank you to my publishing team at Random
House Graphic! Gina Gagliano and
Whitney Leopard and Patrick Crotty!
Thank you to Whitney Coger
for beautiful colors.
Thank you to Holly Bemiss
for being my champion.

Thank you to bees for your honey and
gardens for your flowers and bushes for
your berries and cows for your milk and
barns for your kittens.

Thank you to Warren, who I miss and who
would have been very sweet and very
annoying about this whole book.

Thank you to John and Pal,
who are my faves.

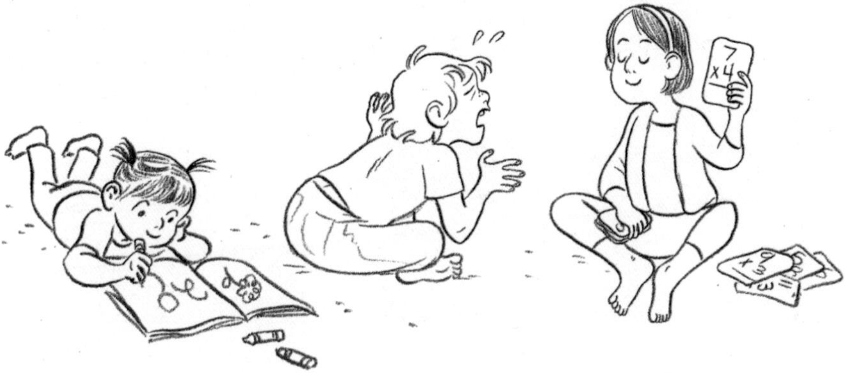
7
x4

Author shown with pencil stubs
used during the making of this book!

About The Author

Lucy Knisley grew up with one foot in New York City and the other on an upstate farm.

An only child with divorced parents, she was an avid comic book and fantasy reader, who began to navigate the unfamiliar world of step-familial melodrama when she was eleven.

She graduated from the School of the Art Institute of Chicago, followed by the Center for Cartoon Studies, and began publishing graphic novels (a travelogue) at the age of twenty-two.

She has always tried to use her work to make people feel less alone through her honest and confessional comics. Her topics range from travel, adulthood, ailing grandparents, foreign romance, wedding planning, food, and reproductive health.

She lives in Chicago, where she likes riding her bike with her son and partner, and reading fantasy novels and comic books.

LucyKnisley.com

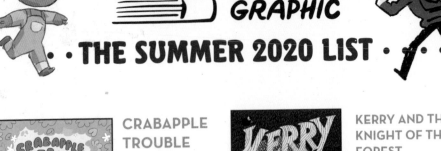

RH GRAPHIC

· · · THE SUMMER 2020 LIST · · ·

CRABAPPLE TROUBLE
By Kaeti Vandorn

Life isn't easy when you're an apple.

Callaway and Thistle must figure out how to work together—with delicious and magical results.

Young Chapter Book

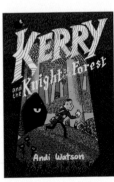

KERRY AND THE KNIGHT OF THE FOREST
By Andi Watson

Kerry needs to get home!

To get back to his parents, Kerry gets lost in a shortcut. He will have to make tough choices and figure out who to trust—or remain lost in the forest . . . forever.

Middle-Grade

STEPPING STONES
By Lucy Knisley

Jen did not want to leave the city.

She did not want to move to a farm.

And Jen definitely did not want to get two new "sisters."

Middle-Grade

SUNCATCHER
By Jose Pimienta

Beatriz loves music—more than her school, more than her friends—and she won't let anything stop her from achieving her dreams.

Even if it means losing everything else.

Young Adult

FIND US ONLINE AT @RHKIDSGRAPHIC AND RHKIDSGRAPHIC.COM